SEEKING COURAGE

For David & Randi,

Thank you for your undying enthusiasm and encouragement for this project. I hope the final edition lives up!

Greg
September 2019

SEEKING COURAGE

A NOVEL

GREGORY P. SMITH

Indigo River Publishing

PRAISE FOR *SEEKING COURAGE*

"*Seeking Courage* by Gregory Smith brings to life the plight of a soldier during the Great War, one who moves from the trenches to take flight over them. As an Aviator myself I can relate to the desire to slip the surly bonds of earth and take to the air over the grit and horrors faced by infantrymen on the ground. This story is more than a tale of one Aviator, it is the story of humanity and the choices we make. *Seeking Courage* is a dynamic historical novel which describes in great detail the life of a young Canadian driven to defend democracy. Fighting on foreign soil he is inspired by love and compassion. This brings him to the realization that he has the chance to pursue life to the fullest and the freedom to make his own choices. At times, this novel is a painfully honest factorial portrayal of what life was like when the world was at war a hundred years ago. The first mechanized war was promoted to be over swiftly as a result of new killing technology and machines, but war dragged on; lives were interrupted, families destroyed, and empires ended. Gregory Smith ably demonstrates the changes in one mans values and his growth through personal experience. I am impressed with the way the subject matter has been handled, it is not overly technical nor ghoulishly morose; it is not bound up with politics or military minutia, rather it balances both the historical and technical details with a humane and honest portrayal of life at this time in history. This biographical work is highly thorough yet refreshingly easy to read with the just the right mix of drama and detail."

Gene Demarco—Aviation Consultant & FE2b Pilot

"This is a wonderful novel. It is exciting, engaging, gut-wrenching, enjoyable, and sorrowful to read. I looked forward to continuing the story each time I picked it up again. The best thing about it is that it brings to life what people were experiencing in the First World War. Like Stephen Crane's *The Red Badge of Courage*, this novel gives us truths about being in war that you'll never get from any history text. I could tell that the author had insights -- from actually being in the cockpit of an FE2b -- that I've never picked up in 25 years of studying WWI bombing campaigns."

Steve Suddaby—Past President, World War One Historical Association

Copyright © 2019 by Gregory P. Smith

All rights reserved. No portion of this publication may be reproduced, stored in a retrieval system, or transmitted by any means—electronic, mechanical, photocopying, recording, or any other—except for brief quotations in printed reviews, without the prior written permission of the publisher.

Indigo River Publishing
3 West Garden Street, Ste. 352
Pensacola, FL 32502
www.indigoriverpublishing.com

Editors: Justyn Newman and Regina Cornell
Cover Design: mycustombookcover.com

Ordering Information:
Quantity sales: Special discounts are available on quantity purchases by corporations, associations, and others. For details, contact the publisher at the address above.

Orders by US trade bookstores and wholesalers: Please contact the publisher at the address above.

Printed in the United States of America

Library of Congress Control Number: 2019936676

ISBN: 978-1-948080-87-3

First Edition

With Indigo River Publishing, you can always expect great books, strong voices, and meaningful messages. Most importantly, you'll always find . . . words worth reading.

THE WESTERN FRONT, 1914-1918

Select Locations Appearing in *Seeking Courage*

Contents

Part I

Chapter 1	3
Chapter 2	17
Chapter 3	27
Chapter 4	35
Chapter 5	47
Chapter 6	51
Chapter 7	57
Chapter 8	65
Chapter 9	69
Chapter 10	75
Chapter 11	81
Chapter 12	87
Chapter 13	97
Chapter 14	103
Chapter 15	107
Chapter 16	113
Chapter 17	117
Chapter 18	123
Chapter 19	133
Chapter 20	139

Part II

Chapter 21 149
Chapter 22 153
Chapter 23 157
Chapter 24 165
Chapter 25 173
Chapter 26 181
Chapter 27 195
Chapter 28 207
Chapter 29 215
Chapter 30 223
Chapter 31 237
Chapter 32 247
Chapter 33 259
Chapter 34 267
Chapter 35 277
Chapter 36 291

Part III

Chapter 37 301
Chapter 38 313
Chapter 39 317
Chapter 40 329
Chapter 41 339
Chapter 42 357
Chapter 43 365

Chapter 44	*375*
Chapter 45	*381*
Chapter 46	*389*
Chapter 47	*401*
Chapter 48	*407*
Chapter 49	*413*
Chapter 50	*421*
Chapter 51	*429*
Chapter 52	*433*
Chapter 53	*443*
Chapter 54	*451*
Chapter 55	*457*
Chapter 56	*461*
Chapter 57	*471*
Historical Note	*475*
Glossary	*480*

ACKNOWLEDGEMENTS

Since a boy, war intrigued me; not the gore and devastation, rather a curiosity about why mankind repeatedly engages in it, and why soldiers, especially volunteers, are so willing to fight on behalf of their countries. I turned to my maternal grandfather's war experiences for lessons about fear and courage, for an understanding of why or how one man came to the decision to lay his life on the line and enlist in 1915. Sadly, I had deferred to family taboos ("Hush, he doesn't want to talk about the war") so did not ask him enough direct questions before he died in 1976. Gladly, there exists plentiful reference material covering the war in general, his regiment and squadron, and specifically to himself: one person among millions of young men engaged in the 'war to end all wars' that lasted from 1914 to 1918.

I began to create a documentary style accounting of Robert Courtenay Pitman's war history based on official service records, but eventually found the story lacked flow due to periods where some information on time and people was missing. I decided to write in novel style, which gave me license to develop more flow without sacrificing the very important historical background. But as with most things in life I could not proceed without the assistance of willing institutions and informed experts.

Such resources include *The Library and Archives Canada*, Ottawa, *The National Archives*, Kew, the *Royal Air Force Museum*, Hendon Aerodrome, London, *Cross & Cockade International*, Kettering, the *Imperial War Museum*, London, the *Canadian War Museum*, Ottawa and the *Saskatoon Library*. Although it is not practical to mention the names of all those who assisted, I can assure you that without exception every person at every institution was exceptionally pleasant, professional and helpful.

In addition to general acknowledgments there are a few professionals who provided very specific expertise on key topics. For pretty much everything about the FE2b, from its handling in flight to its complex makeup I thank *Gene DeMarco*, Aviation Consultant and FE2b pilot. For detailed historical data regarding the RFC/RAF in general and 100 Squadron in particular, I thank *Trevor Henshaw*, author of *The Sky Their Battlefield*, Grub Street Books and contributing author to other publications such as the *FE2b Monogram*, Cross & Cockade International. *Steve Suddaby*, Past President World War One Historical Society was incredibly helpful in the final stages of the manuscript with putting me straight on many details about aircraft manoeuvres and bombing operations. See Steve's extensive database by entering Suddaby in the search box at https://www.overthefront.com/. Finally, I thank the person who gave me the confidence to believe this book would one day come to fruition, war historian *Norm Graham*. Experiencing Norm's depth of knowledge while attending one of his WW1 Battlefield Tours in western France and reviewing many of his books and DVDs provided an insight into the Great War not otherwise accessible. See https://battlefields.ca/.

Finally, my supportive publisher! In the competitive world of published works Indigo River Publishing believed in me; not only to sell books but in allowing me freedom to meaningfully participate in the process. Bobby Dunaway leads a great team. Editors Justyn Newman and Regina Cornell both provided a critical eye with a sensitive approach. And the one who found me, Georgette Green.

For all those test readers, you know who you are and know how appreciative I am of your critical feedback. Thanks everyone!

Part I

Chapter 1

16 September, 1916

"Whoa, Pitman! You did it again. You kicked me in the shin." My eyes burst open at the sound of his jesting voice. I had been sitting across from Issy over the arduous journey from Boulogne—eighty miles that lasted thirty-six hours. The hiss of steam and slowing of the train was further bringing me back to consciousness.

In the dark dream, I had kicked helplessly at a faceless, cloaked attacker. I lifted my head off the carriage windowsill and dabbed the beads of sweat tickling my brow as I noticed his typically playful grin. "Sorry, Issy. I am truly sorry. Dunno, I sometimes fall into a deep sleep with visions of being attacked, flinging my feet for protection." A little more relaxed, I forced a smile to rid what I knew was a bellicose look.

"That's all right, I understand. Just try to keep your kicks for the Hun!"

I straightened up and instinctively smoothed down invisible creases in my tunic as the train came to rest at the Somme railhead. The squeal of iron wheels on the rails and smoke wafting sulphurous vapor into the station's vast glass roof warned onlookers of our arrival. Perce sat beside me, his slumped head stirring toward wakefulness with the slowing momentum.

"You ready for this, Perce?" It was really a reflection, a way to face my feelings about going into war. With no prior military experience, I was nervous; we were all nervous. This trepidation was something that officer training couldn't have prepared us for. Soon enough I would be leading a platoon of fifty soldiers. For that, I would need pluck and confidence.

Perce yawned. "No, not really. I don't think any of us will be ready until we face our baptism—you know, out there in the mud."

I mulled on that as I peered out the partially open window. There were young women scattered across the Amiens platform waving white handkerchiefs of welcome. Businessmen bustled here and there, perhaps looking for opportunities to profit. Voices accented in both English and French called out to many of the disembarking soldiers amid the smell of freshly baked baguettes. I expected this would be a pleasant but short-lived contrast to the battlefield climate.

Remaining in my seat while Issy and Perce organized their duffel bags, I continued taking in the activity outside. Eager young men brimming with innocence piled off carriages, each clutching the worldly possessions assumed to see them through these charged times. I knew from my officer's briefing that most had never traveled farther than the outskirts of the small towns and villages which they had so recently left.

I leaned over to the floor and zipped my duffel bag. Issy stood above, looking at me quizzically. "Is that why you have bad dreams, Bob? You know, facing the war and all?"

I thought about the connection between my dreams and my childhood. "I can't really say that's what's prompting them now, but I've had them since I was young." I often wondered if the dreams reflected the timidity I felt in front of my controlling father. He would hold me responsible for the sometimes naughty behavior of my sisters, my status as eldest child making me somehow accountable. He was always too busy to understand, so he would just yell. I suppose it was my ineptitude at defending myself that led to my doing so in nightmares. But in spite of such personal issues, I knew it was now time to practice courage and to do my bit to defend against threats to our democratic way of living.

I put my hands on my knees and looked up. I liked Issy's cheerful demeanor. Now arriving at the front, I was curious about how he viewed our imminent deployment. "Do you ever get afraid about the unknowns of war?" I asked him. "Will we be brave, or will we panic? Will we lead our soldiers into no-man's-land with confidence?"

Perce's hesitant nature came through as he stood beside Issy. "Well, I do. I've been constantly thinking about coming battles and losing a leg, or worse."

"Ha! Me as well, but I'm not going to let you two know that," Issy confidently mused.

I remained reflective. "We are going into the severest war ever known to mankind. Enjoy each day as if it's your last. That's what I say."

Issy had a way about him; he could make the dourest subject upbeat. "Robert Courtenay Pitman, as your mother would say—put a smile on that cherubic face, young man!"

I knew what Issy was on about. Since I was a child, I had been recognized and even teased for my near round face of olive tones, some saying that my hazel eyes were of matching roundness. I was always thankful that my naturally wavy, even unruly, brown hair gave me more of a rambling look. Yet now, with officer standards for oiled-back, Brilliantined hair and a full mustache below my quite prominent nose, I had gained a more mature, manly look.

"Listen here, Lieutenant Malcolm Isbester, you're not going to get my goat with that motherly talk, although you do make me smile." Issy smirked at the uncommon use of his full name.

Perce lazily moved toward me. "Good sport, Bob. Shall you and

I do our uniform check now?"

I grinned about our little ritual and faced him. "All right, let's look you over. Khaki tunic buttoned correctly, trousers tucked nicely into riding boots, mm-hmm." I walked around Perce, who pretended to stand at attention. "Sam Browne squared, cap sitting straight, and brass *Canada* tab fastened properly to epaulettes. Lieutenant stars clipped appropriately to each sleeve. I'd say you pass. Barely."

"You two sound like finicky women," Issy scolded.

"Uh-huh. But you didn't say that when you got a complete dressing down from the Captain for—now how did he say it?—'poor manner of dressing,' did you?" I said.

We all laughed. As I glanced into the mirror to adjust my military tie to a more centered position, I felt I looked older and more authoritative than my twenty-four years. I regretted such fussiness as my reflection gave me a start. Was I ready for this? Months of training in Canada and England, and now the imminent reality of war in France rather shook me.

I held the image of my mother's pained and anxious face as I peered out the window of the train leaving Saskatoon station so many months before. She had pleaded with me to stay safe and to return to my two sisters, Ethel and Hilda. I had to maintain decorum among the others that were also leaving that day. Yet holding back tears was so very difficult; using my white hanky to wave goodbye, I knew it was also there to wipe them away.

That memory lingered as I considered the promise I made on enlistment, the commitment to lead my platoon bravely into battle. I already understood the smell of fear as it wafted up from practice battlefields with the stench of cordite. I had felt its sting as smoke blinded my eyes. I had felt the concussion of explosion and knew the taste of mud. I knew what was expected by my superiors and, more importantly, by my soldiers: a courageous leader in the face of a war like no one—no army, no society—had ever fought before. A leader who could transfer practice skills to muddy trenches, which held deadly machine guns that could spit five hundred rounds per minute, lethal flamethrowers that burned men alive, and toxic gas that lulled victims into a sleepy death.

...

All right, the long wait was over.

I was the first of our small party to descend the wooden steps from the carriage, relieved to be rid of the stress and strain of the journey. Falling in behind a couple of jovial soldiers, the three of us looked at each other and grimaced upon hearing their innocent bragging about all the women they would meet and the medals they were going to bring back. If only they'd had the briefing we did.

Amid a sea of soldiers and civilians scattered across the platform, a young corporal was holding up our colors, those of the Royal Canadian Regiment. Freeing myself of previous somber thoughts, I broke into an oversized smile and strode toward him, relishing the instant feeling of familiarity and inclusion. "Minnie," I yelled over the din.

"Bob! Er, Lieutenant Pitman, it's great to see you. I saw your name on the roster and could hardly believe you were among the arrivals."

I lowered my voice to a whisper as we firmly shook hands. "Don't worry, we'll be on first-name basis while out of the range of the brass. We're all friends."

"Wow, it was November we last saw each other, right? When you left the rest of us to take some course or other in Winnipeg?"

"Yeah, that long. It was disappointing not to stay with our gang of ten from Saskatoon for the Halifax departure."

"We arrived in Liverpool on 15 December. Most stayed with the Princess Pats; I was assigned this May to the RCR."

"Ahem," someone grunted behind us.

I shifted to open up space, forming a circle. "Sorry, lads. This here is Corporal John Campbell Forbes, RCR adjutant."

"Hello, Corporal. I'm Perce, and this here is Issy—Lieutenants Percy Sutton and Malcolm Isbester on your roster. You are, uh, *Minnie*?"

Issy was on cue. "Minnie? As in the nickname for the German trench mortar, *Minenwerfer*?"

"Oh no, no," Minnie said with a laugh. "I would never allow a German nickname!"

Issy grinned as he shrugged. "Then what could your nickname mean, Corporal?"

"Well, it's a long—"

I jumped in. "Listen, chaps, let me help. You see, when we enlisted together back in Saskatoon, our features were recorded—you know, the attestation description. Well, the enlisting officer peered at John for the longest time before recording 'flaxen hair.' There were ten of us that day, all in a spirited mood, so I blurted out, 'Oh, like Minnie,' and it stuck."

Issy and Perce exchanged quizzical looks, simultaneously asking, "Who's Minnie?"

I sighed, feeling responsible for John's nickname. "Minnie is Mr. Omer's little girl in Dickens's book *David Copperfield*, who was described as 'a pretty little girl with long, flaxen hair.' I'm so sorry if this has brought you grief."

Perce and Issy were laughing openly, kindly but loudly.

"Oh no, quite the contrary! When I explain the story to the *jeunes filles* in the local drinking *estaminets*, I attract all sorts of attention."

I grinned but believed it was really Minnie's blond locks and deep blue eyes the girls were interested in. Although he was a serious science student at the University of Saskatchewan, he had a way about him that women loved. Perhaps it was the rugged looks inherited from his native Nova Scotian ancestry or his easygoing ways, but oh yes, the girls liked him. His acceptance of the unusual nickname pointed to the breezy side of his demeanor. With thick skin, he made the best of things.

I beamed. "You know, sometimes the most innocuous utterings get unintentionally sticky. I'm glad you're wearing it well."

Remembering the reason he was at the station, Minnie suddenly snapped to a more formal stance. "Welcome to France, Lieutenants. It's still early morning, so we have time on our side to reach the regiment by midday meal. If you will follow me to the stables."

Outside the station, we heard whinnying and snorting, and smelled the rank stench of urine in the temporary stables that held hundreds of horses hitched to various posts. Grooms were scurrying around with the busywork of tending their officer's mounts: ensuring shoes were nailed fast, no lameness, no saddle sores. Most were work and farm horses, but some were retired show or police horses. It didn't matter; all were army conscripts now, war horses learning equine calmness amid daily strife.

As the horses frisked about with heads waving to and fro, a groom with a distinctive Scots accent approached Minnie. "Yer steeds are all sound as a wee Aberdeen colt, Corporal."

"Thank you, Private. The officers will mount straightaway," said Minnie.

Issy was crooning over an unusually tall and muscular horse. "This thoroughbred is surely assigned to me since it matches my height, wot?"

Malcolm Isbester, known since a toddler as Issy, was born with the stuff leaders are made of. Composed and always pleasant, he was a very determined fellow with a sense of humor born from an abundance of confidence. He stood proud with dark hair, brown eyes and, of course, a thick, iron-like mustache. At thirty, Issy was recently married and older than Percy and me. His being Scottish and we English brought much laughter and jibing in training camp and the public houses in the surrounding villages.

"Er, I suppose, sir," said Minnie. "I had rather a plan for the assignment, but if you officers prefer to sort things—"

Perce lunged forward to an equally tall horse standing neck to neck with Issy's new mount. "Then I'll take this fellow."

Stroking his horse's snout, Issy laughed. "Well done, Perce. 'Take the initiative' is my motto. Show how things get done."

In this manner, horses got assigned to each officer. Mine was not as handsome as the thoroughbreds, but she wasn't as delicate and was full of jaunty spirit. My time spent on the Canadian Prairie gave me an understanding of what separates a good horse from a struggling jenny. I knew my mare was solid.

Minnie yelled above the din of neighing horses and bellowing soldiers. "Officers, your attention. We are to rendezvous with the regiment in Warloy, eighteen miles northeast. The roads are thankfully solid, but they are congested with the mobilization of troops and transport both entering and leaving the front. The odd stray shell does, of course, play havoc."

"Stray shells?" I asked.

The look between the three of us was accompanied by an uncertain silence, finally broken by Issy with a purposely benign question. "Our kit, Lieutenant? We are burdened with His Majesty's best this and that, not to mention our Lee-Enfields and Webleys."

"I'm afraid you will have to look after your own packs, rifles, and revolvers as you won't meet your platoon sergeants until rendezvous, where you and your troops will push on to La Vicogne, another ten miles to the northwest."

We secured our kit and mounted. I reflected that Canada did not entertain the idea of assigning a personal servant to junior officers, rather smartly following the British trend; one out of the four sergeants in each platoon—the noncommissioned officers, or NCOs—was assigned as an officer's assistant while also serving as an active fighting soldier. While I would have been overjoyed with Minnie as assistant, his rank of corporal did not qualify him.

...

Riding out from the paddocks at the canter, the four of us were quickly on our way amid evidence of previous rain. The roads remained hard packed, but the fields on either side were a muddy quag. The smell was stale, not the pleasant earthy aroma after a fresh downpour. In the few places where farms still operated, their green crops showed just how beautiful the rolling hills must have been. Otherwise, the landscape was a slick, brown moonscape.

I thought back to the vast, rolling farmlands of southern Saskatchewan. About the hot summer days under the clearest blue skies that were enhanced by field upon field of thick, fully grown wheat sheaves. At sixteen I learned to ride there during the summer of my emigration from England. The worry of being thrown was always softened by the belief that landing upon a gentle blanket of wheat would mute any pain.

We rode hard east of Amiens for an hour, then slowed to a walk as the roads became congested. A large convoy dominated the road as they traveled west. Our horses swung their heads from side to side, neighing in concert, as the thundering trucks and horse-drawn cannon spooked them. I had to rein in my little mount more harshly than I wanted, but it was important to keep her on course. I thought of dismounting to lead her before I realized that her footing in the quagmire on the side of the road would be surer than mine.

Since we were intermingled with the convoy, we stopped for a water break. I caught Issy eyeing me with that mischievous grin. "Say, Pitman! Do you remember anything from army riding school at Bedfordshire? You're not sitting erect on that wobbly mare."

I straightened my back and puffed out my chest. "You've no idea about riding like we of the Canadian Prairie," I said. "Ha! You grew up lake fishing in northern Ontario. Horses and tin boats are different. What d'you think, Percy?"

"Looks no worse than the plugs I grew up riding. Perhaps she's tired today, eh? Or maybe this is the state of horses at war."

I loved that Perce—born Percy Villiers Sutton just two months before I was, in 1892—spoke with a northeastern English accent, its Geordie inflection close to the authoritative Scottish brogue. The bluster from his native speech masked his more subdued, cautious nature.

With Percy's sort-of support, I looked back at Issy. "By Jove, it takes experience and skill unknown to navigate a mare as wobbly as this little girl! Besides, I'm sure she's missin' her farm, where she undoubtedly lived a grand life. Look at you two up there on your muscular steeds—"

A loud crack barely preceded the *thrump* of a shell landing, sending a sky-high explosion of earth, mud, and debris a small distance away, startling soldiers and horses alike. I immediately felt sweat drip from under my cap, then run down my forehead. Damn! I had been determined to remain calm in front of others, but anxiety presented itself. My heart pounded like a fist inside my chest as the next shells came in with high-pitched whistles, louder and louder, closer and closer. Chaos erupted as men from the convoy impulsively scattered with little place to hide. The air overhead filled with the whining and screaming of shells, while heaves of earth moved and moaned, the ground trembling as heavy artillery assaulted the landscape. Horses neighed and snorted amid the bedlam. Some were still hitched to overturned wagons. Eventually our small pack stopped under a grove of barren trees—sticks, really—mirroring the deathlike mud surrounding us.

Minnie's breathing was erratic as he reminded us of basic protection. "Tin hats on, Lieutenants! Protection from concussion and shrapnel pellets!" He guessed that the convoy had been spotted by enemy surveillance balloons perhaps as far as seven miles away, and we were caught in the middle. Time became irrelevant as the attack stole any sense of order, driving home its intended effect as lorries full of soldiers scattered off the road and into the mud in terror.

Fear took over my being, for what else could one feel? Mounted officers attempted to bring order, yet the chaos was unstoppable. Senses were heightened by the cordite that hung in the air, the universal smell of terror and death. The whining and whistling of shells smacking into the mud brought an impulsive desire to cover one's ears, but that was forbidden by decorum and the need to keep our hands on the reins. A man rising sky-high like a rag doll seemed dreamlike. At first I didn't register the reality of a life blotted out, his body in bits and pieces.

While each of us managed to remain mounted under the trees, my trembling and ooze of sweat consumed me as my body reacted to what my senses were witnessing. My thoughts were racing as I remembered training for this, but death was never then as present as it was in the current reality. I struggled to keep my little mare steady as my nerves contracted and neck muscles bulged. The thought punched at me that this could be it; this could be where I was to lie at rest. Just one well-directed shell could take us down. The Germans were easily exploiting our vulnerability out on that road.

The horses remained panicked. With my boots firmly placed in the stirrups, I leaned forward to stay mounted as my little mare reared. This caused the other horses in our group to become agitated, aggressively snorting the air, flinging gobs of saliva as their heads swung back and forth.

As the spooked horses sensed the attack intensifying, we scattered out of our saddles and huddled under the remnants of a tree, though there was nothing to hide behind, nothing to protect us. It just felt safer being close to the ground. I was panic stricken and sick to my stomach, very much wanting to get away, get elsewhere, *anywhere*, as a shell landed with a dull thud one hundred yards behind us, tearing up the mud.

As suddenly as the shelling began, it mysteriously ceased, but the terror remained. Was this a lull or a cessation? Did we dare allow ourselves some semblance of relief? We stood there under that burned-out trunk in a fog of uncertainty.

Creating an invisible hitch by hanging the reins at his horse's hooves, Minnie collected our horses together, soothing the giant creatures with soft whispers. That emboldened us to sheepishly move toward him as we finally accepted that no further bombardment was coming.

I knew I looked scared in spite of working so hard during training to practice various facial expressions that would mask my feelings. I could tell it wasn't working this time since Perce was looking straight at me with a look of alarm. Thank goodness Issy broke the tension.

"What did I say?" Issy kidded.

"Officers," said Minnie, "those were long-range heavy explosives—heavies—being lobbed in from miles away. The Hun are ranging, attempting to lure us into identifying any artillery positions of our own, and trying for the ammunition convoy as part of the bargain."

That simple explanation allowed me to somewhat manage my senses. Nervous, I attempted humor. "Damn, that is not very sporting."

"Quite some welcome just for us newly deployed," said Issy. "I rather think the kaiser's spies had eyes on our detraining at Amiens for the purpose of laying on those fireworks. I can't wait to put some sparks up his ass, by Jove!"

...

We remained with the convoy for a while, helping to right the turned-over vehicles and ease equipment out of the mud and onto the hard pack. While the four of us were fine, the ammunition convoy was shaken with three deaths and injuries of varying degrees. Ambulance wagons and lorries rushed the worst to Amiens, while the rest were attended to on-site.

It was distressful seeing the vacant look in some of the soldiers' eyes, many with no physical injuries. While I helped where I could, it took a gallant effort to swallow my own angst.

Was it commonplace in war for survivors to adapt to horror, to accept it as inevitable? What I saw on that road were those who didn't seem to connect with reality at all, at least for that moment. I felt sick to my stomach and fought down the impulse to heave as I wondered if I could ever become such a disconnected soul. Yet in spite of those thoughts, I toiled on. Under some guiding hand, I kept busy with assistance for the suffering.

When the wounded were bandaged, I took the initiative to suggest we move on to our regiment. Minnie jumped at the opportunity, but first we would drink some water and have a smoke.

Issy pulled out a rumpled packet of Wild Woodbines, the cigarettes miraculously preserved. "At this point, I don't care about decorum. I'm smoking one of these piss-tasting gaspers. And you, Pitman—look at you lighting your pipe! The officers' calming implement, is it?"

"I stand behind the pipe being the distinguishing and calming implement. Perhaps you might earn its respect some time?" I blustered.

"Officers, time to move out," Minnie yelled. "We still have a few miles to travel, and you'll see that the roads become congested again as we close in on the Warloy junction."

At a gallop, we closed out the morning before slowing to a walk on the approach. We could see the iconic Moulin de Rolmont windmill just ahead, the wartime symbol of protection for resting troops. We dismounted nearby.

"It is now half twelve. The RCR camp is just beyond the rise ahead. Your horses will be watered while you eat before you move out for La Vicogne."

"Corporal, are we to meet our platoons before or after dinner?" Perce asked.

"After, Lieutenant. Your entire company—four platoons—will be assembled on the roadside." Atop his mount, Minnie saluted and smiled my way, a knowing look that acknowledged our common Saskatoon roots. "I myself will leave you at this juncture, as I am reassigned to the Princess Pats engaged east of Albert. Nice riding with you, officers!"

Chapter 2

September 1916

I **was summoned.** Not with the other newly arrived officers but alone. Captain Logan, the company commander, was working in his tented headquarters.

"Lieutenant Pitman, is it? Captain Logan. Welcome to the RCR. Well, Pitman, your name certainly qualifies you for trench work!"

I wore a rather thin smile, aware I showed anxiety. "Yes, sir."

"Have a laugh, lad. It's only war. Be worried, but don't look worried, eh? Play the game, and all that."

The irony was that Captain Heber Meredith Logan was merely a year older than me, yet his position as a senior officer permitted him to call me "lad." A Nova Scotian, he was thoroughly military. Just below his rolled-up right sleeve was the tattoo "V.R.I. Royal Canadian Regiment." His dark complexion, brown hair, and gray eyes highlighted his soft features. Behind the military façade was a kind, understanding person. I felt foolish for allowing my anxiety to show.

Logan reviewed the papers he held, not reading but scanning for the gist, before he raised his eyes to momentarily assess me. "Now listen, word is that you were a little windy at training, a little rattled at times by the war machine. This is your first tour, but you've got fifty men in your platoon, all of whom are relying on you. They will be watching your every move. You are their strength; stand in there for them."

Logan's words unleashed deep feelings as an unshakeable emotion brought back unsettled thoughts. Death certainly was always a concern, but I was more worried about showing anxiety to my platoon and failing to be a good officer, about how I would react to others being torn apart, dismembered, and even vaporized by high explosives as we had witnessed on the road before. It was concern about caring for and protecting my soldiers.

Logan methodically lit a cigarette, a French Gitane with its notoriously strong odor, allowing me a few seconds to pull myself together. "I'm a little nervous, yes, but you can count on me, sir. I am up for whatever this darn war delivers."

"Good show. Last week we saw intense field action down at the Somme after taking over from the Aussies—269 casualties across four battalions."

Against knee-jerk angst, I straightened up, tightening my face in a quizzical look. "That leaves us sorely deficient of experienced men, does it not, sir?"

"We'll be all right. Over one hundred fresh recruits shipped in from England just ahead of you."

It struck me that such a large number of replacements was an indication of alarming casualty rates. "May I understand the RCR's next move?"

Logan stood tall in a thoughtful manner, lips pursed. "We are marching near where the 42nd Battalion and the Princess Pats are engaged, but make no mistake—we will be awaiting our turn to relieve the front line."

I suppose I didn't expect a firm answer to such a provocative question. "Yes, sir."

"All right, tomorrow morning you will lead your A Company to billets at Canaples. In this warm weather, I expect your tents down in double time, ready to be on the move at 0700 hours."

"Yes, sir."

I made my way through the hustle and bustle of the army bivouac. The smell of the ever-present campfire smoke amid groups of blustering soldiers presented a perverse scene that made it seem more like a large gathering of outdoor vacationers. However, the booms of cannon fire piercing the dusk in the distant battlefields was a stark reminder of war.

"Sir. Sergeant Sam Hardy at your service. I am to be your NCO assistant."

I turned to see a bright, eager-looking soldier. "Hello, Sergeant. The pleasure is mine. I understand you served with Lieutenant Lewis at the offensive last week. I'm truly sorry to hear of the loss; I'm told you were close to him. You're highly recommended. I know we'll work well together."

Hardy looked directly at me through eyes that welled up. I saw it as a sign of strong character that he was confident enough to allow his emotions to bleed. "Yes, Lieutenant. I was close to Lieutenant Lewis. We fought alongside each other in '01 in the Boer War as well. I guess that is the problem with allowing friends to team in the same platoon."

"I suppose. However, there is also comfort to be had by serving with close friends. A tough trade-off, perhaps. You're doing well considering the loss?"

"Oh yes. Count on ole Hardy, sir!"

"Good spirit."

"Sir, I'll have my section in tip-top shape for your inspection tomorrow, and I speak on behalf of the other three NCOs in your platoon. Their sections are as well prepared."

"Thank you for being my eyes and ears, Sergeant. You are aware we are shipping out at 0700 hours, so let's be fed and packed ahead of schedule. I am retiring early this evening, but you go and get your grub."

"Very good, sir. Good night."

"Sam? Thanks for being yourself and for making my arrival as easy as you could. Yes, you are my assistant, but we'll move together as a team, understood?"

Hardy beamed. "Yes, sir."

Later, I lay on my cot thinking about the events of the first day in the field and how eventful it was. I felt an immediate closeness to Sam from the way he had welcomed me with instinctive friendliness while maintaining respect for position. I wanted him to know his experience offered me confidence, but hoped he didn't think me too relaxed when referring to us as a team. As I dozed off, I felt comfortable that he would never lose respect for my position but would remain affable.

...

Contrasted against the miles upon miles of brown, churned mud that beset so much of the Somme landscape, our march across the rolling Picardy hills through morning mist was a lovely surprise. In places, late-season wheat remained yet unharvested, the thick, healthy stalks seeming more substantial than those of the Canadian Prairie. Where the golden hue of wheat was not evident, the green grass of farmland contrasted pleasantly. At times, dairy cows looked startled to see a division of the King's army on the march four abreast across the aged Roman pavé.

We had no sooner encamped in the canvas huts in Canaples than Lieutenant Colonel Hill, Royal Canadian Regiment Commander, summoned all commissioned officers to a briefing in the mess tent. Hill opened the session with a reference to how rested and spirited the RCRs looked, amid quite a few doubtful faces. Only a week before, vast numbers of casualties were shipped out from the trenches, many as corpses. No one dared let their feelings out, dreading the wrong side of Hill's intimidating nature. His steely eyes combined with his air of British blue blood reinforced his reputation as a harsh leader. Yet he tried to appear sensitive by stating, "Now, this briefing is to be an open forum, officers. All questions will be answered."

Some exuberant cowboy blurted out, "Can we do something about the rain, sir?"

"The rains are part of the fabric of western France any time of year. And yes, mud and more mud is also part of the fabric." Muted laughter filled the tent.

Captain Logan, who had been standing beside Hill, interjected in a kindly voice, "Ah, Lieutenant Colonel, many of the officers are curious about the recent events that shaped the RCR's first fight here at the Somme."

"Right, well, parts are quite rough, but it's a story that needs be told."

Hill recounted that in the prior week, the RCR, the Princess Pats, and the 42nd Royal Highlanders were ordered to secure the strategic trench at the crest of a steep hill leading to the ultimate prize, Regina Trench, in order to help push the Germans out of the Somme and back across the vast Ancre Valley. He also described the first-ever use of tanks to hasten that success, although they failed miserably. In spite of Field Marshall Haig's promise about being ready for action, most of those armored machines broke down before engaging the enemy. Not only were countless lives lost, but the trench remained in enemy hands.

Hill came across as smug and insensitive about the vast loss of troops. He was known to be intimidating, yet under that façade of an unemotional British commander, surely there must have resided a caring soul, perhaps with sons who were also fighting. Looking at him, I thought the requirement for British military protocol, that image of the stiff upper lip, seemed timeworn. What was certain was that since July, hundreds of thousands of men on both sides had succumbed to the Somme battle with little to show for it but a stalemate. While grieving for those lost souls, we were to step right into that field of action in an attempt to change the course.

"But the good news," declared Hill, "is that British troops captured Sugar Trench."

"Hear, hear!" spontaneously erupted.

I glanced at Perce, who returned a doubtful look based on his prior RCR experience on the battlefield.

"Officers, none of that. We are the humble RCR," Logan chastised. "We do not gloat over victories which cost so many lives."

As Logan spoke, Hill touched his swagger stick to his cap, capturing the irony between the two men. That stick served as a signal of outdated military authority, not the humbleness that Logan personified. I had a high regard for British military brass, the most powerful in the world, but there seemed to be a few leftovers from an older era that carried a Victorian attitude. In contrast, I believed Logan understood that in modern war, tact and listening to men in the field were required attributes.

Captain Logan continued brightening the tone. "Most of you are young, having earned your commissions through school or family." I reflected that I was commissioned after only one year in law school, making me eligible to lead fifty men into battle, unthinkable in peacetime. "You were sent here to fight for a free and democratic life, and we know most of you will have never before seen war, let alone this type of war. The only means we have to prepare you for battle is to be blunt about the facts."

A voice asked, "May we know more of those facts, sir?"

Logan explained the prior battle as an uphill fight against an enemy hidden behind well-fortified defenses. Brave troops were forced over the top of trenches into a steady barrage of rifle and machine-gun fire. In spite of seeing comrades fall, the men continued to attack. When relieved, there was a grim move back to Tara Hill for much-needed rest. "But I'll tell you what it also means—courage! It is hell out there, officers. I won't mince about it!"

There was a momentary lull in the tent as the officers reflected quietly with their cigarettes. I was quite sure they were thinking as I was; Captain Logan represented that strategic, caring type of officer who would ultimately lead us to victory.

We were yanked from our thoughts when Issy stood abruptly with a touch of bravado. "Sir, we are keen to get into that hell you speak of. How long will this wait be?"

Murmurs of support could be heard above the pelting rain on the canvas.

Logan took a long drag of his cigarette, carefully considering the directness of Issy's question. "Officers, the lieutenant colonel and I know you are eager to do your bit. Your time will come sooner than you might expect. Keep your troops keen, well fed, and above all motivated. That will be all for tonight. Dismissed."

Jumping up and saluting the departure of Hill and Logan, the officers filed out of headquarters in anticipation of supper and a night's rest.

Through the evening I thought again and again about the scene described by Captain Logan and the results the RCR had experienced. They conjured images of leading my men uphill into a bloodbath, seeing them slaughtered in random fashion by shells which themselves fell randomly. I imagined seeing a repeat of what I saw earlier out on the road, only fiercer—soldiers, many of them boys, being blown to bits, arms and legs ripped off, the screams of terror breaking through the din of battle.

It was my job to lead them into the horror.

...

The following morning the sound of the bugle pierced the air, signaling réveille. Percy Sutton and I stood at the edge of a grassy field. The morning dew glistened across the horizon, and the damp smell of turf was actually pleasant after tossing and turning under the musk of mildewed canvas.

Percy seemed on edge. His strong chin jutted out farther than normal from his narrow face as he offered me one of his Gitanes.

"You all right, Perce? You seem distracted this morning."

"Lack of sleep. Thinking about last night's briefing kept me way too alert."

I looked directly at him, absorbing his angst. "Yes, I know Hill and Logan's description of hell was not exactly a sleep aid."

He drew smoke deep into his lungs before letting some of it escape through his nose. After exhaling its entirety, he pondered aloud, "I know they felt we needed to understand what we are about to face, needed to be open with us about the atrocities of this war, and that's scary. Really scary."

I scanned the dewy field, not sure what I was really looking at, not at all sure about any of this except that his thoughts were similar to mine. There was some comfort in knowing that I was not alone in thinking about the horrors of war. "Mm-hmm."

"You too?"

"Of course I'm scared. I also lay awake all last night brooding about what we are about to face. Yeah, me as well."

"What do we do?"

"What we signed up for, I suppose. I don't have that answer, Perce. Except maybe we just stay focused on what we were instructed to do and our training will guide us safely. Maybe just stick together out there."

Perce paused in thought before speaking. "You'd think I would be used to this, know what to expect. The problem is that I've seen the horror up close, not as a platoon leader, but as a follower, a regular soldier. But I suppose you're right, stick together. You, Issy, me, and the others. Stay focused."

"I find that I am able to get through stressful things if I focus on what's in front of me for the moment. Doesn't always work, mind you."

Perce became momentarily distant, deep in thought, as he chain-lit another cigarette. Diverting his eyes back toward me, he looked troubled. "Bob, uh, I need to tell you something. Wasn't going to because I didn't want to add more grief, but perhaps you should know."

I was startled, not so much by what he said but by the look in his eyes. "What? What is it?"

"You remember hearing about what happened to your fellow Saskatonian Henry Egar?"

"Yes, God bless him. He was one of our divinity students, you know."

"Yes, well, I served beside a bloke who was with him up at Sanctuary Wood back in June. In the trench, day after day, we talked. He told me about Henry. There was nothing left of him, Bob; he simply disappeared. No inconvenient arms and legs torn off, no mangled body—atomized by a shell."

"Sweet Jesus, I had no idea!"

Tears clouded Percy's gray eyes. "You know what they call that? They call that a clean death. No fuss, eh?"

I felt like being sick. I was thankful I had not eaten, since my mind swirled with memories of Henry. "That is haunting. Bloody awful."

He snuffed the cigarette out in the mud and stared ahead for a long moment. "And you know what the story is? The Pats were isolated in that wood under an intense German barrage. The brass had no idea their boys were being annihilated."

Placing my hand on his shoulder, I looked into his eyes. "That why you're not sleeping?"

"I suppose. It haunts me, you know."

"You've seen the worst; you've heard the worst. You're a good man who will get through this war. We all must believe that."

"This war is total hell, Bob. Total fucking hell." He wiped his eyes on his sleeve. "But we signed up, and we will sure as shit do our best, eh?"

I kept my hand on his shoulder as we made our way back to the camp, both of us silently deep in thought. I knew we were good friends and had become close by sharing things—good and bad—that would always remain with us.

Chapter 3

September 1916

After holding at Canaples for a few days, the order finally came through to march to the Somme in relief of the CMR, Canada's mounted rifle battalion. "Sir, will you carry your pack while mounted, or do you wish it put on the lorry with the others?" Sergeant Hardy asked.

"In the lorry, please." I was trying to learn not to say please to my NCOs, to observe more of the military discipline I was so recently taught. This reminded me of how quickly I had been expected to change from a civilian to a military leader. It seemed implausible that less than a year before I was a law student and now I was about to command soldiers in an active battlefield. "And Hardy, keep alongside my horse. I need you to relay orders to the platoon, and in these rain-clogged roads, the lads won't hear well."

"Yes, Lieutenant."

Reaching the staging area, the atmosphere was tense with the anticipation of battle, amplified by the rumbling of artillery alongside regular flashes that reflected off the low cloud cover. Through rain-muffled conversation, the RCRs spoke of spirited decorum, knowing their time for advancing to the front trenches had drawn near.

In these waning days of September, the Somme battle had been waging for months with no decisive winner. Now with the fall rains, the battlefield would surely be a quagmire. I wondered if there would soon be a winter withdrawal, more of the dreaded stalemate we continued to hear about. Checking my Webley revolver, I heard the sucking sound of boots in mud, footsteps slogging their way toward me.

With his trademark smile, Issy crooned, "I say, you're lost in thought."

"Can't keep down an active mind, you know, what with that constant rumble over at Thiepval," I retorted with a building grin.

We had both attended the officers' briefing that morning for the Canadian Corps' update and the overall strategy for this section of the war. "It looks like the brass smells some sort of success. Think we'll be going in soon?"

I searched Issy for signs of concern, but he was his same upbeat self, which was reassuring.

"The battalions in the field have been out there for over a week, so we know they will need rest soon. That's when we will probably move. You think?"

"Thinking the same, old chap! Say, I've some news—thought you would want to know."

My mind whirled back to my discussion with Perce a few days before about Henry Egar. "What is it? What's happened?"

"I was just in seeing Logan, peeking at the casualties. It seems your Minnie went down during the intense battle last week, just after leaving us at Worloy."

I tensed, not wanting to hear about another Saskatoon friend gone down but needing to know. "No, Iss, fucking hell! Not Minnie—"

"It's rather all right, only a minor one, a Blighty. No limbs lost, nothing permanent."

I livened, relieved of a building agony. "He's alive?"

"That's what I've heard. Bomb wound to the arm. To be transferred to Bristol, they say."

"Godspeed to him. Thanks for the update."

Issy regained that influential, infectious smile. "Let's get our lads onto the parade ground in time for review, shall we?"

...

Logan's strong voice pierced the heavy rain, clear to anyone within one hundred yards. "Lieutenants Pitman, Sutton, Isbester—good work getting your platoons through bad roads. At 1200 hours we will be marching to billets east of Albert."

I instinctively tensed at the announced march to Albert and felt a compulsion to yell through the rain. "Sir, that is the jumping-off location up the Bapaume Road to the trenches. Do I alert my lads that we are going straight into the fight?"

Perce shot me a look that suggested I sounded naive. I watched the captain's brow furrow. Logan was an understanding soul, but the situation was tense. "Lieutenant, the platoon will be issued orders when orders are issued. Understood?"

I felt stupid about losing my composure to ask that question. In the atmosphere of pending battle, I knew it took courage to remain quiet, to accept orders when they were issued, and not to probe my senior command. That is what I was seeking, and that is what I needed to practice. I saluted as I barked, "Yes, sir!"

...

The warm drizzle that unleashed a powerful earthy scent seemed the appropriate background to reflect the somber mood of the troops.

Some would be thinking the worst, that they would not return. Others thought they might get lucky and only lose a limb. None would return unscathed. *C'est la guerre!*

I sat astride my mare on the road to Albert as my men, four abreast, marched behind. Issy and Perce were ahead, leading their platoons in the same fashion. The lively teasing about the state of the horses just a few days before seemed distant memory.

Feeling a need to connect, I called to Hardy, "Sergeant, the landscape change is startling. Just a few miles south of Picardy, and we're in mud and mire."

"Yes, sir. Many times blown to pieces, repaired, blown away, then repaired again. Rain makes moving forward tougher."

I reflected on our surroundings. The once-productive farmland had been ravaged by shellfire, the churned mud composing a monochrome, barren landscape. The trees had become mere splinters pointing to the sky, their threadbare branches seemingly reaching up to the heavens for help. The shell craters contrasted with the flat horizon, creating a lunar appearance. Even the city that loomed ahead seemed barren with no more color than the landscape surrounding it.

"What the devil is atop the church ahead?" I asked Sam.

"That's Albert's most prominent icon, the Basilica of Notre Dame."

"Yes, I have read about it, but what is hanging from its steeple?"

"Was going to say, sir. That is the leaning statue of the Virgin with infant Jesus. It toppled over from German shelling but didn't fall completely off. Many French and British soldiers believe the war would be lost if the statue fell completely."

I leaned over for Hardy to better hear my lowered voice. "By God, that is daunting. Superstitions can be dreadful."

Whether Hardy agreed, I'm not sure, for as we rounded the corner of a sunken road, I heard a commotion. Turning in my saddle, I saw an excited lad a few rows back. He looked too young to even be there. "Hey," he yelled, "look at the sign! 'Road No. 1 to Crucifix

Corner and the Trenches.' We're bloody marching in the right direction! Action at last!"

"Sure, but look here," whimpered another.

Off the opposite side of the road lay a makeshift cemetery formed after prior battles. Rather than leaving the distorted and crippled bodies scattered across the field and in water-filled craters, surviving troops had carefully placed the corpses in rows of aboveground graves. The marching troops stared in silence at the claylike mud that had been hastily shoveled over each mound with a wooden cross inserted as a headstone. The effect was amplified by the absence of vegetation; it was just rows and rows of crosses on rain-slick burial mounds.

The reticence was suddenly broken by a yell from a soldier marching in the immediate-forward platoon. "Ah, you sod! The bastard puked on my boots. It's just a bunch of dirt and crosses, you shit—"

"Eyes ahead, B Section. Keep marching," bellowed their NCO. "This is war. With war, there are casualties. Get used to it."

They didn't listen as ranks broke. The one soldier's physical reaction to an overwhelming reminder of death caused disarray among the others. Their frightened looks risked becoming infectious, which could not be tolerated. "Sergeant Hardy, we require order!"

"Yes, sir!" He ran forward, working with the other NCO to physically turn a few of the soldiers to resume marching order while he barked at the others to form up smartly.

They obeyed. They were trained to follow orders and quickly did so. This was a reminder of how things could fall apart, how important it was to maintain order on the battlefield. Even so, I understood the natural feeling of trepidation.

Sergeant Hardy continued with his stern command. "Forward march, eyes ahead."

...

Over the next few days, we settled into our Albert billets against the close backdrop of artillery and gunfire. To keep the soldiers fit, each platoon lieutenant organized working parties to repair roads and scout the forward areas. Armies did not survive idleness.

One evening I joined a small contingent of officers who took the liberty to visit a nearby *estaminet*. We were free to travel into Albert as long as someone knew where to locate us in short order. In that regard, Hardy proved a good friend.

Issy was balanced on a bar stool, waving his glass back and forth as he spoke. "Hell, Bob, 'ow many pints of this French Pils, wot?"

"I've had a few, but I'm sure you've had a few more, eh?"

He puffed out his chest, almost toppling over. "Yabut, ise a bigger body, I have!"

Perce laughed. "You two sisters at it again, are ye?"

I held up my glass in a toast, stumbling forward as I put my arm around his waist. "Hugs to you, my brother, but sisters don't fight. Just ask my two."

"Bet sey do," slurred Issy. "Tell me about them." He closed his eyes in an attempt to better focus.

"Ah, Ethel and Hilda. They are darlings. Sometimes naughty when they were growing up, but they didn't fight, no sir. Beautiful girls! The elder, Ethel, moved out to the Canadian West before the war and married just about a year ago."

Perce cut in. "That leaves the younger one at home, then?"

"Hilda. What a sweetie. She was so scared when I brought her and Ethel over to Canada. She was only seven. No idea what we were chasing or why we were moving from England. Papa saw a brighter future, that's all we knew."

"And you did well, I'd say ... university and all," said Perce.

"Oh yes, no doubt. I worked hard, though, law clerking while attending classes. Had to focus, if you know what I mean! Ha ha!"

I glanced to my right, where Issy was seated. In the short time Perce and I had talked about my family, Issy's head had slumped into his folded arms on the bar top, the corpulent barmaid laughing jovially. "Ah, will ya look at him! Blast, how do we get such a bulk off the bar stool and back to billets?"

"I got this." In an instant, Perce obtained a couple of mixing canisters from the bartender and clanged them straight over Issy's head.

Issy sat bolt upright, almost falling backward except for Perce pushing up against his back. "Argghh! Are we at war, boys?"

"No, we're at peace, wot?" Perce groaned.

I couldn't help but laugh quite loudly. Percy laughed too, almost letting Issy's bulk slip free. "All right, time we clamber back to billets before the MPs are sent to hunt us down."

We stumbled down the back road leading to camp, Perce and I alternately supporting Issy as he wavered from side to side between us. Luckily, we made it without incident.

The few hours at the tavern were selfishly good for us. The exchange of friendly banter and at times ribald humor was a rare privilege for junior officers, and the diversion allowed us to bury the angst brought on by the coming battle for a small time.

Well, one of us buried it thoroughly.

Chapter 4

October 1916

The next morning was a sunny and warm Sunday, the first day of October, and a fine church service was held in the cinema tent. Shortly after, Perce, Issy, and I were summoned to Captain Logan's desk. He sat there, displaying a Cheshire cat grin while we stood in a row at attention. "I trust you gentlemen are recovered enough to properly absorb this briefing after, shall I say, absorbing a sufficient amount of alcohol last night."

Perce risked a sideways look at me that required no interpretation. How in blazes did Logan know? Since we couldn't check our grins, we examined the floor. Issy chortled. "We officers thank you for allowing a little discretion in our routine, sir."

"Very well, overlooked. I suppose you lads needed an outlet. Now listen, I'm pleased to advise that as of late yesterday, we've had some progress," Logan declared as he laid out the previous day's success in the field.

Although Regina remained in enemy hands, the trenches leading to the ridge had been captured. It was made clear that the cost to the Canadian Corps was enormous. The 5th and 8th Canadian infantries were still battling fiercely.

Issy raised his hands in delight. "Sir, this is great news to tell the lads. With blessings to the poor souls who perished, we are almost at our Somme objective. Forward, the Light Brigade! Charge for the guns!"

Logan delivered a poker stare as he reprimanded, "I will remind you, Lieutenant Isbester, that Tennyson's very next verse is 'Into the valley of death.'"

Issy looked at the captain, his lips pressed together in an apologetic straight line. "Yes, sorry. That is indeed the case, sir."

"Look, all your lads out there need to be buoyed by this news. The Hun continue to be very stubborn about defending what they believe to be theirs." His look was stern, strongly conveying his meaning. "We must take Regina Trench."

The tone in the room was upbeat. Being supportive, I broke in, "We do understand that, sir, and we are daily, hourly, assuring the lads that success is—"

The sound was unmistakable as an artillery shell whacked into the mud nearby, a whistle followed by an explosion. We ran from the captain's tent to find out if this was friendly fire or Hun fury.

Chaos was erupting. Men were running, some directionless and some with purpose. In panic, others had tripped into the mud. Within a moment we knew the deafening sound and stinging smell of burned cordite was from enemy artillery raining shells across, beside, and over us. I looked around, seeking the location of my platoon while fighting the urge to be sick. Yet I held it together, summoning inner strength.

Long, shrill whistles pierced the air overhead as heavy artillery shells dropped around us, sending tremendous amounts of earth as high as the tallest of grain silos. Alarmingly close, one landed some twenty yards behind us. Shrapnel burst overhead, immediately followed by kicked-up earth as its rocketing pellets hit everything in their way. The Huns were throwing everything at us.

My survival instinct kicked in as I focused on getting to the work area where I knew my platoon was. I thought perhaps the prior bombardment had better prepared me, but my pounding chest told me one never got used to this. "Platoon, spread yourselves thin! Now!"

I heard a triple bang as three shells landed in succession, or did I feel them? My senses became muddled as terror brought confusion. Shell upon shell roared overhead, but as I focused, I realized most were rocketing beyond us. I felt hopeful they might be seeking a distant target, but I couldn't be sure since my sight was blotted out by thick smoke and exploding earth. Still, my trembling body moved forward, propelled by an instinctive need to protect my platoon and all the troops in camp. Overcoming my physical reaction, I felt different, stronger than at Amiens.

Others yelled similar orders based on our rote practiced training. *Spread yourselves thin.* Yet there was so little ground to scatter across with so many platoons close by. Soldiers continued to run in every possible direction, but some now stood still in a daze. So many new ones had thus far not experienced shelling, not experienced battle of any kind.

"You all right, sir?" Hardy yelled as he emerged through the smoky veil. I smiled at him, soothed by his experienced, calm demeanor while under fire.

Logan was out of breath as he emerged through the fog and smoke. Through mud-splattered lips, he muttered something unintelligible.

"What's that, sir?" I asked.

The captain glanced at Hardy before looking back at me.

I confirmed, "It's fine, sir. The sergeant is as trusted a soldier as any."

"Well, gents, the heavies are mainly being directed over toward C Company, but how the devil would the Hun know our twelve-inch howitzers are on the railcars they are protecting?"

I stared at Logan for an instant, assessing whether he was remorseful or annoyed about the secret cargo now being disclosed, but was not able to perceive either. "Twelve-inch ... protecting ... C Company? Captain, I—we had no idea."

Logan was now deep in thought. Again, it was difficult to read his mien. He muttered, "How could the Hun have known? And with such accuracy."

No response was expected as the captain was talking his way through the crisis. He was restrained as he assessed the situation. I admired his poise under attack. I felt safe to be beside him at that moment, could see his innate skills at work. None of us in the junior ranks had been aware we were protecting a trainload of heavy guns, but at that point, it didn't matter. "There is devilish little we can do about this, Pitman. Ah, a moment please." Logan turned to a runner who handed him a note; the scribble was in Morse code.

Hardy and I stood before him, waiting for the news, as he dismissed the runner. "Aeroplane reconnaissance has picked up the location of the Hun battery. Our large guns will be retaliating, putting their lights out as it were."

Amid shells still raining down, I wondered at the logic. "Will that not confirm to the Hun that his hits are good ones, and won't that put our men more at risk?"

"Yes, Lieutenant, exactly. So when the barrage lifts, when their guns are silenced, assemble your men and be ready for a march to Tara Hill. Get that message to the other officers, but await my final orders before heading out. Things are moving fast."

As an afterthought, Logan glanced at me before locking on Hardy. "And soldiers, no need to discuss the howitzer affair beyond this circle."

"Yes, sir."

As our guns put down the attack and we got our platoon organized, I found myself thinking about Logan and how he was so naturally effective. While maintaining the necessary level of authority and poise, he validated his team by involving us in some of his thoughts and actions. He was definitely not the Victorian officer that had fought prior wars.

...

The RCRs double marched as horse ambulance wagons swept past with the injured. The air was filled with the acrid smell of smoke, penetrating taste buds and stinging eyes. We arrived at the Tara Hill bivouacs near dark.

Only a few miles from the Somme front, the din of artillery was constant, confirmed by yellow flashes flickering in the distance. The battle hung over us like a cloud as thick cannon smoke was carried by air currents for miles. Chores were attended to with murmured talk as tents were pitched and mess prepared. I asked Hardy for an accounting of our A Company and found we had suffered three wounded, with Private Brown of my platoon in critical condition. I was distraught but not surprised that C Company had taken the worst of the shelling, with eight wounded and four killed. It was not easy to value the cost of those lives against the prized howitzers and undamaged train, which all remained safe. Gloom set itself down across the whole regiment after a Sunday that had begun so beautifully.

As Hardy and I reviewed the state of our platoon, a muffled whimpering came from somewhere in the darkness behind my tent, strange since the soldiers were in mess for dinner. We moved toward the sound, shining an electric torch in the direction of the sobs.

"Private, what's wrong?" demanded Hardy.

The young soldier was sitting upright in the mud, holding his knees to his chest, and rhythmically rocking back and forth, shaking violently. My sergeant looked stern, tougher than I'd seen before. "Speak to us when spoken to. That's an order."

There was still no reply. In the torchlight I could see the fear in this young man's eyes, staring blankly up at us as we knelt beside him. Without notice, Hardy swiftly raised the back of his hand and whacked the lad across the face, immediately drawing blood from his upper lip.

I stood up. "Sergeant Hardy!" I hissed through clenched teeth. "That's just about enough. Can't you see this soldier is in shock?"

"Yes, I can, which is exactly why I need to knock some sense into him. I've seen this in battle many times, particularly among new recruits."

I intuitively understood Hardy's action, the need for military order. Yet it was a shock. The young soldier's raw emotion invoked in me a sudden urge to also sit and rock back and forth, to make things feel better by curling up into a ball. As such thoughts coursed through me, my anger subsided. "I understand. Now leave me with this soldier. Dismissed."

He saluted and left.

The soldier's rocking and whimpering had stopped. I knelt down again, searching his eyes for recognition of any sort. I had no idea what I should say, but I wanted to sound empathetic and also take control.

"Now, Private, you will need to speak to me," I warned, "either by order or by your own will. Is that clear?"

He looked at me with scared eyes and nodded.

"What is your name, lad?"

"S-Spencer, sir."

"That's Private Spencer?"

He nodded yes. Hardy was correct. The lad needed discipline if he was to survive the trenches. Yet I continued to allow emotion to restrict my ability to direct this soldier to stand, to immediately order him back to his platoon. "All right, Spencer. Are you able to tell me why you are back here?"

Spencer was frozen but needed to pull himself together. "N-no, sir . . . I mean, yes, sir. I don't know."

"How long have you been part of the RCR, Private?"

"Six months, sir."

"And how long have you been in the field?"

"One week, s-sir."

"Ah," I said. "And today was your first artillery action, was it?"

"Y-yes . . . er, yes, sir."

"That was a big scare. Every soldier on that field back at Albert felt the way you do now, only they were somehow able to take things in stride. You need to buck up." I felt for him, but my responsibility was to get him back to his platoon.

He stammered between sobs. "Yes, sir, but they didn't have a village f-friend who was s-sent out a week ago, who was my best friend, shot between the eyes as he peered over a parapet. We took our O-Levels together, then p-pipefitting, aw . . . now he's just gone!"

I'm sure the soldier saw the empathy in my eyes. I wanted him to. "No, they did not. You must always remember that friend. Never forget him, but you must stand up and move forward."

"How can I, when it will be me next? Or another friend? Or maybe—"

"Yes, Spencer, maybe me. It could be any of us next time, but that is why you must go back to your platoon, have the will to fight. You have no choice, soldier."

I felt a need to grab this lad, to give him the hug that I knew he was wanting, and to tell him everything was going to be all right, but this was war.

We locked eyes and held them for a fleeting moment before he averted his gaze, unsure of himself. "Are you afraid, sir?"

"You bet I am. I'm just like you, coming to this war from a cozy life in a cozy home. I tell myself every day to be brave. Try to build some courage as if it were an angel sitting on your shoulder."

Spencer remained defensively curled but forced a response. "Yes, sir." The conversation was slipping away from the direction I intended, not bringing strength to his character. I couldn't do any more for him.

I emulated Hardy's stern look. "Now, look at me. Who is your platoon commander?"

"Lieutenant Isbester, sir."

"Yes, a good man."

There was a rustling a few steps away as a figure emerged through the darkness. I recognized Corporal Clancy but couldn't recall whose platoon he was from. "Lieutenant Pitman, sir," he said. "Sergeant Hardy indicated your whereabouts. All well here?"

"Yes, Corporal, everything will be just fine. Just chatting to young Spencer here, one of Lieutenant Isbester's men. Perhaps you could guide him to his platoon, show him the way."

The corporal looked from Spencer to me and back again. He seemed to instinctively understand the situation but respectfully said nothing. "Of course. And a message from Captain Logan, sir. The entire regiment is standing ready to relieve the 5th CMRs in the trenches tomorrow. We will be advised of company assignments during the march."

Spencer glanced up at me, forcing a smile, yet he was not going to speak for fear of crying. I could see in his eyes that he appreciated our talk. I felt good about being able to help a young soldier, the experience reminding me of calming my little sister Hilda, who was so scared of boarding that big ship sailing for Canada a number of years before. In that case, though, I could wrap my arms around her and whisper comforting words.

Spencer had no such outlet. Like thousands of others, he needed to toughen up if he was to survive.

Corporal Clancy saluted as he led him back to his platoon.

...

As I stepped out of the mess after supper with Issy and Perce, I found Sergeant Hardy spinning a tale with a few of the platoon regulars. He was older than most at thirty-eight, a veteran of the Boer War. He wasn't fond of his nickname, Hardknocks, but he earned that brand for his known willingness to stand in front of a bullet to save another man. Indeed, he had reputedly done so. Although never married, I was told Sam dazzled the ladies with his keen sense of humor and rough good looks that were complemented by rich blond hair and deep blue eyes.

"Sergeant Hardy. A word, please?"

"Yes, Lieutenant. And word has it you did good work with that young lad. You've a way about you."

I felt awkward at the recognition. It was something any junior officer would do. "Thank you, Sam. Perhaps I ought to have used more of your tougher approach." I looked at him smartly, turning the conversation more official. "Orders are imminent that the regiment is to relieve the 5th CMRs in the trenches tomorrow."

Sam beamed. "If I may say, sir, that's good news." My tightened face caused him to reflect. "Well, in the sense that at least we finally have orders."

I remained pensive. "Yes, I suppose."

Still, in his excitement at the prospect of getting down to the business of war, he continued with a lilting voice, "Might we know which part of the trenches our A Company will occupy?"

"Not yet. Captain Logan is still working out the details of relief and reserve, and determining which platoons will move to the fire trenches straightaway."

"Good, sir."

While not sharing as much exuberance as Hardy, I knew Logan was the most capable and uplifting of any senior officer. "This will be the toughest four-mile march yet, and this rain is making things quite sloppy."

"Yes, but we are prepared. Sir, may I inquire as to your progress on the letter?"

My mind shot back to the earlier news that Private Brown had succumbed to his injuries. "Ah, the letter."

"I realize it's a first for you, having to inform the family and all. It would be no bother for me to do a revision if you wish."

Hardy was right to bring this up, for I had stalled, pondering what words would be appropriate. There was the British Army standard letter of regret, but I wanted the missive to be personal. How would my folks feel about a standard-issue regret letter?

I pulled the letter from my tunic, glad to hand it over for an experienced review. "Yes, that would be most helpful."

Mr. Alan Moore
Athalmere, B.C.
Dominion of Canada

1 October, 1916

Mr. Moore,

I regret very much to inform you that your nephew, Private Nels Brown, No. 477114 of this regiment, was killed in action on the evening of 30 September, 1916. Death was instantaneous and without any suffering.

The Regiment was suddenly under attack and your nephew's platoon, my platoon, was one of the two which received most of an enemy artillery barrage. For peace of mind, please be comforted in the knowledge that the defense of a strategic asset was successful; your nephew's death was not at all in vain.

On behalf of all the Regiment, I deeply sympathize with you in your loss.

Your nephew always did his duty and now has given his

life for his new country. I do trust you will be able to locate his parents in his native Denmark to advise this sad news.

We all honor him; hopefully you will feel some consolation in remembering this.

His effects will reach you via the base in due course.

In true sympathy,
Robert Courtenay Pitman
Lieutenant, Royal Canadian Regiment

"It's a good letter, Lieutenant. Well said."

"Crap, Sam, I'm bloody concerned. You and I know that Private Brown suffered under injury, dying slowly and painfully at the Casualty Clearing Station."

Sam extended his hands from his side, palms facing out, in mild exasperation. "But it's your job to make the next of kin feel all right about their sacrifice."

"I understand that, but a lack of honesty does not feel right. We were not directly protecting that train, so how can we say the defense was successful?"

Hardy paused, pondered his next words before speaking. "What would you say, sir? 'Your boy suffered such a great deal that I'm sorrier than if he hadn't'?"

I expelled the breath I wasn't aware of holding. "Point taken. Let's put this bloody well behind us and hope I don't do this too many more times."

Hardy lingered, his demeanor slightly changed and awkwardness apparent.

"Is something else on your mind, Sergeant?"

"Sir, will you be on mount or on foot? I ask because it was Lieutenant Lewis's practice to walk the final bit to the front lines."

I was caught off guard, stumbling, yet it was such an innocuous question. "Of course I will travel on foot, Sergeant."

I didn't know what was expected, but I was sure that if the lads were used to their lieutenant walking with them, that would be my practice. Perhaps being on foot in front of my charges would signal a higher level of support for my platoon.

Chapter 5

2 October, 1916

Captain Logan entered the HQ tent amid muffled sounds of artillery shells and bursts of machine-gun fire. Adjutants and staff officers were moving here and there in their busy responses to field telephones, scrambled messages from aeroplane reconnaissance, and trench map updates.

Under instruction from the adjutant, his platoon leaders were assembled. "Officers, this evening A Company marches into battle to continue the assault on Regina Trench. The enemy positions are being defended by multiple belts of wire and by a determined German enemy."

"Will we be taking over the 5th CMR position, sir?" asked Perce.

"Affirmative. Lieutenant Sutton, you will lead your men into that battle with more determination than the most vicious Hun can muster. We must stop our losses, and we must take that trench."

A heavy silence fell among the officers present, but Logan looked alert, the eve of battle bringing ruddiness to his face. With a confident voice, he declared, "You are fresh, and the Hun is tired. You will do well for your king and your troops. Now, let's look at this trench map."

We crowded around the table as he pointed to Mouquet Farm, which would be used as the jumping-off point by all four companies of the RCR. It would also serve as our A Company's reserve location.

"Lieutenants Isbester and Blott, your 2nd and 3rd Platoons will make your way to the communication trench under cover of darkness. From there, a guide will take you on up the fifteen hundred yards to the fire trench. And 4th Platoon—Lieutenant Sutton, you will advance the nine hundred yards to the support trench. Lieutenant Pitman, your 1st Platoon will stay in reserve at Mouquet. Clear?"

A collective "Yes, sir" sounded buoyant, but an uncertain shuffling and coughing indicated ubiquitous discomfort. Issy and Blott knew their orders were to take them over the top, straight into enemy machine guns. Many would not make it. I had no idea how Logan made his decisions, and although I was selfishly relieved to be entering my first action in a reserve capacity, I was anguished about my friends who were ordered directly into the fray.

"Now, we will move out at 1500 hours for the four-hour march to Mouquet, allowing for the heavy rain, mud, and transport clogging the roads."

I forced a cough, muttering a low-key *ahem*. "Sir, I've heard that Mouquet might still be hot, what with the Huns able to pop out of underground cellars. Could that be so?" I had heard that the Germans held the Farm up until the previous week. The rumor was that, although the Canadians thought it was cleared, surprise bursts of machine-gun fire erupted as the enemy emerged from rubble heaps and cellar entrances, creating terror.

Logan held his confident appearance. "I assure you, the Huns were ultimately smoked out and eliminated. The cellars have been routed and sealed. Little credence ought to be given to that intel, Lieutenant."

"Thank you, sir."

Logan looked at the circle of officers standing at the table, assessing our demeanor, and then ordered, "Company dismissed."

Outside, a shimmering orange-and-red glow reflected off the heavy, rain-filled clouds hovering over the Somme battlefield. All of us were in a wistful mood as we gathered in my cramped hut. I offered Issy my chair, while Blott and Perce sat on the cot. Leaning against my folding desk, I broke our contemplative silence by reflecting, "I guess this is it, eh? We're on the cusp."

Perce was twisting one of his brass tunic buttons between his thumb and forefinger while looking from one of us to another. "Yeah, this is surely the beginning of a new chapter."

I forced a smile as I reached deep into my duffel bag and felt for the narrow neck of the bottle, my hand emerging with the scotch I knew Hardy had stowed there while we were in our briefing. The liquid glistened in the candlelight, symbolizing a beacon of our friendship.

"Oh yes, just so," Perce said with a snicker. "Your timing is impeccable!"

"Now, that's the spirit," said Billy Blott, the 3rd Platoon leader.

I held up the bottle in an improvised toast, then took a long pull. With a guttural expiration, I passed it to Issy while wiping my mouth against the back of my sleeve. As it moved around our tight circle, each made a quiet salute with "cheers," "hurrah," and even "amen," before tilting it back.

With a second gulp and smack of his lips, Issy said, "Don't know how you got this, Bobby, but it's a godsend."

"The usually resourceful Sam Hardy at our service. Don't know how the devil he does it—"

"And you're not asking," interrupted Perce with a chortle.

Blott chuckled knowingly. "Well, don'tcha think any good NCO can turn water to wine?"

We managed a laugh before the enveloping silence once again took hold. Billy filled the gap with, "I dunno if you're the lucky one,

Pitman, or if you and your platoon face agonizing worry waiting for your turn to jump in." His unsureness showed in his nervous grin.

I directed my glassy eyes in his direction. "You have a point. Stuck below you for days might be more troubling than being in it."

Issy chuckled. "Don't get too stuck in the mud; we may need you sooner than you think!"

I tried to put myself into Issy and Blott's shoes. They were going straight to the fire trenches in a few short hours. It was difficult to imagine. I was glad the scotch was allowing a little breeziness in the moment.

Our attention was diverted by Sam Hardy rapping on a wood support. "Excuse me. We're folding tent, sirs."

"Thank you, Sergeant Hardy," I said. "Oh, and Sam?"

He turned to look back into the tent. "Yes, sir?"

I held up the now almost empty scotch bottle. "Thanks for this."

Hardy winked at me and showed a mile-wide grin as the others murmured, "Hear, hear!"

I turned back to my fellow officers. "This is it, gents. I'll see you on the other side."

While extending a tight grip, Issy gave me a slap on my back with his free hand. "Good luck to you, Bob."

"And you, Issy. Let's whack the fucking Germans to kingdom come!"

Chapter 6

3 October, 1916

Through the night, the 2nd and 3rd Platoons became entrenched. Heavy rain fell as shelling and constant enemy machine-gun barrages persisted. 4th Platoon, farther from the fire trench but in front of us, monitored the stubborn progress by providing relief for casualties and ensuring the telephone lines to HQ were kept open.

I ventured into the dawn, which revealed the complete devastation of what was once healthy land at Mouquet Farm. Vertical silhouettes of burned-out probes that had once been trees barely contrasted against the horizontal black and brown that had been plowed fields of wheat and wildflowers not so long before.

I was stunned by the mud. I had been told it was unlike anything previously known to any soldier; only the intensity of modern artillery could create such a quagmire. Even prior warnings could not have prepared my senses, as it looked and felt like a dark, sticky caramel. I watched soldiers move in slow motion, their advance paralyzed by boots sucking in and wrenching out. My own hindered progress gave me a sense of their difficulty. The front of my thighs ached as I struggled with a few steps, a violent upward wrenching as each foot brought with it gobs of the sticky substance. How the devil were our soldiers, especially those advancing from the fire trench, expected to capture targeted ground?

Returning to my quarters—a small piece of canvas with wood supports and a duckboard floor—I thought about the here and now, of its urgency. Issy, Blott, and their troops were not afforded the luxury of idle thought, survival being their sole preoccupation, as a machine gun or sniper rifle could bring any of them to an instant death. The grotesque and bleak scene—seas of mud and anxious soldiers squatting in death and decay—was suddenly as lucid as a crystal in sunlight. My thoughts drifted to that grade school memorization made suddenly understandable, Tennyson exhorting, "Ours is but to do and die."

Sitting in the chair at my small desk, I was jolted from my thoughts with the boom of Hardy's voice. "Good morning, sir. Coffee?"

Hardy could put a smile on anyone's face anywhere. I knew we had no coffee but decided to play along. "I'd love a little coffee, Sergeant. A welcome relief from that acorn-infused acid you've been feeding me."

"Ah-ha, this would be the same infusion, sir."

"Just pulling your leg. Tell me, are the lads keeping up the game all right?"

"As best be expected, sir. Some tension among them, you know, a bit rattled. I've seen this before, during this war and at the Boer. Not easy times."

I thought of my troops squatting or standing in the mud with too much time to think. "Quite so, yes."

"And if I may say, sir, the lads attending the wounded coming down the hill on their way to the Casualty Clearing Station makes for a sobering outlook, even among the strong willed."

"Yes, promotes anxiety. We'll keep them busy, checking phone lines, repairing stretchers, that sort of thing."

"Agreed. If I may, sir, how are you holding up?"

I sipped the hot liquid as I pondered the question. "It's rough, rougher than I'd expected. You're good to ask."

We looked at each other, holding eye contact. I hoped my expression was not showing sadness or possibly frustration rather than the compassion I truly felt. Sam and I both knew that things had been rougher for those thousands of soldiers before us who now lay buried in the rubble we stood over, some in pieces, unrecognizable. The Australians, then our Canadian brothers had both repeatedly clawed their way up the slopes of this nightmarish landscape only to be beaten back under intense fire. With both sides holding strict orders to give no ground, to fight to the death, high casualties were unavoidable. Our task to minimize them while taking the ridge seemed daunting.

Sam portrayed the grace of an experienced soldier, his usually mischievous blue eyes now showing kindness. "Most of the regulars understand the anxiety and are a good influence on the newer lads."

"Are they ready for the task ahead, for when we are called up?"

"Yes, sir. They are very aware of the need to take this hill. It's just those casualties coming down are beginning to paint a vivid story."

I looked up at Sam before turning back to my paperwork, trying to think of something, anything, to say that might help. "Perhaps rotate them away from the casualties every couple of hours. There will be no stand-to this morning. There is little reason to expect an infantry attack this far down."

"Thank you, sir. The men will be relieved at not having to slog through the mud."

I worked alongside the platoon for most of the day while we secured telephone lines and muscled cannon through the mud. While explosions and gunfire from up the hill sustained an edgy alert, its continual din became part of a familiar background. Those that might have been jumpy on this first battle day settled in to work seamlessly, if solemnly.

In the brief periods when the clouds parted, I could see our aeroplanes observing, sometimes engaging in scuffles with the enemy. I wondered about that romantic depiction of war, thoughts which kept me occupied. I imagined how exciting it would be flying as one of those knights of the air, gracefully maneuvering or outmaneuvering enemy aircraft. Swooping in and out, to and fro, through nothing but clear air and wispy clouds seemed so exciting. The whimsical feeling that type of warfare invoked played on my imagination as if I could be part of it.

Absorbed in similar thoughts, I had just returned to my tent when suddenly I heard that distinct whistle startlingly close. Hardy was out of breath as he slammed through the canvas door.

"Sir, we are under bombardment! The sky is lit up!"

The next explosion hit behind us, landing just beyond our tents. The shock wave sent me stumbling to the floor as Sam fell to one knee. He was up quicker. I felt my heart racing, my breath quickening, and my gut churning as the intensity built. As I stood, I grabbed my tin hat that Sam held out to me, struggling with the chin strap. We dashed out into the chaos and saw that the whole hill—from the top right down to the Farm—was lit scarlet and yellow, eerily illuminating the bursting shells and the blackness of the cascading mud.

"Sir, your orders?"

"Get the platoon into their defensive positions. The mud is muting the blasts, but oh God, the fury!"

"No direct hits yet, sir."

"You need to send two runners up to get intel from Lieutenant Sutton. The captain will be on the blower, and I need to determine if mud is making the Hun as immobile as we are. Otherwise, they could fucking well run straight down this hill!"

"Right away, sir!"

"Ensure the NCOs keep on high alert for Hun breakthrough. Meanwhile, I got your section. Get the word out. Make sure everyone keeps their damn heads about them, Sergeant!"

Hardy moved away quickly.

I began to realize the enemy barrage was not accurate since their firing was erratic and misguided. I waited with Hardy's section until his return, moving among the men who were spread out for safety. My senses were on high alert as familiar cordite wafted through the air, zinging sounds pierced the rain, and mud was flung up dozens of feet. This strengthened my resolve as I barked orders at this soldier to look up, not down, and commanded that soldier to cinch up his chin strap under a tilting tin hat.

I was still thinning the men into wider positions when the shelling ceased. Sam returned in a few minutes.

"Lieutenant Pitman!" Hardy was severely out of breath. "Our runners returned, advised the barrage was intended to harass us into reacting." He bent over and supported his weight with hands on knees. "Looking to locate our artillery. Lieutenant Sutton sends his regards, sir, feels we're all representing the regiment with decorum through calmness." In typical fashion, Perce had the resolve to send compliments.

"I would agree. Now let's do a roll call. Advise me at once that we are all present."

"Done that already, sir, and all sections confirm our forty-nine accounted for."

Of course roll call was done; this was Sam we were dealing with. "Good show. The ration party will be cleared to move in soon. You'll want to send escort guides to avoid them being lost, then direct them up to the fire trenches. I want our company fed properly."

"Yes, Lieutenant."

I knew Hardy would execute my order with full understanding. With oncoming dusk and a Mouquet Farm landscape that was so churned, roadways were obscured. It was difficult for the ration party to find their way, but I was not going to tolerate underfed soldiers.

"You have pickets assigned for the two-hour rotation through the night, Sergeant?"

"Yes."

We had established a brotherly bond, so when our eyes met, we knew there was nothing further to discuss. "All right. Let's get some rest."

Through heavy rain pounding on the canvas, I remained awake under the distant muffle of artillery blasts and machine gun rat-a-tat from up the hill. The day's attack was a stark reminder of just how vulnerable war made us. In some ways, it was good to ensure we stayed at the sharp edge. I myself felt better as I was evolving and responding to sudden crises with more determination. Being increasingly aware of fear triggers, I was able to block out anxiety. Such reflections allowed me to understand that the war was shaping me into a different person by thrusting me into confidence.

I lay on my cot in the darkness. Very lights reflected periodically through the canvas, a reminder of each enemy searching for the other. I thought of what the next day would bring when we were called up to the fire trench. I would lead my platoon over the top into no-man's-land. I would face the onslaught of German machine-gun bullets hurtling forward in rapid succession, intent on mowing down everything and everybody in their sweeping path. Sleep was not possible, but hopefully wakeful rest had some benefit.

Chapter 7

4 October, 1916

"Good morning, Hardy. What news from the wire this morning?"

"The lads up the hill stood their ground last night, sir. But they're exhausted. And they're frustrated since yesterday's attempts to push forward into Regina Trench were again repelled. Casualties were coming down the hill all night, walking wounded and such. Our platoon is helping as much as we can."

The steady casualties meant we were to be called up soon. I thought of how many times over the previous few days I had thought *this is it*. Well, that day *was* it. I wanted to get busy, to get at it, to bury my angst in work. A few deep-seated breaths increased my confidence as I remembered the sermon delivered by our regimental Sky Pilot. *Let your faith be bigger than your fear.*

Sam glanced at my heaving chest, knowing I was seeking calm. "Good work, Sam. Let's be at the ready for the order."

"Yes, sir!"

"Other news?"

"Sir, 2nd Platoon was tunneling to establish a post in advance of Regina Trench. That tunnel has simply gone, disintegrated from bombardment. Men with it, I'm afraid."

It was not difficult to visualize just how many soldiers had perished in such disintegration. Knowing that would have spread among the troops. "God bless those poor souls. Our lads—are they bearing with that news?"

"Usual grumblings and cursing, but overall, good. One private who was previously popular for his cocky bravado has become very quiet. Reality checks attitude, I suppose."

"Quite. I'll speak to all the NCOs and their sections this morning to bring everyone up to date. Make sure rifles are clean, bayonets fixed, gas masks secure, grenades primed, and packs ready for advance."

"Very good, sir."

The morning progressed under the din coming down from the front trenches, again muffled by cloud and rain. At times Royal Flying Corps biplanes swooped below the cloud cover to observe the enemy. Their flying in bad weather turned my mind to the risk they took flying through clouds with no sight, only instinct. The thought of those flyers being aloft in mere wood and fabric propelled by a single engine both intrigued and scared me. Yet, if there was anything at all exciting for me about the damn war, it was those flying machines.

"Sergeant Hardy?" I yelled. Hearing anything in the driving rain was near impossible. A random shell whistled off to the left, ripping through the air before landing, harmless. The shelling had again increased that morning, albeit erratically. "Where the devil is he?" I mumbled to no one in particular.

After a few moments, Hardy came slogging through the sticky mud. "You called for me?"

"I've received word that the telephone wires are broken somewhere between us and the 4th Platoon. It's taking runners way too long to deliver messages through the muck. Send three of our best to get that break located and the lines repaired."

Sergeant Hardy dispersed the orders and returned to advise that while he and his fellow NCOs were doing everything they could to reassure the troops, the extended battle was beginning to affect morale.

"The increased shelling this far down is unnerving the men," he advised. "And with no telephone, we don't have eyes from up top."

"Suggestions?" I thought about the impromptu scotch meeting a few nights past when Billy Blott wondered whether waiting at the Farm would be worse than being directly in the action.

Sam surveyed the field in front of us, assessing the situation. "I'll work with the other NCOs to reinforce activity. I find that cleaning and re-cleaning equipment brings grumbles but keeps the lads alert. God knows we have enough mud to remove!"

Sam was the veteran, and I was thankful for his indispensable guidance. Although my rank placed me at the head of the platoon, I lacked experience, lacked that hardened mastery learned from years of training. That didn't so much matter on the parade ground, but sure as hell did at a time when we all faced death.

As the artillery intensified, a private trying to catch his breath approached with news that communication was repaired and that the captain requested a word. I ran over to the field telephone with the runner.

Through the crackling wire, I heard a familiar voice. "Pitman?"

With artillery banging louder and louder, I yelled into the mouthpiece, "Captain Logan, Pitman here."

"What's the situation at Mouquet just now? Quite noisy, is it?"

Instinctively looking up toward the hill, I bellowed, "Yes, Captain, the bombardments have been putting a strain on all of us." *Thwack!* "What was periodic for much of this morning appears to be increasing."

"Yes. Look here, be ready to relieve the lads in the fire trenches.

The 2nd and 3rd Platoons are taking measurable losses. We cannot make changes under this bombardment. As soon as it lifts, be prepared to move. On my orders."

"Yes, sir!"

I took a moment to reflect, a split second of thought. All the training, all the preparation over the past year, came down to this. I was to lead my soldiers up the hill and into the line of fire. Every sense in my being was working overtime with keen hearing, smell, and sight. My mind was racing back over my life with thoughts of school, Saskatoon summers, childhood, and the births of my sisters—my dear, darling sisters.

Well, the time is now!

With wet palms, I emerged from the communications hut and moved toward Hardy, who was crouched under the pelting rain having a much-earned Woodbine with a few of the troops. "Sergeant Hardy, we prepare to move up once this parade of shells subsides; 2nd and 3rd are to be relieved." I paused and looked at him with intensity. "We're up."

Sam managed a smile. "Understood, sir."

"Let's gather the platoon and muster near my tent. We need to move instantly on Captain's orders."

As I spoke, artillery shells rained down faster and louder. As the platoon gathered, it occurred to me that the Hun must be aware that our forward troops needed relief. They seemed determined to stop them, to keep a tired enemy prone to mistakes in front of them. They knew the landscape—after all, they had occupied it for much of the war—and seemed to be purposely targeting us, the fresh relief at Mouquet. The earth around us increasingly moved and moaned. The air whistled with shells, landing in the Somme mud. Geysers were thrown skyward, smoke and flame in the midst.

The blasts rendered speech impossible. We were muted by the shriek of missiles coming on with rushes of sound and at speeds that made escape futile. Moving one way could save one's life; the other, immediate death. Through it, I choked on the oppressive smoke, gagging on its corrosiveness.

Still, I yelled, "Sergeant!"

I must have looked animated to Hardy, making all the facial expressions of speech without sound. He seemed momentarily mesmerized before making his way toward me.

"Sergeant, the platoon needs to—"

Shells whizzed and cracked, then screamed into the earth, throwing up mud in blinding flashes. I stood inert and watched some of the troops scatter across the countryside, thinking they could somehow outrun the raging hate that crashed around us. Shrapnel exploded above, rocketing pellets to tear through anything or anyone in their way. That persistent stench of burned cordite reflected a ground blackened under fire.

The landscape exploded, more showers of mud thrown sky-high, cratering the earth. Shells came in fast and thick everywhere we stood.

Can't think. Must think! Must speak, must lead, but who will hear me?

I yelled orders, any orders, realizing they were more for my own duty of command than actually being heard.

Crash! Crash! Explosions caused soldiers to stumble, either from the piercing sound or being hit, I wasn't sure.

It was deafening. It was hard to see with mud covering my face, but I struggled toward a group of men. *Must lead them to safety!*

Suddenly, the ground in front of me erupted. Men and mud were thrown vertical. Some of the shells exploded underneath the thick mud, yet one shell after another burst on the surface, making the sky and earth come together in a ball of fire.

Were those soldiers hurt, injured? Must get to them, must survive this.

I gasped for air as I moved forward against a massive concussion of force before falling over in a tumble. A great heap of mud, heavy as concrete, slammed me face down. Breathing was impossible as mud clogged my nose and my mouth. Struggling to exhale, I spat.

Somehow lifting myself up, I could see Hardy moving toward me. He helped me up. Shells were driving into the mud all around us, whining louder and louder as they got closer. I wanted to scream but couldn't.

Thump! We were both thrown into the slime. Again facedown, I suddenly remembered the pub room braggarts who boasted about surviving being buried alive.

I am buried and alive! I struggled and fought. I couldn't breathe. *Must get my head up!*

My next awareness was of choking, but thankfully breathing. I looked up to see a lad, but only the whites of his eyes were showing through a darkened face. I wondered why the silly boy had covered it in black mud.

Memories emerged of my face being buried in the mud on the rugby pitch back in grade school, the bigger lads gleefully putting their boots to my head to drive my face deeper. I remember being scared, very scared, thinking that life ends when breathing ceases. I remember not being able to get up, their boots keeping me submerged. I struggled, raged with the need for breath. Suddenly yanked up by my shirt collar, I heard Mr. Rafferty scolding the bullies at the same time. *Where is Mr. Rafferty now?*

Somehow breaking free of the mud and stumbling to get up, I saw Hardy beside me and troops all around trying to help amid the continued barrage.

There, almost standing.

Thwack! Down again, this time with the sting of shrapnel pellets on my back as I saw Hardy thrown behind me. Again, my face was submerged, and I couldn't breathe. My hands were clawing, digging, fighting, and scratching at the earth. *Push up, yes, that's it! Push! Surely Mr. Rafferty will grab my collar soon. My arms are weak! Spit out the filth; ignore the stinging pellets in my back. Clear the blockage in my throat. That's better—air, breath, pulse.*

I could barely hear the shells continuing to rain down; then a sudden silence overcame me. *I need to get up, need to lead.* I was weak but standing now. I twisted my head around as Hardy yelled, kneeling in deep mud. *I can see him, must get to him and the lads . . .*

Crash! Down again. Suffocation, deafness, and stinking smells were my only sensations. My will to live was fierce, without knowing if I was hit or bleeding. Was I buried, buried alive?

Push! Dig! Dig sideways, my survival instinct spoke to me, my will to live strong. *I'm OK, aren't I?* Yet I lay there, suddenly weak, strength seeping from me. I struggled to take in air through my mouth. I was aware my nose was covered, but couldn't lift my hand to it. Weakness enveloped me.

Can't give up.

I was aware of explosions, voices, mud flying, death hovering, then blackness as I escaped into nothingness.

Chapter 8

October 1916

"Lieutenant? Lieutenant, please state your full name." I remembered waking up lying in a medical tent, hearing the sounds of nurses and the cries of injured soldiers. The stench of burned flesh and chemicals was overwhelming. I must have dozed—for a minute, an hour, I didn't know. Awake again, the room seemed alive, but I still had little focus.

I jerked my head sideways, listening, not seeing.

"Lieutenant, are you able to state your name?"

I felt weak, so weak, and lay there trying to make sense of the voice. Suddenly, I felt an urge to confirm that I was alive. "Pitman, yes. R-Robert Pitman." I said.

"Lieutenant Pitman, I'm McAskill, captain with the RCR and doctor in charge of the dressing station. If you can hear me, please nod."

I lifted my left hand to my face, feeling softness. Cotton, perhaps. Confused, I lost the ability to speak.

"Lieutenant Pitman, do you hear me?"

Somewhere between a dream state and wakefulness, I nodded weakly.

"Do you know where you are?"

I shook my head as I again moved my fingers across the covering on my face. Yes, it was cotton, perhaps a bandage.

"You are at the Albert dressing station. You have no physical wounds other than back sores, probably shrapnel pellets. Thank goodness for the steel helmet, as yours certainly took a beating. We don't know yet if any of the blasts you were near concussed your head."

I lay on the stretcher, wanting nothing but sleep.

"Are you following me, Lieutenant? Please nod if you are."

I nodded.

"That is some good news. Now, you have lost vision, especially in your left eye. You are trembling, but I'm sure you're not aware."

I forced myself to focus on the doctor's words, which brought attention to the blackness before me. Was I blind? I could not see, but was that because of the bandage or was it forever? Fighting panic, I thought back to the childhood game of hide-and-seek. Even with eyes covered, I remembered lightness. I could feel the fear rising from my gut to my throat, instinctively retching but with no result. Could I go through life without ever seeing again? I shivered in spite of the blankets that covered me, secured me.

"I'm going to ask you a series of questions. Do you understand? Please nod or shake your head accordingly."

I was overwhelmed, wanted escape, but I nodded.

"How is your hearing?"

I shook my head.

"Are you able to explain your answer, Pitman?"

"I-I seem t-to be s-sensitive to noise."

"All right, thank you. I know this is difficult. Make note of the stammering as well, nurse."

I was not aware of the presence of a nursing sister or anyone else. Of course there were others; I was in a medical station. I forced myself to listen as he explained that my symptoms were caused by experiencing intense bombardment.

"W-will I be able to see, Captain?"

I felt the doctor lean in closer, seeming to ensure he was heard over the background noise. "There is no physical damage to your retinas. We find that this is nature's way of protecting vital organs, and it typically clears up with rest. I know you're very tired, but in case of concussion, you will be woken every two hours."

I was buoyed by the news of my sight, better able to listen as McAskill explained I would be sent to a general hospital, but there was a long wait for transport. I drifted in and out of sleep. With each waking moment I became increasingly fitful trying to recall events. The noises in the background—the groans, shrieks, protests—all put me back on the battlefield. As my emotions welled up, my grief bubbled to the surface, and I had sudden visions of men falling around me, mud and flame rising up as high as a building. Where were those men now? Still at war, or did they die? Where is Hardy—

"Hardy! Sergeant Hardy! Are you all right b-back there? You were thrown. Sergeant, answer me!"

"Lieutenant!"

"Hardy, p-please, for God's sake, answer—"

"Lieutenant Pitman, it's all right, we're with you," said the nurse. "You must have been dreaming, thinking of the horror—"

"No, I wasn't dreaming. I've lost my sergeant."

"Who, Lieutenant?"

"Sam, Sam Hardy, my s-section head, my NCO."

"There is no Sergeant Hardy here at this hospital. I'm sure he is fine. Now you need to rest, or else you'll make your condition worse, especially your eyesight."

"Dammit! Please do f-find out about my Sam."

Chapter 9

October 1916

Dozing in the streaming sunshine, I recognized the familiar voice but not the setting.

"Lieutenant Pitman. Captain Scott at your side. I'm sorry to wake you, but I've been looking over your chart and need to examine you. How you are doing?"

I was confused. I knew Captain Walter Scott, an Alberta doctor with the RCR, was stationed with the Canadian Army Medical Corps at the Somme front. It didn't make sense that he was with me.

"Captain Scott, it's n-nice to hear your familiar voice, but we are no longer at the Somme, is that correct?"

"We are at Number 14 General in Boulogne. I was rotated out, away from the intensity for a few weeks. Can we sit you up a little, take a look at things?"

"Boulogne? When did I arrive here?"

"Today, while you were sedated, on the hospital train."

Captain Scott gave me a thorough examination, asking probing questions. I was relieved when he reassured me my sight would return. A nurse reapplied the eye bandage after my eyes were checked again. The captain explained that the stutter I had developed, as well as deep and fitful sleep, was typical of shell shock. He concentrated on my sleep patterns, the nurses reporting that I'd been talking out loud, acting out.

"Ought I a-apologize for anything bad I may have said or done, Captain?"

"Good heavens, Pitman! You were buried alive, fighting for your life amid the hell of a barrage. You needn't feel responsible for having nightmares. That hellish experience would cause anxiety for anyone. I understand your platoon is concerned about you."

"My platoon? Yes, my platoon. Have you any n-news on Sam—ah, Sergeant Hardy?"

"Oh, Sergeant Hardy was your NCO, was he? Yes, he came through the Casualty Clearing Station right around the time you did. Concussed quite severely, result of the blast straight at his right ear. Broken arm as well."

"H-he's alive?"

"Yes, the sergeant is very much alive. His injuries are all physical, so he was sent straight on to mend in Blighty."

"Oh, thank God. I don't remember much, b-but I do recall Sam being blown backward away from me b-before, well, before—"

"Before you blacked out."

"Yes, I suppose."

The doctor left me in the hands of the nursing staff, promising to come around regularly. He had explained that select British Army doctors, mind specialists, were studying the increasing cases of shell shock and advised me not to worry about the war. I knew that meant I was out of it for a while.

...

A few days later, I was up, slowly gaining enough energy to move around the hospital room. "Good morning, Lieutenant." Captain Scott beamed. "Fine Sunday morning. I see you're dressed and moving around; very good. Blindfold off. So, let's see, five days since the injury. How is your sight just now?"

"Good m-morning. I am frustrated, sir. I'm trying to present myself p-properly to meet military requirements. The nursing sisters are not willing to surrender my uniform."

"Your uniform was sent off for a full cleaning and delousing, repairs as well. The convalescent blues are required for all patients, even the typically well dressed. Those are now your military requirements, I'm afraid."

I felt silly wearing an ill-fitting flannel jacket and trousers all in blue; they were rather like pajamas patterned as a suit. "I-I understand, Captain, but with these rolled cuffs and gaudy red four-in-hand necktie, I could be starring in a children's Christmas play."

"Now, now. That sight of yours must be better, eh?"

I grinned, knowing I was being difficult and that having my sight was worth a lifetime of wearing blue pajamas. "Better. Still b-blurry but on the mend, I'd say. I'm relieved to have sight of any kind."

"Good, that is consistent with what we've seen among soldiers that have been exposed to explosions at close range. While some of the senses protectively shut down, we find that once the cause is removed, our brains work to correct the reaction."

I wallowed in the feeling of relief. "That is good n-news, sir!"

"Yes. Now, I'd like to spend some time this morning reviewing your symptoms. During our recent discussions, I felt I lost you on several occasions, especially when recalling the barrage itself. Sound all right?"

"Y-yes, sir."

Captain Scott reviewed my trauma symptoms, which included slight dizziness, stammering, and the feeling of being dissociated from people and things around me. The recurring nightmares were confusing as they didn't seem to relate to my battle experience. All I remembered was the consistent and relentless bombardment, seeing Sam being blown backward, and my struggle to breathe. Yet the doctor felt that recollection was good progress.

He probed about prewar nightmares, wondering if they were different from those after the barrage. I told him that the prior dreams were caused by general anxiety, being worried about a patchwork of little things, whereas the current dreams were centered on a sense of dread and threats of violence.

"Perhaps we can start with current dreams, then, ones that connect to battlefield events. It would be helpful to try to remember at least one of those dreams."

"Since I have also been acting out in my sleep, I have been thinking a lot, trying to remember. There was one in which Sister Mary helped me back into bed while she talked it through."

The captain worked with me to recall the nightmare, helping me through the frustration of not remembering all of the details. We moved to stand near a window, looking out at the Strait of Dover, which was calming for me as it faced the direction of my childhood home in England.

In the dream, I was in a vast ocean surrounded by an endless horizon of dark water. My mind was in turmoil as unknown—imagined and unidentified—danger swirled below the surface, ready to strike. I recalled feeling deep fear before I suddenly awoke, breathing heavily. Then, I remembered that it was the chaos of the water that yanked me out of my self-control—not being able to defend myself, to harness the turmoil. With the help of Sister Mary to regain some control over my senses, my breathing slowed, and I was again able to fall asleep. Later, I had thrown myself to the floor, diving onto the ground and hitting my head on the side table in the process.

The nursing sister had run back into the room. I woke others as well. Everyone was kind, helping me back to bed. But the sister remained after the lights were shut, whispering soothing words, which helped me remember why I had hurled myself onto the ground. Mysteriously, that dark water had cleared and a shark approached menacingly, his eyes bulging as he looked straight at me. In my dream, I gathered strength, enough to kick hard and dive right under his attack. He missed and I survived. I acted out that dive, crashing to the floor.

The captain remained silent after I related my nightmare, both of us peering out the window to the waves crashing ashore. I turned and could see he was processing, deep in thought.

"That was a profound experience, Lieutenant. An extraordinarily detailed recall."

"It seemed r-real enough, sir."

"Yes. I believe it represents how your brain processed your battlefield experience—the threatening bombardment, the sea of mud, diving valiantly to avoid the menace, to survive. Your subconscious invented the shark dream as a way for you to process the reality, to put it behind you."

I shifted nervously, not used to discussing ways of the mind. "I guess I hadn't thought of it that way, Captain."

"It is a guess, but the connection is quite remarkable—a way for you to process fear in a setting you are not used to."

"I see that. It feels redeeming to m-make sense of that nightmare."

"Based on your symptoms, I'm diagnosing you with shell shock and recommending you for a few weeks' rest in Blighty. That will do you good."

"Blighty, sir? Back to England? Is that n-necessary? I'm to be regarded as unfit?"

"Afraid so, Pitman. The 14th General is a good facility, but you need expert consultation. Here we offer good care, but only for physical wounds."

"S-so, you are saying I need an asylum?"

"No, not at all. The British Army has expert ways of dealing with emotional wounds, wounds to the heart, as it were. Specialists are developed in that field. At a dedicated facility, you will get the care and rest you require."

Chapter 10

9 October, 1916

Matron Nursing Sister Kay processed my admission to the Maudsley Military Hospital of the 4th London General at Denmark Hill. The grounds were welcoming with meticulously manicured lawns and bright gardens, the chirp of the birds suggesting a healthy natural environment.

Matron Kay was predictably stern but defied the stereotype of her title due to alluring blue eyes, high cheekbones, and a modern hairstyle. As a pleasant surprise, she had assigned me to a single room in the officers' ward, a privilege when military hospitals were overcrowded. I felt immediately comfortable and safe at the Maudsley.

Over breakfast the following morning, no end of patients offered comments about Dr. Mott. I was to expect a rigid man with a fair complexion, penetrating brown eyes, combed-back white hair, and a distinctive white handlebar mustache. I also learned he was considered eminent across Europe for his knowledge of neurology, which some found daunting. Still musing about those unsolicited comments, I stepped over to his offices for my first appointment.

"Lieutenant Pitman," Dr. Mott's confident voice rang out from the inner office.

I stood and approached the door. "Yes, sir."

Mott moved to the center of the room and shook my hand with vigor. "Come in, have a seat. I understand that you have settled in and had a nourishing breakfast."

"Y-yes, Doctor, I have. I'm still a little exhausted over the travel here yesterday."

Settled into his leather chair, he leaned forward across the oversize desk. "Good, good. That is, good that you had a nourishing breakfast. We encourage our patients to eat and rest well here at the Maudsley."

"Thank you, Doctor." Now that I was before him, I considered the others' references too daunting. While he seemed exacting, he had compassion on his face, which belied any threatening manner.

"I suspect it's more than the travel that has you tired. I understand you had quite the time of it on the battlefield."

I forced a smile and nodded.

Mott leaned back in a contemplative posture, fingers on each hand pressed against those of the opposite. "Now, as I understand, your encounter was a week ago. I see from your attestation that you are a law student back in Canada. Is that correct?"

"Y-yes, sir, yes. That is, until I volunteered for service."

The fingers began tapping each other. "I see. Volunteered, and no prior service anywhere in the Empire?"

"No, s-sir, just three years' militia prior to the outbreak of the war. In Saskatoon. That was more like a drinking club, though!"

Mott ignored my attempt at humor while the fingers froze in place, hands pressed together as if in prayer. "So, no battle hardening prior to our current dust up, eh? You would characterize yourself as not outwardly seeking military service, is that correct?"

Dr. Mott was direct in his questioning. At times he pointed at me with hands pressed together, but there was an enduring tone to his speech. I understood how some might view his demeanor as stuffy and rigid, but I attributed that to being intensely focused on his work. Anyway, I was used to authority figures in my previous dealings with judges at the Saskatoon law courts.

"Th-that is correct, Doctor. I was largely drawn in by loyalty for King and Country."

The hands separated and flung upward. "Yes, yes, that's the spirit!"

The doctor had made me feel comfortable enough to be direct. "I am w-wondering, though, about the reason for that question? Does bravery or leadership or even fear matter when it comes to signing up?"

"Very good question, Lieutenant Pitman—may I call you Bob?"

"Of course, Doctor."

Mott ruminated as he leaned forward into the desk. "We're still examining circumstances that cause shell shock, Bob. Some doctors claim lack of experience makes a difference, whereas battle hardening protects against shock. Others see it as an unavoidable genetic taint that's exposed. Shall we say some men are naturally predisposed to hysteria, as women tend to be?"

I wondered about that statement, thought about my strong, independent mother and about my grandmother who was an accomplished schoolmistress. I had never seen them hysterical.

After a reflective pause, Mott continued, "Now, I've reviewed Captain Scott's notes, and yes, it appears you have a genuine case of shell shock. Perhaps we could speak about what happened over there?"

I noted Mott's reference to *genuine* but set the comment aside, for I knew there were slackers who did try to shirk their duty. "I'm mostly concerned about my inability to remember what happened.

The artillery barrage has been explained to me, that I blacked out, but I d-don't recall the detail."

"All right, lack of memory. And I know you are experiencing a lack of connection to events and people as well. How does that make you feel?"

"Not very g-good, sir."

I listened to Dr. Mott explain how my symptoms dovetailed with characteristics of shell shock. I was interested to learn that with loss of memory came a loss of association with people and things around me, precisely how I was feeling. It was promising to understand that memory returns as dissociation fades. Yet it was how memory would return that I did not understand.

Mott smiled compassionately. "Does that explanation help, Lieutenant?"

I wrinkled my forehead in spite of trying not to frown. "Y-yes and no. I understand the diagnosis, but it doesn't help me feel good about how it looked when I blacked out."

"Tell me more."

I nervously fidgeted with my cap, moving it from hand to hand. "Well, as platoon leader, I worked hard to be brave in battle. I must have shown great weakness lying in the mud, not dead but unconscious. I had a responsibility—"

"Pitman," Mott barked. "You come to me with a reputation for pluck, for discipline, and especially concern that you showed for your men. You were hit, my good man, hit hard. Your platoon knows that and surely holds you with valor."

So this was the sternness now coming out, although the raised voice was offset by a compassionate smile. I collected my thoughts. "Thank you for reminding me of that, sir. Perhaps I'm trying to tidy this up in logic, when I need to consider that it's emotional."

"Yes, this has nothing to do with logic. Be strong. It's only been a number of days since your shock. Your memory loss, dissociation, stutter, blindness—they all sum to neurasthenia. You will require rest for some time yet."

Mott paused to look at me as I drew in his words. Assured that I was attentive, he continued. "I see your case as being treated with rest, good nourishment, a healthy dose of occupational therapy, and perhaps some social activities. I practice an *atmosphere of cure* here, Bob."

"It's all about rest?"

"That's right. There are some hospitals with doctors who practice disciplinary treatment; they use drastic techniques such as shaming and infliction of pain to rid the victim of shock. But not here."

I sat up, taken aback as I visualized such treatment. I controlled my breathing. "What does an atmosphere of cure look like?"

"Oh, relaxation techniques, taking hot baths, eating well, plenty of activity. Over time, we will see you lose the stutter, cease the nightmares. Count on it, Bob."

I expelled a deep breath and smiled. "I'm relieved there will be no shock in the program. Ah, one more question. I've heard that the brass wants us b-back in the trenches soonest, that there is pressure on doctors to discharge soldiers as fast as possible. Is that so?"

Doctor Mott sat back, studying the ceiling for a few moments as his fingers pressed together. "I won't deny that there is pressure on the Royal Army Medical Corps to return soldiers to the front, but in my hospital, I will not certify discharge unless I'm certain of positive integration back into battle."

"Th-thank you, Doctor."

Mott came around to see me out the door. Despite the prescription for social activity—and perhaps as a result of Mott's intense questioning—I wanted to curl up into a ball, to withdraw and sleep. The doctor's expectation of a positive outcome was understandable as it was in his interest to see patients get well using his atmosphere of cure. I agreed, for I wanted to get well, to return to the RCR, and to prove that I had the courage to get up after being knocked down, to get back in the saddle. But I was so very tired.

Chapter 11

October 1916

While I preferred relaxing on my bed during the days, I loathed it at night due to a cycle of nightmares and insomnia, which in turn caused daytime fatigue.

The worst dream since the one involving the shark attack was when I was confronted by a demon coming out of the dark. There was no shape, nothing to relate to other than a growling and guttural hissing that echoed off of unseen walls. It smelled wet, like hot, suffocating air. With imagined senses on full alert, I stood in a defensive position, holding my thick wool coat out as protection.

With my arms flailing and feet kicking, the nursing sister managed to wake me while avoiding a black eye. We talked about it, but whereas I could identify with the shark, this demon's form remained hidden. I could not relate the threat to any particular experience, which made me wonder if my shock was getting worse.

I decided I had better become more active, convincing myself that some fresh air and activity might actually help me sleep at night, so I ventured to the workshop. Assessing things at the entrance, I looked into the vast canvas tent, the only light being the bright sunshine emanating through the open doors and netted windows. As I stood there peering in, I instinctively tapped out the burned contents out of my pipe on the sole of my shoe.

After packing in fresh tobacco, I struck a wooden match and sucked on the pipe stem. The sweet cherrywood aroma delivered a pleasant feeling that relaxed me as I walked in. Everyone in the hut sprang up and saluted.

"Hello, lads. D-do you greet all patients with such high regard?"

A tall soldier, somewhat older with a warm smile, was the first to speak. "No, sir, but we stand and salute officers."

"How d-do you know I am an officer?"

The tall soldier grinned. "Your cap badge, sir."

"And your pipe, sir. It's rather posh!" observed another.

These observant lads with their friendly demeanors put me at ease. "Of course." I chuckled. "However, w-we are all here at the Maudsley for rest and good health, so no need for formalities."

"If you will excuse me, sir," corrected the tall one, "Dr. Mott insists on maintaining military discipline even in our relaxed atmosphere."

I had noted the distinction where Mott spoke informally to soldiers in therapy but maintained protocol outside his office. "Carry on, then. I'm just getting used to the hospital facilities, and I'm interested in what it is you are creating."

As the men drifted back to their work, I wandered through the large tent, pausing for a moment beside a couple of men crafting a footstool. I moved on to a table where a few men were weaving baskets. There was a lone soldier freehand painting in pastel. It was a peaceful scene, one that placed everyone on equal footing in the quest for relaxation.

Though there were moments I had to manage an instinct to involuntarily recoil at some of their shell shock symptoms—facial tics, powerful tremors, sudden spontaneous shrieking, and physically shrinking from notice. Their trauma in dealing with an invisible enemy, a hidden menace, was the direct manifestation of a dreadful war. The visible result was that shell shock was obliterating minds. It made my stutter seem immaterial in the face of what I saw, and I wondered if they had nightmares too.

Deep in thought, I drifted back toward the entrance, when suddenly the tall soldier was beside me with his hand extended in a friendly gesture. "Would you care to join us in some basket weaving, sir? I'm sure by now you've heard the joke that some of us here are called basket cases." His laughter was shared by the others.

"I admire your g-good sense of humor. You strike me as s-seasoned—an NCO sergeant perhaps?"

He beamed with the recognition. "Yes, sir, you bet. Thank you for knowing that, sir!"

I looked at him, admiring his caring eyes and taken in by his gentle mannerism. "Not at all, Sergeant. I'm a r-recent volunteer in His Majesty's service, but I'm beginning to recognize regular, uh, career soldiers. What is your name?"

"Richard Barker."

"Thank you, Richard. I'm Lieutenant P-Pitman. Bob Pitman if we skirt Dr. Mott's rules."

"Well, we'll have to abide the formal engagement, sir. But I'm known as Sarge. Would you care to learn the fine art of basket weaving?"

"With respect to your kind offer, Sarge, I will take a p-pass for the moment as I need time to settle in, stroll the grounds a little more, visit the library, and so on. Trust you understand."

"Of course, Lieutenant. We would be more than pleased to show you our skills when you are ready."

"Very kind, and I bid all of you soldiers a good afternoon."

There was murmuring as I strolled out of the hut into an autumn sunset. I was upset with myself that I had gone in search of activity but didn't commit. Yet I had little desire to mingle with those who were emotionally broken by war, even though we had common grievances. I wasn't ready to become mired in reasons why one soldier or another could not get well, even if that was blatantly selfish.

I justified this attitude because I was still fighting enemies in my sleep, and I desired to be alone. They were nice folks, well meaning in their offer to help me. Yet seeing, feeling, their symptoms reminded me too much of my own anxious trauma, so I preferred to disconnect.

When I returned to my room, a letter was sitting on the bedside table. Turning it over, I saw its return address was from John Forbes at the 2nd General Hospital in Bristol. I hadn't heard from Minnie since parting ways on the day of our arrival at Amiens. I knew that he was in Blighty like me, but was a little surprised he had remained.

Eagerly opening the envelope, I was anticipating good news, especially from a fellow Saskatonian. He was recovering well from his upper-arm wounds and was to be discharged once he was able to again level a rifle at the enemy. Minnie signed off with a desire to meet up in London, either at the Maudsley or a more cheerful establishment, if I was in decent shape myself.

I penned a short note in return, stating that my condition was still uncertain, but I was all for meeting just as soon as I was discharged. Minnie's short letter was like a shot of single malt on a breezy summer day. It gave me a connection to the outside world, to a friend who cared enough to write, and to our shared Canadian past. That was a boost to my well-being.

The thoughts of Saskatoon, of feeling the connection to family and friends, inspired me to be strong enough to write to my father.

Mr. Charles R. Pitman
426-8th Street East
Saskatoon, Saskatchewan
Dominion of Canada

12 October, 1916

Dearest Papa,
Thank you for the letters of August and September past that arrived in the regimental post. Please give my blessings to Mama, little Hilda, and to Grandma Crippen as well. I trust Ethel is doing well out in Vancouver.

Papa, you will by now have received a cable from the war office that I was wounded in action while serving in France. I am not permitted to provide much detail; however, can confirm I was at the Somme, a battle that I know has been described at length in the Saskatoon Star (thank you for sending a few copies). I am currently at the 4th London General Hospital, the Maudsley Military section, under the care of Major Frederick Mott.

Please don't be disappointed that my wounds are not physical; rather, I am suffering from shell shock, or in technical terms neurasthenia, a nervous debility.

There are parts I don't recall (memory loss is one of the symptoms). The record shows my platoon was caught in severe bombardment, resulting in my state of unconsciousness face-down in mud.

As an officer, I am charged with leading my men into battle with a lively attitude, even in adverse circumstances. I put my men before me by protecting them as best I could. The surroundings were horrific: mud, rats, and the stench of decomposing bodies from recent battles. An intense and constant threat to one's life is ever present. Fear is everywhere, but so too the force of goodness to see this war through. Some doubt the shell shock condition, but lest they walk in a soldier of the Somme's shoes, they will know not the truth.

The papers are reporting that the number of casualties being shipped back to England from the Somme has come to a crisis level, you will hear about some that hide among the wounded, preferring to shirk their duty to our King. Those malingerers, by feigning shell shock injury, place suspicion on all sufferers. I am not one of those—never will be—no matter the sacrifice. I remain committed to returning to the front as soon as Dr. Mott deems it appropriate.

I consider myself one of the lucky ones to have thus far escaped the wooden cross. Please accept my condition with the understanding that would accompany physical wounds, for they are equivalent.

Upon discharge from the 4th General, I will need lodgings for a short period and I will contact our good family friend Mrs. Courtenay Clarke for permission to remain with her until the medical board rules on my fitness to return to general service.

Your loving son,
Bob

Chapter 12

October 1916

It was a breezy, sunny day as I strode into the doctor's office and took my usual seat.

"Hello, Bob. How are we today?" He didn't wait for an answer. "Matron has brought me up to date. Let's see, your eyesight has returned to normal, and your stutter has receded very nicely." His grin showed that he was proud of his atmosphere of cure. "Now, what about the nightmares?"

Knocked from my high spirits, my mind raced, at first about childhood dreams, then more recent ones. I remembered dreaming, at a tender young age, that there was broken glass in my father's slippers, ready to cut him. I had woken screaming, sobbing, crying, and ran from the bed. While he gave me one of his perfunctory hugs and assured me all was well—*who on earth would want to hurt him?*—I have always wondered if it was I in the dream who wanted to punish him for his detached nature. My memory would not go that deep.

There were current dreams about fleeing shells that rained down—spheres of hate and destruction. I would try to duck them, to weave, to do anything to avoid the menace, while my unconscious mind smelled noxious chemicals and a toxic mud that would make my face feel like exploding. One dream was about dodgeball, with an endless stream of balls coming out of darkness at me. I moved, kicked, and tried to push them away as they came close. I would run this way and that, jumping backward and then pushing forward, all the while my arms flung them away. It was tiring.

"Bob. I say, Bob."

My head snapped up as I was jolted back to the moment. "Ye-yes, Doctor."

Mott leaned into his desk. "You were gone for a moment, deep in thought. Perhaps you can share. What was happening just then?"

"I don't know if they're connected, Doctor. I mean, two dreams I was thinking about. One a childhood nightmare which saw my father hurt, or almost hurt. Then, I suddenly shifted to a dream about having dodgeballs hurled at me. In both cases, I fled the terror, tried to run away by jumping out of bed. And thinking about it, there was a fitful nightmare on the train coming into Amiens on my first day in France, sort of like these dreams."

As he leaned back in his chair, Mott's fingers pressed together in what I learned was his contemplative posture. "Yes, the nurses explained to me that you have these vivid dreams, but also that you're willing to talk them through. That is a good sign." He looked over at me, ensuring I was still attentive. "It may be you are prone to anxiety for other, perhaps childhood, reasons, and that your shell shock is causing that to surface in an accelerated fashion."

"It's very serious, then? Long lasting?"

"No, needn't be. We all have dreams, nightmares, where some of us fret but don't act out. Those others may suffer with night sweats or tremors. You are a very open person, Bob; you don't hold back. That taking action is, I think, reflected in your dreams."

I grinned. "Yes, I share things easily. An open book, some say. Ha ha!"

He sat up straight and nodded his head in approval. "Well, the good news is that you are not stuttering nearly as much as you were. That tells me you are beginning to relax, normalizing."

Mott continued to steer the discussion away from my dreams by injecting positive aspects of my recovery, for which I was thankful. I knew there were shell shock victims much worse than me who spent all day staring wide-eyed at an open field, waiting to fight in a fictitious battle that was never going to come, and men who dove under tables at the instant of a sudden noise. I was thankful not to be in that state.

I faced the task of accepting that my shock was a normal reaction to the most significant and destructive terror I had ever experienced. I realized that most people, civilians in particular, could not begin to understand.

Dr. Mott reinforced his prediction that the nightmares would subside and my memory and connection to others would improve. Before I knew it, Mott craftily shifted the discussion to his belief that group therapy—the working with others—was good for the soul. That he was a founding member of the Society of English Singers fit nicely with his plan to promote cheerfulness by holding a Friday-evening sing-along in the second-floor lounge. Intrigued, I agreed to attend.

...

Plink-plink-plink! Plink-plink-plink!

I heard the repetitive tuning of middle C on the piano as I drew on my pipe, watching the glow of the embers. The taste of the smooth tobacco seduced my senses into contentment. Again, the *plink-plink-plink* drew attention to the upstairs lounge.

It was Friday after dinner as I sat in the hospital library listening to the notes whispering down. I thought back to my childhood in Walthamstow. There were times, particularly Sundays, when my granny's home school for girls was closed for the day and our family gathered around the black-and-whites for a sing-along.

It was Easter Sunday 1908, just before immigrating to Canada, that I remember most for a wonderful singsong. The entire world was singing then, as prosperity was boosting spirits across Europe and America. We had attended Easter services before walking along High Street, where it was warm enough to enjoy the season's first ice cream cone. Arriving home, Granny and Mama had played a duet on the piano, laughing at their rusty mistakes. It was always enjoyable to watch and hear, bringing comfort into our home.

We all broke into song. At fifteen, I was still getting used to my rough masculine tone, whereas my younger sisters were like angels with dulcet voices. At twenty-one, Eric, our cousin who lived with us after his parents' divorce, brought a wonderful baritone to the mix. The tunes were fresh and mainly from America, and we knew them well.

School days, school days
Dear old Golden Rule days

Every time we got to the third stanza, Hilda would trip over the words and break into hysterical laughter, and Ethel and I would press on with so much fun.

'Reading and 'riting and 'rithmetic
Taugh to the tune of the hick'ry stick

Oh, for the days of Blackhorse Road, for memories of Walthamstow! I remembered my entry to adolescence when Eric was there for me, teaching me everything about growing up, including some predictably naughty things.

Papa was physically there, but Eric was my guiding light. He would divert great-uncle Charlie with conversation while I nicked a candy from his Pitman's Grocery on High Street, or he would steal a kiss from some unsuspecting lass just to see what she would do. It was great fun being with Eric right up to the time of his plans to settle down with Daisy. That was just before our immigration to Canada.

Suddenly, the upstairs lounge rang out with a similar melody, bringing me back to the present.

There is a flower within my heart,
Daisy, Daisy!

In spite of an earlier hesitance, I followed the tunes up the stairs to the second-floor lounge.

Planted one day by a glancing dart,
Planted by Daisy Bell!

Sarge was lingering at the door, playing the welcoming committee as he was when I visited the workshop. "Hello, Bob," he whispered. "We thought you were the musical type. Can't stay away from a good tickling of the ivories, eh?"

"You got me on that one. I grew up around the family piano and fancy myself a bit of an enthusiast."

Whether she loves me or loves me not,
Sometimes it's hard to tell.

"It's great to see you not buried in a library book. Me 'n the lads, we really like you, what with being one of the nicer officers. You know, you respecting us without throwing your position at us."

"All right now, no need to swell my head to that extent!"

Yet I am longing to share the lot
Of beautiful Daisy Bell!

He grinned. "Well, what with bein' accused of bein' a pacifist, I've nothin' to lose with bein' honest, eh?"

"A pacifist?"

"Oh, yes. Was felled durin' a machine-gun barrage. We were pressin' forward in no man's when our own shells dropped down all over us. I was crazy scared, mumbling stupid, cursin' our own artillery idiots. After they got me back to the trench, seems my CO heard me talkin' about a stupid war, a need to end it at all costs, both sides should go bloody home."

"That's it? That's all you said?"

Daisy, Daisy,
Give me your answer, do!
I'm half crazy,
All for the love of you!

"Well, I might 'ave told him to fuck off and die. Before I knows it, the court martial brass call me shell shocked, respectin' my long service the only thing keeps me outta field punishment or the firin' squad. They says I was temporarily insane, and nows I'm here weavin' baskets."

I continued looking at him, empathetic to such a sorry story. "You'd think they'd want solid fellows like you back out in the trenches instead of judging righteousness or personal beliefs, for that matter."

It won't be a stylish marriage;
I can't afford a carriage.

"Nah, not quite. Theys don't want the likes of me infectin' the morale, the spirit of the lads out there. I understand that. Just do my time here, go before the med board with a promise to say nice things about the cause. Be back sooner than Bob's your uncle. A little humor on you there, eh?"

We momentarily held our look and then burst into laughter. "Well, you're a good man, Sarge. I've seen you with the other lads, and you have a way about things. With them, I mean."

"Thanks, I appreciate you sayin' that."

But you'll look sweet upon the seat
Of a bicycle built for two!

In the silence that followed the end of the song, I looked around the room to see many of the soldiers assembled around the piano, some still giggling with the fun of the infectious tune. Others were sitting sullen, withdrawn into themselves. Still, they had made their way to the event. Others, like Sarge and I, were engaged in conversation. It was when Dr. Mott caught my eye, nodding me over, that I realized I had best set an example and lead some of the singing.

I beckoned Sarge and we strolled over to the piano. I still marveled at the thought of such an eminent doctor breaking into song while playing the ivories. He glanced at me, smiled, and then peered around the lounge, seemingly trying to connect with the patients, to encourage participation. While a few of the men avoided his gaze by looking elsewhere or down at their shoes, most had edged toward the piano after that first tune.

While playing a soft melody, Dr. Mott looked this way and that in the image of a real showman, addressing his patients. Taking the tune to a whisper, he ruminated, "Now, many of you have come to know me over the past days, weeks, and, God forbid, months." There was a hesitant outbreak of laughter. "You know my beliefs about the healing benefits of song and how it works to diminish fear through expressing yourselves with simple pleasantries. Much like the soothing baths that I insist upon, I want you to consider these moments as bathing each other's ears with the soothing rise and fall of your communal voices."

This time the laughter was more comfortable, louder. Mott's voice cheerfully rang out. "All right, let's move to a little ditty that was kindly struck by our Irish friends back in '12. Come on, boys!"

It's a long way to Tipperary;
It's a long way to go.

Ah yes, it was so comforting to hear this marching song that meant so much to so many soldiers, each in their own way. Whether it was a Tipperary for all those Irish who had left their homes for opportunities in England before the war, for Aussies who missed Melbourne, or for me longing for a Canada thousands of miles away, it was a long, long emotional distance for all.

It's a long way to Tipperary,
To the sweetest girl I know.

As I heartily sang along, I felt a slight watering in my eyes, not at the passion for leaving behind a sweet girl but perhaps for not having one to leave behind. While I was perfectly happy to be free of a steady date while at university, in the moment I longed for the love of a sweetheart to whom I could write, someone to whom I could return.

Goodbye, Piccadilly;
Farewell, Leicester Square?
It's a long, long way to Tipperary,
But my heart's right there.

The chorus was repeated twice at the end, as the men were enjoying the catchy tune, and the doctor was reluctant to stop a good time. But after a few more tunes, he suggested that a good night's rest and reflection were in order. However, one young soldier boldly suggested a tune that he and his platoon had sung along the roads of Picardy during a recent march.

Private Perks is a funny little codger
With a smile, a funny smile.
Five feet none, he's an artful little dodger,
With a smile, a sunny smile.
Flush or broke, he'll have his little joke;
He can't be suppressed.
All the other fellows have to grin,
When he gets this off his chest, Hi!

Pack up your troubles in your old kit-bag,
and smile, smile, smile!
While you've a Lucifer to light your fag,
Smile, boys, that's the style.
What's the use of worrying?
It never was worthwile.
So pack up your troubles in your old kit-bag,
And smile, smile, smile!

"I must say," said Mott, "that tune always brings up thoughts of making the best of life, whatever cards we are dealt. I wish you lads the best, wherever and whenever your travels take you, for the rest of this war and beyond."

"Hear, hear." The collective voices of the men fell away as they filed out of the lounge.

Mott called after them, "Have a restful sleep."

Chapter 13

October 1916

One day Matron Kay eased up to me as I was studying my Bible in the library. I was never disappointed to gaze into her lovely eyes. She bent over to whisper that there was an RFC sergeant arrived to see me.

An RFC sergeant? I had encountered flyers before, but I didn't recall actually knowing anyone from the Royal Flying Corps.

Tucking the Bible into my tunic pocket, I rounded the corner to see none other than Sam. "My God, Sergeant Hardy! What the devil?"

He indeed was in RFC khaki, dripping wet after coming in from a dank, rainy day. "Hello, Lieutenant. Just dropped around to see how you're faring."

In my enthusiasm, I shook his hand vigorously, thinking about that last day together at Mouquet Farm. Even though the memory remained aloof, I did know both of us could have met our maker. "By Jove, it's so very great to see you! Come with me, there's a little lounge just here." I pointed the way.

We talked for a long while as Sam explained the concussion and arm wounds he had sustained. Barely three weeks after his injuries, he was assigned to the RFC to train as a sergeant-grade air mechanic. It was staggering how quickly things changed during the war. His reputation of having a natural ability to figure things out and to solve practical issues had earned him the recommendation.

Sam asked after my health, explaining that he had been reluctant to visit in case it caused me emotional stress. I assured him that his visit made me feel exhilarated. We talked more about his upcoming assignment, how exciting it was to apply his skills to aircraft mechanics.

After kibitzing for quite a while, Sam's demeanor turned dour as if he was burdened with heavy thoughts. My mood followed, and on my prompt, I found out he had run into Issy in London.

"Lieutenant—ah, may I call you Bob? At least while we are not technically on duty?"

I almost offered a trade, that if he called me Bob, I should refer to him as Hardknocks, but his body language warned me off. "Of course. Call me Bob anytime." I was anxious to find out what was on his mind. "Now, how about that Issy?"

With shaking hands, Sam slowly, deliberately, took a letter from inside his tunic as uneasiness spread across his face. I whispered, "Oh Lord, please don't tell me something has happened to Issy. You mentioned you just saw him."

"N-no, it's not Issy, but the letter is from him and it's bad. It'd be easiest if you just read it." As he moved to the edge of the chair to hand me the letter, his head drooped, his eyes downcast.

Lieutenant Robert Pitman
Royal Canadian Regiment
C/O The Maudsley
Kings College Hospital, London

16 October, 1916

Dearest Bob,

I am just now catching up with correspondence, finding time for letters after the regiment was moved out of the front on 11 October. I trust that you are on the mend, my dear soldier, as you had a mighty blow.

A few days prior to leaving the battlefield, the RCR was deployed in the frontline trenches for a three-day battle beginning 7 October.

I am very sad to bring you news that our Perce fell on 8 October during the time we were ordered to relieve the 49s. Patrols were sent out to no-man's-land to examine enemy barbed wire and advised there were sufficient gaps for a morning attack. Lining up under cover of darkness in the jumping-off point, waves of nine platoons drove across to set the Hun in retreat.

A part of Percy's platoon was cornered at a portion of barbed wire that was discovered not to be broken, receiving intense machine-gun fire from both flanks. Unfortunately, he was among five officers that did not return.

Perce is dead, gone west. He was a fine soldier and a great friend to you and me. His confidence and strength will be sorely missed. He rests at one of the makeshift cemeteries.

We all look forward to your speedy recovery and return to the regiment.

Sincerely,
Malcolm (Issy) Isbester

I was shocked. Percy—the successful schoolmaster who inspired a smile from anyone he met, the one of us to marry just the right girl—was dead. He had become one of my closest friends in the regiment, a confidant in the field, and a leader to all. Cut down by German bullets, dozens of them in the blink of an eye. Oh, but why analyze that? Perce's voice, his laughter, his humility, and his infectious love were gone, all gone.

Sam was so patient, staying with me right up until his train departure.

For days after the news, time went by slowly, and I became lethargic as an overwhelming grief consumed my energy and disturbed my sleep. I asked myself over and over how I had escaped death and how I had come to be hospitalized when not one single bullet had touched me.

My nightmares were vivid. I felt the hell he endured. I dreamed of Perce being cornered in barbed wire, no place to run, no cover, being struck again and again as multiple bullets riddled his being. Sometimes in slow motion, I *saw* the actual bullets as they penetrated his tunic and bore through him into his heart, his lungs, and his soul.

Dr. Mott encouraged me to open up, to speak about these visions lest I lapse back into emotional shock. One discussion curiously helped me to climb up out of my funk. In one of our meetings, when we were referring to Perce's death, I protested, "It's not right!" Mott had immediately shot back, "It's war. What's it got to do with being right?" Reflecting on those shocking words was helpful in accepting that in war, reason gets swept aside.

Still, thoughts continued to gnaw at me, tempting me in a troubling way. I found myself hoping that I could delay my discharge. While good sense won over such emotions, there was momentary comfort in thinking I could prolong my stay in the comfortable atmosphere of the hospital, avoiding a return to the trenches. But I always turned to my commitment of loyalty, not just to the cause but to myself. Were thoughts of delayed recovery a form of betrayal?

I knew I would never go that far, but I wondered if even thinking about prolonging my illness amounted to the same thing.

I shared my doubts with Dr. Mott, who saw them as quite rational. "You have done a good job of facing down your fears, Bob. Except for the grief over Lieutenant Sutton's death, you tell me your nightmares are fewer. And I can see you are more focused, more in tune with your surroundings."

"Thank you, Doctor. I am pleased you recognize the improvements."

"We should now be thinking about transitioning you toward discharge. You will need to adjust to the idea of shipping back to France. Subject to medical board review, of course."

I instinctively shrank from the prospect of returning to the front, but checked the feeling in its tracks. "I understand and feel up to the task."

"Good. I've set your discharge date for Monday, 30 October."

"Thank you." I laughed to mask my anxiety. "Nothing like a firm date."

Mott leaned forward, studying me across his desk. "It's the only way to do it, Bob. Now, have you access to lodgings in the London area?"

I sat up smartly. "Yes, there is a friend of the family, a lady I've always known as my aunt, up in Stroud Green."

Mott smiled, extending his hands in a friendly gesture as if to indicate a great move forward. "Good, that makes the transition easier. We'll see you over the next week. Please continue your cure program until your discharge."

My feelings were mixed. Although I had shaken most of the shell shock symptoms, I still felt vulnerable to the stress and anxiety of the battlefield. Yet a sense of duty charged to the front of my thoughts that allowed me to admit that I was feeling better and fit to fight.

"Thank you, Doctor."

Chapter 14

October 1916

A few days later I woke with melancholy. While nightmare-free for a while, I became plagued with a sadness turning over in my mind about Percy's death. I needed a change of routine. Never mind the public seeing me in my hospital blues, I wanted to connect with outside life. I was confident the matron would issue a pass as my discharge was pending anyway.

It was the sing-along that had kindled my thoughts about my cousin Eric, about the closeness we had shared before I immigrated to Canada. I knew he and Daisy lived close to the Maudsley. The matron helped me locate an address in *Kelly's Post Office Directory* for a Mr. Eric Pitman, a residence about one hour's walk from the hospital. That had to be it!

I easily found the home and instinctively smoothed down my flannel jacket, straightening my tie. "Good afternoon. Daisy, Daisy Pitman?"

The woman had been laughing and playing with a child in front of the house. The boy seemed about six years old, so he had to be young Stanley, whom Eric had often written about. "Hello. May I help you?" she asked with a bright smile.

I became flush with happy memories at the sight of her. My face must have lit up as I blurted, "Daisy, it's Bob. Robert Pitman. I apologize for just appearing like this, but I thought I should come around to say hello."

"Oh, Robert, how did I not recognize you? It's so nice to see you." Surveying my hospital attire, she frowned. "Are you well?"

I decided not to correct her reference to Robert, as that is how she and Eric knew me. "I'm fine, but I had a little scare over at the front and have been convalescing at the 4th General."

"Oh dear, you must come in for tea. You know, I'm so constantly worried for Eric, who is 'somewhere in France' as we have learned to say. Stanley, this gentleman is your cousin Robert from Canada, and he has come to say hello."

"Is that how they dress in Canada, wearing pajamas and a tie?" Stanley asked.

She laughed, rather embarrassed, and leaned down. "No, dear. Cousin Robert has been in the hospital, near the one where you were born."

"Oh." Stanley curled behind his mother's skirt.

"Come in, Robert. Please come in out of the chill."

I followed her into the kitchen at the back of the tidy house as Stanley skipped ahead. "Thank you."

"Oh gosh, it's so nice to see you. I know you and Eric have corresponded, but I haven't seen you since our wedding in 1908!"

A reflective thought shot into me with images of battlefields. "Is Eric well?"

Daisy smiled, her uncertainty showing. "As far as I know. Thankfully, he is not involved in that damn Somme affair. I'm not sure where he is stationed, and his letter last week didn't provide any clues, I'm afraid."

I found out over tea that Eric had enlisted in late 1915 and shipped off to France almost immediately. Daisy showed me the recent letter in which he expected his first home leave in early November. I explained to her the circumstances of my war wound and my pending discharge.

She regained a tentative smile. "Oh, I'm glad you're all right, but I am constantly worried about Eric. Stanley just wouldn't grow up the same without his daddy."

Reaching across the table, I placed my hand over the back of hers and quietly consoled, "I do understand. I know my mama worries about me. Can't imagine little Stanley losing—but let's rather think on his home leave coming up."

Daisy began to tear up, so I changed the course of the conversation. "What do you and Stanley do to pass the time? I imagine he is a handful, looking at his energy."

"Ohhh yes, Stanley is active all right. Well, let me see, we go out for walks as much as we can, as long as the weather holds up. I home teach him, so our days are filled with lessons. And we visit friends as well."

"Sounds like both of you are very active, then."

With an infectious smile, she said, "Yes, and my mum looks after him when I am able to step out with my girlfriends."

I brightened at her expression and the thought of friends. "I'm glad you can get out. Are there any friends I might know from the past, from the ole Walthamstow crowd?"

Daisy gave me a teasing, almost mischievous, look. "No, I don't think so, Robert. But as you're a single man, and a charming one at that, I think you might find my friend Cissy, shall we say, interesting."

"Oh, Daisy. I'm over here to fight a war, and then I'll return to my studies back in Canada. Not sure—"

"I didn't say marry the girl, just said she might be of interest, you old stick-in-the-mud."

"Well, who is she?"

"A munitionette. Just since the war began, of course. She was in service before, an *au pair*. And such a sweet soul with a genuine, happy demeanor. Being with her lets me forget for a moment. You know how this war occupies one's mind."

I held my hands out in affected surprise. "She makes bombs?"

"In a manner, yes. Doing her bit, I'd say."

"She must be quite the character, leaving service for work in an arms factory."

"She likes her independence," declared Daisy. "And the new level of income certainly provides for a grand life as a single girl."

With increasing interest, I pursued, "I've not met a munitionette. That does sound intriguing . . . but it is wartime."

"Now, keep an open mind," scolded Daisy.

And we left it at that, no firm plans but both of us feeling a little awkward about how to proceed. If there was anything to proceed about. Trailing off to small talk, I thoroughly enjoyed the catch-up as well as the tea and sandwiches.

I pressed Daisy to have Eric call when his leave began, writing down the telephone number of Mrs. Clarke.

As I walked back to the hospital, I thought about meeting a girl, especially an exciting, adventurous one. I felt so much better than I had that morning, better than I had felt in a long time.

Chapter 15

October 1916

"Officers, may I have your attention, please!" bellowed Sarge. "You are all requested—ah, *ordered* to immediately assemble in the front entranceway."

Looking forward to a quiet moment, I had just sat down to read more of Kipling's delightful *Just So Stories*.

"That's rather abrupt, I'd say," retorted an officer sitting on the other side of the library.

"Quite so," said a voice behind me. "Are you clear about your instructions?"

Sarge said happily, "Oh yes, from Major Mott himself, it were."

I groaned. "Well, we'd better see what the good doctor is on about."

Arriving in the foyer, we peered through the front doorway, admiring a few motor cars sitting in the drive with a mix of fine horse-drawn carriages, all of which seemed to be related to some anticipated visit.

Dr. Mott strode in from the matron's office, beaming from ear to ear. "Welcome, officers. Thank you for assembling in short order."

"What's this about?" asked one of our hospital blue-clads.

"Are you joking?" asked another. "Look around you, man. This is nothing but a royal visit of some sort. Just look at the colors and the crest on the carriage doors."

"What the devil?" I questioned.

"Definitely a royal entourage," bellowed another officer. "Looking for directions, I wonder?"

Subdued laughter followed while we continued to focus on the developing event.

"Officers," barked Dr. Mott, "may I have you line up on the grand staircase just there, please?" Then, with the tone of a schoolmaster speaking to his flock, "Won't be a moment now before His Majesty pulls up."

"His Majesty," whispered an officer to no one in particular. I, too, was dumbfounded, thinking it might be Princess Louise or the Duchess Alexandra, but the King himself? How would anyone at home believe me when I told them? Did I look respectable, fit to meet our King? What in heavens does one say, if there was to be a chance to say anything at all? Looking around as we assembled on the staircase, I could see each of us was as perplexed as the other.

The crunch of a heavy motor car on gravel pulling in drew our attention to the doorway. We collectively craned our necks to get a good look at the King's Daimler. His footmen stomped in.

"Presenting His Most Gracious Majesty, King George, and Her Majesty, Queen Mary of Teck," announced a Captain Fausett, who then bowed. "Your Majesty, may I present Major Frederick Walker Mott, esteemed head of the Maudsley."

Dr. Mott bowed to the smiling King and hesitated before taking his extended hand. "Your Majesty," whispered Mott in total deference.

King George nodded.

Mott then bowed to Queen Mary. "Your Majesty."

"Sir," said Fausett, looking at the King, "Dr. Mott is treating patients for the increasing shell shock phenomenon."

The King—bedecked in his British officer's uniform, including a Sam Brown and spurred riding boots, and sporting his distinctive mutton chops—spoke for the first time. "Yes, I have kept up on the developments and the work being done by our physicians. We appreciate the efforts being put forth by you and your staff, Dr. Mott."

In spite of his deference, Mott grinned proudly. "Thank you, sir. We are performing different kinds of work here, including a study of the prolonged physical strain on our good officers and men."

"I see," said the King.

"All with the focus on treatment and returning our men to the front lines, based on fostering an atmosphere of cure."

"An atmosphere of cure, is it?"

"Yes, sir."

His Majesty waved his gloved hand across the foyer, acknowledging the group of officers and soldiers before him. "What have we here? A good deal of our British Army present, I would say."

I laughed along with the others. This moment seemed surreal, so unexpected. I could see King George with my very eyes but was overwhelmed to see him looking like one of us, dressed in military uniform.

As the entourage moved across the foyer, I noted the Queen's elegant yet simple white winter coat with ermine collar and her embroidered hat. I thought of the contrast her attire showed against that of the lads in the trenches but cautioned myself against judgment. She was our Queen and ought to look the part.

As the royal ensemble made their way up to tour the treatment wards on the second floor, it struck me why Dr. Mott had positioned us on each step: the King and Queen had to pass us. It was such an honor—goose bumps and all—to shake the hand of the most powerful leader on Earth. The Queen took a great interest in each of the men, compassionately looking them in the eyes. When it was my turn, I could see the tenderness that could not be embellished by words. I was deeply touched.

After a tour of the upper floor, the Queen paused one step above me and the King one step below. He waved his gloved hand up and down the staircase, drawing attention to all of us. For an instant he glanced right at me, making it feel like he stopped to speak directly, but then he directed his voice to all. "Officers and soldiers of the British Army, I do thank you for serving your country during this time of need. The Queen and I offer our wishes for your speedy recovery."

There were smiles and murmurs of approval among those present.

"As your King, I address you in the dearest of terms. To enable our country to organize more effectively its military resources in the present great struggle for the cause of civilization, every able-bodied man between the ages of eighteen and forty-one must now enroll. To you who signed up earlier, I express my appreciation of your splendid patriotism and self-sacrifice."

All the soldiers were speechless, frozen in their attention, although I knew they wanted to cheer.

"That enlistment, over five million men since the war broke out, demonstrates an effort far surpassing that of any other nation in similar circumstances in recorded history and will be a lasting source of pride to future generations. I am confident the magnificent spirit that has hitherto sustained you through the trials of this terrible war will inspire you to endure any additional sacrifice that may be imposed on you going forward, and that it will, by the grace of God, lead us and our allies to a victory that shall save Europe."

A cheer finally burst from the soldiers, whose hearts and minds had listened intently to the King's speech. I felt the sense of collective patriotism that filled the building, as emotional a moment as any. The King shook the hands of a few officers standing there. I instinctively held out my hand, which he readily took, and I felt my smile stretch from ear to ear.

The King and Queen gracefully descended the staircase and took their leave after thanking Dr. Mott again for his work at the Maudsley.

Chapter 16

30 October, 1916

"Here is our lieutenant. You are looking so well, Robert, so very well with those rosy cheeks." Mrs. Clarke had stridden to the front gate as soon as I rounded the corner off Scarborough Road as if she had been lying in wait for some time. Perhaps she had. "Give us a hug!"

More of a command than a gesture, I obliged, managing to squeeze free after a bit.

Mrs. Clarke stood back, giving some distance as she appraised me. "My, what a handsome young man you have become, all grown up since I last saw you as a sixteen-year-old going off to a new world. And now look at you in your smart uniform!"

I couldn't help beaming, standing there on display. "Yes, I am feeling rather well, Mrs. Clarke. The hospital offered me wonderful rest. It is so good to be in the city and so good of you to put me up until I return to the Continent." I explained that I was to stand before a medical board on 25 November, which meant I would be staying for a few weeks.

Mrs. Clarke seemed to take delight in that. Reaching up to pinch my cheek, she retorted, "Nonsense, Robert! You're like a son to me. Your mama, my dear Annie, must be so worried about you fighting overseas. Oh dear, how is she?"

"I'm sure she is well. Papa would have said otherwise in his letters. They are now calling me Bob, not Robert anymore."

"Oh, Bob, you will always be Robert to me. However, if it must be Bob, then Bob it will be. Bob, Bob, Bob."

After settling my few effects in the bedroom, we spoke for over an hour about the past year. I was reticent to explain too much about the war in western France, as I had found many British civilians preferred to shun the conversation, yet she needed to understand the horror if she was to understand my shell shock.

Although determined to be the strong soldier I wanted Mrs. Clarke to see, I found that talking about battlefield experiences with her elicited deep emotions in me. She reminded me that she had nurtured me since I was born and told me not to hold back. I explained exactly what had occurred and described the symptoms. She surprised me with her understanding.

"You have gone through hell and are to return to hell. You know, that braided wound stripe on your sleeve sets you aside as a warrior who survived."

"I had no idea—"

"Some civilians do understand a bit of what you have experienced, even if we cannot fully comprehend. Wear that stripe proudly."

I felt safe enough with Mrs. Clarke that I cried; actually, I sobbed with relief at what she said. I had held back so much at the hospital in my desire to prove I was well, that I was worthy of again wearing an officer's uniform. My recuperation at the hospital was necessary, but it was that moment when I realized every single one of us was fighting for all of England, and that all of mankind was fighting for civility and freedom. I felt I had come through the hell and could return to the front with courage.

I was relieved when Mrs. Clarke finally served supper, as that gave me a chance to change the conversation. Through the meal she hinted at some financial concerns, and although this was a deeply personal issue, I probed carefully.

"Well, I've managed to hold on to this house. It's a struggle to make ends meet after so much was lost during the financial crisis. When Mr. Clarke died earlier that year, I was left quite sound, with savings and, of course, the life insurance proceeds. He cared for me very well."

"What happened then?"

"On the advice of my bank manager at Coutts, I was to diversify, putting a little bit here and investing a little bit there. 'Safe bets,' I was told, although at the time I did not think about the word *bet*; rather, I felt secure with the regular income coming in. Oh, Bob, everything was good until that nasty Bosnian murdered the poor Archduke."

"Did things change as suddenly as that?"

"Yes, it happened quickly. Banks were closed for a while, but even when they opened again, withdrawals were restricted. In spite of the losses, I'll be all right as long as I continue my clerical work at the post office. I daresay male labor shortages have helped me to make ends meet."

"Indeed, but surely that will halt when the lads come home. Are you worried you will be set aside in favor of soldier re-employment?"

"We will have to wait and see what happens then, but for now I will carry on. I am so much better off than you lot who are saving our civilization, you who are giving your lives. We will never forget that."

Over the next days I settled in to a pretty good routine: going for walks to familiar haunts such as Walthamstow while Mrs. Clarke was at work, helping her prepare supper, and trying to locate friends who weren't serving overseas.

Returning from a walk one morning, a neighbor greeted me on the sidewalk with an urgent message, handing me a slip with the telephone number. For an instant I wondered, but realized that although most homes had telephones, the line itself was shared between two or more neighbors. No name was provided, so I wondered if it might be the medical board.

A male voice answered that I instantly recognized as Cousin Eric, my caution turning to excitement. We chatted for a few minutes, then agreed to meet at the Strand Palace on Tuesday, 14 November, where he had already arranged to meet some friends. I was eager to soon link up.

I sent word to both Sam and Minnie about the night out and urged them to join. I knew Sam was training in the London area, so was looking forward to seeing him again. As the only contact I had for Minnie was at Bristol, it was unlikely he would make it, but I was hopeful.

Chapter 17

14 November, 1916

I exited the Charing Cross Station in order to walk the short distance to the Strand Palace Hotel. I understood why Eric had chosen this location; it was accessible by the Underground, then by foot, a requisite since taxis and buses did not operate after dark. Due to London's being the target of zeppelin bombing raids, street lights were shut off or kept dim. In fact, the streets were so dark in places that sometimes pedestrians collided.

The crowded, smoke-filled club held patrons of all kinds, as many military as civilian. The round tables, each covered with dark cloth and a center lamp, were crammed, many with ten patrons seated in the eight available chairs. Daisy saw me enter before I had my coat off and pushed her way through the crowd. "Hello, Robert," she sang. "Over here. Come, we have a table!"

I was surprised, pleasantly so. "I did not expect to see you. I thought it was just Eric coming." We shared a long, loving hug.

"Mum's babysitting."

Following Daisy to the table, I looked around the night club, admiring the wonderful décor and feeling the beat of the four-piece band playing in the corner. As we arrived at the table, Eric, in uniform, stood up to take my hand and pulled me toward him for a slap on the back. Over his shoulder, I noticed a naval officer, a gentleman in civilian clothes, and a young lady strikingly dressed in the vogue of the day.

I was awestruck by this young lady smiling directly at me, hopefully not so absorbed that the others thought me rude. Her yellow dress, which offset her dark brunette hair, was clasped at the shoulder with delicate fasteners, leaving bare shoulders, arms, and neck. The finely pleated material flowed like a waterfall from her bustline, down through a tightly cinched belt and on to mid-calf.

"Robert," chortled Eric. I knew he had caught me red-handed, staring as I was startled back to reality. "Thanks for coming. It is so wonderful to see you after all these years. And spiffy for us to get together after serving time in that dreadful French mud, I daresay. And how are you, cousin?"

I knew I was blushing, forced myself to direct my attention to Eric. "Rather quite well. Recovered from a month in hospital and feeling mended. What about you? How long is your leave?"

Eric shrugged, accepting his destiny. "I return in two weeks, I'm afraid, so am making the best of it, being able to spend time at home with Daisy and Stanley. I'm so glad you popped over to see them. He was quite intrigued by your hospital pajamas, I daresay. Now, might we know anyone at this table?"

I extended my hand to the civilian gentleman, who looked at me with a grin. "Robert, it's Tom, Tom Wellum from Blackhorse Road. You surely remember?"

I recognized him through his more mature features before looking over to the naval officer and then placed both of them. "Percy Wellum from our Marsh Street Academy, and your big brother, Tom! After all this time! How are you both?"

I suppressed the mixed feelings I experienced with so recently losing one Percy in my life, then meeting up with another. I shook hands and semi-embraced Percy Wellum, my Walthamstow school chum, as the excitement of the evening grew.

"Robert," said Daisy, "we can't forget my very good friend, Miss Cissy Anne Taylor. She lives near Eric and me."

If Daisy only knew the restraint I was keeping while waiting to be introduced. Surely this was the munitionette friend she had spoken of. I tried to keep my composure and not splutter her name, but was unable to shed a silly grin. "Hello, Miss Taylor, it's very nice to meet you." I hoped that stick-in-the-mud look I had given Daisy didn't re-emerge.

"Hello, Lieutenant. I have heard so much about Eric's younger cousin. Oh, but do please call me Cissy. I find those Victorian formalities a tad boring."

"In that case, Cissy, call me Bob, which is my Canadian name now." I glanced around the table. "I'd be pleased if everyone called me Bob."

Cissy was delightful, full of that new self-awareness that so many young women were expressing. She was slender, of medium height with a round face and blue eyes under long eyelashes. Her brunette hair—in contrast to the upswept Edwardian pompadour look—was cut short, meeting her collar at the back and sweeping up under her chin to a point on each cheek, highlighting her upturned mouth, with bangs covering her forehead. Her skin was white and satin-like, her whole look sharpened with lip salve of a rouge tint. She was beautiful.

"Well," said Eric, "now that's settled, let's have a drink, shall we?"

His timing was good. I am guilty of not knowing how long I may have been staring and smiling. When the drink order was placed, we all got to talking. "Cissy is a munitionette," said Daisy, "doing her bit for the war and all."

"I certainly am, and not just for the war, I might say. I'm quite happy to pocket the wages from the Brunner Mond munitions factory over in Silvertown, which are much more than I earned working in service for a Belgravia family from '09 to '14. This freedom is wonderful! And what about you, Bob? You are Canadian, I understand?"

I'm not sure if I could have brightened any more, but hearing Cissy say my name seemed to make it that way. "English by birth, now living in Saskatoon, Canada, which is why volunteering for service was an easy choice. Like you, I am enjoying newfound freedom to pursue dreams over there."

After more familiarization, I turned to the Wellum brothers to learn more about their current lives. Tom, being four years older than Percy, was now holding a mechanical engineering degree and employed for strategic war purposes at a supply factory in Sheffield. There was little disclosure beyond that, presumably due to the Defence of the Realm Act. Percy, my schoolmate who was born only one month later than I, attended university like myself, which is why he was chosen as a naval officer. He expressed displeasure that his service thus far was with Home Establishment in London. He wanted to see action on the Continent.

Shortly thereafter, Sam arrived. As expected, he fit in well with everyone and soon had them laughing about tales of the war and other exploits. I envied how he could go through the same experience yet retain such lightheartedness. Perhaps it was because he was a career soldier, or more likely it was his inherently pleasant, breezy demeanor.

Sam was relating a story about training in boot camp, making the bayoneting of straw-filled sacks seem as interesting as a night at the pictures, when I saw Cissy rise from the other side of the table and move toward me. "Well, Lieutenant Pitman, I suppose if you are not going to ask a girl to dance, then a girl must do the asking!"

I knew I was blushing—again—but eagerly stood up to take the challenge. "Of course, Cissy. How inconsiderate of me to leave you sitting there listening to war stories." It was obvious that Daisy had arranged this meeting, but I didn't mind one bit. We laughed to mask the bit of awkwardness as we stepped onto the dance floor.

Cissy and I danced a couple of numbers until Tom excused his way in to dance the one-step, which was fine as I needed to direct some attention to my friends. In this way, Eric, Sam, and I were able to catch up. The conversation migrated at times to more somber talk about the dread of war and of returning to France. Sam enlightened all of us to the excitement of serving in the RFC with its fast-paced tempo and less formal regimen, at least compared to the infantry.

Yet I wasn't going to let any of the men steal away my chance of having the last dance with Cissy. I joined her on the floor for a slow waltz that allowed us to talk. Holding her, feeling her toned body—presumably from laboring at the factory—was tonic better than a month's stay at the Maudsley. We spoke of her lifelong friendship with Daisy and their enjoyment together while attending sewing club or stepping out to London nightlife. We agreed to have tea the next day. We both knew things were moving fast, but that was expected in war-torn Europe when family and friends didn't know when they would again see each other, if at all.

Sam and I left the Strand together for the walk to the Underground, both of us taking the Piccadilly Line, he traveling west while I was headed north to Finsbury Park. "You didn't tell me about your cutie, you ole dog, you!"

"I had nothing to let on about, at least until this evening when Daisy introduced me to Cissy."

Sam lightly punched my arm in objection. "Aw, come now. She was all over you! There must have been some history there, chappie!"

"No, really," I protested. "Although I admit that Daisy let on about a friend of hers who was quite fun—"

"That she is, Bob!"

I smiled mockingly. "Truthfully, when Daisy mentioned

a munitionette friend, I expected a well-built bruiser dressed in trousers and carrying a wrench!"

"Ahem," Hardy scolded. "If you didn't see for yourself, she is well built!"

"Not in that manner, you silly goat," I kibitzed back.

"Soooo?"

I grinned from ear to ear. "So what, Hardy?"

He jumped in front and turned, walking backward with the mischievousness of a Cheshire Cat. "So, when will you see her again?"

"Uh, perhaps tomorrow?"

"I knew it, you sly dog! I knew there was something there."

"Well maybe, but we have a war to fight, don't we?"

He moved beside me again. "A little diversion is a good thing, Pitman!"

We entered the station while still in animated discussion. Sam's train was pulling up to his side of the platform. "Enjoy, my friend, do really enjoy yourself. For once let things go and throw caution to the wind. I needn't tell you that we only have one life, Bob. Seize everything about this girl." He grinned as he saw me recognize his double meaning.

"All right, Sam. Let's stay in touch. And thanks for being a good friend!"

Chapter 18

November 1916

"Earl Grey, please," said Cissy, "with a little lemon and sugar on the side?"

The waiter glanced at me. "The same for me, thank you," I said, "Perhaps some savories and scones?"

"Very well," said the waiter. "It shan't be a moment."

Awkwardness hung in the air, each of us feeling a little nervous being alone without the crutch of surrounding friends. We both looked around, taking in the ambience of the room; it was filled with small tables covered by white lace tablecloths and other patrons conversing in lively and gay whispers. Our eyes caught and lingered on each other for a confident moment. "I know I said this, but it's so wonderful to meet again, Cissy, and exciting to get to know you."

"I'm as pleased, Bob. I'd be fibbing if I said I wasn't looking forward to it," gushed Cissy, "and at such a posh tea house!"

"My grandfather Crippen would bring me here to Fortnum &

Mason as a child. He would pick up his bulk tea and treat me to a sweet."

"That is sweet. Oh, sorry to be silly. You meant *candy* as you would say in Canada." Her laugh was so natural.

"It's all right. It was always an exciting train journey from Walthamstow on a Saturday, fond memories which I still cherish."

The silver tray of pastries and rolls with butter and jam on the side was deftly placed on the table. I was famished but held back, allowing Cissy to make her first choices. The ham salad was exquisite.

We momentarily ate in silence, each of us careful not to clumsily drop anything. "Do you have a close family, Bob?"

"Oh, I wouldn't say that, not so much. I was close to my mother's parents, the Crippens, and, of course, Cousin Eric. He lived with us for a while and was a great mentor to me. But my papa's parents were not there as they both died before my time."

"Oh, that is sad."

"Not really, I didn't know them. But now I have a wonderful closeness to my grandma Crippen, my mama, and my two darling sisters, all back in Canada."

I pondered Cissy's eyes, which flashed a sadness that made me cautious before asking after her family. "Do you have a large family, Cissy?"

She examined the *petit fours* delicately held between her thumb and index finger. A glimmer of concern that I was probing too deep crossed my mind, but then she raised her flickering eyes to meet mine.

"I don't know who they were. I was raised in a home for girls—oh, there were so many of us. But when I was fourteen, I was taken in by a wonderful family in Belgravia, the Beauchamps. For a few years, I was groomed as an *au pair*. Well, they called me that even though I'm not from France, of course. When the children arrived, I became their caregiver."

I finished a last bite of buttered bread. As I held Cissy's gaze, I was gushing with compliments about her, but at the same time didn't want to sound desperate and foolish. "Well, you certainly are a wonderful and fun lady. So smart, and beautiful too." I flushed, but in the spirit of Sam's admonition to throw caution to the wind, I simply had to say it.

"Oh, Bob. Daisy did say you were kind, but really, you flatter me."

The waiter returned to ask how we were getting along and if we would like anything else. We both indicated no. "Just stating what I see and how I feel. And your work? You are down at Silvertown, at the munitions factory?"

"Yes, at the Brunner Mond, doing my bit for the cause. Not as much as you boys over in France, but doing something."

I leaned in to the table to emphasize my sincerity. "And as much as we are doing our bit, we appreciate the bravery you and your sisters are showing. Not a very safe occupation, I'd say."

She beamed with thanks at the recognition. "It's allowing us sisters to contribute in ways we ought to have long before the war. We are grateful for that now, but we should have been able to do so before this." I pondered how strong and articulate Cissy was.

We absently sifted through the remains of the food left on the table as we talked, neither of us wanting the afternoon to end. While our discussion took a rather serious turn, it was energizing to understand Cissy's beliefs.

"Well, you'll be voting soon enough. That's the assent you deserve."

After contemplating the leftover crumbs, she looked up from her empty plate. "Yes, we will. Why, some of your own Canadian provinces allowed the female vote just this year."

Recent economic advances across the Western world had provided a platform for women to be inspired, to demand what was their right. It was with some pride that Canada was among the leading nations to grant women the vote, and I hoped the war did not close down this liberal process from developing to its fullest.

"Quite so. You are well informed. And there is talk in Parliament just now about granting women the right to vote federally."

"Oh, yes, there have been charged times! We actively honored the brilliant Emily Davison after her tragic death with our march in the summer 1913 Women's Suffrage Pilgrimage, which gave her legacy definite purpose."

"You marched in the Pilgrimage, Cissy?"

"Not the national trek, just the Hyde Park portion; Mrs. Beauchamp was so gracious to grant me some free time."

I looked into Cissy's pensive eyes and ruminated, "Let's keep the hopes up. However, I fear the war cause will dominate the English government for the moment."

"Mother England will do the right thing. She must!" Cissy insisted. Glancing at the fashionable watch strapped to her left wrist, she declared, "Oh dear, just look at the time."

I peered out the vast multipaned windows and realized we had been sitting at the table for a long time, pleasantly immersed with solving the world's concerns. The afternoon was turning to a winter's early dusk. "Golly, we've been here for almost three hours."

Cissy extended her lower lip to mimic a sad look. "I'm so sorry, but I must return to the factory dormitory. Thank goodness for the new Bakerloo Line."

After seeing Cissy to her Underground station, I reflected on how giddy I was feeling. She seemed so interested in me, which was exciting. But was it happening too quickly, especially when I knew I was to return to war soon enough? Ah, but *throw caution to the wind.*

Cissy ensured that I understood her work days were a long twelve hours, but her weekly leave was every Wednesday and Thursday. She also just happened to mention that she and her factory friends went to the Strand for evenings of fun and dancing on most Tuesday and Wednesday nights.

I felt exalted. To be friends with Cissy would bring me that sense of hopeful passion for a sweet girl that I had wished for. How quickly things can change!

...

For a Tuesday night, the Strand dance floor was packed. "I feel so very safe in the arms of one of our King's officers. Somehow the woolen khaki gives a lady great security."

I instinctively drew her closer. "I'm pleased, and I attest that an officer also feels safe being held by the slender arms of a British munitionette."

"It must be terribly frightful being in a shell bombardment. I don't know how you men don't just curl up and weep. Daily, I see the munitions leaving Brunner Mond, and to see how many are shipped is itself a dreadful thing."

"Yes, fear is so very much a part of this war. The business of being able to avoid funk is part of survival." Cissy made me feel comfortable, and I felt that I could trust her with my feelings. "That's why we only go into the front trenches once every few weeks. Before going into battle for the first time, I thought I was in touch with my feelings. Yet I have never felt as frightened as I did over in France, a feeling you don't recognize until the possibility of death is real."

"Oh, Bob . . ."

We moved together across the floor, at one with each other in both touch and emotion.

"So many have fallen, yet the men go bravely forward when ordered," I said.

"You are strong. I can see that in your eyes. They are so very kind."

"I try to bury my angst by keeping busy at what I do, persisting at a task. Like right now, to keep busy swaying to and fro with you should be continued for as long as possible. The burdens of war will not overcome me!"

We laughed, both having so much fun. Her carefree way took

me away from the war and gave me strength. For her, it took her away from the monotony of twelve-hour workdays. We danced and talked and talked and danced. It didn't matter where this was leading or how things might develop. My medical board was on Saturday, which meant when declared fit, I would be quickly shipped overseas.

The next night we again met at the Strand, she arriving with her factory friends. The dancing and talking was as wonderful and memorable.

Cissy accepted my invitation to supper the following Thursday at Mrs. Clarke's home, who had encouraged me to bring friends around. I would invite Eric, Daisy, and Stanley since Mrs. Clarke would remember Eric from our Walthamstow home. I wrote out the address for Cissy, mentioning I would send word if my return to France was accelerated. Cissy boldly suggested she would make the visit in any event, as she was confident I would still be in England.

...

"Lieutenant Pitman," said the Royal Army Medical Corps staffer, "you may go in now for your review. Follow please."

I entered the dark-paneled room, made darker by limited natural light due to the late, overcast November day. Three somber medical board officials were seated behind a wide desk. I saluted smartly.

"Right. Sit, please."

I nodded and took the only seat in front of the desk. The first to speak was a sullen-looking man of about fifty with veins protruding from his red cheeks and an unkempt mustache that was in keeping with his balding head. "Now, Lieutenant, we have in front of us the proceedings of the board which met on 25 October, finding you unfit for general service for one month, and also your assessment from Dr. Mott of the Maudsley. You're feeling how, Lieutenant?"

"I'm feeling very well, Major Donald. Despite the severity of the shell shock injuries I sustained at Mouquet Farm, I feel completely mended under Dr. Mott's care."

Seated beside the major was a younger, sprightly officer who carried a caring smile that made his gray eyes seem to dance. "Indeed," Captain Davis cut in, "Dr. Mott speaks very highly of your progress and your health. Are you able to describe how your demeanor is and how you feel about returning to battle?"

I confidently sat forward, connecting with Davis. "I am ready to return to the front, back to my regiment."

Two things were clear: One was that Major Donald and Captain Davis were conducting the Board. Perhaps Major Brown was merely clocking time. The second was that Captain Davis, a medical doctor, seemed endeared to my cause.

Davis continued in a clear, compassionate tone. "How are the nightmares and the general malaise you were feeling just after the injuries? You are aware it is difficult for a board to assess, ah, psychological disabilities, Lieutenant."

"Yes, I would imagine it is difficult to become of one mind with me; however, I assure you I am very fit for service."

Major Donald blustered into the conversation with a commanding voice. "No loss of masculinity, Lieutenant? No open dread? No risk of breaking down in action?"

Of course I had fears—lots of them—but I also had sense enough not to speak of them to a medical board. I smiled to project a positive countenance, checking any irritation as I answered confidently, "No, none, sir."

"You didn't wangle your way into convalescence to the detriment of your service and your duties?" Donald bristled.

I held my smile, forbidding this naysayer from getting to me. I slowly drew out my response. "No, sir. I believe the record shows clearly that I was subjected to intense bombardment under enemy shelling. Few in that circumstance would have kept up the pluck and the concern for the platoon that I did, Major."

I glanced at a nodding Captain Davis to maintain a calm demeanor in front of the implacable major, who himself had probably not been in the front lines, at least not in this war.

The captain interjected, "Lieutenant, you understand this board must interview soldiers like you who suffered from severe trauma and exhaustion while under fire, but also identify soldiers who use shell shock to wangle, using the major's term, their way out of duty by feigning shock when, in fact, they are malingerers with invented or imitated symptoms."

Captain Davis's steady and empathetic voice was calming. I held my direct contact with him. "Captain, I assure you that had I not lost consciousness on the battlefield, I would have remained steady in my duty."

"Thank you, Lieutenant."

Major Donald cut Davis off. "Right, the fifteen minutes have lapsed. Let's convene, shall we?"

He rang a service bell. Immediately there stood the staffer, beckoning me to follow him out of the room. I visited the toilet and upon return was escorted straight back into the boardroom.

"Lieutenant Pitman," snarled Major Donald, "you may remain standing. You are informed that this medical board finds you to be in A1 condition and fit for general service in the British Army."

I remained at attention but gave a slight bow, acknowledging the confirmation. "Thank you, sir. I am relieved and pleased."

"Now," said Captain Davis, "let's discuss your integration back into service. We acknowledge your request to rejoin the RCR in the field, and we will do our level best to secure that for you. Meanwhile, you are assigned to the casualty company at Brighton, where you will train and harden up before shipping back to France. The company there specializes in remedial gymnastics and physical training. Welcome back to the army, Lieutenant."

Major Donald looked up at me and exhorted, "You will have a

few days to get your affairs in order and report to the CO, Brighton, on Friday, 1 December."

"Yes, sir."

I saluted and took my leave into the dreariness of the Strand, where I strolled through the drizzle without umbrella in the direction of Trafalgar Square. I was relieved to again be fit for active service, but felt a slight gnawing in my stomach at the thought of returning to the mud and slaughter in France. As I'd done in the past, I steeled myself with the personal understanding that I had signed up to fight and to maintain the will to honor that commitment.

As I passed the Strand Palace, my mind was swept up with images of Cissy. I was to meet her on Thursday at Mrs. Clarke's, a day before my travel to the Brighton coast. That was a blessing I would cherish.

Chapter 19

30 November, 1916

An unexpected rap on the door roused me from the thoughts of joy I was feeling about dinner. I jauntily crossed to the front hallway, wondering who was calling in midafternoon.

"Cissy, you're here? I wasn't expecting you until 5:30 with Eric, Daisy, and little Stanley." I had just returned from a walk to the High Street market, where I collected the necessary vegetables and trimmings for the roast that I planned to slow cook starting at three, two hours before Mrs. Clarke arrived home from work.

She was beaming at me with that beautiful smile. "Well, Daisy told me that you will be departing for Brighton tomorrow morning. Having all day to myself, I thought I would sightsee in one of the better neighborhoods, and, well, that led me to your door!"

The smile, the surprise, and the delight all pounced on my emotions as I became aware of my heart thumping inside my chest and my breathing quickening. "It's Mrs. Clarke's door, and I'm just not sure it's proper for you to arrive unaccompanied." I didn't mean for that to sound surly. I was nervous. Oh God, she was beautiful!

Cissy ever so confidently stood at the threshold, her fingers interlaced at her front. "Daisy knows where I am," she teased, "and besides, it's 1916, not the fuss and feathers of the Victorian times, I daresay."

I suddenly became aware of the kettle whistling with impatience. "All right. As long as Daisy knows, then I guess we are in good hands." At that moment I knew all too well that I was in very good hands. "I was just brewing some tea. Would you like to join me in a cup?"

"If that is an invitation from a gentleman to enter, then I accept."

"Oh, I'm very sorry. I completely forgot my manners. Do come in."

Cissy looked ravishing as she passed me at the door, her *eau de cologne* sensuously following. She was wearing a fashionable silk dress in mauve and black, buttoned at the front below an oversize white open collar, low enough to expose her long neck. The dress was pleated below the waist, stopping mid-calf, while the ribbon belt accentuated her lithe body. The wide-brimmed hat, with ribbon to match her belt, highlighted her bangs, while her high-heeled shoes and caped overcoat made her look as much high fashion as any of the lady shoppers at Selfridges.

"Would the lieutenant relieve me of my cape?"

I was still trying to work through my nervousness and become comfortable with Cissy's sudden arrival, her stunning looks, and, above all, the confidence she exuded. I felt like a little boy in the presence of a sophisticated lady.

"Y-yes, of course, forgive me."

We sat in the front parlor, sipping tea and engaging in small talk. The conversation turned to Cissy's interest in how my medical board went, where my service would next take me, how long I thought the war would last, and if we would win.

She was most outspoken about her work at the munitions factory, stating that women deserved better working conditions and increased safety protection. While she had somehow escaped the dreaded yellow skin coloring that afflicted some of those who handled the sulphuric acid embedded in TNT, many of her friends did show such signs. She was also articulate about the high risk of explosion.

We were eased out of such somber discussion by the sun peeking through the rain clouds that were rapidly clearing away, and decided to go for a walk to nearby Finsbury Park. "I'll just get your cape. I placed it in my room."

"Thank you. I'll need that, unless you are offering your tunic?" she teased.

We laughed as I went to my room at the back of the home. Lifting the cape off the bed and turning around, I was surprised by Cissy standing right there in front of me. "I was only gone for a moment. Is everything all right?"

"Everything is just wonderful. For you as well?" She placed a white-gloved hand on my tunic, running her fingers across its brass buttons. She reached to my shoulder with her other hand, moving her face in closer to mine. Her rouge-tinted lips hovered razor close. I was at the same time frozen and very excited. "Kiss me, Lieutenant. Or shall I have to kiss you?"

I leaned across to lightly brush her lips, afraid of smearing her rouge.

Cissy's voice dropped to a whisper. "That's hardly a kiss, Bob. Let me show you how a lady is to be kissed."

Before I could take a breath, her lips were on mine. It was heaven, it was passion, and it was like I'd never been kissed before.

"There, that's better. Did you like that, Bob?"

My whole being, every sense I had, was roused as I stood there in a shiver. "Yes, I did," I whispered nervously. I wanted more, wanted to again feel the softness of her lips, but realized where we were. "I-I'm not sure about being so intimate in Mrs. Clarke's home. She will be home at five and—"

Cissy affected a coy look as she murmured, "I've seen the way you look at me. I know you like me. Besides, five is more than two hours away. A lifetime."

I gave in, losing all inhibition, becoming absorbed in Cissy as I looked into her gorgeous blue eyes, her round face bordered by those full bangs, and her assertiveness being as desirable as her physical appearance. I kissed her tenderly, she responding with her own kisses, sometimes briefly, other times for long, passionate, breathless moments. Two became one, clutching and holding and caressing. The only noise being lip upon lip and the crinkle of silk as we became entwined.

I was scarcely aware of how we became prone on the bed, looking into each other's eyes, bodies pressed close, so close. The world outside our shared aura did not, for that moment, exist. I pressed myself into her, testing, looking for approval. She didn't resist. With tunic off, my tie loosened and askew, there was no stopping. Cissy helped me lift her dress, petticoat included, and guided the way.

Later, after catching our breaths, we both lay there staring at the ceiling. Cissy began laughing. I turned to her, grinning in complete satisfaction. "And what is so funny, Miss Cissy Anne Taylor?"

"Oh, I am thinking that you had no idea how your day was to turn out. Did you?"

"No, but the question is, did you?"

She gazed at me from under chaotic bangs. "Not exactly as things happened, but I'd be lying if I didn't tell you I arrived here this afternoon with a very open mind. Do you think less of me for that?"

I propped myself up on one elbow and stroked her rosy cheek. "Of course not. It's just that I'm not familiar with the new demeanor of London women, what with me now living in the backward Canadian Prairie."

Kissing my hand, she breathed, "That's what is intriguing about you. You are so experienced and smart, but you have an innocence about you that is so very attractive. Not like so many of the London men I encounter."

"I hope by 'men you encounter,' you don't mean—"

Cissy held her smile, feigning a punch to my shoulder. "I am pushy, yes, but I hold strict values. I am very selective, Bob." She clasped my hand and lifted it to her lips for another delightful kiss.

I noticed on my wristwatch that the time for the roast to be put on had passed. With a "Sweet Jesus!" I jumped off the bed and extended my hand for Cissy to join me. She straightened her dress, then excused herself for the toilet. I attended to the dinner before we left for the walk to the park. We had decided to meet Eric, Daisy, and Stanley at Finsbury Station.

The dinner went very well, everyone pitching in with the preparation as well as the cleanup. Eric and I had a chance to speak about the days to come, he traveling directly to France in two days and myself leaving for Brighton in the morning.

At about nine I walked the Pitmans and Cissy to Finsbury Station. At the last moment before the train departed, Cissy placed her hand on my tunic as she had earlier in the afternoon and kissed me ever so briefly, ever so tenderly. I looked up and caught Daisy looking at me with an all-knowing smile, the kind that a woman displays when she, well, just understands.

I walked back to Mrs. Clarke's home with a cascade of emotions. It was too early to say I was falling in love—unless it had been love at first sight? I felt strongly about returning to war, but now I felt a new closeness. Neither Cissy nor I made any further commitment, but it was Daisy's knowing look that told me there might be something there to pursue. I felt ever so good.

Chapter 20

December 1916

Amid the winter bluster of English Channel winds, I had arrived at the Brighton Training Grounds. The second week of the month had me fully engaged in gymnastics and training offered by their professional staff, and it felt good to be active. In addition to daily runs along the seacoast, prison-like push-up drills, and calisthenics, we got out onto the playing fields for house-league matches, both football and cricket. The high skill levels shown by some of the men—from bowlers and spinners to strikers—made the games quite competitive.

However, one morning I felt off. It wasn't a headache or fever, but rather a general feeling of malaise. Upon rising from a good night's rest, I noticed a little smarting while passing water. I hoped this was a fleeting issue since I didn't want to miss my reporting to the RCR Depot at Le Havre, where I was scheduled to sail from Southampton in a week. Since the regimen did not require me to attend every activity, I opted to remain in quarters that morning and write Cissy a letter.

Miss Cissy Ann Taylor
C/O Brunner Mond Munitions Dormitory
Silvertown, West Ham

8 December, 1916

Dear Cissy,

I trust you are well, working hard for the cause, and enjoying your one or two nights out with your friends. I am doing well, settled in at the Brighton training facility. It is such a nice feeling to think that I can write to you while I am deployed, remembering the tenderness we shared.

I have thought about you often, about your wonderful sense of humor and your quick intellect. You are a beautiful person, and I am so privileged to have spent such intimate time with you. Daisy was so right to make the introduction. Now it is up to us to decide how the rest is to unfold.

It is a comfort to hold intimate thoughts about you as I proceed to France and back into battle. No matter the outcome and no matter what future is written for you and for me, fond memories will endure.

You may write me C/O Royal Canadian Regiment, Headquarters Le Havre. Correspondence will be forwarded from there to wherever I may be in the field.

Yours,
Bob

I thought about my words for quite some time, wondering whether they were too forward for such a new relationship or perhaps too rigid in my desire to avoid sounding wanting. Cissy and I had shared an experience that most couples would have been more cautious about, but we had succumbed to it because of wartime circumstances. I decided to post the letter and see what response I would receive, if any.

Strength training and outdoor physical exercise continued into the new week despite the wintry coastal rains that at times pounded the fields. I preferred these strenuous workouts to Maudsley bed rest. However, the smarting that began a number of days before had developed into outright pain and burning while passing water and was now keeping me up nights.

I checked with the Brighton doctor. He turned me away, stating that he only dealt with training mishaps such as sprained ankles. In fact, he was completely uninterested in being involved in my internal issue and suggested I await diagnosis when transferred to the RCR Depot.

...

I was picked up from the bustling Le Havre port by the CO's adjutant, who drove me to HQ. As it was just the two of us in the army car, I decided to explain my condition. When I looked over I saw his face had turned an angry red. "You mean to say, Lieutenant Pitman, that you have had a burning sensation down there for a week now?"

I felt I could trust this staffer and that opening up was the right thing to do. "Yes, as well as having to get up three or four times during the night."

He snapped his head in my direction. "Why didn't you check yourself into a hospital?"

"I tried to get medical attention at Brighton but was advised that, unless it was a military emergency, the two hospitals there would not see me, being reserved for the Imperial Indian Army and for the Aussies."

The vehicle lurched to a stop in front of the HQ building. I felt demoralized as we walked in silence until we arrived at the adjutant's office, where he lit up again. "Dammit, Pitman. Caught quickly, this could have been nipped in the bud. Now it likely means you will have extended hospital downtime."

"Caught what, sir?"

"Venereal disease! Gonorrhea. VDG! You have the classic symptoms, which if caught within three or four days, well—"

"Gonorrhea? Are you sure?"

"No, I'm not sure! I am not a damned doctor, but I've seen so many cases come through this depot I'm familiar with the symptoms."

I was shaken, stunned by his prognosis. "But how could . . ." I trailed off, feeling stupid. My thinking became like mush, wondering if the emotion triggered in the adjutant was born from intense morality or from a secret checkered past. But it didn't matter. He began to speak between clenched teeth, forcing the words out through puffed, reddened cheeks.

"You tell me, Lieutenant! Just when we had you traveling up to Arras to rejoin the regiment, you bring me this news. Dammit!" He stood two feet away, staring directly at me. "We need officers in the field. You've let your regiment down."

I felt a need to explain, as awkward and embarrassing as the situation was. "I was with a girl only once, a couple of weeks ago. A good girl."

The adjutant stood rigid. "Well, not that good a girl, is she? Tell me, where did you find this whore?"

I had to control my emotions so as not to make things worse. While I wanted to protect Cissy, I had to have the understanding of the commanding officer's assistant. I breathed purposely, trying to be calm. "Sir, she is a friend of a friend, actually a friend of my cousin's wife. We met during my convalescence. It was innocent, things happened."

"I am spitting mad. You recovered from shell shock, which I understand. However, with leave on your hands, you couldn't seem to keep your—your pants—well, your *health* straight. Get yourself over to Number 39 and let them deal with you."

...

I was admitted to Number 39 General in Le Havre, where the diagnosis of gonorrhea was confirmed. I felt horrible and disgusted and spent a fitful night worrying over the circumstances that placed me back in hospital. The frustration was not so much about the disease itself, but rather the shame of not being a good officer who was expected to show leadership.

My mind was in turmoil. I had been in training and then saw action with no leave for a year, not dating any girls and certainly not seeking any professional love. Unless there was some immaculate process at work, I could only have contracted the disease from Cissy. Had she known she was infected and simply didn't care enough to inform me? Had she lied about encounters with male companions, about her holding strict values and being selective about whom she embraced? Could she perhaps not have known that she was infected? Many more troubling thoughts attacked my overactive mind.

At my initial examination, I was bristling at being questioned about Cissy and lost control of my demeanor. However, after a level of mutual trust was built concerning the circumstances of my activity, and after a sensible discussion, the doctor and nursing sisters were understanding and professional. I learned that a woman is sometimes unlikely to know she has that particular disease.

As my thoughts turned from frustration to grief, I became concerned about Cissy. The medical staff assured me she would be contacted at the Brunner Mond factory to "have a word," but I was under military order not to contact her for fear she could react "irresponsibly, perhaps run." That was harsh, and I felt trapped.

After another bedridden day, the adjutant arrived, turning my pensiveness to anxiety. Sitting up in bed, I tried to smile and remain humble. Donning the hospital blues made that easier.

"Lieutenant Pitman," barked the adjutant, "I have come around to discuss your situation."

"Captain, I . . ."

He looked at me with a level of haughtiness and an impersonal distance. "No need to explain or justify. I've done this dozens of times. The examining doctor has apprised me of the circumstances, and although he is convinced you had a somewhat innocent dalliance only once with your little munitionette, you have let your regiment down."

My smile waned but not my humbleness. "I am so truly sorry."

"I am not here for that, Lieutenant. What occurred was unfortunate but not in violation of military law. As you did not conceal the disease, there is no offense, but you will be subject to hospital stoppage. Since your disorder was not connected with military service, deductions from your pay will offset the medical costs. Is that clear?"

"Yes, sir."

"Captain Hume advises that you will likely be resident here in Number 39 for up to four weeks, after which you will be assigned according to CEF needs in the field. I am afraid you lost your appointment back to the RCR."

After the adjutant left, I felt a little better, the same way perhaps a school boy would feel after having his punishment completed. I was still left with guilt, but not completely sure why.

Had I not sacrificed a lot for King and Country? Was I not willing to continue that pledge? Were changing societal morals allowing for physical contact between unwed couples not gaining a level of understanding, if not acceptance? Was there no consideration that soldiers who could die at any moment might take sexual risks?

I reflected on where I was laid up: Le Havre, the Haven of Grace. While the physical location of a hospital is meaningless, there seemed some solace in being surrounded by grace.

I was sitting up, reading an old copy of *The Telegraph*, which a sister had so graciously found for me, when the doctor appeared at my bedside. "Good morning, Lieutenant. Captain Hume, I'm head physician and will be taking over your case. I understand the adjutant has dealt with your military issues. Let's dispense with that and work on getting you better. We don't judge here, just treat." Hume seemed genuinely nice, not just in a doctorish way.

"Thank you, Doctor. That is some comfort."

"Now, we will be applying several treatments to rid you of this bacterial infection, and I ask you to be strict with the process. That way we will have you cured and on your way." He examined me behind the closed curtain, but a couple of times, in spite of his being gentle, I gave a painful start. "Your medical history shows you've just been released from the London medical system for shell shock concussion, so I'm sure you want to re-employ as quickly as possible."

With the examination over, I leaned back against the pillow. "Yes, that's exactly what I want. More than ever, I need redemption through getting on with what I set out to do here in France."

Hume patted my forearm while looking at me with kindness. "You are a good man, I can tell. That positive attitude will be a key piece of your cure."

The doctor reviewed the treatment, which included good food, fresh air, and silver solution injections that would stimulate my immune system. "I'm embarrassed, but thank you for looking after me and for your kindness."

He nodded his acknowledgment. "Lots of bed rest and a worry-free mind, Lieutenant. Light exercise, no cricket, no football, no running. I find walking along the seacoast to be rehabilitating. One sees many hospital blues along the boardwalk."

I kept to the strict regimen prescribed by Dr. Hume and began to feel better after the first week. However, because there remained evidence of infection, I needed to stay the course and be patient. I wanted the bacterium completely out of my system.

Yet the companion to patience is time. With time on my side, I thought a lot about Cissy. How was she doing? Had the authorities contacted her? Who were the authorities, military or the national health board? Thinking of the adjutant's attitude, were they kind or rough?

I wavered in my intense feelings between anger and compassion, which confirmed at least one thing: I cared about her. If she had known she was carrying the disease, I would be devastated, since that meant she didn't care about my welfare. But if she was innocent and didn't know, then I needed to be a comfort to her. But how could I help when I was forbidden to contact her and was shortly to be assigned to a battlefield?

...

I welcomed the 1917 New Year in a quiet fashion from the hospital grounds in Le Havre, followed by a mid-January order to report by shuttle lorry to the nearby Canadian Base Depot. I marched out that day in full uniform, feeling relieved to finally be returning to my military duties yet unsettled about the two recent hospital visits on my record.

I began my journey under a cloud of confusion about what was to come, what was before me. I struggled to keep my emotions in check, to not sit in the lorry and sob my heart out. I felt guilty, remorseful, embarrassed, and uncertain as I sat beside the driver, reflecting on what was to come. I wasn't just scared about my immediate future; I worried over Cissy.

I wanted her to be clear of responsibility, to have been as surprised as I was about the disease. I wanted that shared innocence to spawn a new world for both of us. Yet I felt desolate at not being able to speak with her, hold her, and hear her weep out the straightforward truth. I felt as anguished as on that day at Mouquet Farm when I was buried by enemy artillery. I again felt buried, this time with emotion.

Part II

Chapter 21

January 1918

"Pitman, is it?"

I saluted sharply. "Yes, sir. Lieutenant Pitman reporting, Major Deedes."

Major Henry Granville Deedes was born into the Indian British Service and later immigrated to the Dominion of Newfoundland. Now at thirty-five, with military tattoos on both arms and piercing blue eyes, he looked a formidable CO.

"Please sit, Pitman, let's talk. Welcome to the 12th Reserves."

"Thank you, sir!"

Crumpling the top of the report he had fished out of my file, Deedes peered at me. "I have reviewed your medical history. Quite a scare you had at the Somme, eh?"

I shifted in my seat, anticipating a reference to the *other* hospital stay. "Yes, it made me understand just how mechanized this conflict is."

The major smiled, perhaps with fond memories of past service. "Quite so. Not like sepoy command in India, I daresay."

"I suppose not, sir."

"Lieutenant, we need to speak frankly. Please be at ease."

I felt a twang of dread about what was coming, about how it would affect my next assignment. Only God knew how much I didn't want to be a paper-pushing adjutant. "Yes, sir. Yes, of course."

"Most of our Canadians discharged from 39 General are sent up here to the 12th Reserves, a great number of which have been afflicted in a similar manner as you, so I've heard the usual apologies, remorse, and wishes of turning the clock back."

Would it sound too defensive to, well, defend myself? "It's not—"

Deedes peered up from my file. "Your service record tells me that you've had legal training, so you understand frankness. You had a dalliance, you paid dearly for it, and we need to move on. Are you following?"

Through the staccato of Deedes's voice, I realized what he was doing. A feeling of relief swept from my brain to my feet, causing a slight sweat but eliminating the dread I had felt only moments before. "Sir, very much so."

"Good. Now, the RCRs have moved north. You've missed them, I'm afraid. Their next initiative will be months ahead, but we cannot keep you in reserve waiting for some unknown request to backfill casualties, as inevitable as that will be."

I looked at him hopefully. "Sir, are you thinking of assigning me to an alternative battalion?"

"In a manner. You see, Pitman, the war in the air is key to achieving our victory. Sadly, the Somme conflict seriously reduced the number of available flyers. Just now, transfers to the Royal Flying Corps are a priority, and I believe you would be a good fit."

Gads, I was not expecting that. My mind flooded with thoughts and images. "With respect, sir, the life expectancy of a flyer is known to be quite short. Are you suggesting this because of my recent condition, a sort of penalty for my dalliance, as you mentioned?" Damn, I didn't mean to sound defensive again.

The major grinned. He was really quite affable. "Not at all, it is not as simple as that. You've had a devil of a time dealing with shell shock, but you pulled through. Some would not be as willing to return to the front. Many agitate for Home Establishment duties."

I looked down as I twirled my hat in my hands, thinking that this was the moment to ask for home duty, to be safe in England if that was what I wanted. I quickly dismissed the thought. "I consider it my duty to return to the front, sir."

"You've obviously a way of overcoming the things that must haunt you, the things that haunt all of us. You've a logical mind that is capable of grasping map reading, mechanics, reconnaissance, and bombing techniques, so you profile as a pretty good RFC candidate."

My mind was reeling. I was flattered to be spoken of in such high regard, but I wondered why I gave the impression of managing affairs so well. I had heard that before—that I portrayed confidence even while my gut was churning over some event or other.

I remembered back to when I first became aware of that. It was after immigrating to Saskatoon, when I was up at Redberry Lake Camp with a few school chums in the summer of '09. During routine riding lessons, we had taken turns on a young stallion that had barely been broken. All the lads had difficulty staying in the saddle, and when my turn came, the beast had not at all settled down.

Climbing up onto an old harvesting machine, I had slipped over the saddle while others held him steady. When they let go, he bucked and kicked like the devil, and in short order, I was thrown to the ground. I was trembling, and my heart raced; sweat dripped off my forehead and down behind my ears. I inwardly sobbed as I could hear the others chanting my name, over and over, as I kneeled in the dust. *Pitman, Pitman, pity Pitman!* Somehow, I rose and, without looking at anyone, climbed that harvester and sat right back in the saddle. I was not going to quit.

Later, the lads had gathered around and congratulated me on my persistence. What they hadn't known was just how afraid I was, how it took all of my gumption to get back on that horse. I guess it was pure determination that had given me strength; it looked like courage when really I was full of fear.

"I understand, Major Deedes. I appreciate the acknowledgement."

"Bluntly, Pitman: we have a shortage of flyers and you're a damn good candidate. The type that can grasp the concept, absorb details, and survive in the skies. And you are a fully trained machine gun officer."

Deedes shuffled through a file in front of him, evidently finding what he was seeking. "Let me see . . . Lewis Machine Gun Course at the Canadian Military School, Shorncliffe, and another Lewis course at the 2nd Army School, British Expeditionary Force in France. You've been squeezing the ole trigger with zest. That gunnery expertise is quite valued in the skies!"

My mind was flashing through so many thoughts, so many scenarios, about what this type of commitment would bring—a completely different form of fight, both exciting and differently dangerous. One that would see me acquire new skills and catapult me into the heavens, flying over the enemy at speeds as fast as a train, maybe faster. Controlling an aircraft while fighting, risking the likelihood of being shot down or just crashing. Perhaps being flung out of a cockpit with arms flailing while soaring to a horrible death.

But as quick as those thoughts came, a more calming sense took over. I had thus far survived by keeping focused, by being busy in order to find courage. Yes, this flying assignment would work.

I looked at the major with a huge grin. "All right, sir, I'll give it a show. I'm ready to be a flyer."

"Well done, Pitman! I'll have my adjutant draw up the papers and see if RFC HQ over at St. Omer agrees with my recommendation. Meanwhile, you will remain in active duty here at Le Havre assisting in the training of freshly arrived troops."

Chapter 22

February 1917

The interview at St. Omer was detailed but seemingly scattered. The RFC commissioner wanted to know how often I had been in battle, what sporting games I played, if I could balance on a jittery horse, and what other coordination skills I possessed. I thought back to the summer of 1910 when I stayed with friends down at Little Manitou Lake, who taught me to shoot game while mounted. The commissioner was intensely keen on the details of that venture.

And he continued: Did I have good eyesight, hold enough knowledge to recognize military units of all nationalities? Did I think I could interpret the significance of infantry developments when viewed from the air, and did I think I could apply my machine-gun training to a flying situation while traveling at eighty miles per hour? He questioned my education at both the Winnipeg School of Law Clerks and the University of Saskatchewan. He wanted to understand my motive for transferring from the infantry.

He was more thorough than I expected and ended the interview precipitously.

Meanwhile, I endured tedious Canadian Base Camp duties while clinging to the anticipation of transferring into the RFC. But warm quarters and routine hours afforded plenty of time for letter writing and catching up with Issy, Hardy, Minnie, and letters home. One unremarkable day was pierced with the excitement of a letter from Daisy Pitman.

Lieutenant Robert Pitman
Royal Canadian Regiment
C/O Canadian Base Camp
Le Havre

27 February, 1917

My Dearest Bob,
    It is with my deepest sympathy and understanding that I am writing you about the situation between you and Cissy. She was hospitalized but is now near the end of her convalescence in London.
    When I visited her, Cissy confided the circumstances. The medical board contacted her just before the New Year, and after an examination, determined she had venereal disease. While they did not disclose your personal particulars, she is sure that based on their questioning and the timing of their visit, you became infected.
    The board stated they are convinced that her partner, you, was not infected prior to the intimacy. She accepts that and admitted to them that she had a dalliance in October past. Unfortunately, that soldier could not be reached. Cissy wants you to know that she is terribly sorry, and that if she had been at all aware of being infected, would not have put you in such a situation.

She feels the pain this has caused you, and that you are not inclined to have anything further to do with her. She wanted you to know she received your affectionate letter of 8 December and that she feels the same; however, she recognizes that it expresses your feelings prior to being aware of these current circumstances.

Bob, Cissy is my dear friend, and despite this angst, I'm so relieved she escaped that nasty Silvertown business. It's a blessing that she was not at the Brunner Mond factory on January 19 when the TNT explosion occurred. While I feel deeply for the souls that died, I am thankful she was at that time hospitalized.

Before I sign off, let me say that I've known Cissy for most of my life and can say that her apology is sincere and truthful. In the event it matters, this has shaken her to the core. She wishes you well and desires that you remain safe.

Eric and I join together in expressing our love for you.

Daisy

Silvertown explosion? Workers dead? Of course, I had read a brief article in *The Telegraph*, but I was so wrapped up in my hospitalization it didn't register. Oh yes, I too was very much relieved that Cissy was spared. It clearly resonated that this war was not confined to the battlefield but extended to the homeland. The hardships and risks that women were enduring in their factory work under zeppelin night attacks and in sourcing enough food to feed their families were a testimony to their contribution and their strength. How could our men in Parliament continue to deny women their equal rights?

Yet in the days and weeks that followed, my mind was harangued with a range of emotions. While I knew Cissy would be interviewed about the disease, I couldn't have known when, and I had forced myself to avoid thinking about it. I wanted to understand and accept that it was all right that there had been others before me, at least one.

I was frustrated with wild, random thoughts. Was she telling the truth? Was she really sorry or just remorseful because she knew she was infected and got caught out? Did she really feel the same as I or just seek sympathy and understanding? How could she simply assume I wanted nothing more to do with her? Dammit all, did I?

Daisy vouched for her, and I respected Daisy. I read and reread the letter, holding it, clutching it, in an attempt to feel its sincerity. Did any of it really matter at this point?

Yes!

On discharge from the 39th, I had made a vow to follow up, to reach into her soul. Wasn't this the opportunity to do just that? I knew just what I needed to do, and I would find an opportunity to do so.

Chapter 23

April 1917

The Royal Flying Corps training aerodrome to which I was attached was located in a farmer's field near Hythe on the shores of the English Channel, the 1st School of Aerial Gunnery. The location was the nearest to the Continent, which meant two things: that we were as close as anyone to the fighting and that, when graduated, we would be deployed to an aerodrome in France. I was not going to Africa or Asia.

"Pitman!" yelled the captain.

"Present!"

As one of fourteen prospective gunner/observers in training, I had been surprised at the sophisticated syllabus that seemed more consistent with an engineering discipline than with navigating an aeroplane.

"Now listen up, officers," bellowed the captain. "Let me be the first to formally welcome you to flying school. You will find that becoming an aviator involves a degree of culture shock as most of you have come from the trenches. The contrast of being stationary in a trench versus traveling at high speed several thousand feet above can be daunting. For some of you that will be disorienting, perhaps overwhelming."

"Will you be training us, sir?" questioned a newbie.

The captain walked down the line, stopping to address the trainee. "Sometimes, Lieutenant, and at other times you will be piloted by one of the other experienced officers."

"Captain," another emboldened recruit sputtered, "man has only been flying for about ten years, so how is anyone considered experienced?"

Our CO turned to the other end of our line, strutting through the grass. "You will find, cadet, that this technology is revolutionary in a permanent way, and once you understand the basic rules of flying, experience builds rapidly."

"Exciting!"

"Yes, it is, and it is my job to make it safe as well. Traveling at eighty miles per hour some ten thousand feet in the air, any doubt will be replaced with courage, gentlemen. Accept that now and you—we—will win control of the skies."

I caught myself gulping but was fairly sure no one saw. Standing out on that blustery spring day under billowy clouds amid blue skies, we periodically gazed upward as we heard the captain explain that our two-month training was to include reconnaissance and application of Morse code. For the first time during this dreadful war, I began to realize that the reason officers were selected as flyers was related to the need to grasp technical concepts, which sometimes coincided with advanced education.

The captain blustered, "Other skills taught here include navigation, bomb sighting, and machine gunnery—both on the ground and in aerial combat. But before you undergo your baptism of fire, there will be two weeks of classroom theory."

A collective groan was expressed in typical schoolboy fashion, completely ignored by the captain. We were encouraged to poke around the aerodrome, observe the aeroplane in all aspects of flight, from takeoff to landing, and learn its mechanics, its very fabric, before venturing skyward.

The discipline in the RFC was casual when compared to the infantry, yet all of the cadets took their training very seriously because if we didn't, the chance of surviving the skies was diminished. The end of each day was a pleasure. We would retreat to the mess for a few beers and a great cook up, and continue to learn from one another's experiences.

...

Mail was dropped daily, left in the mess in time for midday dinner. Since the moment Daisy had acted as go-between, the most special days were when Cissy's letters arrived.

Lieutenant Robert C. Pitman
C/O RFC Headquarters
London, England

22 April, 1917

Dearest Bob,
It was wonderful this morning to receive your weekly letter in the post. You are such a sweet man, and I always look forward to hearing about your training exploits. It must be so exciting that you are to soon soar high up in one of those majestic biplanes!
You have been so kind to me over the past weeks with your thoughts and wishes that keep me going and get me through each long day. Nottingham is terribly different from London,

but the girls are nice and we have many friendly ventures out to the pubs and such.

The factory is a monster, employing thousands in pursuit of the war effort. Even with the problems you and I faced, perhaps more so because of them, I continue to take up my support for women of all classes and the inevitable vote we will soon be granted. I believe that.

And thank you for recognizing the Silvertown horror, as I was close to a few of the girls who perished. After crying for them, we are compelled to pick ourselves up and continue the work. It remains risky, and the pressure continues to produce more and more explosives, but I'm sure that now the Ministry will increase safeguards.

Do keep writing, my darling. Does it feel strange to hear me call you that? We have known each other for longer by letter than in person, yet I feel closer to you as the days pass.

Take care and be safe, my strong flyer! I so look forward to a reunion just as soon as you can manage a reprieve from your work.

Yours,
Cissy

I wallowed in that one word, *yours*. I was thrilled. I had known what I had to do those many weeks ago and was proud I'd had the courage to follow through. Reaching out to Daisy was the first and most difficult part, as I knew she would get a message to Cissy and I wasn't certain about the response. In that first letter I was very blunt about my disappointment with being infected since that unbearable memory had usurped such a pleasurable, intimate meeting between the two of us. But it had to be addressed.

Yet I had held out an olive branch, stating that I understood how such grief could happen and that I believed in her and cared, not just in my heart but for her safety. I knew she had been granted a healthy discharge but also that she was ordered to relocate to the National Shell Filling Factory at Chilwell, near Nottingham.

While we had not seen each other since our farewell at Mrs. Clarke's, we so desired to. I could feel the passion in her letters, and I eagerly responded in kind. I dreamed of her beauty, of holding her. My days were filled—consumed—with thoughts of moving forward with each other. My training was enhanced as my heart was flying as high as the aircraft soaring above the aerodrome.

...

With the completion of classroom instruction, we were eager to get airborne. My first flight would forever be etched into my mind. The Avro 504J two-seater biplane was capable of traveling at ninety-five miles per hour, faster than any train I'd traveled in. I felt safe sitting in the seat behind my pilot, Captain Walker. It was almost like being enveloped in a cocoon except that there was nothing above my shoulders but open air.

The power of the 100 hp Gnome engine, as it noisily sparked to life after the air mechanic primed it with a spin of the propeller, was exhilarating. Vibration riddled the aircraft as the engine raced wide open until Walker "blipped" it down. I had been versed in this particular engine, which required the use of a Coupé button to continually blip the engine on and off, controlling its revolutions. While that now seemed awkward, I had been told that it made for smooth flying. The captain twisted to face me, giving a thumbs-up.

"Ready, Pitman?"

I felt the leather flying cap tighten against my forehead as I beamed a massive smile. "Yes, sir. Ready!"

"All right, let's see what the heavens are up to today."

I hoped he meant the rhetorical version.

On command of Captain Walker's controls and expert blipping, the craft moved forward across the flat, grassy plain. Racing toward the corner of the field, we cleverly spun around with a deft coordination of power blast and rudder control, facing into the wind. We momentarily sat there as the increased engine noise and a smoother vibration made it feel as though we were all-powerful, but going nowhere. Yet.

After straining, begging to move, the aircraft suddenly lurched forward and we were hurtling across the field toward the barracks. About two-thirds of the way across, the back end sank into the ground, or I thought it had, but it was the front end lifting up, and before I could think about anything else, we were above the barracks. Looking over the side, we seemed to be careening past the shoreline at a reckless pace, but that image slowed considerably as we gained altitude.

The sheer joy of losing myself in the moment was delightful, and looking at the billowy clouds set against the clear blue sky was breathtaking. As we increased height, looking down on those wisps of white was absorbing, making it feel as if we were floating in a timeless capsule. Turning this way and twisting that, dipping down and rising up, were all part of the experience. The wind sailing across my leather helmet and goggles and against my face was as pleasurable as anything I'd ever experienced. That is, once I learned to keep a closed mouth to avoid inhaling and gasping at the rushing air. At one point, Walker turned to look at me or to determine if I was still with him, I'm not sure which, but I gave a meek wave that he responded to with a determined thumbs-up.

Thoughts and feelings were buzzing through my mind at a speed seemingly as fast as the aeroplane. I felt free, as free as the birds I had watched for as long as I could remember, gliding through their own air space. In spite of this being the most dangerous thing I'd ever done, the flight gave me courage, a feeling of power. I realized that being aloft on that peaceful, lazy day would seem like child's play against what was to come over enemy lands, but somehow I felt I'd be more in control flying over top of them than fighting on the ground.

Forcing my mind back to the task, I remembered to gaze at the few gauges and dials located in my seat, the observer's office. I saw from the altimeter that at one point we reached eight thousand feet, and later, that the airspeed indicator registered seventy miles per hour!

After what seemed like five minutes, we began our descent. We had actually been airborne for thirty-five minutes. Approaching from the east along the English Channel coastline, we passed Dover, those white cliffs gleaming in the spring sunshine. Closer yet, we soared over the Martello Tower. We circled the aerodrome a few times, and with each pass, dropped lower until the people on the ground became larger than miniature toy soldiers. We were coming in off the sea, facing into the wind with the barracks in front of us.

Looking over the side, it seemed we were traveling at a horrific speed that could only end in a crash. We landed quite abruptly as the machine bumped down hard, flew up twenty feet into the air, and bumped hard again, followed by a series of smaller bumps until we were rolling across the grass in what I later learned was a perfect landing. We pulled up to the crowd of waiting men. After watching Walker climb down out of his cockpit, I copied his grace and also descended to the grass amid cheers and congratulations, the very same as those offered to the lads who had gone up before me.

Chapter 24

23 June, 1917

I caught up with Sam Hardy's RFC progress from a letter, which triggered in me the idea that I might be able to influence my own service. Hardy had completed his mechanics training weeks before and was now attached to the new 100 Squadron, the first to be formed exclusively for night bombing. He was posted to St. Andres-aux-Bois, their first French aerodrome, some thirty-five miles west of Arras.

Knowing I was training as an observer and hearing that his new squad was on a recruitment push, Hardy made clear in his follow-up letter that I would be a perfect candidate and encouraged me to put in a request. He was thrilled with his posting amid the constant excitement at the base. I could feel the enthusiasm in his words.

On a warm day in mid-June, we cadets assembled in a straight line on the grassy airfield, feeling very unfettered without our caps and tunics while standing at ease as the captain reviewed our progress. As aircraft buzzed in the background and lorries thundered by on their supply deliveries, my name was called first.

"Lieutenant Pitman?"

I took one pace forward, looking expectantly at the CO, knowing my future was about to unfold. "Yes, sir."

The captain grinned knowingly. He had seen my hungry look hundreds of times before. "Pitman, I am pleased to advise that you have from this day been accepted as observer on probation, to be attached to the Royal Flying Corps in the field."

The other cadets applauded, which continued for each officer cadet as the captain moved through the roster. We had all made it. We were all to be airmen! "Lieutenants, you will be based in western France as our initiative in Messines will continue for a while yet. Accordingly, you will report Monday, 19 June to the No. 1 Aircraft Depot at St. Omer for further instructions.

"It's been a good class. Good luck, lads! *Bonne chance!*"

Chaos erupted as whoops and congratulations broke out; slaps on backs and good wishes were shared freely. When things settled down, I strode forward. "Ah, Captain, may I have a word?"

"Yes, of course."

"I mean in private, sir."

"Fine. Let's stroll over to my quarters." He moved quickly across the grass, seemingly to prove that his definition of stroll was different from mine. "What's this about, then?"

I gathered my thoughts, choosing my words carefully. "Well, I've a friend who has been selected for 100 Squadron, and I would like to request a posting there."

The captain stalled, thought about my request, then said with uncertainty, "Damned good of you to come forward, Pitman." He looked me over, perhaps not wanting to spoil a great day. "I, ah, I'm afraid that's not my decision. You'll have to take that up with the Depot."

"Yes, sir. Very well, sir." I knew I looked downtrodden, disappointed that I couldn't secure a posting right then and there. After saluting smartly, I turned toward the door, becoming aware of the mess, where there was a lot of cheering and celebration.

The captain's voice stopped me. "But I say, old chap, there's no harm in asking. I'll send word on your behalf."

I turned quickly, aware that my grin must have stretched from ear to ear. "Thank you, sir!"

After spending too long in the mess, enjoying too many drinks, I later lay in bed. The excitement made it difficult to sleep, so I just stared at the ceiling, mentally composing my next letter to Cissy. As I did, something triggered a thought in my mind that seemed to address a nagging feeling I'd had for a few weeks.

In spite of the excitement that flying brought, I knew the expected *usefulness* of an airman at this point in the war was perhaps a few weeks, maybe a couple of months. Word had it that lads quickly became fatigued and made mistakes, some literally going down in flames.

This thought of death was different from the infantry. Falling from an aircraft, or worse, having to jump into the skies to avoid being burned inside a flaming machine, was suddenly going to be a possibility. My mind was churning. I knew the workings of the aeroplane and knew its shortcomings as well. It was not difficult to visualize being hit by anti-aircraft shells—nicknamed Archie—or enemy fighters or simply losing power as an engine overheated. Or tumbling out on landing after hitting a rut!

Sleep would not release me from negative thoughts, and I lay there trying to get control of the anxiety. I remembered a trick Matron Kay had taught me, which was to be aware of my breathing to bring my heart rate down. As she had coached, I thought of a safe place, one where people believed in me for holding a calm, confident demeanor. Thoughts of Cissy and her many letters were calming, which brought the good feeling I was seeking. I drifted off to sleep sometime before the early-June dawn, and upon waking a couple of hours later, I felt refreshed. I knew I would have the pluck for the airman's job.

The St. Omer Depot was an exciting hive of activity. Urgency seemed to be everywhere, with lorries lumbering and officers barking orders. This shouldn't have been a surprise when twelve hundred aircraft were kept operational in western France and one thousand new ones were delivered each month to keep up with attrition. Feeling like bowling pins bouncing away from this rushing person or dodging that swerving motor car, we Hythe graduates made our way to the observers' pool to be advised of our squadron postings.

Waiting in the stark, windowless reception area was nerve-wracking. One by one, the lads before me emerged from their interviews, smiling about their new assignments. I thought of Hardy as I waited, not wanting to jinx things with too much ambition, but I had enough hope that I would make it into 100 Squadron.

As the cadets dwindled to just a few of us, I pondered the CO's name on the closed door—Lieutenant W.F.C. Kennedy-Cochran-Patrick—and wondered whether he had three mothers or was descended from a long line of aristocrats.

I was finally summoned with, "It must be Lieutenant Pitman."

I thought that was very astute since I had just congratulated the only other cadet-lieutenant as he strolled out of reception. I saluted, and we shook hands. The CO exuded a pompous air, so I decided he must have had that aristocratic, triple-barreled pedigree.

I was curious, hopeful, and confident, all at the same time. "Yes, sir. Lieutenant Pitman reporting."

Gesturing to a chair in front of his heirloom desk, Kennedy-Cochran-Patrick barked, "Sit, Lieutenant!" He looked up from the file with a thin smile. "Well, well. I see you've done well in your training."

It wasn't what he said, but rather how. I concentrated on smiling since he held the cards to my future. "I enjoyed the time, sir."

"So modest, Pitman. Come now, lad."

Keeping cheerful, I pondered that this CO was about my age and of same rank, yet I was a *lad?*

"Dossier states you excelled at most of the aeronautic subjects and did really well at gunnery. And, my Lord," he scoffed, "look at this—says here your airborne skill with the Lewis machine gun is excellent." He waved my Hythe file in the air as if it somehow created my good record rather than my skills.

I was not sure why his tone was offhanded, but I thought it could be from envy because he was stuck behind a desk. No matter. I kept up my poise as I declared, "Well, yes, the Hythe CO was quite pleased. I was asked a few times to lead the team with training exercises in the Fee." A plug for the FE2b was a shamelessly calculated comment since that was the only aircraft flown at 100 Squad and I wanted in.

K-C-P sat back to ruminate. "Ah yes, the FE2b with observer in front of the pilot. Sweeping skies in front of you, slipstream in your face." He looked at me and smiled. But the sincerity of that expression was absent, subtly transformed into a pretentious grin.

I knew he was toying with me, knowing then that he was aware of my request. "Yes, an aeroplane which requires solid teamwork." I explained I felt confident sitting in the front nacelle with the ability to maneuver the gun from right to left, from below the machine to above, and to raise the rear-facing gun to shoot behind. All while the pilot commanded control of the aircraft.

He waved me off, agitated by my enthusiasm. "Very good, Pitman. Now, you must be anxious to know what the future brings."

Of course I was; he knew that. I instinctively, perhaps nervously, adjusted my seated position. "Yes, sir."

"You are aware that the premier RFC night bombing unit is 100 Squadron?"

I grinned, knowing then that I was to team up with Hardy. Not able to hold back my joy, an unapologetic smirk covered my face.

"Well, Pitman, you have been selected to join them as an observer on probation."

"Yes, sir. That is exciting, if I may say?"

"You may, Lieutenant," offered the CO. "Mind, you will need to impress the squadron CO before you are awarded your observer's wing. That means flying at night, in all seasons, over enemy territory before returning safely to your base aerodrome. A tough assignment for even the best, Pitman."

I was impatient to join the other newly assigned flyers over at the officers' mess. "Yes, sir. Understood, sir. This is great news! I can't wait—"

"You won't have to wait, Lieutenant. You are to report immediately to Trezennes. Good luck!"

"Tre-zens, sir? I understood the squad to be at St. Andres something."

"No, no. Your friend has moved along with the squad to Trezennes in the Lys Valley, about six miles south."

The emphasis on "my friend" felt like a slap, but I didn't play in to this desk jockey. "Thank you, sir. I will report there tomorrow."

I stepped into the summer sunshine and threw my hat straight up into the air. A couple of passing flyers looked at me as if I were crazy. Meeting up with my graduating class in the mess, we all agreed the CO was a prig, but we were too excited to give him more than one passing thought. I was the only observer going to 100 Squadron, but quite a few of the lads were joining a sister unit, the daytime bombers of 55 Squadron.

After again too many drinks, I did not feel like turning in early due to the long June evening. I took a full glass of whiskey and found a table in the aerodrome offices, where I sat for some letter writing. I wanted to have a clear mind, so my letter to Cissy was last. There was no use writing Hardy since I would see him sooner than a letter could be delivered. My letters to Issy and Minnie responded to their last writings, when I had found out Issy was still battling with the RCR, but Minnie had moved to the Princess Pats.

Writing to Cissy was more intimate, and it helped me fight

back my still-raw emotions about Percy, knowing they were made more intense by the alcohol. After writing to my circle of friends, I felt sad with the painful recognition that he was not among them. Yet letters to Cissy always took me away to hope for a better world to come.

I gulped a mouthful of scotch before putting pen to paper. I thought about Cissy's last few letters to me, imagining her settled in with friends who introduced her to fun and activities during time off. I could feel her infectious laughter when she wrote about boating trips on the River Trent or dressing up for a night on the Strand at Chilwell.

My letter was full of excitement and optimism as I described my posting to a new flying unit located in France and how I was going to give the Hun what for in order to do my bit to win the war. I was careful not to say too much about when the two of us might meet, for I would be weeks in practice, having little idea about when leave might be possible.

I followed Cissy's lead in the salutation, opting for her word *Yours* instead of risking something more intimate. I felt proud that this would be the first letter she would receive from me postmarked "France."

Chapter 25

June 1917

"Lieutenant Pitman, welcome to 100 Squadron," greeted Major Malcolm Christie. "I trust you've been shown your quarters?"

"Yes, Major, and in passing met 2nd Lieutenant Frank Wells."

"Quite so. Frank is one of our best, and a gentleman at that. He'll be a good roommate." Christie assessed me with an up-and-down look. "Welcome to Aire!"

"Thank you! But Aire, sir? I understood we're in Trezennes."

"Yes, yes. Trezennes is located in Aire-sur-la-Lys, the Lys River area. Ha, the French! They are a confusing crowd. Easier to say Aire, don't you think?"

I grinned, more at feeling comfortable with my new surroundings than with the immediate conversation. "I agree, sir."

"Now, Bob, you might drop some formality, loosen up a bit. Flyers are a little more relaxed than other units of His Majesty's whatnot. Prefer our lads to think on their feet, well, in the air, as it were."

I noted that in spite of the admonition to be less formal, I was not given permission to respond to him as Malcolm. "All right, Major. Less formal it is!"

Christie surrendered to deep thought, which I took to mean I was dismissed. Without waiting for a reply, I saluted and excused myself. As I walked across the aerodrome grass to my hut, I thought about what an intense man he was. His vivid black eyebrows over dark eyes gave him a mysterious persona. At the same time, he spoke softly and had gentle mannerisms, supporting his reputation as a fair commander who was respected immensely. I liked that.

"Howzit, Pitman?"

The voice emerged from the bright sunlight as I was unpacking my meager belongings, a soothing accent that was both sing-song and uplifting. Hearing footsteps, I turned around to a grinning boyish face. "Hello, Frank. Just moving my things in."

"They call me Wellsey. You will too. And they call you . . . ?"

"I'm Bob to my friends, just Bob."

"All right, Bobby, what say you get finished up there and we go for a suds?"

Our two-person hut was one of many that were erected along the west side of the airfield, downwind of the officers' mess and the CO's headquarters. I was intrigued by the wooded area behind, which appeared to be teeming with birdlife among the thick vegetation. Wellsey saw it as a great place to hide if we received a surprise visit from enemy aircraft. I was anxious to walk over to the opposite side of the field, where the aeroplane hangars were and where I knew I would find Hardy. But Wellsey, in his affable manner, convinced me to join him. Walking over to the mess, he explained that on nonflying days, officers were encouraged to enjoy a drink or two.

The mess was alive! From the entrance, I looked around and saw flyers sprawled all over, some lounging on couches, others standing engaged in animated discussion, and still others sitting erect playing whist or leaning against the long bar. In the middle of the room was a massive wood-burning brazier with mesh screening around its circumference and armchairs pulled up. I could see how important that would be during cold, rainy nights.

Wellsey led me over to the bar, where the duty soldier poured us each a whiskey. I learned that Wellsey had enlisted in his native Cape Town in a similar manner to my enlisting in Canada. However, he was focused from the get-go on joining the RFC, having obtained his pilot's certificate from the Royal Aero Club in South Africa. "And you, Bobby, what's your story?"

I knew straightaway that this was going to be such a different experience than the infantry, and the much less formal manner of the RFC was welcome. "English by birth and Canadian by transplant. Fought at the Somme, where I sustained injuries, and here I am."

"Major says you did well at training, is it? You've got balls, do ya?" Wellsey didn't probe about my injuries or my hospitalization. I didn't elaborate, at least for now.

"I did well with the machine gun, also scored high on navigation."

"Come on, Pitman, loosen up. Ya did great, chappie." His voice was full of mirth, teasing me along. "You're such an old man, Pitman!"

The bartender was hovering, listening to the banter. "You twins need a top-up?"

Wellsey and I looked at each other as we broke into laughter. "There's something there, Bobby!" I, too, saw the connection, the sharing of similar, if not quite twin-like, features. While the mustache generally gave officers a homogenous look, in our case we also shared hair and eye color, as well as skin tone and build.

I grinned. "Another, Wellsey?"

"You bet!" I noticed the drink had brought out his Cape Dutch brogue. After a while chatting, another couple of flyers entered the mess and made their way to the bar. "Wellsey, how you doing? Knew we'd find you here!" jested one of them. He turned to me, overtly sizing me up. "So, this is our new boy?"

"I'm hundreds, Ace, and *ja*, this's the new one, my bunkmate. Careful, he's an old man!" Wellsey's infectious laugh had us all chuckling.

I was introduced to Ken Wallace and Charles Lunghi, both observers in the squadron. Like so many of us, their RFC appointments followed time in the infantry. Before the conflict, Ken had been a practicing engineer, while Charles had been an engineering student, typical of the type of background we all shared.

Ken was the more outgoing. "So, we have another old man from the trenches to loosen up, do we?" With a winning smile, he extended his hand. "Welcome to 100 Squadron, Bob. We were briefed about your arrival."

Charles also stepped forward, his Italian accent dominating. "Welcome Bob, we are-a looking to you for good-a friendship here."

"Thank you, Ken, Charles. Wellsey, you referred to Ace—"

"Ah yes, old man. Ken here is our token squadron ace."

I scrunched a puzzled expression.

"*Ja*, token because we are a bombing squad. Ha! We wouldn't knock out five enemy aircraft no matter how hard we tried!"

"All right, but why Ace?"

Wellsey looked at Lunghi and sang, "Lunghi, do tell."

Lunghi had a shy smile. "Well-a, they have-a fun with my accent. I met-a Ken, and I called him Wall-ace! Not like the Wall-ass you would-a say. So-a Ken is our Ace." Lunghi was pleased with himself, willing to take in stride the ribbing about his accent.

I offered a warm smile to Ken. "Well, Ace, I'd say camaraderie is as good as or better than any medal or title!"

"Quite, good way to put it," said Ace.

We talked for some length, and I thought the warm relationship that was quick to develop was indicative of what would become a close bond. We had a daunting task ahead of us with dropping bombs in the dark on industrial targets behind enemy lines, and knowing there was an *esprit de corps* made the task more sufferable.

...

Crossing to the opposite side of the grassy airfield in the bright July sunshine, I was excited to seek out Sam and reconnect after so many months, and after our near-death experience on the Somme. Enjoying my pipe, I approached the Bessonneau hangars, which were erected along the eastern side of the field, all looking identical in their dark-green canvas coverings.

I entered the first amid the drone of an aircraft engine and the bustle of activity as mechanics clambered on top of, over, and behind the various FE2bs being serviced. Yelling over the din, one air mechanic knew exactly where Hardy was, directing me to the third hangar down the line. However, he diplomatically requested I remove the lit tobacco from the area, correctly citing the danger of explosion. I was new and green.

Coming in from the bright sunlight, my eyes adjusted momentarily before distinguishing Hardy from the rest of the blue coveralls buzzing around. His joyful voice bellowed from the middle of the structure. "Bob, over here! Hey, guys, this here's my old platoon officer!"

I felt a little overwhelmed as Hardy and his mechanic friends gathered around to greet me, all so cheery and welcoming that one would hardly believe they were the least bit troubled by an annoying war waging a few miles east. As they drifted back to their work, Hardy said he had arranged with his lieutenant for a break to see me settled in. I was learning the ways of the RFC with its emphasis on teamwork and somewhat-flexible work arrangements.

Sam indicated he would fetch me in an hour and we would find a suitable tavern.

I was chatting with Wellsey in our hut when I heard the pitched whine of a downshift. I looked out, and there was Sam astride one of the black Douglas motorcycles that were plentiful around the aerodrome. "Hop on, Bob!"

I looked somewhat quizzically at him astride the one-seater, but quickly determined I was to sit across the metal carryall over the rear tire. I waved at a grinning Wellsey as we roared off, leaving a veil of summer dust behind.

While I attempted to determine exactly where he was taking me, talk was near impossible over the pitch of the two-cylinder engine. Besides, I needed to hold on. The four-horsepower machines could top out at seventy miles per hour, and I knew Hardy was more than capable of trying. I soon saw the parish church steeple over Sam's left shoulder as we pulled up safely to an *estaminet* near the Aire-sur-la-Lys bell tower, which hadn't been rebuilt after a fire in 1914.

The inside of the tavern was homey with walnut-paneled walls, beige tiled floors, and wood tables for two that could be pulled together for larger groups. We chose one of the two tables alongside the open French-paned windows, brightened by the evening summer sun amid a cool breeze. Sam placed the flower vase on the sill as it annoyingly blocked our conversation.

It was good to experience Hardy's lightheartedness again, his cheery disposition had so positively affected all of us in the RCR, even when a dark cloud hung over the battlefield. Explaining his new vocation, he talked with excitement about being responsible for preparing the powerful aeroplanes sent to the skies each day. So much good had happened to him since we talked at the Maudsley some months before.

As we caught up I waited for the inevitable question, knowing it was finally coming after a pause in the conversation when Hardy grinned warmly. "So, tell me about Cissy. What's the story, old sly one?"

If Sam knew, was aware of the whole story, what would he think? Not just of me, but of Cissy. I stalled by lingering over the *vin rouge*, sipping it slowly. "Well, we write to each other regularly. You know, 'can't wait to see you' and 'do keep safe' kind of stuff."

"Come on, now! There must be more to the story. When I left you at the Strand, you were as lively as a boy who just got a first kiss.

Well?"

"Well, what?"

"Oh, you are difficult! How many times did you see her again? Did you get that kiss, you know, *that* kiss?" Hardy studied me for a moment, a sparkle in his eyes that betrayed his thoughts. "You did, didn't you?"

I grinned, buying into Sam's mischievousness. "Did what, Sam? I respected her like I would any lady, you know that."

"You did, I know it. You did, you ole charmer!"

In spite of the effect of the wine, I felt stressed, my countenance changed to reflect my anxiety.

"Ah, but why suddenly so glum, my friend? Has something happened?"

I was on the verge of spilling everything, thinking it would be a relief to have a confidant to share my grief about what exactly did happen. Yet I just couldn't open up, not now. I had to deflect.

I did my best to smile even though I knew it was a forced grin. "Sam, Sam, Sam. I grant you are perceptive, but let's talk about the aerodrome. Tell me about the Fee." We talked about 100 Squadron and how, in spite of being such a new squad, an incredible team had been built up. This was especially significant because of its newness as the first RFC night-bombing unit. Sam felt I was incredibly lucky to be bunked with Wellsey since he was one of the most competent pilots at the base and simply a nice person.

After finishing our second bottle of wine, we roared back to the aerodrome with the last bit of daylight disappearing behind us. Although the long summer days made it seem early, it was actually nearing 2200 hours, so we walked the motorcycle from the entrance to avoid waking anyone. We slapped each other's backs as I thanked Sam for a very warm welcome on my first day. "Good night, Sam."

"Good night, Bob. It's great being together again."

"It sure is, and thanks for inspiring me to request the 100 Squad. It all worked out so well."

"I knew the post would come through—I worked on Christie enough!"

"Sam, you devil!"

"Ha ha!" He started to walk off but then turned. "And oh, I should tell you that the lads here have figured out my nickname, so I'm Hardknocks to the squad. Yup, I let that loose under the duress of a glass or two!"

Chapter 26

September 1917

I had been at the aerodrome for two months, through my twenty-fifth birthday in July, which was now a fond memory. Birthday wishes had arrived at the aerodrome every day for a week, mainly from family at home, but also from Issy, Minnie, and a special card from Cissy. How my mama was able to package up an angel food cake in a tin to arrive whole was nothing less than magic.

I had built up knowledge about the workings of the FE2b, the bathtub with wings fondly known as the Fee. It wasn't just the daytime practice runs but also an understanding of the inner workings of the aeroplane that were important. To force land in a farmer's field without basic mechanical knowledge could make the difference between life and death.

The evening of my first official sortie, I was nervous while walking toward Hangar No. 2, which housed our assigned aeroplane. In the Ops Room, Wellsey and I had reviewed area maps, memorized our sortie notes, and synchronized with the other flyers for the mission.

"You set the pace here, Wellsey," I deferred. "You're the veteran."

"*Ja*, rare comment as I've only been on two priors!"

"That's two up on me, *mon pilote*!"

"Fair 'nuf, now let's get this baby looked over, eh?" We walked the circumference of the machine, looking for obvious defects—cracks in the struts, fraying of the wires, or tears in the delicate wing fabric. We did not expect to find any since the mechanics were ever so thorough in their preparation. Still, flyers wanted to see for themselves.

The Farman Experimental FE2b began war service as a fighter due to its rear-mounted propeller that allowed a 180-degree forward gun range. But after the invention of the synchronized gear—which allowed a machine gun to fire through the propeller while aiming the newer, faster single-seaters straight at the target—the Fee became obsolete as a fighter. Yet the old girl won back admiration for her phoenix-like reputation as a strategic bomber, a solid, worthy, and accurate workhorse.

Amid the late-day shadows that were cast over the Fee's starboard side, a cough emerged. From the lit portside, we peered into the darkness to see Hardy lift himself up, grinning. "All well with this bathtub? Find any flaws, gents?"

"Ah, Hardknocks," said Wellsey, "you serviced this machine, *ja*?"

"I and the other mechanics, yes."

"Good on ya, Sam—er, Hardknocks," I corrected. "We're blessed to have your hands on our safety."

He looked over at Wellsey, who confirmed, "I'll say. You mechanics with your dedication and commitment are a godsend."

Hardy grinned proudly as he asked, "May I help?" Without waiting for an answer, he showed us how he had inspected the propeller and the parachute flares, and also the wingtip flares. We crouched down under the nacelle to ensure the center 230-pound bomb and the wing-fastened Cooper bombs were secured. Hardy showed me how to lightly pull on the bomb cable release to ensure it was taut. Failure to release the bombs at the precise time would result in a wasteful, blundered sortie.

The warning buzzer from the CO's barrack warned us we were to dress for takeoff. While we were not yet to bear the weight of the winter Sidcot suit, we did require warm protection. Suddenly, air mechanics came from behind crates and out of the shadows, forming teams to roll the Fees out to the grassy field in front of the hangars.

Dusk was advancing as I looked up toward the cockpits. Standing on the landing gear strut, then onto the tire, I remembered to avoid getting caught up around brace wires and control cables. From there, I ambled up onto a higher strut to then heft myself onto the wing root, being ever so careful not to crush one of its ribs or puncture the linen fabric. I swung my leg onto the pilot's seat in the rear cockpit before rotating my other leg into the front section of the nacelle, using the edge of the ammo box for support. With no seat or bench up there, I knelt on the floor.

My stomach felt taut and my pulse raced at the thought of actually going into battle. I tried to calm myself by thinking about Ace and Lunghi, who had been up on their maiden sorties over the past two nights and returned safe. Still, my gut churned. I made myself busy, checking and rechecking the two Lewis guns, ensuring the mechanisms were clear of jams, and that the shell collection bags were fastened tight. Shells blowing behind would destroy the propeller, a mistake that could be fatal.

Seeing that my flying clothes were cinched tight so as not to flap in the slipstream and that my leather flying helmet with goggles was fitted, I said a prayer and thought of Cissy. She was my talisman, my safe place, my inner courage that would bring us home. I gave Wellsey the thumbs-up he was waiting for.

Hardy was ready at the propeller.

"Switches off!"

"Switches off. Suck in now," thundered Wellsey.

Sam swung the propeller around a few times, priming the engine for ignition.

"Switches on!"

Away went the propeller at one thousand revolutions per minute before Wellsey throttled it back to an idling six hundred, giving it a few minutes for warmup. As we awaited the go signal, I could feel the Beardmore run up again to full revs as the throttle was pushed forward. I turned around to gaze behind Wellsey, and my attention was caught by the fiery red flare that was shooting out from behind the twin exhausts, highlighted against the blackness of the night. A powerful signal of His Majesty's air strength.

We were signaled to follow the fifth machine. With the first four now circling the aerodrome to gain altitude, we swung around into the wind for takeoff. Feeling the full force of the throttle, I leaned back against the wooden cockpit interior, my hands tightly gripping the side of the nacelle in anticipation of takeoff. After a few bumps we were skimming along the field, then climbing into the darkness.

Suddenly, I heard Wellsey wail something. Exactly what, I'll never know. But instantly I knew from the tone of his voice that things were not good. As I was gulping down my panic, realizing the heavily laden Fee wasn't climbing, there was a sharp crack like an electrical zap. Amidst sparks flying all around I heard the engine quieten as it was throttled back. Being out front, I knew we had burst through telegraph wires and could do nothing but watch as Wellsey steered the wobbly craft through the darkness. In an instant we slammed into a ditch!

I was dazed, not really sure what had happened, but I knew I was alive. Wellsey was out first, holding a hand out to me as I climbed onto the field. I momentarily stared at the broken aeroplane, nose down with a crumpled and splintered nacelle. He jabbed his left fingers forward, pointing to a broken undercarriage, and then at the heavy engine lying behind, making me realize how close we came to being crushed. He abruptly pulled me away with his right hand. "The bombs, Bob!"

In a fog of confusion, I looked at him as the events of the past few moments tumbled through my mind. Why was he concerned about not dropping our bombs? We were obviously done for the night and weren't going anywhere in that mess. As Wellsey yanked on my sleeve, I stared in bewilderment at the front of the aircraft, its front pointed into the ground. My eyes moved toward the rear, saw it was elevated in an unnatural way, and my mind caught up with the scene. The Beardmore engine was weighing heavy on the explosives. "Oh fuck, the bombs could go off! The bombs are triggered for detonation!"

"My point, old man!" We ran like stink across the farmer's field back to the aerodrome, meeting the ground crew who had run out to assist. With enough distance, we looked up to survey the situation and saw that we had failed to clear the telegraph wires above the farmer's land. They were now dangling dangerously onto the ground.

Hardy ran up. He ensured we were not injured, then explained the bombs would not detonate in their current condition as there was no fire and nothing touching their fuses. However, it would be a delicate operation to defuse and dismount them in the recovery process. He joined the other mechanics that were cautiously approaching the downed aeroplane.

Wellsey delicately touched my head. "How are you? You're bleeding above your ear!"

I instinctively touched my head and then stared at the blood on my fingers while I gathered my thoughts. "A little dazed and perhaps a little bruised. Christ, I think I whacked the side of my head on the front of the cockpit as we hit. I'll be all right. You?"

He winced, seemingly not wanting to draw attention to himself. "My reputation is severely bruised, old man! I hadn't expected that damn crate would fail to climb; it seemed all right during warmup. We checked her over thoroughly and we know she was serviced properly. I'll make my report straightaway, get this behind us."

Walking back to the Ops Room, I realized that the other eleven aircraft had carried on with their planned sortie. Not so for our registration 4936, a complete wreck. The ones taking off after us must have wondered, uncertain. Lunghi and Ace behind us must have been worried sick but realized that war stops for no one.

The medic gave Wellsey a clean bill, observing that he was better protected, positioned immediately in front of the engine. I was ordered to sit out the next few days to ensure my little head bump didn't turn into something worse. Privately, I was all right with that. I needed to get my pluck back before the next mission.

...

Miss Cissy Ann Taylor
Women's Dormitory
National Shell Filling Factory
Chilwell

5 September, 1917

My Dear Cissy,
Your letters are such blessings. They keep me going, and I look forward to them in each mail drop. And if I daresay, I know my return letters are as welcome! I know you understand that I am unable to verify just where I am located other than somewhere in northern France.
If you saw me just now, you might laugh as I have gauze wrapped around my head! Oh, don't fear—it is only a superficial wound. My pilot, Wellsey, was taking me up on my first sortie when we encountered engine trouble and crash landed. The aeroplane has gone to heaven, I'm afraid, but we are all right.
As my confidante, I will tell you I was scared out of my

wits. With the occurrence of a split-moment life-ending possibility, I realize how those few seconds of terror can affect one's whole being. The medics must be used to that since they ordered me grounded for a few days.

I lay upon my bed that whole evening not sleeping a wink, living and reliving the moment. Even by morning the fear had not subsided, with nausea welling up from deep in my stomach. Yet I managed to hold things in.

I won't say I am chomping at the bit for the next sortie, but I will tell you that I am looking forward to getting back up on the horse and riding with purpose. It is my duty and sacrifice to do so with courage.

Well, I must go meet Wellsey for a hearty breakfast and heartier chat. That bloke is always up and feeling chipper by dawn, even if he spent half the night flying over German territory! Take good care of yourself, Cissy. I always look forward to your precious letters.

Until we are able to meet, I am yours.
Bob

...

I wandered over to the mess. Approaching the side of the building, I was greeted with, "Well, time you got outta that warm bed and joined us, old man!"

It was such a pleasantly warm fall morning that Wellsey, Ace, and Lunghi had commandeered a table set up in front on the lawn. I took the only vacant chair as they all grinned at me. Ace quipped, "You look like one of the battle-fatigued officers in those silent pictures they are showing."

Everyone was laughing, and I laughed along. "You three are damned comedians, eh? Doc says the headgear comes off today, getting ready for more follies." Wellsey and I had spoken of the need to get airborne again after our disaster, the sooner the better.

I listened to the murmur of their conversation, eating bacon, eggs, and kidneys, while reflecting on Wellsey's affectionate reference to me as "old man," as he had branded me so quickly those few months back. Not only was I a little younger than him, but he was married while I was not. Yet I knew he was referring to my old-soul attitude compared to his less serious, take-things-as-they-happen approach. He captured my character so well, exposing it kindly, which allowed me to permit myself to be a little more lighthearted.

"Look, we've lost him," said Ace. I took my gaze away from the airfield and looked back at my friends at the table.

Lunghi grinned. "Oh ya, just-a look at his frown."

Wellsey remained grinning. "I tell you, he is an old soul," he said as he leaned toward me. "But you are a champ, walking away from your first crashed aeroplane—and on your first sortie! I think there must be some kind of a medal for that, what say?"

As we laughed, I could see the fondness in Wellsey's eyes. "Quite," I said breezily. "But you ought to have a medal for not flipping that old Fee on top of us or detonating those pills." I looked around our little table, eyeing Ace and Lunghi. "That, my friends, is the skill and courage of a medal-winning pilot."

...

"The old man's back!" yelled Wellsey as he strode in through the mess door. "Thought I'd find you here, Pitman." Flyers in the mess raised their heads, some recognizing the quip he directed about me, others frowning in confusion about what he was on about.

A week after the crash, eight Fees were to attack aerodromes in the Lys Valley. Wellsey had since gone on a short sortie, but the squad had been grounded for a few days due to dud weather. He bounced over to join me and Ace.

"Feeling fit as a fiddle." I grinned confidently in my desire to ensure those around that I was in fit flying form. "Wouldn't sacrifice a sortie for the sake of a little more downtime if I felt I needed it."

Ace chimed in. "Yeah, good on you for facing the devil in this."

"We've got an easy enough sortie tonight, gents," said Wellsey. "A little run across the valley over the lines into enemy aerodromes, the Lys River our guide. Good way to ease back into things, Bobby." I understood what Wellsey was doing, his gentle demeanor providing encouragement in support of my professing readiness. I was up for it, but Wellsey knew me well enough to sense I was hiding a residual bit of fear.

A baritone voice broke the moment as the CO's adjutant inserted himself in our tranquility and bellowed across the mess. "Attention, officers!" Major Christie's arrival for dinner was always announced, signaling our need to stand-to.

The fifty-two of us shuffled to the main table, quietly listening for Christie to begin his flying-night sermon. He admonished us to keep vigilant as it was to be a dark, hazy night. He warned that enemy aerodromes would be heavily defended with searchlights and Archie. Our leader, Lieutenant Kent, had made the run up and down the Lys Valley many times, so we were to follow his guidance closely.

"Any questions, gents?" The major's pause was not long enough to even beginning moving one's lips. "No? Well, let's get to our supper, shall we? First wheels up at dusk, 1940 hours. Lieutenant Lunghi, your blessing, please?"

"Come-a, Lord Jesus, be our guest and bless what you-a bequeathed us."

Lieutenant Hyde, a new recruit thundered in with, "Father, Son, and Holy Ghost, the one who eats the fastest eats the most!"

"Ah-ah!" said Christie, barely hiding a burgeoning grin.

...

The eight black bombers had been pushed out onto the field in front of their respective hangars. Dusk set in, but few lights were illuminated to keep the aerodrome safe from the chance of a Hun attack. The bombs were inspected by observers, four 20-pound Coopers to each wing.

Amid the chatter and banter under torchlight that preceded our sortie, I was buoyed by the camaraderie of the flyers, the mechanics, and the ground crew. We were a true team, all depending on each other. But none depended more on that teamwork than the flyers who had to get airborne, drop bombs, and return to the airfield, all in darkness. While the blackness made it too dangerous to fly in formation, we did follow the same direction at five-minute intervals, keeping a distant watch on each other.

Standing in front of our newly assigned A796, Hardy raised his right arm to alert us as he yelled a blessing for the flight home. I responded with two thumbs up. He called up, "Switches off, sir!"

Wellsey checked that the engine ignition switches were indeed shut off. "Switches off. Suck in," he yelled.

Amid the wires and tail booms, a couple of mechanics strained at the big four-bladed propeller to turn over the pistons of the 160 hp Beardmore, coaxing it to suck in petrol. After forcing it around a few times, the mechanic raised his thumb to Hardy, who then yelled up to Wellsey.

"Switches on, sir!"

"Switches on."

I could hear the ignition switch click behind my right ear; then Wellsey began winding the starting magneto. I heard the first cylinder fire, and then the other five came to life in quick succession as vibrations rippled through the craft. Wellsey opened the throttle as I looked behind to see blue smoke followed by the red flame firing from the exhaust. With the engine and coolant up to temperature, Wellsey signaled for Hardy to pull the chocks away from the wheels.

As we traveled across the rutted field, I could feel the tension build from the top of my stomach to my chest, then spread across my body. Wellsey tapped me softly on the head as he sensed my apprehension. He yelled something that included "old boy," but I couldn't hear. The words didn't matter, but his soothing voice did.

From the far corner of the aerodrome and facing into the wind, Wellsey opened the throttle, testing the engine again for any sign of misfire. We were damn well not going into the telegraph wires tonight. Suddenly, the flare path lights were thrown on from blackness and we were speeding along the field back toward the hangars. With a feeling of lift, we were away.

The warm breeze flowed through me, settling my stomach. After circling the aerodrome to gain altitude and await the last two aircraft, our eight teams zoomed into the blackness—and it was black!

I directed us on a safe heading to cross the lines at 21-Lighthouse near Ypres, signaling in Morse and receiving a "good to go" response from the tower. Peering over the nacelle at eight thousand feet, I could see a few campfires and the odd artillery burst, unlike the daytime view of zigzag trenches. Time seemed so distant, yet it was only one year before that I, too, had sat down there shivering with my platoon, wondering about the aeroplanes we frequently heard. I was now in that proverbial aircraft, feeling more cheerful than if leading a ground platoon. Each presented different risks, but my feelings dovetailed much more with those in the air. I was confident and secure at eight thousand feet.

Yet thoughts of platoon life brought the sadness of Perce's life's being snuffed out, as did the thought that he was buried down there in that mud where his family would never know, could never know, the brutality and horror that defined his death. That his loss was repeated over and over with a devastation conscripted upon a whole generation of young men could not be understood by folks back home.

I fought back tears lest they mist up my goggles. I needed to concentrate on getting us safely to our target. The thirty-eight miles to the Hun aerodrome at Courtrai took only forty minutes; however, because the enemy was keeping things in blackout, we circled for quite some time with wingtip lights extinguished. I kept watch on both sides of the aeroplane for the green bombs-away signal from our leader, Kent. I knew the enemy aerodrome could hear the roar of our machines but were disguising their location by not opening up their searchlights or firing their Archie.

The tension mounted as the minutes passed and our flight leader still did not signal with the Very pistol, the other bombers circling in the same hazy blackness. I stood up in the face of the slipstream and pointed out to Wellsey the red signal from Kent's aeroplane, the indication we were to abandon the target and follow him to the prearranged alternate. I felt a little relief as the tension waned, but I knew all that had been achieved was to delay an attack. I remained with my hands on the Lewis gun in anticipation of encountering enemy aircraft.

A few miles farther we found the German aerodrome at Marche Sterhoek, its illumination signaling it was waiting to receive its own returning night flyers. Their bad luck, as we now had a line on a target.

Searchlights sprang to life as the enemy realized they had been made. Kent gave the green light. We were circling, circling, waiting. After what seemed like an age, it was our turn to dive.

About half a mile from target, Wellsey began the descent and cut the engine. With Hun searchlights flicking back and forth, we sailed through the blackness in silence, dropping altitude quickly. I was terrified and excited at the same time. The whistling of the wires as they vibrated against the night air brought an eerie presence, but the thought of dropping my bombs on enemy aircraft and facilities for the first time was somehow intoxicating.

But suddenly we were caught by searchlights, trapped in a flood of brightness. Too late to sideslip, to escape sideways, we had to stay on target. My training kicked in as I aimed my Lewis as best I could at the lights. I had to shoot for the middle no matter how much it blinded me. Short bursts from the Lewis; no need to overheat or, worse, jam the barrel. *Five rounds, release. Five rounds, release.*

Wellsey was yelling, "Prepare to drop the pills, Bobby, prepare to drop."

To concentrate on the bomb release wires, I had to let go of the Lewis, which made it feel as if I might as well stand up in the cockpit and flail my arms around to alert the enemy of my now-exposed self. *Got to get the bombs dropped; waiting for Wellsey's signal.* Could he see anything through this blinding light? Was he simply acting on impulse, perhaps counting the seconds that he knew it took to descend to the correct altitude, the right place? Worse: Would we get a direct hit before we drop and pull away?

"OK, now. Go. Fucking now! Pull up on the releases!"

I yanked the starboard release lever to feel the first bomb fall away, then yanked it three more times in rapid succession. I quickly swung the Lewis out of the way to grab the portside releases. One-two-three-four and they, too, were away. I gave a thumbs-up without turning around and then concentrated on my Lewis. The Beardmore kicked into life, and as we lifted away, I stood in the cockpit to fire downward, continuing to fight off the searchlights. At this vulnerable altitude of five hundred feet, I saw tracer bullets rising, miraculously missing me even though I heard the odd ping against the engine block and whistling as a few ripped through the wing fiber.

I continued firing short bursts—*five rounds, release*—then suddenly we slipped again into the blackness. We had broken clear of the lights and were free to continue our ascent, to gain altitude on the homeward course. A shiver of relief overtook me, as though I had withstood a great scare. Well, I had! Still standing, I turned to look at Wellsey, who was illuminated by the cockpit lights. He was smiling, actually laughing.

"You did it, Bobby, you old bird! You fought off the blasted Hun! Let's go home." The silver ribbon of water—our guide, the Lys River—was easily found reflecting the now-moonlit night sky. I knelt in the front nacelle, feeling joy, relief, and courage for facing the enemy and doing our bit for victory. We fought the wind blowing in from the faraway English Channel, slowing our pace. But the worst was over. Crossing the lines, we re-engaged with 21-Lighthouse.

I thought of how quickly the bombing had started and then was over. In the moment, it had seemed as if time had stood still, yet only minutes had passed. Sitting up front of the aeroplane, staring into the wind, I began to choke up thinking of my family. What if I had died? Would my sisters have been proud to tell their friends they'd had an older brother who fought in the war but was shot down while bombing German territory? Would my parents have erected a small memorial somewhere in Saskatoon, perhaps on the banks of the Saskatchewan River, remembering a son who fought for freedom?

But there was no need for such thoughts. Shaking them off, I realized we were over top of our aerodrome. Wellsey signaled with the correct wingtip lighting, which caused the flare path to light up for landing. Bumping a few times across the field, we taxied to the sheds for the welcome by the mechanics and the other flyers that'd arrived before us. It was 0100 hours, and under a well-lit moon, all eight bombers pulled up to the hangars, returned safe.

Chapter 27

September 1917

I was aware of Wellsey lying on his bed, watching me sit at the little writing desk in front of the hut window. "Are ya gonna read that damn letter hundreds more times, Bobby? She must be a right doll for you to gloat over her words like that."

It was only when we had checked in with the Ops Room after our sortie that the adjutant handed me the letter. Major Christie had a rule that no personal mail was to be distributed during the day of a sortie in the event bad news might affect a flyer's focus.

5 September, 1917

Dearest Bob,

How are you, my darling? Your letter arrived this morning. How quickly the mails are keeping us in touch. I was so distraught about the news of your crash that I wept. Not just for that accident, but also for the reminder that you are in constant peril for what you are doing over in France. Oh, how do you flyers do those sorties, taking such risk?

I am so glad you are all right. Do look after yourself and don't let that Hun do anything to you. My sisters and I at the factory are working hard to ensure arms are manufactured and sent to you at the front. Straightaway!

You would laugh a little if you saw me just now, for I have taken on a slight yellowing of my once lily-white skin. Nothing drastic and nothing permanent, just a little side effect of the TNT we handle—your own little canary girl! Yet I am one of the lucky ones, being promoted to trolley train driver. Oh, I can see your questioning eyes! I drive around the factory floor pulling flat cars on a track, loaded with bombs ready for shipping. In my fantasies I pretend I am you, soaring high above with my bombs loaded. Yet I daren't take my mind off things lest I crash. Oh dear, I am rambling. I do keep up the happy façade, for losing it to the sadness which surrounds us – the grief of women who've lost brothers, sons, husbands, and the crippled warriors who still want to work for the cause – would be to give up caring and feeling and, mostly, hope.

I know you are not able to tell me when we will see each other, yet it keeps me going to know that there will come a time when that will happen. Isn't it interesting, dear Bob, that we have been able to develop such a closeness more through letter writing than being with each other? As they say where you are, "C'est la guerre!" Perhaps with winter coming in a couple of months, you will get leave. Let's have faith in that.

It is so sweet of you to tell me as much as you do about your life over there and to trust me in that way. And yes, I do want you to continue because I am interested, and as long as it helps you survive to talk about it. I know you cannot confide such details to your parents or sisters for fear of worrying them *silly. That wouldn't be fair as they are at such a great distance from you, whereas I am close. Be safe, my darling.*

*Yours,
Cissy*

"Yes, my good man. It keeps me going, keeps my spirits up, as you do, but in a different way." I turned around and winked at him. We had only known each other for a few months, yet it occurred to me that when one works with another in the face of death, friendships becomes good, strong, and wholesome. "A nice balance, I'd say."

"Yes, old man, you are a balanced one." There was that endearing phrase that I'd come to enjoy. And in this case, it was ironic since he was as excited as I to read and reread letters from his wife and family back in Cape Town. We all reread our letters.

We were interrupted by a tap on the open door. "Hello, chappies. Having a little rat-a-tat with each other, are we?" Hardy was leaning on the door frame, listening for how long, I didn't know. "Fine day for such camaraderie, I suppose."

I knew that air mechanics seldom got time away from their hangars, especially in the early afternoons. "Hello, Hardknocks. What brings you out of the hangars so early?"

"Our technical lieutenant feels we all need a little R&R once in a while, and I got tapped today. Say, you chaps want to take a walk in the woods down by the Aire Canal? It's similar to the woods back in Blighty, quite pleasant."

"Ah, you fellows go," said Wellsey. "I think I'll rest up for tonight's follies. Besides, I have a letter to write!" When I shot him a look, he jutted out his chin in mock defiance.

Hardy and I strolled across the fields through the afternoon sunshine, finding the wooded trail leading to the canal while sharing home news along the way. Coming out onto the narrow flats that edged the canal was like finding magic, a little natural heaven that defied the existence of wartime France. Wildflowers were in late-summer bloom, richly colored against the green grass over which they swayed. The glass-like water waited in anticipation for the inevitable ripples that would break out from passing canal barges.

We didn't break conversation as we sat on the flat granite surface of a large boulder situated beside an outcrop stream that flowed lazily into the canal. The peaceful scenery and the understanding that had built up between Hardy and me through shared battle experiences provided the setting for us to talk about anything and everything.

"Things are going well with your Cissy? Wellsey says you sure perked up when handed her letter last night."

I could feel the blush of embarrassment rising from my neck into my cheeks. Sam talked of relationships, whether for overnight or longer, as if they were just part of natural conversation. It made me wonder why the rest of us recoiled in embarrassment with emotional issues. "Things are wonderful with her. She and I write regularly, way more than with my family."

"I think that's expected. Ya know a sweetie like Cissy doesn't just come along with the regular tide, eh? Lots of time to write home, but you need to cherish that one for now."

I nodded, accepting that advice. "Quite so. What about you? Any steadies in your life?"

Hardy thought for a moment, then threw a pebble that he had been kneading out into the water. "Nah, too busy knocking around aeroplanes. Don't really want the commitment just now. Besides, there's lots of girlfriends a bloke can chase in the French villages, my friend." I felt him looking at me, studying my face. "Except, if I had a Cissy . . . say, wait a moment."

I jerked my gaze away from the canal, forcing a smile. "What is it?"

"You've turned as glum as a nun caught in a bad habit! Ha!"

"Aw, it's just a bit of stress, nothing really."

"I'm not buyin' it. C'mon, what's on your mind?"

Looking at Sam, my closest friend in France, I deliberated. "I don't know. Really, I don't. Yet I'm caught in a trap of silence. No one to confide in."

Sam momentarily touched my shoulder, confirming our connection. "All right, now we're getting somewhere. Next move is yours. Time to open up."

I stared at him, studying his bright eyes, his optimism confirming trust. "Not a word to anyone, Sam. Not a word, I say."

Hardy nodded, assuming a sincere look to show me he understood the graveness that was etched on my face.

"I have—or had—VD. Gonorrhea. Shameful, I know, but that's the truth." I searched Sam's face for his reaction as I so very much wanted a sincere one, even if judgemental.

"My God, I'm so sorry. Now it makes sense why you were delayed in your assignment after being hospitalized—for shell shock, I mean. How are you now?"

"I'm fine, but it's not that. It's the feelings that linger, the reputation, the shame."

"Listen, many of the lads have experienced this. You're not alone. I remember talking to Captain Logan before you arrived about why so many apparently healthy lads were being shipped off to hospital. He told me that as many as twenty percent of Commonwealth troops had been infected in this war."

I bowed my head thoughtfully. "I can understand that, but being an officer, that's cold comfort as I'm supposed to be leading by example."

"You are, Bob. Look at how many rally around you, who like being with you and respect you. They respect your confidence."

I looked up and cautiously nodded at a grinning Sam. He could get anyone to smile at any time.

"Say, is Cissy involved?"

My head shook back and forth as I confirmed, "Oh no, Cissy is fine. She is healed as well."

I explained the whole situation from the encounter at Mrs. Clarke's to the awful response by the doctor at Bristol, the attitude of the RCR adjutant, and the convalescence at the French hospital. Sam was surprisingly well informed about the issue and had heard that women were sometimes not aware of carrying the disease and were therefore victims in a worse way than men. Our talk gave me comfort.

We sat there for a while, gazing at the water in quiet reflection. Sam broke the silence. "Who knows? Does Wellsey?"

"No, you are the only one, and I'd prefer to keep it that way. Except Major Christie, of course." I grimaced. "It's in my service record."

With his hand back on my shoulder in empathy, he said, "I'm so sorry to hear about this. But listen, my chum—it's over. You must look forward. And going through this with Cissy, well, having her comfort and understanding, and yours for her, is very special."

"You know, that's a very good point. In these circumstances, she and I share a very unique intimacy."

...

Wellsey was spinning a tale about his grandfather teaching him to hunt guinea fowl in the Western Cape when the adjutant strode into the mess, his presence signaling there was a sortie planned for the night. "The following flyers are to report to the Ops Room at 1700 sharp!"

We continued tea until reporting time, Ace, Wellsey, and I debating where our sortie would take us. Lunghi was booked off again, a concerning pattern, but we decided not to judge him as we all had tolerances and we were not going to question his.

We walked across the soggy grass to the Ops Room. I glanced skyward and declared, "A haze is building, which I hope won't develop into anything serious. Difficult navigation in that stuff."

"Yes, old man, just enough to provide cover for us as we zoom into tonight's target." There he was again, Wellsey always seeing the positive side.

Major Christie stood in front of the long table, absorbed in the large map of France and Belgium. I followed his eyes, scanning locations marked with colored flags, identifying first the sentry lighthouses, then the trenches at the lines, and finally some of the enemy's aerodromes. So that was it—we were to return along the Lys Valley. The officers fell quiet as his booming voice broke through their chatter.

"I am handing around reconnaissance photographs of tonight's targets, which begin with the Bisseghem Dump in Courtrai and continue with stations and trains south of Lys Valley. The identifiable landmarks are clearly shown, so please memorize them. Questions?"

Ace questioned, "Sir, what exactly does an ammunition dump look like? I cannot see anything obvious in these photographs."

The major stood tall, smiling at the scrutiny. "Well observed, Wallace. The enemy is not going to place out welcome flags for your benefit. Their ammo is purposely obscured."

Christie explained the use of natural landscape as camouflage, yet distinguishable to the trained eye. A shallow excavation was typically covered with a wood frame roof and packed over with loose sod and earth. Less evident in the dark, except that the existence of the fresh earth lying next to the aerodrome was a giveaway.

Captain Scudamore added detail. "A word from the wise—drop your pills from a sensible height, and don't linger. A direct hit will blow sky-high, and you don't want to be in that brouhaha!"

"Very good, Captain," said Christie. "You have the flight lineup. Bushe and Colbert will lead, locate the target. Their phosphorous bombs will light up the skies. When you see that, get in and get out!"

Scudamore again: "And be aware Captain Schweitzer will be following behind with his pom-pom rig. Dismissed."

We met Hardy at Hangar No. 2 for a walk-around of our Fee, and when satisfied it was in top form, walked across the grass to our hut. As tonight was to be freezing at eight thousand feet, we decided to suit up well. For the moment, the fur-lined flying boots and Sidcot suits made us hot and sweaty, but this was a minor irritant compared to the cold slipstream we were soon to encounter.

We got off at 2035, Ace and his pilot, Bean, just ahead. I kept vigilance through the haze and increasingly cloudy skies. Peering through the darkness, I found what we needed and yelled behind to Wellsey, "There's our signal; there is 21-Lighthouse."

I followed each blink of the Morse, *dot-dot-dash-dash-dash* followed by *dot-dash-dash-dash-dash*. With twenty-one being the correct number, I signaled green from the Very pistol to indicate our friendly status. We were cleared to sail through to the lines, following the Lys River as best we could in the haze, backed up by compass and wristwatch navigation.

Thirty minutes brought us closer to our target, when I lifted my left arm above Wellsey's small, curved windscreen and pointed to my wrist.

"What are you thinking, Bob?"

"It's time, time to descend. Luck be with us, eh?"

We dropped speed and descended to twenty-five hundred feet, just in time to see the wing lights of the aeroplane ahead of us. "There's Ace and Bean, dead ahead."

"Right you are. Any action?"

That was right—we were out there looking for action! With the calm ride over the line, I had momentarily shed the angst that comes with flying a sortie, but it was never far behind as we prepared to dive into battle. "Not yet, we're just a little too far to see, but they must be dropping their pills about now. Thing is, everyone ahead must have missed the mark. No fire, no phosphorus, but the searchlights are active. Puffs of Archie as well!"

"I'll drop to fifteen hundred. Keep your guns ready, eyes on target. When over it, drop 'em quick. Damn, there must be a dozen searchlights looking for us. Our boys in lead gave the Hun lots of notice."

Wellsey cut the Beardmore to silence. It wasn't that the Hun weren't aware there would be more of us following, but if they couldn't see or hear us in the darkness, we had a better chance of surprise. Through the eerie quiet, the rigging strained and the wing fabric whistled. My senses reacted, involuntarily causing my pulse to race and stomach to churn. Somehow a roaring engine provided a sense of power, of being more in control and able to zoom away from danger. Yet that was just the point: we were not there to sidestep danger. There was no time to indulge fear since so many were depending on us. Our task was to maintain the courage to fly into the face of it, to conquer. I steeled myself to focus.

I caught Wellsey's attention. "Lewises ready, bombs ready, hand on release lever. I'll raise my left hand as soon as my right releases."

"Steady on, old man, steady on."

We were moments away from release when suddenly one of the searchlights caught us, completely blinding our sight. Timing was critical lest the target be lost. Archie streamed up at us, not very accurately, thank God. The little Fee bucked and bumped in the brightness, catching us in its clasp. Another and another as the lights triangulated our presence. Hope and prayer were our only friends now. As I yanked up the starboard bomb lever with my right hand, I shot my left arm skyward and then dropped it to the port release. The two 112-pounders broke free just as Wellsey fired up the engine, allowing us to climb away. Lady Luck was holding.

Locking my flying boots into the metal ringlets on the sides of the nacelle, I stood up to lean precariously over the front, balanced only by my Lewis. I felt us lift away from danger, bursting shots down onto the direction of the lights. I trembled at the thought that, should the gun mounting give way, I would be hurled off into the night, German soldiers below following my silhouetted figure with their lights and applauding my demise. I refocused on the rising machine, which offset my downward fire, but I kept blasting in five-shot bursts. The searchlights persisted as we attempted to escape their grasp, Archie bursting around but still miraculously missing us. Blackness couldn't arrive fast enough, finally showing its emptiness as we broke free of the lights. I caught a rearward look at the flaming red exhaust against the inky sky and slumped hard onto the floor of the cockpit, exhaling in one deep breath followed by short shallow ones.

Wellsey yelled into the slipstream above the engine noise, "Catch your breath, old man! Steady your breathing!"

I hollered back. "Quite, Wellsey. I'm focused."

"Deliver us to the next phase, Bob. Let's go get ourselves some steely rail, shall we?"

I sat there for a moment, not wanting to get up and let Wellsey see my tightened face that marked anxiety. We had achieved our objective, so why would we run off looking for trains and railway tracks? Why would we go looking for more danger? I owed Wellsey a response even if I thought he was being cavalier. I clambered to stand up as I confirmed, "Right, then!" Looking at him as I leaned over the windscreen, I forced a smile. I would not let him or our squadron down.

We flew south of Courtrai, knowing we would pick up the Scheldt River as we got closer to Tournai. I thought back to the many times I had tested my memory, visualizing the map lines that represented the river and canal systems of France and Belgium, mentally comparing the weaves and turns to make sense of the ribbons in the darkness below. Very shortly, I saw the definitive right turn of the Scarpe River where it broke off from the Scheldt.

I turned backward against the slipstream, cupping my hands to be heard. "Bank starboard. We can pick up the river over toward Ascq. Stay at two thousand." The Scarpe was a navigator's blessing with its numerous east-west canals cutting a straight line to Lille, whose subdued lights we could just make out in the distance. The double rails of the German-controlled Lille-Tournai line soon appeared before us, but I was unsure what I was looking at. "Keep steady. I can see something down there. Wait, is that a rocket? What the devil?"

Eagerly standing up in the front nacelle, I was amazed at what I was looking at. It was the unmistakable silhouette of a Fee strafing a moving train, but the powerful blast from its cockpit was unfamiliar. There were bursts of red from its tail as it accelerated then slowed, and another fiery blast from its front. I turned to speak to Wellsey, seeing his wide grin illuminated by his cockpit lights. "Fuckin' crazy, Bobby! That's Schweitzer with his pom-pom. Look at that baby go! Who knew that one-pounders could carry such a wallop? Damned rocket launcher, that Fee is!"

As Schweitzer blasted the train from five hundred feet, Wellsey swooped down to join the fray as I momentarily crouched, clutching both sides of the nacelle. We leveled at one thousand feet, and I ensured both my Lewises were ready, focused for the attack. We circled over the moving train as it attempted to accelerate away from Schwietzer's threat. Tracer machine-gun fire spat from between a couple of its carriages in an attempt at retaliation.

I was excited as seeing this new weapon sent spurts of adrenaline through my veins. "Pull up five hundred yards behind Schweitzer. When he blasts the next pom-pom, the machine gunners will pop up and I'll try to mow them away."

"You got it, Bob!" We were at five hundred feet, and I was ready to pounce. The next pom-pom missed the target, but we provided cover against the retaliatory machine-gun response.

Wellsey was yelling, waving a free arm for emphasis. "Good shooting, Bobby! Short, steady bursts! You held 'em down. Schweitzer turning port; I'm turning starboard. Hold on, old man!"

We swung around to see Schweitzer blink his starboard wing lights in acknowledgment of our presence. Wellsey throttled back to allow him to line up once again behind the train, determined to immobilize it. We flew in at five hundred feet, again trailing Schweitzer. Seeing the pom-pom rocket blast, I opened up with short bursts whether or not the machine gunners were returning fire. Schweitzer launched a second one-pounder, this time straight into the steam engine, before circling off into the night. Wellsey's high-pitched yell marked his excitement, as frenzied as mine. "I'm staying the course, Bob. Keep the strafe up; keep the pressure on."

I kept blasting my Lewis, balancing against the rocking of the aeroplane. I knew I had enough ammo to keep the bursts up before changing drums.

Suddenly, an eruption came from the locomotive, its force bucking us up as if we had been shot from underneath. I fell backward into the nacelle and then kneeled up as we veered off, my Lewis swinging wildly in the slipstream. Peering over, I noticed the locomotive falter along the dirt, derailed from the track, before it lay over onto its side, taking with it the firebox full of red-hot burning coal. The train had hissed to a standstill by the time we disappeared into the darkness.

I remained kneeling, facing Wellsey as he yelled the obvious, "Schweitzer got that last one directly into the loco, old man. I'm going around to keep up the pressure. It must be a troop train; otherwise, ammunition stocks would have blasted skyward by now."

I managed to stand ready with my Lewis when I saw Schweitzer come around just ahead of us, roaring to the left side of the train and unloading pom-pom shells into the carriages as fast as he could reload. Wellsey and I were on the starboard side, blasting machine-gun fire into the carriages. Our two Fees were like a couple of wolves moving aggressively on a felled deer.

Dark figures ran in every direction away from the train as we continued strafing aside Schweitzer, but it was not long before the Hun organized ground-based retaliatory machine-gun posts. We veered away as our job was done and our ammunition running low.

Chapter 28

September 1917

I relaxed my vigilance as we neared the lines, standing with my back against Wellsey's cockpit. With the aftereffects of the adrenaline rush, I remained warm even with the frigid slipstream pushing into me. I turned and said, "We're a damn good team, Wellsey! And Schweitzer, whoa boy! Gutsy man!"

Wellsey grinned as he nodded, pointing ahead.

"Ah, 21-Lighthouse at starboard." I loaded the Very pistol with green shot.

"Right-o, Bobby. Homeward we sail."

We arrived at the aerodrome and blinked our wing lights. The landing T lit up the welcoming flare path, and at about fifty feet, I released the parachute flare to light up the grassy field. We bounced twice before taxiing up to the hangars, the last aeroplane to arrive.

Hardy and another mechanic helped us out of our sweaty Sidcots and fur boots, leaving them hanging over the tail of the Fee to air out. After we filed our report in the Ops Room, we met up with

Schweitzer in the mess. Although it was after 0100 hours, we were looking forward to a drink or two.

Tonight was typical of any after a sortie—glasses raised, pipes lit, and conversation robust as small groups sat or stood facing each other. The brazier held a crackling fire, but I couldn't imagine being chilly after tonight's excitement. I walked from the bar to catch up with Wellsey and Schweitzer, who were with Ace and Bean. Schweitzer turned to open the circle for me.

"Successful night, Bobby! Good backup on that train. I wasn't sure if I could continue alone until you showed up. Thought I might have to abandon a precious target!" Captain Viktor Schweitzer was of German heritage, and his family resided in Winnipeg. His broad figure, blond hair, and blue eyes told of his ancestry, and his humble demeanor was indicative of his family's Canadian background.

"Oh yeah, Vik, what a night! Damn, I was taken by surprise when we came out of the dark to see you blasting those one-pounders. Never would have thought they could destroy a train."

"And when I first saw them last week, I never thought the ole Fee could withstand the pom-poms' strong kickback, what with bucking around like that," reiterated Wellsey, "let alone being able to shoot accurately."

Schweitzer looked around our excited circle, not used to being in the spotlight as the night's hero. "Yes, but be mindful that it takes a very lucky hit to do what I—er, what we did tonight," he said humbly. "Only one shot in ten strikes the target, so it's especially hard to take out a loco."

The captain had us all riveted to his story as he explained that the pom-pom had to be lined up from behind the locomotive's firebox and aimed as conditions allowed. The gun had no lateral movement, so the aeroplane itself had to adjust the aim. And the Maxim one-pounder shell without shrapnel was ineffective against anything but a direct hit on a target. Another challenge was the inability to carry an observer since the gun muzzle protruded through the front nacelle, which meant the pilot needed to fly and shoot at the same time, with little accuracy.

Schweitzer continued, "So, you see, the gun can level a train, but it needs perfect conditions and teamwork from additional, uh, support Fees. Having Wells and Pitman work along to distract the loco engineer and keep their machine gunners subdued allowed me just enough time to line up and shoot."

Wellsey, who had seen the gun work before, continued the narrative that, although the nature of the cannon's pom-pom sound can strike terror into the enemy, its cumbersome need of reloading and re-aiming was why the weapon was seldom used. His perspective was that a skilled shooter operating the Lewis gun was much more effective.

As the conversation had become technical, and the hour late, it died away. Characteristic of his perpetual wakefulness, Wellsey was game for another drink. I cheerfully obliged. We walked over to the bar that was bereft of officers, and although exhausted, we found our second wind and digressed into family matters. "What of your wife, Frank? How does she deal with being all the way back in Cape Town while you're here in Europe?"

"Ah, that's the thing. Letters and packages go only so far, you know. Having a wife far away where you cannot visit on leave is damn difficult."

"Not being tied down myself, I'm not sure what it's like for you. Did you marry long before the war?"

He chuckled. "*Ja*, we were married young, before war clouds massed over Europe. I wanted to be a flyer down home, you know. Got my Royal Aero Club ticket, was on my way."

"You could have stayed, yes? Could have served in a South African home establishment?"

Wellsey stood up straight, confident in his answer. "Nah, wasn't going to be. It was my wife who encouraged me to do my bit. I don't know. I don't know at all if she regrets that now. Still, we don't question it, just reassure each other there will be an end to this chaos and I'll be returned home."

I looked thoughtfully at my friend. "I suppose that's all you can do. I can't imagine what it feels like for her, not knowing whether you are safe, trying not to think of some dreaded telegram."

"You have your Cissy, and you have family far enough away that you can't visit on leave, either."

I thought that over, knowing it was true but having buried its reality. "Quite so, yet it's not like I've made a life commitment to a lady. Cissy and I haven't known each other long and are still in the beginnings of—of what, I'm not sure. It's difficult to develop a deeper relationship through letter writing, as you can imagine." Glancing across the now almost empty room, I looked dreamily back at Wellsey. "I do know I care for her a whole bunch."

He affectionately slapped me on the shoulder. "That's obvious, old man! Your pondering her letters is striking. She's certainly got your attention."

"Oh yes, Wellsey! She's beautiful, has a sharp mind, and stirs me like I've never felt before. Quite the suffragette. A strong woman, which I think is a good part of my attraction for her. And so I'm rambling now, *mon pilote*. Time we retire, don't you think?"

...

Miss Hilda R. Pitman
426-8th Street East
Saskatoon, Saskatchewan
Dominion of Canada

10 September, 1917

My Dear Hilda,
Plain and simple, I miss you so. I imagine that at this time when summer is coming to a close you will be thinking of fall activities. I miss the autumn in Saskatoon, and I imagine it to be colorful and beautiful as always.
France has autumn, of course, but much of its beauty has been marred by the destructive forces of war. It makes me pine for the peacefulness that defines Canada. I'll see you just as soon as we put an end to this madness.
I'm so pleased you are there to be with Mama and Papa. It must mean a lot to have their youngest child with them. You are seventeen now, my little darling. In spite of war, these are the best years a young lady has. (I pause as I reflect on now referring to you as a lady, as it seems we were playing hopscotch together not so long ago.) Enjoy them!
I am doing well, as well as expected in the thick of things here in western France. We are flying sorties over German territory in an attempt to wrench from them the very land that they so destructively stole from France and Belgium in 1914. I'm forbidden from telling you more or where I'm based, but be assured I'm safe. As safe as possible.
Do take care of yourself and stay well. If you feel up to it, another tin of that Saskatoon berry jam would be most welcome.

Love to you,
Bob

...

10 September, 1917

My Dearest Cissy,
   As always, I woke this morning with you on my mind. Wellsey and I returned from a successful sortie last night and sat up talking about relationships and distance.
   Wellsey's wife is alone in South Africa, for which I feel sad as he cannot see her due to the great distance. Even with leave, there is insufficient time to travel home. That is the fate of Commonwealth soldiers, I'm afraid.
   Their situation is not different from ours as circumstances dictate our emotional distance must remain wide. Yet we are lucky being only a few hundred miles from each other, and there must come a time when I am granted leave. I'll be in Chilwell before you know it.
   I only need close my eyes to see you, and I only need to think of you to get through the most difficult moments of our increasing number of sorties. I do trust you are keeping well and keeping that tractor on an even keel as you send more bombs to us at the front. I am proud of you, Cissy, and I told Wellsey that. You mustn't think I go around talking to others too much about you, but they are curious about our frequent letter writing. Not much is private on an aerodrome. Mere distribution of the weekly mail brings teasing questions!
   Around the airfield, word has it that 100 Squadron is to be quite busy supporting the ground offensives reported in the newspapers. Our job is to cease or at least slow the ability of the Germans to move matériel to the current struggle at Passchendaele. We have been successful in our own small way and will continue to bring justice to our foe. So please be patient with me

if letters are not as regular. And please do not worry, as we are camouflaged nicely in the blackness of night.

Well, my canary girl, I wanted to let you know you are in my thoughts. There is nothing that could change my feelings for you.

Yours especially,
Bob

Chapter 29

September 1917

After the night of the train, the squadron was quietly thankful to be grounded as weather conditions worsened over the following days, providing a reprieve from the intense strain and tension of prior nights. Major Christie decided on a little in-house celebration. I was to learn of the small blessings that separated junior officers of the Royal Flying Corps from those in the rest of the British Army—a fine table, wine, spirits, and joviality.

I felt spoiled, pampered, and gluttonous as I looked across the table, catching Vik's eye during a rare moment of silence in an otherwise uproarious couple of hours. "That was one of the best poached-fish dinners I've ever had, Vik. Is this typical of squadron custom?"

"This is just the beginning."

I donned a puzzled look.

"Yeah, the beginning of a squadron tradition every once in a while."

"*Ja*, I've heard," said Wellsey. "It's jolly tonight, I'll say that."

In the momentary quiet, Wellsey probed Schweitzer about his accomplishment of completing twenty sorties to date, no small feat as the squad had only been operable since the spring. Schweitzer felt that, in spite of the tension that came with our bombing campaigns, he was driven to build on that record. "As long as the major promotes cheery evenings like these," he offered.

Schweitzer continued a strange—and seemingly morbid—line of discussion by adding that these soirees were where aviators came together to accept their mortality, to accept that they flirt with the leading edge of danger, and to understand that bravado is needed to boost courage. As he did so, he had a wide grin while he encouraged us to join in and keep to the spirit of the night.

The happy tension built as I looked at Wellsey. "He's right, you know. Just let go and see what the night brings!"

Major Christie rose grandly from his seat at the head table, instantly causing the room to silence. "Gentlemen, the Airmen's Toast!"

"The Airmen's Toast!" roared the room.

That was evidently the signal to chug our drinks back and continue standing as we sang "God Save the King." Cheers went up immediately after the anthem concluded, making it reminiscent of an English football game opener. The evening was opened for festivity.

Ace wandered over to where Wellsey, Schweitzer, and I were gathered and whispered, "Keep your wits about you."

We studied him for sincerity. "Now, why is that, dear Ace?" snickered Wellsey.

"I've been secretly warned there is a ritual for us squad newbies, and I understand that the more you resist, the more ribald the act. I must warn the others. Gotta go, cheers." He staggered off.

"What the devil? Secret warning?" I questioned. Wellsey and I looked pointedly at our veteran, Schweitzer, who was not even trying to hide the smirk on his face. Something was afoot. For me it was exciting, similar to joining the Saskatoon Fusiliers with their induction or the boyish behavior directed at university freshmen by seniors.

Wellsey responded, "I've no idea. Some sort of initiation, maybe?"

We looked back at Schweitzer, his smile spreading from cheek to cheek. Before we could press him, the room erupted into song.

I'm sorry now that I'm a flyer;
I don't want to get shot down.
Now, I'm really very willing
To make myself a killing,
Living on the earnings of obliging ladies.
I don't want a bullet up the rear end;
I don't want my bollocks shot away.
If I've really got to lose 'em,
I'd prefer it was with Susan,
Or Dolly or Polly,
Or any whore at all!

This was getting raucous. I joined in with glass raised amid laughter and song, anticipation rising. Soon enough, we heard the tinkle of spoon on glass, growing louder as more airmen joined in. The squadron's longest-term flyer, Boret, shouted, "It's time, gents!"

As he and Schweitzer moved toward us, I instinctively turned around to peer behind me to see who they were after, only to belatedly realize it was Wellsey and I. I chuckled as they jostled and taunted us, all of it friendly jesting. I was giddy, partly due to drink and partly due to being roughed up in a manner that I could imagine was from an older brother.

I burst out a guttural shout as we were set off balance and wrestled to the ground. Amid our half protesting, half laughing, we were de-shoed and de-socked, then carried to the brazier in the room's center, its door now open. For a moment a wave of panic crossed over me. Surely they weren't going to brand our feet? Dammit! I had never checked the feet of a 100 Squadron flyer.

I could hear Wellsey's distinctive voice say, *"Fuckin' hell!"* followed by robust laughing and shouting useless protests. The more he groused, the more he was jostled, so I decided to keep my mouth shut. Yet I couldn't stifle continued laughter and grunts as I knew in my heart we were not to be harmed. Well, that was my belief. At one point I heard Ace protest, but he was upended on the other side of the brazier, too far for me to see due to the blurry tears in my eyes. Someone grabbed a blackened log from the firepit and began rubbing the soot on the bottoms of our feet. They held us upside down while a tall wooden stepladder appeared. As Wellsey and I were held down beside each other, a look of resignation passed between us. After all, we'd been through worse while aloft. Up, up, up I was hoisted until the ladder bearer grabbed my legs and stabbed them at the ceiling, others below holding me up by the shoulders. He held them in place on the ceiling while grinding them upward. I wriggled with laughter. Next was Wellsey, feet stabbing the ceiling. He was laughing so hard they almost dropped him. I thought, *well, at least my feet aren't ticklish!*

We were released from this carnival as quickly as we had been captured, and the group of bandits moved on to other plebes. It was at that point when I believed we had truly become part of the squadron, our black footprints imprinted on that mess ceiling with those of all the other flyers who had been initiated since the beginning.

More of the captured were dragged to the brazier and stabbed up to the ceiling. What a display of chaos! In spite of our lingering laughter, sobs of joy, and related tearing of the eyes, we managed to return our footwear to its appropriate place. Wellsey and I agreed that if this was the extent of our initiation, we could take it in stride. "Can I buy you a drink, old man?" Wellsey asked.

"I'll take a two-fister. Make it the *vin rouge, s'il vous plait*," I said.

Wellsey stood up off the floor, extending a hand to pull me up beside him. "Let's sit at the bar for a minute and take the heat off our feet, if you know what I mean," roared Wellsey. Our gaiety continued amid increased consumption as we compared the experience to growing up, to being accepted into this team or that club. Reliving the event and howling as we looked up at the ceiling was as much part of the camaraderie as the stunt itself. We both felt accepted and damn good about being part of one of the best squadrons in the RFC. Our kibitzing caught the attention of Schweitzer, who was sidling up.

"Well, lads, you've been added! Can't say whose soles those are up there anymore, but I know mine are among that blackened mess."

"Ah, I appreciate the double meaning." Wellsey chuckled. "As long as our soles are protected in the mess, our inner souls will be protected in the dark night?"

Schweitzer laughed as he nodded approval. "Hadn't thought of that one, my boy, but it stands to good reason."

"I've got to say, Vik, that with all this whooping it up and acting silly, the boost to morale is wonderful," I offered. "Makes you feel closely attached to 100, what with sharing moments like this."

Someone yelled for "The Bold Aviator," which was responded to in a rip-roaring breakout of song.

Oh, the bold aviator lay dying
At the end of a bright summer's day (summer's day!).
His comrades had gathered around him
To carry his fragments away.
The crate was piled up on his wishbone;
His Lewis was wrapped 'round his head (his head!);
He wore a spark plug in each elbow;
'Twas plain he would shortly be dead.

Schweitzer produced a song sheet with the lyrics bold enough to read in the dim light, so Wellsey and I joined in the discordant anthem.

He spat out a valve and a gasket
As he stirred in the sump where he lay (where he lay!).
And then, to his wondering comrades,

> *These brave parting words did he say:*
> *'Take the manifold out of my larynx,*
> *And the butterfly-valve out of my neck (from his neck!).*
> *Remove from my kidneys the camrods—*
> *There's a lot of good parts in this wreck.*
> *Take the piston rings out of my stomach,*
> *And the cylinders out of my brain (his brain!).*
> *Extract from my liver the crankshaft,*
> *And assemble the engine again!'*

The inimitable Ace with his playful character decided to lie on the floor mimicking the dying aviator, pretending to pull aircraft parts from his body, creating more jostling and laughter as he did so.

> *'Pull the longeron out of my backbone,*
> *The turnbuckle out of my ear (his ear!).*
> *From the small of my back take the rudder.*
> *There's all of your aeroplane here.*
> *I'll be riding a cloud in the morning,*
> *No engine before me to cuss (to cuss!).*
> *Shake the lead from your feet and get busy;*
> *There's another lad needing this bus!'*

Around three in the morning, we somehow navigated our way to our hut. Lying on our beds in silent drunkenness, Wellsey unexpectedly felt the urge to speak. "That song was a sobering end to the night, eh, Bob?"

I rolled on my side, facing the edge of the bed. "Yeah, I was thinking the same. Can't get the tune out of my head, and the lyrics were haunting . . . so much reality in their meaning. The facing down of death . . . that ballad made me literally see it. What do you make of it?"

Wellsey got drunkenly loud, but as articulate as a school master. "What I think? Being an airman, being a squadron member, is like being part of any team, say cricket or rugger. Someone gets hurt, he gets carried off the field, attended to, of course, but replaced with another. The game carries on all the same. Being sorry for oneself is not on. A sense of cheerfulness is demanded as a way to keep the morale strong for the bigger cause—ya know, the need to carry on, to play the game."

I sat up, fighting an alcohol-induced spinning, looking at Wellsey's profile illuminated by the full moon that filled the room. "That's well thought through, eh?"

Wellsey continued his inebriated but lucid enlightenments: "That bold aviator who lay dying keeps the morale of the squad going. That's his last responsibility. He makes sure the rest of us keep together, keep the ball rolling, that's all. We face what we face, we fight for what we fight for, and if God is with us, we continue. But the truth is that the squad carries on no matter if we live or die. We must! G'night, Bob." Silence filled the dark room. "Bob? Hey old man, you awake? Ah, talkin' to myself, am I?"

Chapter 30

September 1917

14 September, 1917

My Dearest Bob,
 I received your letter today and was so warmed by the thought that you wake with me in your thoughts. You are on my mind throughout each day, which helps me to get through the long hours, but at the same time gives pain to not know when we will meet. Oh, when we do, it will be heaven sent.
 The news that you are to be yet busier flying sorties over German targets is worrisome. Sometimes I look up at the black night sky and wonder what it would be like to sail through the air toward a distant enemy. I imagine you doing so, and I sometimes try to work out the puzzle of how you guide your aeroplane in different conditions, whether moonlight, starlight, or cloudy darkness. Why, I can't at all imagine what it would be like to fly!

Life up here in Chilwell is edgy as expected but teeming with wonderful people, some single like me, some grieving for lost ones, and some just accepting the moment, but all of us pulling together as a team. Lord Chetwynd has done such a marvelous thing with building adequate dormitories and feeding us well. Do you know there are ten thousand working at the National Shell Filling Factory, a majority of which are women? That makes for a lot of female talk in the local pubs! It's fun and refreshing to go out, but oh, I do miss dressing up for the London crowd.

I am excited to tell you that for my two days' leave last week, I traveled down to see Daisy. Eric is still off fighting "somewhere in France", but as far as we know, safe. Little Stanley is growing up so fast and is such a gentleman. Do you know he put out his little hand to greet me? And on hearing your name, he jumped up and down while saying "Uncle Bob, Uncle Bob." You left him with such warm feelings, as you do others!

Well, I must sign off. A few of us girls are going down to the Charlton Arms for a whist competition. Oh yes, we girls have penetrated an exclusive man's domain and some of us are really quite good at it.

Be safe, my darling.

Cissy

...

19 September, 1917

Dear Cissy,
I received your letter this afternoon as I was sitting down to again write you. The squad is still grounded due to terrible weather blowing in off the North Sea. After seven straight days,

everyone is fidgety. However, tonight we have been ordered back up to the skies. I am quite concerned but take solace in the fact that our CO would not send us into more danger than we usually face. I know you pray we will all be safe.

It is quite funny that you mention whist, for to pass some of the time, we have been playing too, along with gin rummy. The CO keeps a close eye on our betting as he feels too much can lead to bad morale. I do see his point, especially when one loses!

It is wonderful news to hear Eric is safe. I often think of the infantry stuck in those trenches, especially in the kind of weather that is now upon us. I wish there were better news about an armistice, but the commanding officers on both sides appear dug in with their beliefs that the stalemate will break—in favor of their particular side, of course.

But I digress. I am happy that you could spend time with Daisy. I can only imagine hearing you two catching up on this news and that scandal. Friendships are such precious things, often taken for granted, but not in the current troubled times. Our individual sacrifices make us sure to cherish what is dear to our hearts. And I am flattered that Stanley loves his uncle!

Well, sweetness, do take care. You, too, be safe. You are dealing with some nasty materials, which I hope your supervisors understand well enough so as to protect you. I know you understand that, but I do worry.

Bob

...

While watching Hardy and his crew push the Fee out of the hangar, I noticed the blustering wind lift the starboard wing and then ease off, gently rocking the craft in periodic gusts. The atmosphere was currently dry, but reports all day from the coastal weather station had alternated between dry and wet conditions with wind warnings.

Looking upward at the fast-moving clouds against a darkening sky, Sam commented that once airborne we would be carried quickly over the lines to our target. He intended it to be a helpful comment, but it made me mindful of the extra effort it would take to make the return. I would be watching our petrol supply with extra vigilance as flying into strong westerly winds would make the Beardmore work longer and harder than usual.

Sam and his crew ensured the Fee was shipshape—pistons turning over in their usual rhythm, propeller snug in its bearings, and wing fabric fastened against its ribbing. He had seen me gaze up to the windy conditions and would leave nothing to chance. I was just thinking about Wellsey, who had been quite some time in the Ops Room receiving final orders, when he came strolling across the field.

The usually calm Frank Wells had a look of determination on his face, but it changed to a smile as he approached Sam and me. He explained that there had been a heated conversation in the presence of Major Christie about conditions, but eventually the pilots had acknowledged the need to get up over the night's target. This was to be a trade-off between bad weather and supporting our ground troops in the current offensive. In a show of support, Captain Tempest, whom we knew to be a rising star in the squadron, volunteered to be our wing commander.

We had clouds between three thousand and four thousand feet on the way out. It remained dry, but visibility was challenging. Being last in the roster meant we would learn from those ahead of us. For the journey over the lines, I kept sight of the distant wing lights of the Fee flying in front of us along the Lys River, then crossing over Armentieres, where the lighthouse could be seen a few miles away at Locre, our crossing point.

The thought of attacking enemy billets at Rumbeke and Hooglede was unnerving. Thus far we had bombed industrial plants and aerodromes, targets that did not house as many Hun soldiers as would be resident in sleeping quarters. While the military mind saw them as just another enemy target to be taken out, the thought of destroying so many lives at one time with a few bombs weighed heavy.

Yet I was in this. I knew what answer I would give to the question of what I would do if I were instead the enemy ordered to bomb France or England. Indeed, the Germans had done just that, except they included civilians.

We avoided the searchlights of Menin and Courtrai amid a sudden worsening of visibility through dank haze. Ground landmarks were now all but hidden, so as we dropped to twenty-five hundred feet, we relied on compass and time/distance to the target.

Heading northeast at seventy miles per hour with the wind was smooth, yet the filmy blackness of the night surrounding us was eerie—black above, misty sideways, and murky below. Our red-hot exhaust must've looked like a comet when viewed from the ground. I kept watch over the side for landmarks, but in the mist, none were obliging. In addition to poor navigation, we became aware that, although dressed in our warmest flying gear, the wind-boosted slipstream was creating extremely cold conditions. "Take her down, Wellsey. We are in vicinity."

I turned to face Wellsey, nestled in front of the hot Beardmore radiator, and in the dim illumination saw his comforting smile. "Copy that, old man!"

We dropped to eight hundred feet where the billets at Hooglede ought to be, but had difficulty finding them. Our lead machines should have been over, placing the Hun on defensive. But here it was quiet. All lights were extinguished. Sailing through the quiet, dark canvas was ghostly, but then I heard the familiar rat-a-tat of a machine gun in the distance, its faintness growing louder. Then, the telltale sign.

"Tracer bullets, Wellsey! Ha! We got 'em! Go around a second time, same bearing."

I twisted my head and shifted my body around as the aeroplane made the tight turn, then craned in the other direction, refusing to lose sight of where I remembered the target to be. I then saw two other aircraft in the sky near us also circling, now in behind us observing our activity for guidance. The distinctive silhouette of the Fees instilled me with confidence, for even if we missed the target, our bombs would light the location for those that followed. Wellsey did not bother to cut the engine since the enemy knew we were right there on top of them, and we would want to climb out fast after bombs were dropped. "We are lined up exactly, Bobby. Give 'em hell when you want. Nerves of steel, now!"

I could see the red tracers again, threatening to catch us or any of the Fee's vulnerable engine parts. I couldn't release too quickly, had to have steady hands, needed to fight back the urge to let loose. I managed to stay the course.

I could just make out the dark outline of buildings and tents as we came screaming in at the target. I pulled the release levers again and again to ensure all the pills dropped as planned, hearing each one rumble off the rack and away from the aircraft, imagining them guided down by their little spiraling propellers. We were up and away, but as I looked back, I could not see any obvious damage, just the explosions themselves.

I leaned over the small windscreen and grinned at Wellsey. "Fair target for the others now!"

"Well done, Bobby. We've done our bit tonight."

"Yeah, the big work now is to get home in this bloody wind."

With the sheets of rain picking up amid the ceaseless gale, Wellsey decided to drop south to follow the Lys River, even though that placed us directly over the probing Menin searchlights. I crouched down as we battled forward, struggling to read the map under torchlight and directing Wellsey with finger points on a southwest heading. After a while, I saw blurred lights ahead.

I scrambled off my knees so Frank could hear me. "Menin, it

has to be Menin, which means the Lys is coming up portside. From there we can run straight down to Armentieres and home."

We managed to pick up the Lys, but the wind was severely hampering our progress. At times, it seemed as if we were standing still even when stressing the Beardmore at thirteen hundred revs. Sitting in the front was miserable with little to do but look out for enemy activity, albeit unlikely. With no windscreen and no protection from the blustering wind, driving rainwater streamed across my goggles. My flying suit was drenched, leaking into my underclothing in places. I battled the wind to keep my head above the lip of the nacelle when suddenly the sky lit up.

Wellsey leaned as far forward as he could and yelled, "What the fuck?"

Kneeling, I held the wind-whipped map in one hand and the torch in the other while I struggled to determine our location. I flipped my goggles up on my forehead to see properly, then turned and shouted, "Rough guess says we are over Wervicq, hostile batteries. Enemy must've been alerted by our earlier attack, perhaps by telephone. Amazing they can hear us."

With the suddenness of the searchlights, I was vigilant, forgetting my numbness, instinctively knowing we had to remain and fight. Fleeing into the clouds could be fatal. I stood and, with fully extended arms, directed the Lewis gun straight down, pumping bullets five at a time into an unseen target. I was unable to stand upon the edges of the nacelle to increase the downward arc as it would have been suicide in such slippery conditions. I only had the handle of the Lewis to support the weight of my body, trying not to slip on the rain-soaked floor. Wellsey instinctively knew to keep the machine steady—no sudden moves—with the courageous nerves required to fly through puffs of Archie.

I slid in the wet oils of the smooth spruce nacelle flooring, losing grasp of the Lewis as I crashed to the floor. Damn the fastidiousness of the British mind that everything had to be perfect. Would it have been weak to have installed rough, unfinished planks that would allow a firmer footing?

The wind was howling as Wellsey shouted encouragement. I managed to first kneel and then stand to grasp the handle of the Lewis. I fought to hold firm, to stop the gun from whipping sideways, and to get it placed downward for a fair shot.

With small bursts, I pumped a full drum of bullets down into those lights, but they held us. As we ran through the gauntlet, their glow bounced off the low cloud ceiling, illuminating our little aeroplane from above as well. We pushed on, painfully slow into the wind and the pelting rain, expecting to be hit at any moment. As I knelt to change the Lewis drum, Wellsey was able to zigzag and sideslip our machine in an effort to wrench away from the menacing glare. He leveled the machine, but I stood too quickly, again losing balance.

I slipped, wincing as I slid down on one knee, the Lewis swinging freely of its own accord, again whipped by the wind. I momentarily thought of the other Lewis, but realized it was only useful to shoot rearward. I staggered to my feet, reaching out over the nacelle to catch it, grabbing but missing. I slipped on the wet pine-tar flooring as my head bounced off the side of the nacelle, necessity causing me to ignore it. I heard the Beardmore throttle down as Wellsey took one hell of a chance by lowering speed to allow me to gather myself. Up on my knees then standing, it worked. I took hold of the handle and heard the engine rev up again. I pumped more bullets downward.

After what seemed like hours in the Hun crosshairs, we freed ourselves by turning sideways across the wind into blackness, our nighttime friend. The balance of the journey back over the lines was not as perilous as over Wervicq, but the pace was unnervingly slow. I reflected on what had happened, suddenly gripped by the thought of falling over, out into the blackness and completely helpless. A disturbing sensation emanated from my groin, a feeling of exposed vulnerability forcing me to change my thoughts to those of getting home. Yet that physical feeling remained as those overriding panicky thoughts drove sickness up from my stomach, which I discharged into the slipstream.

Hearing the engine's roar, seeing the red exhaust, and feeling the power of the thrust confirmed progress, which eventually settled me, even though forward movement remained painfully slow amid driving sheets of rain. Bitter coldness took over as I sank low in the nacelle, my back to the pilot's cockpit. Wellsey kept checking on my spirit by patting me on my right shoulder, which I acknowledged by squeezing his hand. He was positioned cosily in front of the heat of the radiator, just inches from his backside. It spirited me to know he was safe and able to maintain control.

We pushed on until I saw faint light. "The lighthouse, Wellsey. Starboard!"

"Give 'em what they want, Bobby."

With gloves off, I fumbled in the darkness for the Very pistol cartridge, feeling the correct rippled design that indicated red. I loaded and pulled the trigger of the wide-barreled gun, momentarily lighting the sky as the charge soared skyward. Our go-ahead response came quickly, opening the gate for the run to Trezennes.

Over the aerodrome we flashed code with our wing lights, a request for a lit flare path to guide our landing. I asked Wellsey if he might have got it wrong, and he flashed again. Nothing but darkness was the answer. I had been anticipating our landing and now felt colder due to the delay, but then I realized perhaps the 'drome had been under attack. While we circled overhead, we watched our reserve petrol gauge and realized we had minutes before being forced to land.

Suddenly the flare path lit up, went out, and lit up again. Something was wrong, but we had to get in. Facing west into the wind, the aircraft bucked like a prairie stallion as we reduced altitude, the vibration so strong I was sure it was about to break apart. At fifty miles per hour, the treetops and the huts disappeared behind us at a lightning pace. We bumped, catapulted straight up into the air, and then came down hard again. Surely this baby could stand the abuse;

surely we weren't going to come to a very nasty end.

Yet somehow Wellsey throttled down and kept the machine on the grass, rolling forward. With the path remaining lit, what we witnessed was alarming—two machines smashed, completely obliterated beyond recognition, pieces lying all around. It became clear that we had been held back because aircraft remains were scattered across the flare path, making it impossible to put down. We pulled up to the hangars and jumped from our machine, our souls filled with anxiety, dreading very bad news of the crew.

Major Christie held a focused, commanding presence. "Right, Wells and Pitman safe. Who remains?"

"Kemp and Scudamore, sir!" snapped his adjutant.

"Quite sure they are about to come in just now, sir," I interjected. "Saw another Fee circling the 'drome as well."

"Very good, Pitman. You two file your report. We'll take it from here."

"What of the crew who were in the crashed Fees, sir?" asked Wellsey.

"Alive, Lieutenant Wells, alive. Captain Tempest was unhurt and is in the Ops Room, while Captain Barry and Lieutenants Carpenter and Reece were retrieved from their wreckage and are now in the hands of the Royal Army Medical Corps. Due to the blustery conditions, we anticipated trouble and had a motor ambulance on standby. Good thing, too."

I wondered why, if he anticipated trouble, we were even flying tonight, but I kept silent. Wellsey read my mind, perhaps my body language, and shot me a warning look. "Bless them. I wish them well, sir."

We filed our report and knew enough not to immediately inquire about the fate of the damaged machines since tensions were high. It was only 2000 hours, but it felt as if we had been on the sortie for a full night. We struggled out of our wet flying clothes, put on tunics, and dashed into the cold, wet night to the officers' mess.

Shortly Kemp and Scudamore entered, joining the rest of the flyers. The questions asked around the hut were the same—why the devil were we out there flying in these conditions?

The mess fell silent as Major Christie joined us with a confident roar, "Eleven of you ventured out, eleven returned. I am relieved. Barry, Carpenter, and Reece are damn shook up, but no physical damage, no bones broken, and no internals. They are to remain at the clearing station overnight. I'm afraid we've lost three machines. Unfortunate, but *c'est la guerre*."

"Sir?"

"Yes, Captain Tempest?"

"I'm speaking for the lads here. Some are wondering why a sortie was undertaken in these weather conditions and on a nonindustrial target, sir. It seems—"

"Yes, Captain, I understand and appreciate everyone's concerns. Army HQ is unfolding a major plan that required our air support. Gentlemen, have a drink and get some rest. It will not be long before you understand the larger initiative, just not tonight."

After the major left, the reaction to his words ranged from grumbling to outright anger. Captain Tempest attempted to reason with the ire, but some persisted. Tempers flared and emotions ran high. Every officer in the mess understood military authority, which contained the situation for the most part. Yet some were willing to speak out.

"I think you-a need to speak to the major," said Lunghi. "You-a need to tell him we all have family and don't need to be fucking-a sacrificed this way."

"Second Lieutenant Lunghi, I understand your frustration, but as the major said, all our flyers returned tonight," reasoned Tempest. "And he also reminded us that this is the way with war."

"But tonight was just stupid-a. All of us could have gone down in the wind or gone off course to force land in the dark with no petrol."

Officers began to gather around, many siding with Lunghi, frustrated at the seeming ill regard for our safety.

"Now, look," said Tempest as he scanned the group, looking with purpose at many of them, "you and the other flyers did God's work tonight, finding your target and returning. It was a bad situation, but I ask you to consider that Major Christie is under intense pressure from Command."

I could see Lunghi softening a bit, his face a little relaxed as the alcohol no longer directed him. Captain Scudamore stepped forward, leading him by his left arm as he murmured, "Charles, Charlie, let's go outside for some air. Let's call it a night and begin again tomorrow, what say you?" The group dissipated as Lunghi slowly nodded. Finishing what was left of our drinks, we all eventually drifted to our quarters for needful rest after a stressful night.

...

20 September, 1917

My Dearest Cissy,

Darling, I am sorry to bring you grief, yet I need to vent, and my family would not understand as they only receive milder news. I realize it appears I am saving them from anguish and using you for that selfish purpose. If I make you feel that way, please forgive me.

You see, last night a great number of aircraft were sent over the lines in an attempt to destroy enemy dormitories. While that itself is disturbing, it can be justified as a necessary act of war. What is troubling is that we were sent over with full knowledge that a wicked storm was blowing in, yet we were sacrificed for the good of the cause.

We are thankful that no lives were lost; however, machinery was written off. I am not permitted to disclose to what extent, but the wreckage was bad. There were times on the return from our target that I felt like giving up, as cold, miserable, and fearful as I was. It is uncanny to think an extreme situation could cause one to abandon caring. Yet a simple thing like feeling Wellsey's hand on my shoulder was enough to bring me around.

Some of the boys remain hopping mad this morning, and although I understand their feelings, we need to rally together as a squadron. I do believe Major Christie is a kind soul underneath his army façade, but that he is being pushed beyond all expectations. He needs his flyers' support.

Yet perhaps the dismay we are feeling should be directed at the brass and, for that matter, at the politicians who are ultimately enabling them? Have they now become as careless about human life as to willingly sacrifice soldiers with little regard? I know even English citizenry are beginning to question the validity of this damn war. Yet I also know that we are fighting for our freedom against a nasty dictator, to push back crushing German tyranny. Oh, these are complicated and troubling times.

Cissy, I am so lucky to have you as my friend, my intimate friend who is as beautiful inside as out. Thoughts of you warm me to the core and bring me out of the despair I sometimes feel. You give me courage.

Until your next letter,
Bob

Chapter 31

September 1917

We were sitting on the step of my hut. Hardy slid his plate to the ground to let one of the stray hangar dogs finish up the balance of his egg and chips, after which we watched it happily trot across the field in search of some other treat. "These are the moments when I miss home," he mused. "Just seeing the in-the-moment joy of a dog. Even if it is a French dog!"

"What's that mean, Hardknocks?"

Hardy tugged at his oily coveralls, thinking through his comment. My question had caught him off guard. "Oh, just thinking French dogs should carry a little attitude, but they are just like English dogs, don't you think? Slurp up anyone's leftovers."

I laughed. "Yes, always scrounging, never tiring of food, making us feel like it's us they come to see. But that reminds me of people—French, Germans, Canadians, the whole lot. At the end of the day, we are all quite the same, what with our needs and wants and wishes."

Hardy looked at me with a frown as he was not inclined to deep discussion. "Better sortie last night than the one before, eh?"

"Yes. Weather still violent at times, but at least Christie held us back until there was a clearing period." In spite of the major's difficult position with respect to the prior disastrous sortie, he showed empathy by ensuring conditions were acceptable the previous night. "We got up and down just fine. This morning our reconnaissance reported twisted track in the Wervicq area."

Hardy turned to look at me. "Ha! They'll have that repaired in no time, I suppose. Your machine was still warm when I took my shift at 0600 hours. Late night?"

"Yeah, we were last to return, 0540, I think. Is she in shape for tonight?"

"Almost, just waiting for the wing dope to dry. You took some machine-gun fire, a few rips in the fabric to patch up."

I shook off the alarm. "Ah well, you're the man for it!"

"You all right, Bob? You sound a bit unsettled this morning."

"I'll be all right, just having a bit of a blue time. Happens to the best of us. Weather spooks me, I suppose."

I lit a pipe as we spoke of the coming onset of winter and how the poor weather would become more frequent. While most of 100's flyers were annoyed at being sent up in treacherous conditions, Hardy and I agreed that we'd all best get used to it. The only reprieve would be when the generals decided to dig in for the winter stalemate, yet even then it was possible that air attacks could continue.

"As I've said, you have the best in Frank Wells. If anyone is capable of surviving violent skies, it's you two as a team."

Hardy was offering too much credit, typical of his nature. "Bloody kind of you, but you are part of our team, my friend. Without you boys on the ground servicing our machines as well as you do, well, I don't want to think what might happen."

"All right, I'll take that. Remember you have Cissy to buoy you too—isn't that right? Perhaps if you write to her—"

I perked up, feeling the smile spread across my face. "Done that. Done that many times over!"

We strolled over to Hangar No. 2 as dusk laid itself across northern France. Conditions were much improved, as was my state of mind after talking things through. Wellsey was already at the Fee, walking its circumference with Hardy's team while other flyers were descending on their machines. I suited up as this was to be an early sortie.

Hardy climbed up on the port foot step and yelled, "*Bonne chance!*" over the noise of the Beardmore, giving Wellsey and me a thumbs-up before jumping down to remove the front wheel blocks. Standing in front of the machine, he gave Wellsey the all-go. The other mechanics let go the wings, and we were down the flare path and away.

The night sky was full of activity with sister squadrons, reflecting a massive coordinated initiative. Crossing the lines at the lighthouse, we were quickly over Ypres. We kept an eye on Tempest and Barry in front, who led the way to our target, the Menin-Ypres road. At times we could see enemy movement but were not given clearance to drop bombs. As we approached Gheluwe, however, Tempest signaled with a Very green. We were free to attack.

Tracer fire rose from the ground as I assessed for maximum effect. Troops and transport were lined up along the road. Bottlenecked, they were bloody sitting targets! As Tempest dove, I saw Huns scatter into any possible cover, fleeing his threat. Looking over each side and then in front as Wellsey descended toward the road, I needed to quickly seize a target. No time to defend against the tracer coming at us. Thankfully, there were no searchlights out on the country road.

And there it was, a particularly narrow section of road with open fields on each side, exposing an enemy who had fled seconds earlier, now with no cover.

I yelled behind me, "Steady, Wellsey, steady . . . Keep at eight hundred feet."

Machine-gun fire was streaming around but somehow did not get a fix on us. I released just ahead of target, feeling the 230-pound heavy clank away from the rack underneath. I immediately pulled on the secondary levers, setting free the twenty-pounders. Our objective of ripping wide holes in the road, trapping the enemy with no ability to move their heavy equipment—lorries, cannon, and weaponry—was successful. Yet I knew the night's job wasn't finished. Wellsey climbed up out of tracer range. "I'm circling back so we can strafe them with Lewis fire."

It dawned on me what Wellsey instinctively knew: if we didn't keep up the pressure on the Hun, he would pick himself up and keep moving toward his objective of obliterating France and England. "All good up here in front. I'm going to give 'em hell. Fly over and leave it to me."

As we approached the road with its newly made craters, I opened up the Lewis with constant bursts, ignoring the possibility of a jam. Tempest and Barry were doing the same. I fired down onto the road, arcing the gun back and forth over men, horses, and machinery, at times standing up to mow down everything we flew above. Somehow, we managed to evade a serious hit from their guns even as we made a second pass.

As we completed the mission and flew away, I realized I had unloaded three drums. I didn't recall reloading; I had been in a trance, grasping at the need to do my part in putting an end to this struggle. The thought rolled around in my head that we were trained to fight this way because that is what war had become: mechanized slaughter.

I sat down and leaned back against the cockpit framework, breathing heavy, sweating in spite of my Sidcot. My pulse raced as we made our way toward the lines. A couple of times Wellsey tapped me on the shoulder as a signal of support, but I'm sure he also wanted to see that I was alive. I knew we would be commended for courage under fire, but the thought somehow felt shallow.

I was alert for enemy retaliation, perhaps aeroplanes from one of the nearby Jasta squadrons, but my mind could not shed thoughts of the chaos a few miles back. There would be injured men screaming for help as field medics attended to as many as they possibly could, prioritizing those they could save. There would be dead infantry, leaving behind mothers, fathers, sisters, girlfriends, and wives in Germany, Austria, and perhaps Istanbul. Dead horses, maimed horses, and mules with broken legs. What a mess, what a bloody fucking mess this whole business was.

Yet those thoughts were unlikely to be shared by some of the others at the squadron, who might protest that striking first and fast was essential. That there was simply no alternative when facing an enemy as determined to obliterate your life as you were his. I remembered a career soldier who had said we were not the top species on this planet because we were nice; as humans, we were wired to kill when survival was at stake.

I was so deep in thought that Wellsey had to control the aircraft while leaning far forward to rouse me when we crossed the lines. "Hey, Bobby. Yoo-hoo! Pitman. Anyone home?"

I scrambled to my feet to shoot the Very pistol as we approached the lighthouse. On landing, we were not surprised to learn that another sortie had been ordered. After all, it was a beautiful night for flying, wasn't it?

After warming sips of cocoa, we were airborne again by 0130. I was thankful Wellsey let me be without any focused discussion, talking only about aeroplane operational issues like refuelling and makeshift wing repairs. He definitely had an intuitive mind, knowing when to engage, what to say, and what not to say. I appreciated that.

On the way out I thought of Lunghi, who had committed himself to the infirmary after the first sortie that night. Everyone knew he was feeling the stress; I had certainly seen it when he left the mess the other night. Symptoms of shell shock were evident, an infliction of fatigue increasingly affecting flyers. Perhaps a few weeks in Blighty and an assignment to Home Establishment were in his future. Once an airman becomes overwhelmed, a recovery back to flying was improbable.

The skies remained crowded with aircraft as both 100 and 101 Squadrons completed second sorties. It was a godsend that the Germans did not deploy their fighters to counteract our initiatives. We reached our target, Menin Station, and returned to Trezennes in good form just before 0400.

We struggled out of our flying suits in a state of exhaustion, put on our night clothes, and tumbled into bed. I was tired but not sleepy, and when I drifted off, would wake in a sweat, drenched with nightmares of war. Dreams of the menace were manifested by images of horror—falling over the nacelle, being burned by enemy fire, bullets slamming into me like Perce's final experience—that kept me on edge.

I lay there thinking about the night's first sortie, about our "success." Wellsey was snoring, not as shook up. From his cockpit behind me, he could not have seen the carnage five hundred feet below our Fee. But I saw, and it was I that faithfully prosecuted this new form of automated war, mowing down tens if not hundreds of souls in one sweep. Scything machine guns, lethal long-range artillery, chlorine-gas-laden artillery shells, and fearsome mass tank formations had all changed the face of war forever. It was easy to see that this was to be a race among nations to invent ever-worse instruments of death under a new discipline of *military science.*

In those wakeful moments I asked myself over and over if I had guilt. Never mind that annihilation was being done by all of us on both sides of the conflict. What mattered was whether I had committed an offense by carrying out destruction on behalf of my leaders. Did it make a difference if everyone was committing the same atrocities that were justified behind the veil of warfare? In the rising dawn I convinced myself that what we were all doing was validated and would continue to be until an armistice was declared. There was no other way for a sane man to feel about this; since the declaration of war on that August day in 1914, this was the reality of our abyss.

...

Bumping along the wet road was fine if one was in control of the handlebars, but for the passenger holding on, it was a challenge to stay seated. Still, I laughed heartily at every swerve Hardy took to miss the muddy puddles, which sent me unbalanced toward the wrong side of the Douglas. But he managed to keep us upright. I grimaced and chuckled as he hooted and hollered like a boy on a Ferris wheel.

It was such a fine September afternoon that we took a table on the front terrace of the *estaminet* and ordered a bottle of claret. The rain and wind that Major Christie had submitted to, finally grounding us for two days, was clearing away. But we were still not to fly, not yet.

Taking a moment to calm down after the wild ride, we contemplated our surroundings for a few moments, admiring the stateliness of the belfry at the end of the cobblestone street and the fountain in the square in front of us. Hardy broke the silence with small talk about my health, paying particular attention to the despondency I had been showing. I acknowledged my funk over the past couple of days, but I was feeling quite cheerful at the moment. What I liked most about him was that he had a direct manner when asking about sensitive personal issues while being most pleasant about it.

"I see your spirits are up, but you looked like a troubled tiger for a while, and it wasn't just the rain getting you down."

I smiled back at Hardy's blue eyes, sparkling in the sun. "Yes, I was, although I'm not sure what a troubled tiger looks like."

"Figure of speech. Are you going to tell me?"

"You already know most of the story. After the sortie a couple of nights back, my mind was left with the horrible images of men scurrying away from danger, from death by rapid fire. Bombing them does not seem as bad, but I don't know why as it's the same fucking thing!"

"Well, I've seen a lot of destructiveness in a lot of fighting, from the Maxim in the Boer to the Lewis in this war. Sure, the thought of a machine gun mounted to an aeroplane was unthinkable just a few years ago, but it's become routine now."

"That's what bothers me: these weapons of destruction are now routine."

"I know what you are feeling. Same as I did in the earlier parts of this war and others. You are a good man with a solid focus on right and wrong, and you are being asked to do things you wouldn't in peacetime. Few would."

"I've thought about that thoroughly and dispensed with any guilt for what I'm being asked to do, but this whole nasty business still leaves me feeling sad. For both sides."

We debated the vagaries of war and its immediacy that had spurred some brilliant inventions, except for the irony of their purpose—effectiveness to kill. Some would likely be put to peaceful uses when the war ceased. Still, it was difficult to understand how such inventions as the Lewis automatic machine gun—used with high-speed airborne vantage—could possibly find peacetime uses. It was easy to agree that the means of warfare had changed forever, but the same principle of kill or be killed remained.

It was a beautiful afternoon with the sun shining down on our exposed faces, which constrained our discussion and kept it brief. I was describing the flyers' black-feet initiation ceremony and had become so engrossed with mirth that I failed to notice the *jolie fille* who had been filling our wine glasses and keeping the aperitif plate full. But not Hardy! On one pass by our table, I caught him eyeing her and she boldly eyeing back with a beautiful smile.

I leaned in and waved to get his attention. "You listening to me?"

"Of course I'm listening. But I can do that and make use of my eyes, can't I? Genevie is the oldest daughter of the tavern owner.

Pretty girl, eh?"

I grinned with both palms facing up in a questioning gesture. "What? You know her?"

"I don't '*know* her' know her. Just the few times I've popped over here for a visit, well, we—"

"We what, Hardknocks?"

"We've gone for walks. Nothing serious, we just talked—well, tried to talk as my French is not good."

"I can see you two have 'talked' all right. Sparkling eyes tell everything, my friend. Good on you, Sam. How does her papa feel about this?"

"Cautious. We're allowed to walk over to the canal, but I know and she knows that every villager and farmer around Aire is watching. So we . . ." Hardy sighed heavily. "Well, just talk!"

"Sam looking for love, eh?"

"Whoa! Look at you—you and your Cissy."

I smiled broadly, proud that she was my girl.

"See? You're grinning like the devil himself. And you ask me of love!"

It was great to kibitz with Hardy; he was a good friend who reminded me of the good things about life. After a time, we needed to report back to the aerodrome for dinner. He gave Genevie a couple of intimate kisses on each cheek, while those I gave her were a little more perfunctory. We raced off into the afternoon brightness as I clung to the back of his jacket.

Chapter 32

September 1917

The next evening presented clear conditions and a bright moon, perfect for flying. We arrived at the hangar to help Hardy and his team finalize the check of our A796. The squad was sending up seventeen aircraft, each loaded with one 230-pound and various four-finned Coopers, the agile twenty-pounder that was the first high-explosive bomb adopted by the RFC. 101 Squadron were equally equipped and coordinated their sorties with ours.

I felt the calming vibration of the synchronized pistons with Wellsey seated in his office and Hardy positioned on the ground waiting for the ground tech's flash of light to signal our good-to-go. I felt good, well rested, as I checked the swivel of both front and rear Lewises, their mountings secure.

As soon as the aeroplane in front gained altitude and disappeared over the hangars, the tower flashed our number. Taxiing out to the T end of the flare path, we gyrated into the wind. At about fifty-five miles per hour, I felt the ground cease to rumble, and we were off once again into the heat of war.

Through the moonlit night, we brushed past gathering mist on our approach into Wervicq station. On the way over, I reflected on my building confidence with these sorties. Anxiety, yes; angst, sure, but as my experience and skills continued to build, I became better able to manage the perils that accompanied any mission. Yet the trepidation of facing unknown dangers lingered.

Cutting the engine, we dropped to twelve hundred feet amid heavy Archie, but I maintained my concentration on dropping our pills, ignoring the threat. The involuntary fast breathing and the punching within my chest were both there—couldn't be helped—but I leaned far over the front of the nacelle to get an eye on the lit train station.

"Hold on, Bob! Keep steady, old man," shouted Wellsey from behind.

I waited, mentally calculating the distance and trajectory, anticipating a hit on the station and tracks together.

Damn! Enemy searchlights locked on us, making it difficult to eyeball the situation. Without the advantage of our descending from blackness, I had to guess at the correct angle. I yelled without turning around, "Here goes!" I pulled up the middle bomb lever to release the 230-pounder and then methodically yanked up the others to release the Coopers, four to port, four to starboard. With a clunking surrender from the rack, they were behind and dropping fast when I realized I had been holding my breath.

Expelling air from my lungs, I felt the Fee swing around. I grabbed at the Lewis, pumping rounds into the luminescent glare on the return over the station. We knew the ole bathtub was too slow to easily escape their grip, so the best defense—the only defense—was to turn into the light and dive. The going was precarious, and after leveling out over the station, Wellsey again drove the machine in a tight turn. "Lean, Bobby!" he demanded. With my stomach pressed tightly against the gun post, I forced the Lewis downward as far as it would extend. Ignoring the threat of a jam as I held the trigger fast, pumping rounds down into the blinding illumination. *Breathe. Remember to breathe!*

I shot out one light, which caused the second to momentarily waver. I had the curious thought that perhaps its operator was astonished, wondering how this Englishman could have scored a direct hit! Miraculously, he lost us in his instant of hesitation. I quickly kneeled back down into the nacelle, knowing that Wellsey would level out at full throttle to soar away from the danger.

I clung to the port side of the nacelle while sticking my head over to peer behind. Catching my breath, I saw a raging fire. It looked as though we hit the station directly, which added to the brash feeling from taking out the searchlight. Relating the news to Wellsey, he sported his infectious Cheshire cat grin. I smiled back at his confidence and tremendous instinct for survival. With adrenaline-filled bodies, we headed home to Trezennes.

With a quick refueling, we were back over the Locre Lighthouse at 2300 hours. Christie had ordered a few of us to return to raid the Menin area, particularly German transport facilities. We were one of three aircraft to join Captain Tempest on a strafing exercise over the Ypres-Menin road to interrupt the flow to the front. We were to again strafe infantry and equipment at high velocity. As we closed in, I checked my two Lewises while feeling my belly wrench and my pulse quicken, a bead of sweat trickling from my forehead down my cheek. Yet I was prepared, knowing what was expected.

We knew the Hun would be on alert due to our earlier sortie, so I focused on searching the sky for enemy aircraft, unlikely in the starlight. Something, or some thought, pulled at me, causing me to turn around. Looking backward in the direction from which we came, I peered between the top and bottom planes and could not believe my eyes.

Silhouetted against the subdued moonlight were rising towers, the bulging threat of cumulus clouds that were moving in from the coast. I waved at Wellsey with alarm, catching his attention. "Threat at our tail, and it's ugly!"

He held his composure. "If it was threatening aircraft, you would be on the gun by now. What've we got?"

I swung my arms in a wide circle as if drawing the immense blobs. "Dark clouds stretching above us up to who knows how high, with a flat base low enough to bring more damn rain—looks like lots of it."

Frank Wells wasn't alarmed, seldom was. "We best get in and out quickly, old man. I'm peddlin' this crate as fast I can."

The threat of another rain-driven return to the aerodrome seemed at odds with the starlit night into which we flew, and the thought of flying back toward the storm nagged at me. We followed Wing Commander Tempest as he veered south before Ypres to pick up the road to Menin, Harmon behind us some distance. Tempest flashed his wing lights before extinguishing them, which we did for Harmon in turn. Tension built as we all knew we were upon the target.

Wellsey slowed the Fee and dropped level with Tempest at eight hundred feet, the ribbon of dark road rising up to us. Suddenly, a great flash burst ahead of us, followed by tracer bullets rising up in response to the threat. Tempest was climbing away as I steadied myself to pull up on the bomb releases, apprehensive. Being first, the Tempest bombs stirred up a hornet's nest, so I knew we were flying straight into Hun hate.

I looked quickly back at Wellsey, who gave me a supportive thumbs-up. I held back, saving the release for the string of lorries I could see along the road, thinking how painfully slow we seemed to be traveling. Machine-gun tracer was slamming up at us, trying to find our altitude, not quite able to pin us down. Thank God!

We moved in closer, just ahead of the ground vehicles coming toward us, timing just about perfect. I pulled the lever up, then another and another, dropping our load to explode one after the other along the roadway. As the upward blast from the explosions reached us, ground machine-gun fire increased. It came from both sides of the road, perhaps hidden in the shrubbery. The Hun had quickly set up emergency nests after Tempest had attacked.

I grabbed the Lewis and returned fire, not sure where to aim in the dark. I began to panic as I realized I couldn't defend both sides of the aircraft. Wellsey was softly rocking us back and forth, perhaps in an attempt to shake off the tracer, I wasn't sure. My senses were keenly alert; I heard bullets ripping through wing fabric, yet I couldn't possibly tell from which direction. I swung the Lewis from side to side and across the front of the nacelle, blasting downward in blind defense.

Just as my gun ran dry, I heard pings as bullets hit metal, bullets stopped dead. They had to have struck our only metal component, the Beardmore. Yet I had no time for those thoughts. That would come later. I had to control my breathing, to steady my hands as I fumbled with a new drum. I slammed it down onto the top of the barrel, hearing the click as it fell into place. I stood up again and rained down hate, not seeing any target, just pelting shots down.

With relief, I realized we were fast gaining altitude as Wellsey hammered on the throttle. Slowly gaining control of my senses, I turned to glance at him, at the same time noticing through the planes that Harmon was now descending on the roadway target, an unnerving scene as his Fee gleamed under starlight. I shuddered to think we had thought all along that we were shrouded in darkness when we were so clearly outlined in silhouette.

We had to make the run across the lines to the aerodrome. My mind turned to the weather, seeing the cloud mass looming in the night that we were now racing toward. I leaned over the small windscreen to work out the plan with Wellsey and saw concern, so rare from the effervescent South African. "You all right, Wellsey?"

He looked pained, a rare display of uncertainty. "Fluid on my seat, Bob. Can't quite make out what it is, where it's from."

The main petrol tank was below us, so fluid on the seat meant that was not the problem, a relief. In that critical moment, we both looked up at the reserve gravity tank in the top wing. Wellsey showed alarm. I must have as well. If it had been hit, a vapor flash from petrol spilling onto spark plugs would engulf the wing fabric in flames.

My pulse quickened, but my mind was clear as I thought through the situation, rejecting thoughts of having to jump from a burning aircraft. Seconds seemed like minutes while I stared up at the top plane with empty blackness beckoning behind, taunting us to join it. As my gaze followed the struts down to the cockpit, I glanced at Wellsey, then behind him. In one of those moments not understood let alone explained, I knew I was staring at the problem: the Beardmore's radiator!

I pointed, but Frank just looked puzzled. I yelled, spluttering out the words, "The radiator! The Beardmore's radiator!"

As Wellsey stared at me, I jabbed my finger into the air in front of me. "The fluid, it must be water."

He removed his glove and brushed his finger against the seat, bringing it to his nose. "*Ja*, no smell. It's water, old man. Christ, the rad's shot through!"

I let out my breath, feeling relieved, but then realized a leaking radiator couldn't be good. "W-what does that mean?"

Wellsey shrugged, back to his composed self. "Fuck, I don't know, but let's get the hell home."

We planned to make a straight run over the line, ignoring any Archie in our way. We had no choice. The engine was already running hot as water slowly leaked from the rad. As the storm's effect increased, I had this irrational thought that perhaps its bitterness would have a cooling effect to keep the Beardmore running. With the machine bucking violently at times from gale-force winds and driving rain, it was impossible to look at the map, so I kept a keen watch for the Lys instead.

In time I made out the lake that formed part of Armentieres, knowing its source was the Lys River, our path home. Fighting against the gale coming hard at us, I was able to use compass and time to determine our distance to Trezennes. But that would only matter as long as the engine continued to help propel us there.

Wellsey bellowed, "Water holding, but temperature's up more. Distance?"

"I make forty miles, maybe forty-five minutes in this gale." I hollered against the clanking of the engine and the howl. "Fuckin' winds are a curse. In this squall, we could miss the lighthouse at Locre."

"We have what we have," quipped Wellsey.

I retorted, "Without Locre, we have little chance."

"Understood. But we stay the course or face doom. Meander in these conditions, we could end up back over the line."

I knew I was sounding concerned, perhaps panicky. It was one thing to be in the pilot's seat with the belief of being in control. But to be up front in a gale with nothing to do except watch and wait was unnerving. Human nature was to control things, to use intellect to manage against peril. I forced myself to keep alert, at times standing straight up into the oncoming wind, supported by my Lewis gun while scanning each side of our small craft. We were being tossed about in the manner of a trawler caught in a North Sea squall. Anxious trembling was detracting from my will to stay warm, but I had to keep focused.

I could feel the engine struggling to propel us forward. The pistons were starting to miss, losing their natural purring. My mind was racing through many questions: How long could this craft keep going? What happens when a radiator runs dry? Could we safely force land? What would POW life be like, even if we survived a landing? Minutes seemed like hours. Although I knew checking my wristwatch would not quicken our progress, I kept looking, kept wishing for time to advance faster.

I couldn't stand the wait. Conscious of short breaths emanating from my stomach, I sounded shrill. "All right back there, Wellsey?"

"Struggling. Water near boiling; gauge pointing up against its stop."

I leaned over the low windscreen, making myself heard. "I make twenty miles out. Hit-and-miss river guidance is blotted out by driving rain, thick mist, but I can pick it up often enough to confirm we are on—"

Suddenly, the aeroplane bucked wildly, and the engine gave an angry loud bang.

"Fuck! Wellsey, wh—"

Frank offered a tentative smile. "She's not happy, Bob. Water boiled away. Oil smells burnt; pistons pumping in its boil."

"How long before the thing just melts away?"

"Fucked if I know, old man. Keep pushing the limit, whatever that is!"

I momentarily stood there looking backward behind Wellsey for any sign. Of what, I'm not sure, but I felt that by watching I could will that propeller to keep revolving, to take us home. Eventually I turned around to refocus on the ground below, looking for any landing opportunity. Mist obscured a clear view. I decided to pull the scrunched map from my Sidcot pocket, not caring at this point if it blew away. With the help of my torch, I found the lake at Armentieres, and with a frozen finger, followed the Lys to Aire. It was a guess, but there appeared to be farms and fields that might suit a forced landing.

Kneeling upright to again look over the side of the nacelle, relief washed over me as the mist cleared ever so slightly to reveal a welcome sight. The subtle straightening of the river where it met the canal, that very canal Hardy and I had sat beside a few weeks past. The Aire Canal! I jumped up and excitedly faced Wellsey. "The Aire Canal! Turn to port, follow canal, and descend to eight hundred. Wingtip lights on!" I barked out orders and directions in my excited state.

Wellsey sat there composed, only a slight smile giving away his cool demeanor. "No lighthouse, old man?"

"No idea how we missed it; don't care, Frankie! We're home, we made it!" Whether it was my excitement or that he himself was awash with relief, he chuckled, then broke into a full-on laugh.

When I was sure we were over Trezennes Aerodrome, I pressed a flare through the chute and quickly looked over the port side, then the other. What a sight, what an ecstatic feeling, to see the ground light up, the flare slowly descend under the guidance of its little parachute. Through the rain, familiar ground.

I was pointing left and yelling, "Still to port, Wellsey, keep turning."

I could feel our turn. I watched the ground below, but my euphoria faded. No flare path, no aerodrome lights, no welcoming glow at all. But then Wellsey's loud but gentle reprimand brought me back to reality. "Bobby, a little haste before they think we're enemy."

I realized I had forgotten the signal light, the landing request. I was breathing excitedly, *but what was I thinking?* Once the red Very light was propelled into the rainy sky, the flare path lit below us. We were not yet landed, but relief continued to rise within me. But then I turned and realized the Beardmore was silent.

"Wellsey, wha—"

He was struggling with the controls, trying to keep the craft balanced. "Engine seized . . . no prop . . . can't circle; got to land this bucket on a straight drop. Wish us luck, Bob. We fucking need it."

I felt my elation melt away as I thought about coming this far in these conditions only to die on our own airfield. We were to land without the leveling thrust and controlling balance of the propeller. My mind shot back to the crash on our first takeoff together.

The night sky was violent, but in the eerie silence of our aircraft, I could hear the rain hiss as it hit the melting Beardmore, no longer able to offer us comforting power. The whistling of the rigging did nothing but add to the tension. I felt like my head would explode, racing with ugly thoughts. Wellsey was totally concentrated, but I knelt up front, tormented.

A sudden drop out of the sky could see the 650-pound engine slam on top of us, mashing us into the ground. Landing without power could flip the machine over. I was terrified.

Still, Wellsey managed a sideslip, keeping the front up and lowering the ailing machine toward the lit path. Flares whipped past as we touched the grassy field; we bounced upward ten feet, then twenty or more before slamming down again. The third bounce drove our machine straight down onto itself, buckling the undercarriage, a distinct crack as the wheel struts collapsed. Somehow, I hung onto the side as the Fee slid sideways on its belly out of control along the pathway, leaning to port, the lower plane digging into the rain-slicked field. Coming to a stop, we both sat there stunned as relief washed over us.

The air mechanics were all around in an instant. I felt arms in behind my shoulders lifting me up, while others took hold of my legs, easing me down off the mangled craft. The hissing sound of the Beardmore under the pelting rain spat out in the darkness, its unique death knell. They managed to lift Wellsey out. He was jammed tightly into the crumpled cockpit. Frenzied activity all around made us aware of the pending fire risk.

Stunned but largely unharmed, we sat upright in the Crossley tender on the way to the Casualty Clearing Station, where someone handed us each a flask of whiskey. The medic and nursing sisters looked us over, wiped grime, oil, and sweat off our faces, then cleared us for good health. Major Christie strode in, a frown on his face.

"You gents have a good flight?"

"We brought your old Fee back with all the parts you entrusted to us, sir," Wellsey said while using his sleeve to wipe a whiskey spill from his lower lip. "Although on inspection you may find a few of them, ah, remodeled."

I was surprised he had the gumption to respond back to the

major with an equal dose of facetiousness, yet Christie laughed. "I earned that, Lieutenant Wells. Tempest tells me you two did very well with your second sortie in spite of conditions. I congratulate you, and I daresay we are pleased to have you returned safely, if shook up. Not so for Harmon and Stedman, or for Archibald."

I interrupted a gulp of malt to ask, "What about them, Major? Not bad news, I hope?"

"No sign of either machine, I'm afraid. Even under these conditions, threat of a retaliatory bombing of our aerodrome is forcing us to remain dark. Difficult on the return, I suppose. Possible they put down in some other 'drome."

Wellsey and I exchanged looks expressing our mutual feelings. That could have been our outcome, or worse. The storm had risen quickly, taking us all by surprise. Christie was under tough orders, and although protocol prevented him from expressing his feelings in front of his flyers, his anguish was clearly evident.

"That is rough, sir," I said. "God, I hope they are safe."

"Well, there is nothing you lads can do, any of us can do for the moment, so finish your whiskey and get some rest. There are plenty of ground troops searching for them. Sleep well."

Chapter 33

September 1917

After waking in our sun-filled room, I lay about, thinking over the previous night's events and about how Lady Luck had extended Her hand once more. I appreciated the discretion to loll around in bed until we felt like facing the new day. Well, until a sharp rap on the door disturbed my reflections. I rolled over to see what urgency was visiting.

Wellsey murmured something unintelligible as he pulled a pillow over his face. Ace was at the door, pale as though he had not slept a wink. He was agitated, wanted to talk, so I swung my legs over the side of the bed and sat up. With deep emotion, Ace explained there was still no news of Harmon and Stedman and wondered when we last saw them. I recounted the horrific time we had wrestling ourselves away from the surprise machine-gun fire, but I did recall seeing their aeroplane behind ours as we climbed away. I had no idea what had happened to them after that except to speculate that they had faced the same intense tracer hate.

Wellsey pushed the pillow to the side of the bed and sat up, a little groggy. He looked at Ace compassionately, knowing he was a close friend of Stedman's. "I'm sure the Germans would have reported by now if they had force landed behind the lines."

Ace wrung his service cap in his hands as he stood there looking downcast, listening to Wellsey.

"The order of attack on the roadway last night was that Tempest and Barry led, followed by us." Wellsey pointed to himself, then me. "Harmon and Stedman were in anchor, so there was no one behind them to see what happened. That is the hard reality, I'm afraid."

I was struggling for comforting words but could only come up with the facts. "We had no time to stick around as we were badly shot up. We barely made it back. Perhaps in this case, no news is good news. Let's hope for the best." I knew my words were not coming across in the supportive way I intended and lacked the comfort Ace was seeking. Yet I connected with his feelings as they were the same as mine were for Perce. The unspoken despair was that the missing flyers had been shot down and were prisoners at best.

Ace remained discouraged. "Well, I was just wondering if you remembered seeing anything of them."

"Remember," said Wellsey, "conditions had deteriorated with visibility almost nonexistent in the gale. And with the intense German defense, we were not able to go back to—"

"I know, Frank, I do understand." Ace was sad, but we were at a loss to provide the comfort he sought. "I understand survival was at stake for all of you. Still, I'm dreadfully worried for Alex. Terrible loss if he—well, the two of them have gone west."

I looked over at Wellsey, who gave a slight nod in response to my hidden shoulder shrug. I tried to draw attention subtly away. "What of Archibald? Any news?"

Ace perked up a little. "Oh yes, Arch didn't make it back, but he's all right. He forced landed near here in a farmer's field at Saint

Venant. Managed to get to an army field post and ring the 'drome in the wee hours. Lucky bloke, especially since he was flying solo."

"Well, there you go; that gives hope for the others. You know, Ace, as difficult as this is, we must be positive. Our squad loses few compared with the fighter squadrons. I know that doesn't make this easier, but losing comrades, well, is reality." I gave Ace as big a smile as I knew how, but he still looked dreadfully busted up.

Ace merely nodded and said without conviction, "Oh, CO wants us assembled in the Ops Room at 1400 hours."

We pulled ourselves together while the aching in every bone known to our Creator reminded us of our landing debacle. We managed to tie our ties and head over to the mess for some grub.

...

26 September, 1917

Dearest Robert Courtenay Pitman,

Hello, my Bobby. Forgive me for addressing you above with formal salutation. I wanted to see your name written out in full. I admit to you here and now that I repeat your name as I go about my factory work, driving my little train and willing away the constant clanging of machinery. Thinking of you, thinking of the time we spent together, of the sadness we shared that spawned the happiness we now share in our letters—well, that keeps me going. I know you cherish our closeness as much.

Oh, darling, as I rattle on I think about your last letter, so sad I felt for you and your squadron facing that wicked storm. It's enough that you must fight off the heinous Hun, yet more intolerable that you boys must be placed at more risk.

Oh no, you do not bother me with your grief, my lieutenant. On the contrary, I am flattered that you treat me with equal deference as you would your male friends. Try not to feel distressed; you need all of your energy to maintain your courage. I know I couldn't possibly put myself in your place to understand what it is like to fly into battle, but I try. Do not let doubt enter your mind as you need the pluck to carry on and win the war for us. All of you boys do.

If I can be of any help to you, it is to be your guiding light, to provide encouragement. Think of the happy places you've enjoyed. Think of a walk in Finsbury Park with birds chirping and children playing under billowy clouds, or perhaps a picnic on the grass alongside the banks of the Serpentine on a warm summer evening. You will enjoy these simple pleasures soon. That works for me when war gloom seems overwhelming over here in our homeland.

So don't be dismayed. You are fighting the good cause, for civilization and for liberty, for all of our citizens. Take the courage you say I inspire in you and build it higher and higher. And come back to me. I know you will.

Yours,
Cissy

...

The silhouette loomed large as Major Christie's frame emerged out of the afternoon sunlight through the doorway into the dim room. He looked weary and strained yet retained a level of focus that most would have quickly lost under the severe demands coming out of London's war office. "All right, officers," he bellowed.

Silence fell over the room as Christie addressed the previous night's nasty sorties and thanked the flyers and staff for their effort. His stressed demeanor made him sound a bit patronizing, but I took him as sincere. My interaction with him when arriving at the aerodrome had given me a glance into his soul, his kindness reflected in the way he handled my medical digression.

Christie broke out of his solemnness with a brief smile. "I've just heard that Harman and Stedman have been located and are being transported back to the aerodrome." A roar went up across the room. To lose crew was bad, but not to know their fate seemed worse. I looked over at Ace, who was brimming.

"Let this be a hard lesson: we don't take shortcuts." We stood rigid as Christie explained Harman and Stedman took undue risk by returning on a shorter, unknown heading. In the gale, they not only missed the mark but veered off in a southerly direction before being forced down fifty miles off course near the Ardennes. Things could have been much worse, but I couldn't help wondering if Christie might have taken a similar action in those circumstances.

"Now, brass has been pushing us hard." That was the first time I heard the major admit to the stress he was receiving from above. As I surveyed the room, I saw that other officers held the same understanding look, a few nodding. "Allow me to review the current state."

The room was silent as Christie expertly stitched together events, which had either unfolded or were in the course of unfolding. German submarines had bombarded Yorkshire on the English coast, and their aeroplanes had bombed London by night. A developing revolution in Mother Russia was creating low morale among their soldiers, and they sometimes refused to leave their trenches to fight. In spite of the heavy rains that created unsuitable conditions, our infantry had been making headway in the Ypres Salient.

"Yes, flyers, the Hun is stomping up to our front door at home, and we have all but lost our Russian ally. The Americans are on their way, but it will take time for them to fully deploy."

Christie had always made it known that these briefings were open, that the men were free to probe. Bean stepped forward. "How long before they arrive, Major?"

"I am not privy to that, Lieutenant, but I'd be surprised if they were not a dominant ground force within a few months. 1918 could see significant change in the prosecution of this war."

I wondered how they might be an influence in our bombing drive, how they would integrate. "Major," I queried, "will the Americans be bringing their own aircraft? Will they add bombers to our forces?"

"Well, Pitman, that's sticky business. The US doesn't have bombers to speak of—a few fighters, perhaps. Where they will bring strength is with fresh, well-trained flyers. And we will welcome them." I appreciated the candor but wondered if there would be conflict if the fresh American flyers pushed aside British and French officers, yet there was no denying we needed their help. Perhaps the Americans would be most effective with their ground forces. Christie continued, "Study your bearings, know your navigational aids, and stick to known practices. We wrote off three aircraft last night. Let's keep ourselves safe."

In the sobering moment it took the officers in the Ops Room to reflect on the fragility of both men and machine, Captain Tempest moved to the front of the room. "No offensive tonight. Poor weather and battle fatigue are grounding us. Spend time with your mechanical crew and get rested." The reprieve was an unexpected gift.

...

The Pitmans
426-8th Street East
Saskatoon, Saskatchewan
Dominion of Canada

26 September, 1917

My Dear Family,

Papa, Mama, Ethel, and Hilda, I think of you all the time. It is approaching two years since I enlisted to fight in this war, but it feels like I've aged twenty.

Thank you for continuing to send me copies of the Saskatoon Star, keeping me current with local events. Harvest festival in England was last week, reminding me that Thanksgiving will soon be celebrated in Canada. I just need to close my eyes to see the miles upon miles of golden wheat fields, I suppose now just harvested.

Remember, Hilda, that in the September before I left we would roar across the open prairie, you on your little pony trying to keep up. I would race ahead, only to turn back to fetch you or to await your catch up. We would laugh, and then I would cajole you into accepting another race, which you would also lose. But you were always a good sport and learned from those experiences! And afterward, I would take you to Delaney's for one of the new ginger ales. You must look very grown up now that you're seventeen and working at the oil company!

I won't carry on too much, but the memories help me get through this war and give me pleasant thoughts, a safe place in my mind. Since earning my observer's wing as an RFC flyer, I have so far been across the lines on one bombing sortie or *another for a total of eleven times. I won't pretend that each one isn't daunting, but I do have the comfort of knowing that each night I return there is a warm bed waiting.*

Our CO, Major Christie, gave us a long briefing during which he sounded upbeat about our prospects. We are pushing the Germans back in places, although they are still firmly rooted in France. We do our bit by punishing them when they bring troops forward and by bombing their factories and airfields. We will continue to do so with the spirit of bringing peace to all of the democratic powers.

*Your loving son and brother,
Bob*

Chapter 34

September 1917

In the final week of the month, we resumed our bombing attacks in the Wervicq and Menin areas in a continued effort to thwart German troops from reinforcing their Ypres Salient ground effort. Wellsey and I felt these raids were purposely subdued, likely a strategy by Christie to rebuild 100 Squadron's confidence and *esprit de corps*.

But after a couple of nights attacking those easier marks, we were ordered to a more difficult and dangerous target. For the first time, we were to venture farther east of the front lines into long-held German territory to attack Hun infrastructure and stop its use against our ground troops and innocent citizens.

Army intelligence and air reconnaissance had identified the Gontrode Airship Sheds near Ghent as housing a large number of zeppelins and Gotha bombers that had bombed Paris and London many times. We were ordered to rain terror down on those sheds, to pound them into oblivion. Night after night we were active with little sleep, but the squad shared a sense of euphoric victory as we flattened aircraft and sheds with relentless tenacity.

The last day of September was a beautiful Sunday with sunshine splashing across the grassy airfield and glistening through the red and gold leaves of the nearby woods. Through the stubble of harvested wheat fields, Hardy and I returned from a walk to the canals, his Genevie remaining close to her papa's *estaminet* these days.

Sam left me in front of my hut and wandered off to coordinate the servicing of the Fees for the night's sortie. I sat on the small steps, leaning back against the doorframe with the southern sun caressing my face while birds chirped above me on the peaked roof. I thought of Cissy, dreamed about how we would love to share a moment like this. We had only been with each other during winter when time together indoors was enduring, but summer moments were meant for deeper memories, which surely must come. I ached to be with her, to feel the wisps of her hair against my cheek as she laid her head on my shoulder. I closed my eyes and thought of her tender skin as my hand brushed her arm and the feel of her lithe body as we walked arm in arm. Although I had never felt this way before, I knew I was in love.

Suddenly yanked from my reverie, I heard the South African singsong. "You in love, chappie? Just look at that dreamlike smile." I opened my eyes to a grinning Frank who was nothing short of mischievous.

"Perhaps, Wellsey. Perhaps in love with life itself, eh?"

He chuckled. "*Ja*, my friend. I'm just *snaaks* about this weather, you know. Shall we go poke and prod our Fee?"

The orders were for the 100s to head out over Locre Lighthouse for an all-out punch on the Gontrode sheds. I released my rancor about involving citizens in war since the Germans were violating that in spades when they terrorized women and children. A punishing attack was appropriate; we knew 101 Squadron would be following our charge later in the night, which meant there would be thirty-three aeroplanes involved.

We flew over the lines under a bright full moon, where the trenches were a visible reminder of our infantry. Knowing firsthand the mud, rats, lice, and prolonged struggle of wits gave me a momentary shiver. Following the Lys River led us to the Scheldt, where we would turn north to approach Gontrode from the southwest.

Within minutes, I saw explosions flash in the distance as our forward aeroplanes dropped their bombs. Searchlights scanned the darkness as Archie exploded in puffs of black. I knew this was going to be a hot one. I felt good.

Wellsey signaled for my attention. "We'll glide to eight hundred and drop our 230."

"Right. See there ahead? That's Bean and Ace flashing their wingtip lights. They are dropping in ahead of us. We'll follow."

Frank cut the engine as I kept watch, grasping the spade-like handle of my Lewis, ready for any threats. Suddenly, the forward machine flew erratically, zigzagging back and forth over the target as Archie shells burst on both sides of his Fee. I yelled, "By God, Bean's under attack! We've got to concentrate on that shed."

"Let's get 'em, Bobby!"

Our top and bottom planes gave out little shudders of protest as their fabric strained in the wind, wires whistling and struts creaking as we descended through the night air. I knew our protection—the only shelter we had against Hun Archie—was surprise, to swoop down out of the darkness in spite of their knowing we were somewhere out there. As seconds ticked away, I alternated my focus between defending with the Lewis and attacking with our bombs.

Even as we remained in obscurity, Archie was coming up thick as the Germans were anticipating our squadron's continued attacks. To direct Wellsey, I pointed to the southwest corner of the giant shed where Ace had evidently just scored a hit, a fire lighting the surrounding area, giving us a clear target. It also gave the enemy a clear view of our Fee.

Having moved their attention away from Ace's fleeing machine, searchlights locked on us. Kneeling for protection but looking over the nacelle, I was half blinded by the massive lights that were dangerously close. Yet I could clearly make out the fiery shed, enticing us to blast it to bits, to raze it once and for all. The intense danger spurred me to action, focussed for a direct hit as I yanked the lever to release the large bomb. As I turned my attention to the Coopers, my brain registered vibration as the Beardmore sprung to life. Wellsey was getting us the hell away. As we began our climb, I released the small pills over the airfield itself.

But just as we were climbing into the black night, two searchlights crossed, holding us in their grip. I stood up, pulling the Lewis with me, pointing downward and pumping bursts into their glare, moving the gun across the arc as we swung up portside to get away as quickly as we could. A shiver of relief flooded through me as the lights turned away to focus on the next attacker. I barely had time to think about their fate when Wellsey bellowed, "Fuck! Bobby, turn around! Fire at port—lower plane, I think!"

Hearing the panic in his voice, I turned around quickly but could see nothing. He did say port, didn't he? That wing wasn't visible in our banked turn. I released my grip on the Lewis to kneel and, against all logic, allowed my weight to shift me into the portside turn, gravity pulling me against the low nacelle where it would be easy to tumble out into the night.

Looking intently to focus on that side, I saw it. Brightness had spread to illuminate the whole lower wing. I looked back and yelled, "Damn, you're right, but I can't see flames! Level 'er so I can get a look." With a rush of momentary relief, I felt the aeroplane straighten itself, allowing me to relax my grip.

We knew this was perilous since a burning aeroplane meant sure death, either by burning in situ or by jumping away from the flames.

My mind raced with thoughts of parachutes with which I could jump to safety. While provided for those in observation balloons, they were forbidden to flyers lest courage be squandered. *I wish we had them now!* Fighting back panic, I continued to search the wing, determined to find the cause. Every second it did not break into flame was a blessing.

Survival instinct consuming his thoughts, Wellsey did the only thing he could: he pointed down with his middle finger as he plunged the little aircraft into a steep dive. Grasping the Lewis handle with one hand and the nacelle with the other, I peered down to scan the moonlit landscape for a landing.

Fixated on the glowing wing, I hung on, praying we'd land safely, my mind racing with thoughts of pending disaster. I was barely aware of the sweat escaping from the edges of my leather helmet or my heart pumping anxiously through my whole being. Would we crash? Would we burn? If we did land so far behind the lines, would we be taken prisoner or shot on the spot for having just rained terror on our very captors? Yet I allowed a tiny sliver of hope to rise from my churning stomach as the thought of landing seemed possible.

Hurtling downward, my sight was steeled on the ground, ready to give Wellsey the sign to level out at the right time, a race to land before flames erupted. His altimeter would give him our elevation, but he wouldn't be aware of any hills before we smacked into them. I was so focused on observing the ground that I didn't see the sudden change at first. It was only when Wellsey screamed, "Bob, Bobby, we're clear," that I looked at the port wing. I felt the change as Wellsey leveled the aircraft. The flame was gone, mysteriously gone.

I peered portside to see that the once-bright wing was just as dark as the others. Wellsey throttled up to regain altitude. I looked over the nacelle and, with the most incredible relief, saw a parachute flare drifting downward on its illuminated journey to the ground.

I faced Wells and swore in sheer relief, "Ah, fuck! It was one of our parachute flares. Bloody hell, that was absurd!" I exhaled heavily, expelling all the grief of the past few minutes.

Wellsey leaned forward and yelled above the accelerating engine roar, "You mean to say that nasty little flare was lit while still on the wing?"

"Yes, I saw it drifting toward the ground. Enemy fire must have hit the damn thing and set it alight!"

Wellsey cried out, again loud enough to be heard above the fully throttled Beardmore, "Ohhhhhh Lordy! Let's go home. We are survivors, my dear man."

I stood up and leaned back against his cockpit, turned my head toward him. Heavy breathing made speech impossible, yet we managed to laugh in relief.

...

Beginning at the entrance, then fanning out across the room, voices dropped and silence prevailed as Christie strode into the mess. Unusual for the time of night. "Officers, I regret to inform you that Second Lieutenants Bushe and Colbert failed to return to the aerodrome. We are doing our level best to locate them." He nodded and abruptly left with his adjutant trailing him.

The reaction was mixed. Some retreated into silent reflection. Any of us could have force landed or been shot down. Others talked quietly in small groups, while still others carried on playing games of whist or rummy. But the room was quiet as everyone said a silent prayer for our two colleagues.

Our little group talked, musing about what might have happened. After all, it was a bright, moonlit night with little wind and no gale to blame. The intensity of the raid could have resulted in many outcomes for our flyers, but one team distinctly remembered them climbing away from the shed after their bombs dropped. We knew there was little we could do and that army intelligence would not rest until they determined the outcome, however grim.

It had become expected that, with so many active 100 Squadron flyers now operating increasingly dangerous night raids, there were bound to be losses. None in our close group knew Bushe or Colbert very well, but we did know the grief of losing friends. "Another grim reminder that not all of us will make it home, Bob," said Wellsey. "Not all of us will get back to our loved ones."

I stared at Wellsey, assessing his mood. He was seldom this somber. "I suppose, but we mustn't let ourselves get run down. We really are forced to take every day as it comes, to live in the moment so as not to worry over what may or may not come in the future."

The reason for his gloom became evident. "Right, but that's not easy when one has a wife to provide for."

Taking the pipe from my mouth in a contemplative gesture, I thought about that for a moment. I wondered if there was more will to live if one had a spouse or whether the desire to survive for the sake of oneself was equally important. Wellsey needed support at the moment. "Quite so, but your comment makes me think we all have reasons to survive—desires to fulfill and achievements to attain regardless of marital status."

I remembered having to sit down with my father on a hot summer's day to hear one of his forced life lessons. With birds chirping and kids playing in the streets, he wanted me to know that a man needs to build his nest, to make something of himself before entering family life. He awkwardly explained in a cold and mechanical manner that seeking a heart's desire, a one true love, before earning those responsibilities would make them later unattainable.

I didn't often pay much attention to my father's prophecies, but this particular talk resonated. Perhaps it was hidden frustration at being pulled away from my friends at the time that heightened the memory. Or perhaps it did make sense— well, until this war changed everything. I thought of the flipside—for a man on the front lines to achieve success but to die loveless was a dour thought.

Frank continued his thought pattern: "Do you think this war has stolen so much time and energy that your plans are rattled, or do you think you will slide right back into your studies and carry on?"

"I dunno, Frank. I've so concentrated on surviving that I've lost my sense of the future, of how it will be possible to go back and simply sit down at a desk to read law again. You?"

"*Ja*, I think about it. I think about how my *vrou*, my wife, exists on my measly war salary. So I force myself to think about a return to the clerking job I was pursuing, building my career as an insurance professional."

I put my hand on his arm and gave him a supportive smile. "You know, I was envious of you lads who have wives back home. When I was in hospital with shell shock, I wished I had a sweetheart to write to, so lonely and depressed I was then."

Wellsey put his hand over mine. "Yet you have your Cissy now; you have your sweetheart. You just said to take each day as it—"

"Oh, I know. I do that. But when thinking of the future, where then does our relationship lie? I can't just take her over to Canada. 'Hey, Papa, hey, Mama, look who I brought back from the war.' Well, can I?"

Wellsey moved his hand to my cheek and gave me a fond pat. "Why not? More than anything, this war has upended all chance of attitudes and beliefs returning to how they were. Things have changed forever. Unlock your wishes. You—we *all* deserve it."

"We'll see. Funny, I know I'm in love with her, but we haven't spent much time together. So far it's been a long-distance affair, just characters on a page."

He poked me in the chest. "You need to get over to see her."

We finished our drink and retired to our hut. I lay in the darkness, unable to sleep, as a subtle doubt returned, making me vulnerable to a mistrust I had fought off before. I had fallen in love with Cissy, a beautiful, intelligent, intuitive, and enterprising woman who knew what she wanted and how to get it. But that strength was where the mistrust grew. Was I just something she had wanted for the moment and I had naïvely followed? If that were the case, she was shrewd, not innocent. And if she weren't innocent, what if she had known she carried that dreadful disease yet ignored the risk? I was tormenting myself with these irrational, returning thoughts. That itself gave me guilt since I wanted, needed, to trust her.

I tossed and turned and grunted so much that Wellsey hurled a pillow across the room, hitting the wall beside my bed. I startled and mumbled a quiet apology but couldn't shake my thoughts. If Cissy had ignored the risk, then I was wronged in a most terrible way. I lay on my back, watching a shadow moving across the ceiling; the subdued night watch light at the hangars was making its circular rounds.

I knew in my heart that Cissy had shown no sign of being shrewd, either when I was with her or in her many letters. Perhaps I was thinking this because of feeling so close to her, feeling vulnerable and not wanting to get hurt. I had to see her.

Chapter 35

October 1917

The Crossley tender was idling on the side of the airfield, waiting for a final safety check before pulling out on the 235-mile journey south. Sitting up in the cab on the passenger's side, I had an expansive view of the bright-green airfield and the eighteen Fees lined up outside their respective hangars. They would follow in a couple of days with their pilots and air mechanics. Hunched over in close examination of our Fee, Wellsey and Hardy were busy adjusting the rudder. We had said our goodbyes a few minutes earlier.

Now a few days into October, we were heading down to our new aerodrome at Ochey, in the Nancy area near the Vosges Mountains. Our work at Trezennes was done, as the battle at Menin Ridge had wound down and the Gontrode Air Shed lay in ruins. Ochey was close to the Alsace-Lorraine region where the German industrial base lay and where we were to now wreak havoc.

The lorry driver had stepped up into the cab, and we were ready to follow those pulling away just ahead. I took a last look across the field and saw one of our flyers, I think it was Bean, talking excitedly to Wellsey and Hardy, others gathering around. Sam looked over to our lorry convoy, hesitated, then broke into a run toward us.

The driver looked mildly annoyed as I ordered him to wait, holding the convoy lined up behind. Hardy approached from the front with arms held up, signaling for us to wait. He was out of breath, his chest heaving, as he jumped onto the running board. "Good news! They've been located. Bushe and Colbert are alive!"

"By God, that is great news! Wonderful, indeed!"

"Seems they force landed near Thielt, missing the Lys River before engine trouble set in," said Wellsey, who had caught up with Hardy.

"Are they returning to us soon?" I asked.

"Ah shit, Bob, that's the bad news. Surrounded by German troops, they gave themselves up. POWs, I'm afraid. The major just received a telegram from the Swiss Red Cross."

"Damn shame. They will be in for a rough time of it."

The lorry driver signaled his impatience and pulled out as Hardy jumped down with a wave. I sat in the opposite seat for a couple of hours, reflecting on just how close Wellsey and I had come the other night to being POWs ourselves. The driver looked over a few times but remained silent in respect of my pensive mood. I tried to imagine what the future would be like for Bushe and Colbert since it was known that the Germans were facing severe food shortages, even in their home country. POWs must surely be at the bottom of the food chain.

...

"Is there an emergency, Lieutenant?" asked Major Christie.

I thought quickly. I couldn't lie, but the need was overwhelming. "No, sir. I have some business in England I'd like to attend to. Perhaps I'd say it's an urgent request for leave, but no, not an emergency."

"I've got my whole fleet absent. Now located, thank goodness, but sitting up north waiting for this weather to clear. And two Fees at Remy if you don't mind!" 100 Squadron's Fees, which had left Trezennes three days prior on a flight that ought to have taken eight hours, had temporarily vanished in bad weather. 101 Squadron finally located them in a farmer's field way north at Fismes.

I should have anticipated his mood. "Yes, of course, Major. I was putting myself first."

"Look, Pitman, I know others have had leave. Yours is in the queue. You've put your squadron ahead of everything else, and I appreciate that. But my hands are tied. We have an aerodrome to set up and sorties to fly."

I walked out of squadron HQ into a light drizzle that reflected my mood. I had known the chance of leave was remote, had guarded myself against a probable denial, but its confirmation was disheartening.

I settled in to assist with assembling the aerodrome at Ochey, one of the largest in France. It was home to 100 Squadron's night-bombing Fees as well as 16 Squadron's Handley Pages and 55 Squadron's DH4s, both day bombers. There was also a French Escadrille. It was a pretty setting located just outside of the Ochey village of a few dozen houses. Being so close to the Vosges, the surrounding countryside was hilly and thickly wooded. About seven miles to the north was the army center of Toul, which had quaint cobblestone streets and an architecturally stunning cathedral with lots of shops.

I constantly thought of Cissy, wishing I could see her, talk to her, but I respected Christie's denial of my leave since assembling the aerodrome was a major undertaking. Already two Fees in the fleet had been destroyed while landing in bad weather, which sent shivers through me as yet another reminder of how fragile war flying was.

We were settled in by mid-month, but bad weather postponed the start of operations, leaving plenty of time to participate in leisure opportunities. The officers' mess was a large and airy space. In the middle was a massive brazier, larger than at Trezennes and composed of a big, open basket of wrought iron that could host a very large fire. A phonograph with song cylinders such as "Auld Lang Syne" and "Keep the Home Fires Burning" was in one corner and a relic of a piano in the opposite. Cuttings from English and French illustrated papers were posted on the walls showing recent news. Scattered throughout were card tables—at least, tables where cards were played.

The rainy days were long, and we looked forward to the evenings when we enjoyed dinner followed by sing-alongs until the wee hours. I joined in by leading with a few tunes. We had English, Scots, Canadians, Afrikaners, Australians, Indians, and the like, so there was no lack of colorful song material. When words were not understood, we just hummed the cheery tune. During breaks in the singing, tall tales came from a good repertoire of experience, mixed with gales of laughter.

During the third week of October, restlessness crept in. It was twenty miles into Nancy where the lads knew of a brothel reputed to welcome Allied flyers. Well, didn't they all? I thought it uncanny how news of such service traveled so quickly into an RFC squadron; Ochey aerodrome had only been in existence for a few weeks. The problem of transportation was solved by Hardy, whose resourcefulness would be well rewarded. With three sitting up front of the lorry and ten crammed under the canvas cover of the cargo area, we made our way through the hilly farmland into Nancy in less than an hour. Our evening meal was exceptional, duck and potatoes at Le Coq, a bistro, followed by a Calvados digestif.

Hardy put his hand on my shoulder. "What do ya say, Bob? You coming along for some more dessert?"

"I'll follow in a bit, but only for a look, my friend."

His grip tightened as if to emphasize his sincerity. "Cissy won't have to know, Bob. Besides, it's been a long time for us."

"Thought you had your Genevie up in Aire?"

"You mean the girl with the papa attached to her sleeve? Not a chance with her!"

I laughed heartily. "I could have guessed."

"C'mon. They offer protection, you know. Don't have to worry about things. The French are open and sophisticated about such matters."

I smiled and shook my head. "Just the same."

But I joined in to support the team; they moved in formation down the street to the blue light above the ornate door. The madam greeted us with a warm, "Bienvenue, aviateurs Anglais!" At the same time she cleared the tables by shooing away her regular French patrons. All was fair in love and war, *oui?*

I was dazzled by the rich décor seemingly from a bygone palace, or perhaps the bordello was indeed one hundred years old. Amid the velvet curtains and ornate finery decorating the walls and ledges, the *mademoiselles* happily flitted among the lads in an attempt to flourish affections that would lead to important business transactions. In time, the population of flyers in that room dwindled as did the *filles*. I winked at Hardy as he grinned his way to a cloistered door, a lace-clad belle with matching headband clutching his elbow.

I sat with Wellsey and quipped about whether they would emerge in time to catch the Crossley back to the aerodrome. We devised a backup plan in case Hardy required liberating from the delayed clutches of love since he was the driver and needed by 2200 hours. We bided our time while Madame offered encouraging prompts. But after tipping an affectionate brunette for emancipating my lap, we proffered polite smiles and made our way behind the thick curtain out to the street.

We walked in silence back to the *estaminet* for a drink while we waited. The cool, misty air felt good against my face, for I was mildly troubled to have been in that amorous atmosphere. The lads needed their ardent adventure and release after each had felt the tension build up over weeks of service, knowing he might not have another day to live. I wondered if I would have joined them, enjoyed the temporary comfort of a female companion, if it weren't for my previous circumstances. And even more fundamental to my state were thoughts that perhaps there was promise with Cissy, and I wouldn't jeopardize that for the world.

Yet those thoughts were clashing. I knew she was a wonderful girl whom I wanted to be with. Perhaps tonight's exploits were intensifying my feelings as the longing in my heart extended to physical needs as well. I thought of being with Cissy in that exciting way. But then a burst of shame befell me because of the doubt I held about her innocence, albeit meager doubt. I wanted her, wanted us to be together with trust and respect and all the things that come with love. I needed to see her, needed to talk, to touch, and to understand her.

...

Next morning, the participants of the Nancy venture had aching heads and poor memories, to no one's surprise. It was unfortunate, for the major ordered practice runs. Although raining, I looked up to the skies and saw clearing patches. It was time to familiarize ourselves with outgoing and incoming landmarks surrounding Ochey.

Sam peeked out from behind the propeller of our Fee, breaking into a boyish grin as Wellsey and I approached. "How's your head this morning, Hardknocks?"

His grin grew wider while his chest, under loose coveralls, seemed to expand with pride. "Fine, just fine. Didn't drink so much. You know it affects your, ah, shall we say accomplishments?"

"You are a naughty one, Hardknocks," said Wellsey, "but a good air mechanic. Our baby in tip-top shape for our run today?"

We traveled east at thirty-five hundred feet for about twenty miles until Luneville, eight miles from the lines. We saw the sadness of that devastated town, as it had been shelled for three straight years, the spire standing before a burned-out church and châteaux in the countryside reduced to rubble. I then realized that Pozieres and Thiepval must have looked the same from the air while I was fighting on the ground a year before at the Somme.

I scribbled notes, documenting landscape and landmarks, how to distinguish the Moselle River from its tributary, the Meurthe, and where the distinct chalk lines of the zig-zag trenches demarked the lines, which mountain peaks belonged to each village, and how to identify the Toul cathedral for the return to Ochey.

It was refreshing to fly during the day, a totally different perspective than at night. While locating silver ribbons of river and dark blobs of wood presented a clandestine element to our night sorties, seeing the farmland and mountains in the light of day was a thrill. After an easy landing, our Fee was pushed back into its hangar while we made our way to the mess.

Our days were filled with similar practice runs and reviewing bombing targets. The task was to delay, destroy, and interrupt the flow of German resources from the Alsace-Lorraine area. Its Saar Valley was the industrial and transport center of a massive coal basin that provided the Germans with much-needed iron and steel products. Direct attacks on the Völklingen Steelworks along with the destruction of trains, junctions, and sidings between Falkenberg and Saarbrücken would support our troops in the northern battlefields. The trouble was the weather, which continued to hamper our ability to fly at night.

During the last few days of October, the weather finally cleared. I hadn't expected that I would welcome the change as much as I did, and I looked forward to our anticipated sortie. Perhaps it was the comfort of having learned the aeroplane's complexities or my hardened experience after many near misses, but I became emboldened. For the first night's return to the skies, 16 Squadron, with its giant Handley Pages, were assigned the Burbach works in Saarbrücken, while 100 Squadron's FE2bs were to attack railways in the nearby Rhine and Lorraine regions.

Hardy stood behind our Fee. With switches off, he swung the propeller to prime the engine. With switches on, the Beardmore roared to life. That feeling always put a jab in my stomach and a lump in my throat as adrenaline coursed through my body. I adjusted my position on the floor of the nacelle as the tower gave the green light. Taxiing to the flare path T, we spun around 180 degrees and throttled into the pitch-black sky, climbing into a night filled with stars. It felt good to be back doing our job after such frustrating weather delays.

The silver line of the Moselle four thousand feet below looked peaceful. It was a fleeting vision as we journeyed once again to pour devastation onto an enemy we had never seen and would never see up close; we just knew he was the enemy.

I triggered our Very pistol as we passed C Lighthouse at Nancy, climbing to eight thousand feet. Farmland and hills dotted the ground below, the dark blotches of woodlands becoming more prevalent. Kneeling against the slipstream while peering over the side, I thought how different from the Somme it would be to wage a ground war on that forested, mountainous terrain. Wellsey brought my thoughts back inside the aeroplane with a tap on the shoulder and a baritone voice.

"Flashes of light ahead, Bobby. What do you make of it?"

"Been periodic for a few minutes now. I reckon it's the Burbach Steelworks."

"*Ja*, that's 216's work, old man. We'll save ours for the darkness of Saarbrücken Station."

In time I knelt taller. Turning to Frank, I bellowed, "Approaching. In five minutes we drop to four thousand. Follow Drummond and Ace. I saw their wing lights flickering through broken cloud; they're descending now."

The glide a few miles out of Saarbrücken began with that familiar silence but grew to a pitching whine as gusts of wind pushed us forward in an erratic manner, making the Fee rock back and forth. Abandoning a surprise approach, Wellsey fired up the Beardmore for better control as we leveled out at twelve hundred feet. I stood up and fired bursts from my Lewis when the Saarbrücken searchlights caught us in their crosshairs.

Dodging puffs of Archie and ground machine-gun fire, we surged in for the kill. I pulled up the middle bomb rack lever, but it didn't respond. It wouldn't budge, wouldn't release, the cable cutting into the webbing between my ungloved fingers. With frustration building, we raced over the target.

Wellsey had urgency screaming out in his voice. "Drop the pills, Bob, drop the fucking bombs!"

I yanked up on the lever and released it quickly in an attempt to loosen the bomb spring, irked that I could visualize but not see it below the nacelle, willing it to release. I felt it give a little but not release as I yanked up on it again. I realized I was perspiring in spite of the cold, feeling the sweat roll down from under my leather helmet. With no support, nothing to hold on to, I grabbed the lever with both hands, pulling up again and again as the cable grew slippery with my blood. Finally, the spring underneath moved, and I felt the missile break loose of the rack for its journey down to the enemy. But I knew it was too late. We had missed our mark.

"Damn!" I yelled. "Wasted. Totally fucking wasted."

"Ah-ah, no time for that; we still have work to do with those Coopers."

That *ah-ah* made me feel silly, as if my grandma had just scolded me, but he was right. "Just so, but it would be foolish to go back on that station. Too hot and too angry now."

"Understood."

"I say we swing around and follow the Saarbrücken line back toward Falkenberg where there's bound to be opportunity lurking!" It was satisfying that, although this was new territory, I had managed to memorize and recognize key landmarks.

I became aware of a squishy feeling as I replaced my gloves and calmed down after that rush of energy, realizing that my frustrated method of releasing the bomb lever could very well have resulted in a totally different and devastating outcome. If my hands had suddenly slipped when I violently yanked on the release, it could have resulted in me flailing through the dark sky to face certain death. It was not a courageous action; it was stupid, and I was lucky.

I shouted as we headed westward, "This wind is turning into a gale. Do we have ample petrol?"

Wellsey nodded. "Yes, and the going will be slow."

"All right, I'll guide us along the rail lines as best I can. We need to drop the Coopers before too long. I'm not happy to land with them attached."

Wellsey took his hand off the controls, offering a gloved thumbs-up. "Check, old man. You find the target, then let's get home."

We maintained low altitude in the building storm, keeping below the cloud bank that was obscuring the previously clear sky. I scanned the ground, watching the tracks as their steel periodically reflected random light. As a blade of moonlight broke through parting clouds, I saw movement ahead and a flash of brightness. My mind struggled to process what I saw in the brief moment.

I stood up off my knees and turned to yell over the windscreen, "Ahead! I'm sure that's a train!"

He shook his head. "Nothing from here, Bobby. Nothing I see on the tracks."

"Yes, for an instant it flared red. Must have opened its furnace door. Lower, Wellsey, drop us down. It's down there and won't hear us coming from behind!" We dropped lower, and, in time, there it was. We soared out of the blackness onto the rear of a long cargo train. These were the opportunities our major had spoken of. Redemption for tonight's missed opportunity.

At five hundred feet we slowed to pace the train, the wind acting as a brake. With hands on both release levers, I waited patiently, the wetness gone as the blood had absorbed into my gloves. *Not too quick. We have one chance, must hold back.* We crept up on its back, seeking its vulnerable neck, the rear of the locomotive and its fuel car. *Patience.*

Now! I pulled each lever once, twice, and again until the Coopers dove onto the back of that iron horse. I had a good feeling. I knew we had struck since the explosion was louder than our bombs. Wellsey acted quickly, rising up away from the impact as I signaled for us to go around to view our attack, aware of the danger of retaliation but too curious not to.

I released a parachute flare to light up the area, and there it was—the train hissed as steam escaped its burning corpse, lying there with its front completely destroyed. I stood up, grasping the Lewis with both hands, awaiting machine-gun hate that would surely come up if we overstayed our visit. But none came.

I turned to face my pilot for an instant. "Wellsey, what a team! Let's beat it back to safety, fight these winds." He raised his right thumb in agreement and took us home.

We pulled ourselves out of our wet Sidcots. I headed to the infirmary, where the nursing sister bandaged my hands, shaking her head in wonderment at how I'd made such a mess in the folds between my fingers. I had elevated expectations as I headed to the mess to meet up with Wellsey and to kibitz with the others.

I met a somber tone. Eerily the same as our last sortie out of Trezennes, this first out of Ochey ended with a cloud over our heads. Flyers were again missing, this time four. Archibald, Archie, who had experienced a forced landing just back in September. Greenslade, poor Greenie. Tonight was his first sortie since engine failure near Trezennes. Would luck hold again for these two flyers, or had they realized their ultimate fate?

And then there was Jones, our new lieutenant on his maiden sortie, now missing. As was his observer, Godard, who had just returned from extended leave since August. Surely not all four of our fine squadron had gone west tonight?

...

16 October, 1917

My Dearest Bob,

Oh, how I fretted when I didn't hear from you, but today I received your last three letters all at once. I now understand that your squadron moved to a place called Ochey and the mails got delayed. I think it was a good idea for the RFC to acknowledge that since the enemy knows of our squadron locations, our civilians should as well. I attended the local library to look at a map of France, and it was exciting to be able to see where you are. Well, at least on a piece of paper.

I trust you are fit, my dear, as fit as can be expected in war conditions. You keep up a brave front in your letters, but I do worry for you because of the responsibilities you must endure. And yes, I, too, wish to see you as soon as possible! I have taken little leave lately in the expectation that I will have banked time to spend with you when that does happen.

Life at the factory is bearable. I covet my driver's position even when a few women scorn me. Some accuse me of using my femininity to savvy favors. Well, they are wrong and are typically the same women who threaten to strike over poor wages and who cause trouble by getting in arguments at the pub. I don't think it fair that women are paid only half that of men either, but striking is not the answer. Do they not think about how the much-needed bombs are to be made, about loyalty to our soldiers?

No, I prefer to hold my head high and work well, which adds cash to my pay packet. "Performance bonus" they call it. Well, I'm not at all sure what I will do when this dreadful war is over and I return to London, but at least I have been able to sock away some savings and have acquired some very useful skills. Have you thought recently about what you will do after the war, Bob? Return to Canada, I suppose.

Oh, an exciting activity happening here at Chilwell and at some other munition factories is the formation of a women's football team. And yes, I am trying out for a position! It's so thrilling and makes twelve-hour work days more bearable. As you can imagine, there are many more girls trying out than positions, so I work hard at it. They say there are enough teams to perhaps form a league, and there is also talk of a Munitionette Cup.

Well, my darling, I reluctantly must go, but I look forward to your next letter. And do keep working for leave. I hunger to see you.

Cissy

Chapter 36

October 1917

The black cloud of anxiety that cloaked the officers' mess reflected the rain clouds that hung over the aerodrome. Losing four colleagues in one evening was devastating, and it showed in the faces of the flyers. I felt an urge to get out for a walk. Perhaps the wind and rain echoed my mood in the same manner that sunshine would entice a cheerful stroll. I gathered Wellsey.

"I am having trouble, Wellsey. With my feelings, I mean. Fear for our lost boys makes me obsess about our fate. Over and over I think, what if it was me and you? It seems cowardly to put my worry ahead of our missing."

"I'm not an expert on feelings, but I know when I am in the presence of a coward. You are not a coward."

"How do you know? How can you tell? Do you have these thoughts as well?"

"Seems not as deep as you, old man, not so much. But a coward does not move willingly into genuine risk, does not accept the real possibility of being killed. You do, we both do. We do that every night we are up there flying over enemy lands."

I kicked a pebble along the field. "I see. I understand that, but my emotions sometimes trump reason, clouding my thoughts, making me crazy with fear, with—oh, I don't know."

We walked on. "If we were cowards," said Wellsey, "we would not line up our Fee toward the enemy, fight off inner demons and stomach cramps to dive at their throats as we did last night on the back of that train. That, old boy, is not cowardice."

"Hmmm."

Frank grabbed my arm, stopping our stroll for a moment. "You are a precision machine yourself, operating that Lewis and lining up those bombs, yanking the hell out of the bomb lever at the precise moment, don't you see that?"

I looked at him, blessed to have his perspective. "Yes, I do keep focused under stress, on what needs to be done without thinking consciously about it. Even as a little boy, I would think ahead, kind of an instinct about how not to fail."

We turned back in the direction of the mess. "That's your survival technique. We all act differently, yet we get things done in the manner that we are comfortable with and in support of each other. That is the courage which creates success. Never doubt that, for doubt will blind you to courage."

"Thank you, Frank. I guess I just needed to be reminded." He shoved me into a massive rain puddle as he casually strolled around it, and with me now sporting flooded flight boots, we made our way back to the mess in a much-lighter mood than when we left.

"Where have you two sweethearts been, eh?" Major Christie seemed in a cheerful mood given the loss of four men.

"Taking a breath or two of the French air," said Wellsey as he smiled.

"I have news of our missing flyers, which I've been explaining to the others here."

"Oh, what say, sir?"

"All have been accounted for. Jones and Godard force landed near Saint-Avold, straight into enemy-held territory. Taken as POWs, I'm afraid."

"But they're alive and well, sir?" I asked.

The Swiss Red Cross confirmed that Jones walked away from the crash, but Godard was reported injured, now in the hands of the Germans. Archie and Greenslade were hit west of Saarbrücken, forced down and immediately surrendered to the Hun. As Christie spoke, I thought about the prospect of being confronted by hostile Germans on the return from a bomb attack on their facilities, about how they would react knowing that some of their brothers would have just been hurt or killed. I silently wished them well, as prison camp would test them to the extreme.

...

25 October, 1917

My Dear Cissy,

How are you, my darling? I received your letter in which you sound full of life, full of energy. I think that perhaps working in a munitions factory is not really your life's desire, but as it supports the cause and gives you a sense of accomplishment, then I am so happy for you. But I know you are destined for bigger accomplishments. I feel poorly for you with having to deal with others' jealousies, so try to ignore them and surround yourself with those who bring you affection.

My day is brightest when I receive your heartwarming letters. Thank you for being such a devoted and caring friend. It sounds like you are having a bit of fun pursuing football in your spare time. That is exciting, and I have fun imagining you in football boots and trousers, when you were in heels and lace the last time we met!

My family write regularly, so I am able to keep up with news from Canada. Things are well for them, although they are subject to food and goods rationing as much as you are in England. They, too, have many women working in factories for the war cause, although my sisters are fully employed in their own pursuits, which they sought before the war broke out. The Pitman women are strong ones! You would get along swell.

I remain devoted to securing leave, as I desperately wish to see you, yet the weeks go by without its granting. Thank you for thinking ahead to bank a few days' leave as they will be precious. I sense my time will come in due course since the weather for flying is becoming seasonally poor. I do trust the brass will see to it to allow us to stand down a bit for the coming winter.

Until then,
Bob

...

Before posting it the next morning, I read and reread my letter, as I did not wish to sound too determined. I wanted Cissy to know of my need to see her, to speak with her, but at the same time I did not want to portray a sense of urgency. I remained conflicted between my growing love for her and concern over betrayal. I again felt ashamed to even think she would lie to me, yet my emotions continued to drive my need to hear her tell me she was innocent. There was nothing my intellect could do to overcome that emotionally driven feeling, even though I knew all possible reason pointed to innocence. And I knew that if I sounded or behaved accusingly, I could destroy our relationship and lose what I really felt: love.

I heard a loud yawn behind me. "Ah, Pitman," said Wellsey, "why is that electric light radiating across the room?"

I turned in my seat. "Good morning, Frank. Not very often I greet the morning before you, eh?"

He sat up. "What the devil are you doing hunched over like that?"

"Finishing some paperwork."

Swinging his legs off the bed, Wellsey chuckled. "Aha, letters to your girl are now just paperwork, old man?"

"Just an expression. You ready for some grub?"

The mess was busy as flyers awoke early, there being no prior night sorties. Discussions were lively due to the announcement of a new ground attack near Passchendaele, where Canadians relieved the exhausted Anzac Corps. The push was to gain higher observation positions and win drier land in preparation for the coming winter.

Listening to the chatter again took me back to thoughts of a rain-drenched, cold and miserable infantry knee-deep in mud, waiting for the whistle to send them over the top directly into the aim of the Hun's deadly machine guns. How many men—boys, mostly—would give up their lives, lose limbs, sight, or their mental well-being in order to gain a few feet of better positioning, ready for more slaughter in the springtime? The horror of it—the lives lost, the distraught families, the waste—was deplorable.

Feeling restless, I withdrew from the table to walk about the mess, thinking it unfortunate the rain kept us indoors. Taking pleasant pulls on my pipe, I moved slowly around the adjacent reading room, glancing at the various front pages posted across the wall. With so many flyers receiving newspapers from their home countries across the world, we always had an interesting display. I passed by the ragged page that was ripped from a *Punch* magazine when something caught my eye. I retraced my step and focused on "Take up our quarrel with the foe, To you from failing hands we throw, The torch . . . ," reading it with new reflection.

The late Canadian military doctor Major John McCrae beseeched us, ordered us through his burial service poem "In Flanders Fields," to continue our fight for freedom even with individual sacrifice. Taking a contemplative draw from my pipe, I stared at the quote, realizing it was for me a sign that, although there was more death to come, victory was imaginable.

"Ah, there you are, Bobby. I guess you heard?" Wellsey asked as he entered the room.

I turned away from my reflections. "No, I stepped away."

"Well, no surprise that we are not flying again tonight. At this rate we won't see many sorties before the end of the year, I'd say."

"You may be correct. We may be stuck for a while."

"Or granted leave, old man, or granted leave."

We remained grounded but kept on alert through to the last day of the month, which we were to find out was indeed the squadron's last sortie of the year. Wellsey and I joined nine other aircraft to lay down bombs on the Völklingen Steelworks just over the French-German border near Saarbrücken. The factory was brightly illuminated from some distance, presumably shedding caution after many attack-free nights. One after another we swooped down in the customary silence, pounding their infrastructure right through their belated reactionary blackout.

I decided to concentrate on the powerhouse, where we dropped our 230-pounder. Smoke and machine-gun fire prevented a clear observation of the results, but we were sure the enemy's electrical power was disrupted. Swinging west for the return, we saw a stark difference from our incoming flight: the whole Saar Basin was now in blackness, which confirmed the Hun had developed an emergency communication system, perhaps born from fear-filled defensiveness.

While we were ordered to remain on alert for possible bombing opportunities through November, the month was quiet, as the four-month battle at Passchendaele had mopped up for the winter stalemate. Movement of German troops and transport had quietened down as a result. For most of 1917, the Germans had avoided attacking heavily defended British and French aerodromes, but that changed. In the middle weeks of November, the *Luftstreitkrafte* targeted our aerodromes, hitting Ochey on three occasions. When the lighthouse alerted us to their approach, we would take refuge in the nearby woods. There was little damage and no lost aircraft, but the terror effect was profound.

Part III

Chapter 37

December 1917

In spite of bitterly cold Channel winds, I was content to stand at the prow of the ship overlooking our progress toward the great white cliffs rising vertically from the blue waters. I had been entertained during the afternoon watching destroyers circling our troop ship, now silhouettes against the lights of Calais behind us that twinkled in the late-afternoon dusk. From Dover I would take the train into London to lodge with Mrs. Clarke for a couple of days until Cissy's leave commenced. Her supervisor was most gracious in allowing her a few days' family leave on top of her banked days, even though I was not at all the brother she said was visiting through to late January!

The wind whipped at my greatcoat as I thought about what was to come, nervous but looking forward to a harmonious reunion. I knew there would be emotion; there had to be considering our history. Her letters were so caring, so delicate, and so full of energy that I felt things would go smoothly. I just needed to get that gnawing question behind me.

Darkness fell as I reluctantly made my way inside the ship, loathing the idea of sharing the stateroom with three other officers. Not because I did not like them—I had exchanged polite introductions when I dropped off my bag—but rather dreading the inevitable swapping of war stories. I knew I had to return at some point, even if to offer a perfunctory good night before retiring. But not quite yet.

I packed my pipe as the bartender quietly placed a whiskey on the table. I nodded a thank you as I glanced at the front page of *The Telegraph*, which offered a detailed analysis of the Passchendaele battle with its recent two hundred thousand British and Commonwealth casualties. The packed page also contained various articles about Lenin's withdrawal from the war and his freeing up of much-needed resources to feed and control the Russian people. A good omen was the increased support of the Americans, finally declaring war on Austria.

Sipping a second whiskey and well into the newspaper, I turned to a long article by a British war correspondent who was traveling through the Western Front. In addition to the reference to the German bombings of our aerodromes in November and the continued air attacks on London, the chap did a good job at describing the nature of the war to this point. While his editors closely censored what could be printed in the British newspapers, I was struck with the level of detail printed about the comparative difficulties in prosecuting the war at both the Somme in 1916 and Passchendaele a year later. Both battles were extensive in duration, horror, and casualties.

As the ship gently bumped the dock in the early hours, I was already up and dressed, bidding my bunkmates *adieu*. With my duffel bag over my shoulder, I stepped lively through the dimly lit deck to the gangway.

...

Mrs. Clarke was her usual gracious self, ensuring I was comfortable and well fed, and expressing curiosity at my being a flyer. I supposed she had tales to tell among her post office colleagues. After a few days, I left for my scheduled trip to Chilwell, telling Mrs. Clarke a white lie about visiting a friend in the Midlands. Well, that was not completely untrue.

I was pensive during the long train ride with thoughts wavering between ambiguous doubt and expectant joy. So many questions flashed through my mind, yet Cissy's letters were clear about her excitement of seeing me. What if I looked different to her with my added muscle weight? What if seeing me caused anxiety, even though I could feel the excitement in her words? What if her new friends doubted my presence even though she told me they were happy for her?

In the end, joy won out as I stepped down from the train at Beeston Station, buzzing with anticipation. I walked the length of the platform with a spring in my step that did not reflect the dreary winter day. I stopped momentarily to read the directional signposts offering a choice between the River Trent, the University of Nottingham, or the High Road. A makeshift sign indicating the direction of the National Filling Factory No. 6 was clumsily attached to the High Road posting. I supposed anyone with business there would know its direction. A gloved hand tenderly touched my right arm. "Looking for directions, officer?"

Her voice, her melodious whisper! Breaking into a mile-wide grin, I twisted my head before turning and in so doing abruptly pushed her off balance. As she teetered, I dropped my duffel bag and caught her around the waist, drawing her so close I could smell the sweet scent of roses. "Oh, Cissy! Darling, it has been so long!"

We hugged and closely held each other, both breathing heavily while nuzzling one another's necks. "Is that all the welcome you are capable of, Lieutenant Pitman?" Cissy placed both hands to the back of my head and drew me in to a kiss, a long, sweet, and savory kiss. Releasing me and pulling back to catch her breath, she said, "That's better!"

At that moment, I lost all concern about questions of innocence and doubt and fear and misgivings. I just wanted to hold her. I could feel tears forming in the creases of my eyes, thinking about the excitement we had shared and the grief we had endured. Yet here she was!

I slung my duffel bag over my left shoulder while my right arm wrapped her in close as we strolled the short distance to the Chequers Inn on High Street. We kibitzed about her fashionable clothes, looking like a London model up here in the middle part of the country among thousands of munitionettes and other arms workers. Her felt French beret made her look like an artist, while her heeled shoes defied any sort of winter practicality. Cissy exuded a femininity that raised my heart rate to a pounding level.

Stepping inside my room, we laughed like naughty juveniles at the innkeeper's expression when I had registered as a single. Cissy and I could indeed be taken for siblings, but his mischievous wink let me quietly know he understood the situation. It seemed that in some circles Victorian morals had thankfully collapsed, perhaps one small positive of an otherwise brutal war.

I took Cissy's coat, laid it at the end of the bed, and stood back to admire her gorgeous dress as she twirled to show it off. With no need for words, no need to talk, we embraced with a lingering entwining of bodies that encapsulated our deep feelings as we hungered for each other. Our kisses were long and deep, then short and light, touching forehead, eyes, lips, cheeks, and neck. There was so much to catch up with, so much time lost to this war. We fell back onto the bed.

"Bobby, wait, please wait a moment." As she made her way across the room seeking her handbag, my eyes explored her shapely shoulders and back, now exposed by the lowered zipper of her dress. I could see her muscles through her chemise. How fit she had become.

Returning to lie beside me, Cissy noticed what my hand now held in front of her and giggled. After leaning over to kiss me, she pulled back to show me that in her hand was the same: a condom. "Great minds think alike," I snickered. "And I think we are in good hands. If the Germans only knew that we use their superbly fabricated brand of protection!"

It was late in the afternoon when we woke to the warmth of the sun. Its rays had burst through the window as it set on the horizon just below the cloud bank that had threatened rain all day. What a pleasant way to awake!

...

The next evening we sat down to dinner in a quaint restaurant on High Street after a full day of walking along the banks of the River Trent up to the Wilford Suspension Bridge, then over to the University of Nottingham. Cissy had asked me whether I thought she might one day qualify to attend university, and I said I felt sure of it, especially since so many barriers were breaking down and providing increased opportunities for women.

I had been indecisive all day about when to broach the subject. I just had to get it behind me, and with a pre-dinner drink in hand, I stammered, "Cissy, I'd like to speak to you about something. Won't take but a moment."

"Of course. We've talked about many things, yet there are many more thoughts to share."

I was nervous, but knew I had to remain calm and not speak matter-of-factly with just a soothing tone. I knew if I did this wrong, things could end badly. "It's about our encounter and the disease. I'd like to talk about it, to clear the air, so to speak." Her cheeks flushed as she became instantly and visibly upset. I worried I had done the wrong thing, perhaps chosen the wrong time or the wrong place, allowing anxiety to muddle my intent.

Cissy's look portrayed a nasty defensiveness. "What is there to speak of, Bob? I was shocked to have those health police come to Silvertown, the ones you sent to see me and who escorted me from my dormitory."

"Cissy, I—"

She sat up dead straight. "I'm over that now, and I thought you were; otherwise, why are we here? All those letters from you, all those pleasant—"

"Don't you think that we need to speak of the issue to ensure there are no misunderstandings? Why, already there seems to be one with you thinking I sent the health authorities. I didn't."

Cissy leaned into the table, affecting a vicious whisper through clenched teeth. "How did they know it was me? How did they know where to find me?"

Being completely distraught, I could have cried, but I needed to resolve what I had started. "Cissy, please. I got very ill, hospitalized. It is natural they would ask questions—"

She retorted, "Fine, you had to answer their questions. Could you not have let me know?"

I held my hands out and shrugged defensively. "No, that was not possible since I didn't know what was happening until I was in the Le Havre hospital. I was under orders not to contact you. But even if I wanted to, there was no telephone, no way to reach you." I tried hard to keep my voice calm, feeling increasingly helpless and wishing I had not asked the question. "There was no way to reach you, darling. Surely you can see that?"

Cissy remained defiant, angry that I had questioned her honesty. "I see that, but I also see there is no need to open this painful door again. Do you not think I went through the same hell, the same investigation about how this could happen?"

"That's just it, that's what I need—well, would like to know." I knew I was sounding desperate. "Were you aware of having—"

Cissy's tone didn't yield. "Having the disease before I slept with you?"

I looked around the restaurant, aware that others were turning their heads. "Shhh . . . please lower your voice lest we attract attention."

"Is that it? You have a need to question me, and you choose to do it in a public place, where you tell me to lower my voice. Take me to my dorm."

"Oh, Cissy, that's the last thing I intended. I didn't mean to—"

"Now!"

We walked in silence, neither of us even looking at each other. I tried to take her hand, but she angrily pulled it away. We arrived at the dormitory gate, where a few of her friends greeted her with hellos and giggles as they looked at me. Fighting back tears, she turned on her heel and walked away.

Most of the night I lay awake questioning my actions, asking myself if her anger and protest was born of pure innocence or if she was hiding a truth that she did not want to expose. No, I had already decided that she was innocent; she showed that in her reaction. It's just that I wanted her to say that to me. Why was I so needy that I had to hear Cissy's answer instead of relying on trust? I had pushed her faith in me to its limit.

The next morning, I decided to remain at the Chequers Inn through my paid-up time, holding on to hope that Cissy would want to mend things. I knew she wasn't working, as she was on leave. I went for a long walk, keeping a keen eye open in the event, the hope, that I would bump into her. As I dropped a note at the guard hut, I again questioned myself: Why could I not have just accepted Cissy's bold, outgoing self, who was obviously able to put things behind her whether or not it was good or bad? Why did I ache with a need for certainty? Why could I not just accept her affection as the truth? Even if she had made a mistake, she clearly loved me.

On the second morning after that terrible dinner, the innkeeper strolled into the bar to hand me an envelope addressed in Cissy's handwriting, grinning as he did. I would have punched him in the nose if he'd made a comment about my sister. Instead, I let him leave in peace as I turned the envelope over. I didn't care that it had obviously been steamed open and resealed.

Bob,

Received your note. I would like to meet, to talk. As my dorm is not suitable, I will arrive at your lodging at eleven this morning. If this is not acceptable, please advise innkeeper.

Cissy.

It was abrupt, but it was a message I was relieved to receive. I finished my breakfast, thinking about how she knew I was still there, but it didn't matter. Of course I would accept her proposal.

...

She arrived at eleven sharp. With an austere look, she turned her cheek when I leaned in to kiss her. I led her past the innkeeper, who was absorbed in the *Nottingham Daily Express*, a distraction I appreciated. In my room, I took Cissy's coat and was amazed to see her attired in a worker's uniform that was both functional and trendy. Her trig knee-buttoned trousers and skirted blouse laced at the front wouldn't attract attention on the factory floor, but on Cissy and in my room, it was a statement of strength. Her beret and high laced boots added a level of dominance, which could be viewed as sensual. As I knew her intention was far from that, I gathered the strength to busy myself with draping her coat over the footboard.

I knew my voice held a nervous tone when I spoke. "Cissy, I—"

"No, Bob, I'd like to speak first," warned Cissy. I nodded. "I believe what you said to me was accusatory and unnecessary." She held up her hand to silence my impulsive interruption. "I suffered as much as you, perhaps more if you consider the unfair treatment of women. Judgements such as *whore* and *loose* and *tramp*, the whispering among the hospital staff... I could go on."

I felt terrible for the injustice she had experienced. I held back tears. "I'm so sorry."

"I lay with you that day because I cared for you. You who were traveling back to war and might never lie with another. Oh no, it was not sympathy—it was a blossoming love that I felt. I am an honest woman with integrity, and I would never have knowingly compromised you."

I felt a wave of relief sweep over me, which I attempted to hide as I did not want to give the impression that, because I now had my answer, all was good. I knew she had her own emotional needs and that I had hurt her with my inept question. I felt shaky, felt I could lose her, but also knew I needed the strength to rekindle our relationship, reconquer her love.

Cissy maintained her dominant stance, looking sternly into my eyes. "You questioned my activity prior to meeting you, Bob, and I will tell you. There was an army private who worked at Silvertown alongside me. He had lost a leg in the Battle of Loos but still wanted to serve his country, so he came to work at the arms factory. We became close friends, and one thing led to another late one night in the ladies' dormitory. He shouldn't have been there, and I had no intention—"

I moved forward, my hands outstretched to embrace her.

"No, Bob. Please hear me out."

Cissy's speech became rapid as she unleashed years' worth of anxiety and grief. The trust she sought but never quite received from her family employer, the growing up in foster care, and the uncertainty about from where her next meal would come. It all tumbled out. Her ability to function well, to take advantage of the rapidly changing world, was a testament to the inner strength she had developed over those years, that and her acumen. She broke into tears. I held her while she sobbed, not letting go until long after my shoulder was soaked.

"I want you to think I'm a good person, to deserve the respect you offered me." After a sob escaped from her stomach, a single teardrop rolled down her cheek that she wiped clear. "So many men had only one thing on their mind, but you, you were gentle, never persistent."

"I was stupid in my rush to ask questions to satisfy my own selfish needs. I never intended to push you away, to hurt you."

Between sobs, Cissy spoke into my shoulder with muffled words. "I sat in my dorm for a full day, thinking that I had lost you. It took all the courage I had to write that note and deliver it in the early hours. Oooh, and to hand it to that creepy innkeeper—"

She looked at me through swollen, bleary eyes at my twinge of smile in response to that last comment. It opened the way for both of us to laugh. We continued our embrace and made fun of the innkeeper, agreeing that, although ghoulish, he was simply lonely and harmless. It was such benign conversation that provided the moment to break free of the sadness.

We leaned back to look at each other, still locked at the hips. Passion and desire rose quickly as our breathing hastened. Moving in to kiss her, I felt our hearts beating in rhythm. We tumbled onto the bed, I on top of her, locked in a kiss that seemed to last a lifetime. I unlaced her blouse, and she helped me raise it over her head, followed by her chemise, as she helped me from my buttoned shirt. More kissing, more caressing, hands exploring, leaving no chance of neglecting any area of her soft skin.

When it came to her bottoms, I was at a loss and paused in wonderment. Cissy broke into laughter as she sat up, her naughtiness expressed by just leaning back on her hands, leaving me with the responsibility to figure out how to liberate her from those trousers. "What's the matter, Lieutenant? Can't breach the target?"

I so adored her and her natural mannerisms. I watched as she eventually stood up to unlace her boots and unbutton her trousers, staring in awe at her perfect form. I thought I would burst.

Lovemaking is special between two caring souls, but especially intense after stress and anger gives way to passion. I believe we wrote a book that afternoon, a caring, sensual book that only she and I knew how to read, a memory to last forever.

...

By 22 December, Cissy's leave was over and she had to return to work. While that was disappointing, we had done so much in so few days and had grown even closer. We knew separation would be difficult, and we were careful not to make promises in case circumstances forced us to break them. But I had leave until 21 January and was determined to spend as much time with Cissy as her work circumstances allowed. As we stood on the platform at Beeston waiting for the London train, we both realized we had become secure in our relationship.

"When we were talking the other day, there in my room when we got things sorted, you said something that I am curious about."

Cissy had that mischievous look about her, as if she knew exactly what I was about to say. "Yes, Bobby?"

I shifted nervously. "Well, when you were explaining why you lay with me the first time, you said it was because you cared for me . . ."

She held my stare, grinning at my awkwardness. "Yes?"

"Well, you also talked about a blossoming love."

"Yes?"

"I just wanted to say, um, just wanted to leave you with a thought before I board, well um, I'd like to say . . . I love you, Cissy."

Her gloved fist slammed into my left chest, reverberating at once through my greatcoat, my tunic, and my shirt. "Bob, you fool! How long was it going to take to tell me how you feel?"

I looked into her beautiful blue eyes and saw the softness of her soul. "I love you, Cissy."

"And I love you."

Chapter 38

25 December, 1917

"Bob, come in! Merry Christmas!"

"And Merry Christmas to you, Daisy." I grinned at Stanley clutching his mother's dress, half hidden behind the pleats. "And hello, young man. Merry Christmas."

"Is that for me?" asked Stanley.

Daisy leaned over, pointing a scolding forefinger. "Stanley, that's not polite!"

Stanley wrenched his eyes away from the wrapped present and looked at the floor. "Yes, Mummy."

I knelt to present the small gift. "Go ahead, Stanley. This is for you." I hoped that an introductory Meccano set would be of interest to a seven-year-old.

With the smell of dinner in the background, I held Daisy's shoulders as I gave her a kiss on both cheeks. She embraced me and said how lovely it was to be able to get together for Christmas dinner when so many other families were without their sons or husbands.

I wondered whom Daisy was entertaining for her dinner; she was known for her generosity. She turned with a wide smile after hanging my coat in the front hall.

"Come through to the family room. I've someone for you to see."

We turned the corner, and my mouth gaped. I looked at one, then the other and back again. My body froze, as I wasn't sure which way to move.

"Go ahead, Bob, give your Cissy a hug," said a beaming Eric. "Daisy told me all I need to know about you two. I can wait."

I almost ran across the floor of the small room, tears welling up as I embraced her. After a few unabashed moments, we released as Cissy urged me over to Eric. I took his hand, then pulled him to me for another embrace, different, of course, from the one I had given Cissy. "Eric, I am surprised, so pleasantly surprised, to see you here at your home."

"On home leave, Bob. Invalided with wounds. Afraid I lost a leg at Langemarck back in August. Oh, I'm doing all right. I'm just so happy my discharge from Le Havre was in time to be home for Christmas!" He hobbled across the room and back, showing that his wooden leg allowed ample mobility. "And I'm glad to be here with my Daisy and my Stanley, Bob. Damn happy!"

"I'm sorry, Eric. I admire your pluck. I know things could have been worse."

"And indeed they are for many others, both men and their families. Now go and catch up with your girl. Daisy and I have a few things to do in the kitchen."

Fussing with my cap between my thumb and forefinger, I turned to Cissy just as she was about to speak. "Well, Lieutenant, do I have to ask for a kiss hello?" Snapped out of my fog of disbelief, I embraced her tightly. "Whoa, fella! I need to breathe."

I pretended to pout as if I were a scolded schoolboy. "Oh, sorry. I'm excited to see you, and puzzled."

"It's simple: the factory is closed for Christmas Day in a gesture of compassion by the Ordnance Board. On Daisy's invite, I caught the train this afternoon and, well, here I am."

I again squeezed her hard. "For how long are you here, darling?"

"First train back in the morning, Bobby. My supervisor was not pleased when I said I would arrive at noon. Of course, I received his scolding, 'only because it's Christmas.'"

We laughed as I stood back to look at her, never a disappointing sight. An ankle-length red dress wrapped across her chest in a bow before falling in two layers, a black fringe made up the shorter front, and all was complemented by a solid rose-colored chemise. Its sheer full-length sleeves were also fringed in black. A thin fabric headband and matching shawl, both in black, were offset by very light brown shoes. "Cissy, you are a sight—such an adorable, beautiful sight. How do you manage such fashion at these times?"

"I make my clothes."

I looked at her in disbelief. "You make—"

"Yes. Butterick posts me the pattern, and Mrs. Crawley at the dressmaker's is able to bring in fabrics of many choices. For the parts that I cannot finish by hand, she allows me to use her Singer."

Holding her left hand, I stood back to again admire her dress. "You look wonderful, my darling."

Eric hobbled around the corner. "Dinner is served, you two."

We said grace, and I extended my apologies for Mrs. Clarke's absence, as she had prior arrangements with a neighboring family. Dinner was grand, especially when food was severely rationed. Daisy winked when I inquired as to her source. The highly animated chat allowed us rare moments of levity, but as expected, the conversation eventually returned to the war. Our final toast over a wonderful Christmas trifle was the wish that 1918 would see an armistice.

Although it was late, Cissy accompanied me to my Finsbury train before she retired. Her morning would come early, as she had to rise at four to be organized for her Beeston train. We strolled slowly in an attempt to delay our inevitable separation, basking in thought about our few stolen hours together. Standing on the platform, we embraced. I promised to again return to Chilwell before my leave was up, even though Cissy's had run out. The inevitable whistle forced us apart. From the window, I waved my white hanky as Cissy turned to leave. As we chugged forward, I glanced Eric leaning on a walking cane just outside the station gate. The gentleman had arrived to escort the lady home. Cissy was sure to give him hell.

Chapter 39

January 1918

"Are you sure this is what you want, Wellsey? You were on top of your game when I last saw you."

"I'm as sure as rain. Yes, I was on top, we were both in the thick of things, but by the time the squad stood down for the balance of the year, I had already begun questioning my resolve."

The waiter placed our drinks on the round table, his a scotch and mine a G&T. I pondered the Savoy Bar, full of London patrons who were either in cheerful animated discussion or in serious negotiations of one sort or another. Looking back at Wellsey, I scolded, "You didn't speak of this before, Frank."

"That is true, but you were scheduled for leave and I didn't want to do anything to delay it. And now, well, it's only the first week of January, so you're not too far behind with my news."

"That's thoughtful—"

"I wasn't just thinking of you, old man. I knew that when the now Major Tempest took over as CO from Christie, he would be the one to better understand my request, as he was also an active flyer, perhaps also worn out. Well, he took the desk job for some reason."

I smiled at the thought of Tempest being our CO, as he was such a good man. "You are worn out?"

"In a way, yes, I feel I have a kind of shell shock. I dunno, call it flying fatigue."

Wellsey described difficulty in dealing with the intensity of the night-sky battleground and of losing some of his fervor. I knew there was talk that a wartime flyer was only good for a few months before becoming exhausted. I wondered what had happened to the happy warrior who had been my role model, that uplifting figure that so motivated me. His explanation that the surface did not always reflect its contents was understandable but a surprise, nevertheless. However, I respected his reasoning that high levels of anxiety and flying dissonance could affect his judgment.

Wellsey's brown eyes seemed darker against flushed cheeks. "So I'm off to 48 Wing, Home Establishment, which is starting up on 1 February. I'll serve by training recruits, providing coastal protection or other benign duties."

"We won't be all that far apart, then. What of the others?"

"Well, you know Lunghi was having the odd fit here and there, emotional outbursts at times. He's been found permanently unfit for flying and posted to Home Establishment, a technician, I believe. Ace is in hospital for a minor case of nerves and will also be transferred to Home Establishment."

I whistled, thinking about all that had occurred in just a couple of weeks. "Well, the lot of you are out. Looks rather like the break in action allowed for deep reflection and a turn in one's outlook."

"I suppose. What of you, old man? Where does your future lie?"

A second round of drinks was set in front of us as I confirmed that I would return to 100 Squadron. I felt I had more work to do there in spite of Wellsey's stating that there was no shame in asking for a transfer since, after all, twenty-two of the squad's fifty-two flyers had done so before year end. The news set me back since I had believed we would all return to the squad and resume our service. The war was wearing us down, which I hoped would not break up the will to win, the drive to overcome the evil before us.

I felt apprehensive as we continued our conversation. I knew a request to serve in RFC Home Establishment would likely be granted and would allow me to be closer to Cissy. But I still had a drive that influenced my compulsion to return to France, to the squadron. Wellsey questioned my need to prove myself, which made me a bit defensive. Was I acting out a childlike fear of not doing well enough when others saw that I did?

My papa had been hard on me. Small things such as accusing me of tripping my sister on the ballfield when she had fallen of her own accord or leaving the door open to mosquitoes when the latch was clearly broken. He would lay out the accusation, which I would deny, then admonish me for lying. One after another, day after day, the seemingly inane issues would bind together like a growing ball of elastic bands, straining with each small piece that was added. I'm sure my mama knew the truth, but she allowed him to continue using his eldest child to wage some unspoken internal struggle about power or insecurity.

My resolve to return to active battle—to honor those like Perce, who had fallen; like Jones, Godard, Archie, and Greenie, who were all rotting in a Hun prison camp—was as strong as ever. I knew that, in spite of my love for Cissy and my sisters and my fellow soldiers, this was the time for courage. Grit and determination to stay alive were part of that.

Wellsey leaned across the table, waving his hand in front of my face. "Bobby? Where did you go? I've been talking to you, but you went trance-like."

I smiled to confirm I was still with him. "Not really, just something you said earlier causing me to be reflective."

Wellsey stood up and, fetching his coat from the back of the chair, beseeched me with, "Do think about what I said. Sorry, I have to go."

"I will, I promise, but don't count on it."

"All right. Look, I've also requested a return to Cape Town to serve with Home Establishment there. Should that come through, things could happen quickly. Here's my address down there in case I go. Good luck, old man."

He placed a card in front of me and put his hand on my shoulder as he had endearingly done so during the many times I sat in front of him, my back against the nacelle after we had just escaped harm. He smiled warmly and left as I looked down at the card. *Frank William Wells, 25 Balfour Street, Woodstock, Cape Town, SA.*

...

Via Royal Post Office:

MISS CISSY ANN TAYLOR
WOMEN'S DORMOTORY
NATIONAL SHELL FILLING FACTORY
CHILWELL

7 JANUARY, 1918

CISSY
MY ARRIVAL CHEQUERS INN 14 JANUARY AFTER MRS. CLARKE VISIT STOP LEAVE FOR DOVER 20TH FOR RETURN FRANCE ON 21ST STOP BOB STOP

...

I was enjoying a cigarette while passing the time standing in front of Chequers when she approached out of the dusk. "Darling, I came as quickly as I could." Through her open coat, I could see that Cissy wore the knee-buttoned trousers and laced blouse whose effect was emblazoned on my mind from before and would be forever. I wondered if she knew only too well how that image stirred my passion. "As soon as the shift siren blared, I ran to the dorms and cleaned up quickly."

With my hand gently on her back, I guided her into the Chequers pub. "You look as beautiful as ever. Shall we have a drink before dinner?"

Sitting at a corner table away from the noisy factory crowd that was beginning to enter, Cissy gazed at me through deep blue eyes. "You're so sweet, Bob. You're always so sweet to me. I've so missed you."

"Sweetness comes naturally in your presence."

"You are flattering me. Do you still love me as much as you did at the train station?"

"More, but do you need to ask?"

"No. Well, yes, because I like to hear you say it with your Canadian accent."

"Canadian accent?"

"Well, more Canadian than English." Cissy giggled. "So, how was your time in London since Christmas?"

Over our dinner of meat pie and chips, I held Cissy's interest with tales of adventure over the past days. I had gone with Daisy and Eric to see *Chu Chin Chow* at His Majesty's Theatre on Haymarket, a comedy and pantomime musical based on the tales of Ali Baba. The excitement, especially for the soldiers in the audience, was the many scenes that involved big dance routines and exotic costumes.

Seated between Eric and me, Daisy teasingly squeezed my hand and grinned when the pretty, scantily dressed slave girls entered the stage.

Cissy contrived a pouty, mischievous look. "How scantily?"

"Enough!" As I grinned, she leaned across the table and kissed me.

While Cissy leaned forward with keen interest, I continued my story that Daisy said she felt the wartime climate needed such distractions as *Chu Chin Chow* to keep soldiers' thoughts away from the trenches, even for an evening. Eric and I were quick to agree.

Sitting back contemplatively, Cissy asked, "And how is Mrs. Clarke? She was so kind to me when I came to supper. So long ago ... over a year, I think."

"Yes, she is a very considerate person. She's been like an aunt to me for most of my life." Chequers became crowded and patrons stood between tables as beer swished out of pint glasses. Moving closer to Cissy for more intimacy, I told her about spending rainy evenings with Mrs. Clarke going through old photos while reminiscing about my life in Walthamstow, and how she brought out the good in everything. "Being in her presence is a shelter for me, a safe place in times of stress."

Cissy rubbed the back of my hand as she stared compassionately. "I saw a flash of frustration in your face as you were saying that. Do you want to talk? Will you talk to me about that?"

"There are things one doesn't talk about, things there is no need to talk about. They are past."

"It's good to talk, Bob. I sense you have scars. Emotional scars?"

I fought back a tear of frustration, not wanting to open up. "What makes you say that?"

"Well, women talk. Before I met you that day at the Strand a year ago, Daisy told me a little about your admission to the Maudsley."

"She shouldn't have—"

"She's my family, and she cares. The reason she told me was

because I persisted in knowing why you were away from the front for so long."

I laughed nervously and looked at Cissy in a gentle way, thinking I should not be surprised that she of all people would probe. I was not mad at Daisy nor irritated with Cissy, but rather concerned about being judged for failing my troops. I knew Cissy was a bright, intuitive lady with compassion, but I wanted nothing to upset our burgeoning relationship. I knew I had been forthcoming with others, but I was uneasy—perhaps irrationally—about opening up to the one I had so passionately fallen in love with.

"There is that look of anguish again. I don't wish to force you, but it might be good for you to talk about things."

"I wonder if I have the courage for that."

"I think you do. You are strong, my darling, and caring. I think you must have been just as caring in battle with your troops. That is who you are."

"I don't want to say much, but it was awful. We were pinned down in a heavy barrage, unable to get to each other, to hear each other, and especially to even help each other."

Cissy was drawing me out as I realized she was all compassion, even when I became involuntarily frustrated. She remained calm, not judging—in fact, quite the opposite as she stroked my hand in kindness.

I continued, "The central thing is that I was not able to help my troops. I felt like I failed them."

"Daisy said you were buried, knocked down many times."

"That's true."

"Well, my darling, how could you help them? You know in your heart that your injuries were severe, taking many weeks for you to recover. Try to stop being so hard on yourself."

I looked at her, deeply into her eyes, as my heart beat faster, thumping with passion as the love I felt took hold, dominating the moment. "Oh, Cissy, you sound like an angel."

"You're changing the subject, but that's all right. I've pressed you enough for one night. You've been a good sport."

"If you want to press me some more tonight, I—"

"Ah-ah! You can't use that as a way to beguile me to your room!"

"I'm not sure what you mean by this thing, *beguile*?"

"Ha! You're to be a lawyer and you've a short vocabulary." She let out a mischievous *tsk-tsk*. "Really, now!"

I walked Cissy to her dormitory under a near-full moon peeking out from high cloud cover, thinking it was a perfect night for flying. We strolled quietly arm in arm while I reflected on my pending return to the squadron, wondering what it would be like with so many colleagues having moved on to other ventures and what tasks I would be assigned.

"Penny for your thoughts, Lieutenant?"

"Oh, just thinking about returning to France and thinking what a lovely evening it is, already missing you."

"We've a few days yet. Let's make the best of them."

When I finished a deeply intimate and lasting kiss, Cissy pulled away from under my arms, breathing heavy. "Good Lord, Pitman! What's got into you?"

"Thinking about pressing things."

"Now look, buster, it's time for you to return to your hotel and me to get some rest. Early shift for me, remember? Same time tomorrow?"

I looked squarely at her with a mile-wide grin. "Looking forward to it." I turned to go.

"And don't forget—stop being hard on yourself. You're a good man."

...

The few days at Chilwell were special, as I slept late and enjoyed leisurely breakfasts while pouring over the newspaper. Some townsfolk who were delighted to have a soldier in residence were curious about when I thought the war would end. None seriously thought I knew the answer, but enjoyed the debate. The innkeeper, whom I had considered to be eerie, actually had good sense as he engaged me in discussion about when munitions production would wind down in favor of a return to the local industries of coal mining and lace making. I knew it was more about his concern for the effect on jobs, and therefore on his business, when thousands of munitions workers in the area would leave. He was astute.

And during conversations with him and other locals I learned more about the munitions factory. When I tried to draw Cissy out about the working conditions, she was stubbornly resistant, claiming that it was soldiers at the front who were most at risk. Yet I gathered that the Ministry was pushing its employees to produce more arms faster in order to keep up with demand. That left open the chance that corners were being cut and the risk of accidents rising.

...

One evening Cissy asked if I wouldn't mind accompanying her to football practice. Lord Chetwynd—founder and supervisor of the filling factory—so graciously allowed use of a small pitch located immediately adjacent to the east wall of a warehouse. His benevolence was manifested by allowing the electric lights on the exterior walls to be illuminated for the evening practice until the season began in the longer days of March.

After field drill and ball-handling exercises, Cissy ran up to me, completely out of breath, her short hair askew and sweat dripping from under her bangs. I had never seen her look so casual, wearing men's trousers and an oversize shirt. "What do you think? Do you think I'd make a good player, at least good enough to make the grade?" She stood erect, trying to get control of her breath. "What are you smiling about?"

"You are so adorable working so hard for something you want."

"Argh! Men! I don't want to be adorable. I want to make the team."

"I'm a cricketer. My football skills are not tops, but when I see you play, you are as good as or better than the others. Keep going, girl!"

"Thank you, Bobby. I'll show you all!"

...

Our Friday supper was special, as Cissy was on leave the next day, meaning we had no time restrictions for the evening. It was also only one full day before I was to travel to Dover to meet the Calais-bound ship. At the posh restaurant, the mellow ambiance of our window side table set the right tone for the candlelit supper presented by the family proprietors. The flickering on Cissy's face accentuated her natural beauty.

After local roast duck with all the trimmings and a nice bottle of Chianti, we were well fed and content. "Shall we stroll along High Street, perhaps settle our meal?"

"I'd like that. Oh, it was so wonderful. You really know how to treat a girl."

I looked at her as the flame highlighted her eyes. "I'd like to take credit, but—"

"But you know how to arrange things, Bob. Wonderful memories."

We strolled hand in hand, pausing at times to look into shop windows as my anticipation grew under unspoken expectations. Cissy pointed out her dressmaker's shop, its window draped in rich cottons and silks, which she said had the same effect on her as a candy store had for children, especially for its diversity of fabrics. There were millinery shops, automobile garages, and cafés, whose wartime success was explained in the wealth created by the munitions factory.

We were so absorbed in each other that we found ourselves in front of Chequers with no concept of time, taking little notice of the Friday-night patrons spilling into the street. Moving to the inn's side entrance, Cissy looked at me before reaching for a kiss. No words were required, no need to ask, just a tacit understanding.

There was something different, something less urgent about our lovemaking, allowing us time to cherish each moment, exploring one another. Time was irrelevant. Quietly, forcefully at times, we tossed and tumbled on the oversize bed, the only noises alternating from momentary laughter to pleasurable grimaces and finally to a shared quiver.

We lay there half dozing, mumbling words of comfort amid total bliss. In time we heard the distant midnight whistle from the factory, causing me to instinctively look at my wristwatch in the dim light, perhaps wishing time to ebb back to earlier in the evening.

"I should go. The guard will already look suspiciously at me."

"Don't go. Stay here with me."

"I can't. I want to, I do, but I just can't."

"Sure?"

"No, I'm not sure, but I can't show up in the morning wearing my dress from the night before."

"I could lend you trousers and a shirt."

She slammed the pillow on my head while jumping squarely on top of me. We tumbled and struggled before I gained control and rolled her onto her back. The banter quickly turned to a kiss, then another before looks of desire and ultimately a repeat gift to each other before stumbling out of bed to get dressed. We took turns in the bathroom down the hall, creeping ever so quietly so as not to wake other guests.

The guard was nodding off as we kissed good night, hardly aware of Cissy's return as he dozily waved her through the gate before his head fell again to his chest. Although tired, I felt no urgency to rush back to an empty bed, so I strolled leisurely along High Street in the comfort of memories, images flashing across my mind. I ascended the stairs to my room, finding with a glance of my wristwatch that it was two thirty. We had little time left to enjoy each other. Perhaps in the afternoon we would stroll along the estuary before dining and Cissy's early return to her dormitory. I looked forward to our parting kiss but not our parting.

Chapter 40

May 1918

Hardy held his hand high to draw the Vicar's attention. "Switches off, sir!"

The Vicar leaned over, visually connecting with our head mechanic. "Switches off!"

Sam pointed sharply at his men positioned behind the propeller, giving them the thumbs-up. The prop was swung around a few times, priming the Beardmore, coating the pistons with life-enabling motor oil. I knelt and looked over the windscreen facing the Vicar, confirming flight details that would take us forty-five miles north of our relocated aerodrome at Villeseneux to our target—Mohon Railway Station.

"Switches on, sir!"

The Vicar flipped the magneto to initiate the electric pulse in the Beardmore's spark plugs. Francis Richard Johnson was a tall, blond, lithe individual with a quiet demeanor, the son of a priest at Oxford parish. He himself was a seminary student who had enlisted to do his bit and who readily accepted his nickname rather than his Oxford salutation, Francis.

"Switches on!"

Two thumbs up from Hardy, and the Beardmore roared to life. We were fourth in line with ten minutes to idle. I thought back to Wellsey, when I felt safe in the knowledge that our two-man team had survived so many challenges. The Vicar was an experienced pilot, but we were yet to be tested as a team.

Flying out of Villeseneux was a new challenge, not just due to unknown bearings but because we were so far back of where we were in Ochey the previous winter. The German Spring Offensive led by General Erich von Ludendorff had created temporary havoc for our infantry and air corps, who scrambled to relocate far behind existing lines. However, in a matter of weeks we were successful in arresting that initiative, holding fast to Channel ports and protecting the key Amiens rail junction. The Huns were retreating back in the direction of Berlin, but burning and destroying as much in their path as they could. We were to stop them.

I revisited my frustration at having been held back from 100 Squadron during the Hun initiative, assigned for months to No. 2 Aircraft Depot at Candas, which itself had retreated to a temporary location near coastal Le Havre. While the reasoning was sound—there was little point assigning me to a squadron that was on the retreat—the delay caused me to question my decision to return to the front at all. I could have opted for Home Establishment, nearer Cissy. The moments when it looked as if our troops might be pushed into the sea were the worst, until finally the tide had turned. Ludendorff had overextended and simply could not keep up a war of attrition when his troops were exhausted, hungry, and emotionally crushed.

I was gratified when orders finally came through in April for me to report to Major Tempest, Christie's replacement at 100. Very few of the original lads had stayed on, yet the new bunch was friendly and supportive. A few held me in esteem over my being on a second tour with the squadron, giving me a sort of elder statesman status.

Hardy removed the chocks, allowing us to move forward. At the far end of the airfield, we spun 180 degrees to face the barracks. When the flare path lit up, we taxied to climb into the darkness. I felt great, soaring back into the night to rain justice on the malicious Hun.

Traveling northeast, we crossed the Marne River before seeing the lights of Reims portside. It was a beautiful night for flying—light winds in the pleasant late-May air, cold at sixty-five hundred feet but bearable.

My reverie was broken by advancing mist as we traveled toward Mohon, memories of being distraught in the previous year's storms causing me to gulp down queasiness. I forced myself to be positive; this sortie was an easy run up to the target and back. That ground mist was not the same as torrential rain and gale-force winds. Arriving at the target was disorienting, as all we saw was light being dispersed up through the low cloud, an eerie greenish effect with no clear image of buildings or rolling stock.

The offset to our angst was a lack of enemy searchlights and Archie since the Hun could not see us above the cloud, so we decided to immediately swoop down and drop our 230-pounder on whatever was below, then search elsewhere for an alternate target with the Coopers. With less weight, we quickly soared away and flew down to the nearby Juniville railway system. While this was a clearer target, it also provided the enemy with an equally clear view of us.

As we approached in silence, light sprang up toward us in quick fashion. The Vicar yelled something unintelligible, but I had already grabbed my Lewis to rain bullets downward. We sideslipped to wriggle away, but then suddenly the lights were extinguished and the Archie silenced. We moved closer to the tracks looking for a train, for any worthwhile target.

Seduced lower by the cover of darkness, we realized too late we had been fooled as the searchlights suddenly reappeared and with them, relentless Archie. We were trapped in bright crosshairs, the Vicar yelling to catch my attention. I turned as he signaled to get down to avoid tumbling out as he violently sideslipped to shake off the lights. It succeeded, and we were free, but free with our bomb load.

Around we went, now aware of the cat-and-mouse game the Hun were playing; they waited, they listened, then slammed on the lights when we dove onto the rail tracks. Again breaking out of the clutch of the lights, we knew we had to go back and drop our load. I manned the Lewis in expectation, and as I peered into the darkness, the lights glared in my face, blinding me. I was not able to see anything as my pupils struggled to constrict. I had no accuracy in the face of the multiple lights aimed at us as I squeezed bursts of five, hearing the Archie pop around us, knowing tracer bullets were rising in an attempt to destroy us. It was as if we were in broad daylight! It would be only a matter of moments before the Hun's machine guns ripped apart our Beardmore or hit the petrol tank.

The Vicar clanged on the windscreen with his ring to attract my attention. I looked back to see him thrust his thumb skyward, signaling we needed to clear away, demanding that I sit on the nacelle floor. As the Vicar continued rapping on the windscreen, I peered over the side, then methodically pulled up the port bomb lever, one, two, three, and four as they fell away. I repeated the sequence for the starboard Coopers before tumbling down to the floor. The Vicar lowered the starboard wing as we swooped away into the darkness, shedding the lights without knowing where our bombs landed.

Conversation was lively in the mess with flyers arguing differing opinions about the evening's sortie—slight disappointment to some and complete failure to others. The ground mist over Mohon Railway Station had certainly inhibited accuracy, but for many of the aeroplanes to return to the airfield with their full complement of bombs was seen as abject failure. Major Tempest was furious at those who had compromised the aerodrome and its occupants, vowing that any team who repeated the act would answer to military court.

The Vicar was on edge through our conversation, but I didn't press him. "Just one thing before we retire, Bob," he scolded. "We need to talk about your overlooking my order to sit."

"Our bombs remained intact, Vic. We needed to dispose of them, so some attempt on the target was necessary."

"We could've dropped them anywhere. Instead, you chose to delay our breakaway from the Hun lights. And besides, I gave an order."

"Just a moment, Vicar—we are a team up there, two minds who decide actions with like-mindedness. On our first sortie together, that cohesion might not have surfaced perfectly, but it will in time."

"Not about that. As I said, I called an order!"

I held my patience, thinking the Vicar was speaking naïvely. "That's my point: neither of us give orders when we are flying; rather, we work together. It is a necessity that we operate as equals, complement one another."

The Vicar held his gaze, a slight smile emerging. "But one of us has to rule, eh?"

I wasn't sure if the Vicar was dug in on the point, but decided that since he had phrased it as a question, I would respond firmly. "Look, Vicar—we are both lieutenants, equal rank. But that shouldn't matter when we are looking out for one another. I dropped those bombs because we needed to dispose of them, and we also had an obligation to complete our mission with the best-possible effect."

"Even though we had enemy shells and tracers come up at us in broad illumination?"

"Yes, under enemy fire we needed to complete our mission and then get the hell out of there. To have dropped them knowingly over French soil could have killed innocent citizens, a situation I won't have."

He was suddenly thoughtful. "I see your point, but you need to see mine. We can't both fly the aeroplane; one of us has to be in charge. I had the controls, so that puts me in charge."

I stared in his eyes for a moment, neither of us blinking. Standing down, I deferred. "All right. You are the pilot, and I accept your need to govern. That makes sense. I would ask you, though, to understand why I needed to dispose of those bombs while we were over a known target."

Vic relaxed a little, talking in a more conciliatory voice. "All right, I understand your reason and appreciate you seeing mine."

After this one sortie, this one altercation, I knew that flying with Johnson was to be different than with Wellsey. I didn't begrudge his approach. In fact, I appreciated his focus on safety. I held a lingering doubt about whether a flyer that was inflexible would be able to react quickly in an emergency. Still, I had to respect Vic's role as pilot, and any other pilot with whom I might fly. "Of course. I think we both want what's good for the squadron. I trust, though, you feel good about our efforts tonight?"

"Oh, of course. Just a misunderstanding. I'd say we'll work well together."

I nodded. "Yes, we will."

Vic looked at me with a tired smile. "How about we drink up and hit the sack? I'm about done!"

...

Lieutenant Frank Wells
25 Balfour Street
Woodstock
Cape Town, South Africa

4 May, 1918

Dearest Wellsey,
 I trust you are well and settling in to your life back in your native Cape Town and that your reunion with your wife was as pleasant a dream as you anticipated. I was not shocked to learn of your transfer. I suppose the rapid rise of Americans arriving in France gave the brass confidence in releasing such good flyers as you.
 I've returned to 100 Squadron for active duty. Your local papers will have written about the British, French, and now American successes pushing the Hun back toward Berlin, where they belong. Well, they damn well don't belong in France and Belgium!
 There are many new airmen I am meeting at the squadron, all of whom are eager to do their bit, albeit some wet around the ears. Can't say much more than that, old man (to borrow your endearment)! Yet I do miss you up here, mon pilote. Not the same, you know!
 Wellsey, as a flyer you know me better than most, so I confide in you that I'm experiencing a bit of melancholy. Not the sort that grounds good airmen, but rather that sits in the recesses of one's mind, gnawing away in a subtle manner.
 My relationship with Cissy has blossomed, especially after spending time with her over an extended winter break. I should be pleased about my life! Yet doubts swirl. The shell shock in '16 is part of it, but it is the terrible loss of life that we rain down on the enemy that I question. Every so often guilt rears its head

as I question the mass slaughter. Yet others see me as courageous. As I do them.

At times I feel I have sorted things in my mind as to what is right and faced my actions as a flying fighter. Why does the guilt persist?

When I think this through, I am able to dispense with the concern, as it is my responsibility as a gunner. But that satisfies my logical self, not my emotions. There are triggers that overcome a lucid sense of rightness, causing gnawing anxiety. You know, I volunteered to return to the squad because I wanted to continue my service in honor of Canada. That alone promoted courage. But I now increasingly ask myself whether redeployment to Home Establishment might have been a better course.

Be assured, none of this crops up during a sortie or blurs my accuracy over a bombing target. That's when I'm at my best. Major Tempest paid me a grand compliment in the mess the other day by suggesting to some of the new lads that they could benefit from my experience. That shot of confidence should eliminate my doubts; I know you would believe that too.

I also know you would advise me that it is all right to hold doubts, but that I ought to rely on my skill and experience to make success a part of my makeup, to seek peace with my soul that the deaths caused by my bombing and strafing are part of the cause to ultimately end all of the suffering.

Wellsey, you are not here with me, yet it is because we went through so much together during '17 that I understand the former is what your guidance would be. Simply by posting this letter brings me peace, as your kindred presence makes me feel better.

Do write if you can.

Sincerely,
Bob

...

5 May, 1918

My Dear Cissy,
I received your two letters today. You must really miss me, my favorite girl—I know by saying that you will now be asking out loud who my non-favorite girl is! There isn't one, silly!
I am so pleased that you made the grade with the football squad! Well done! I can see you pitched against the Carlisle Munitions or the Vaughan Ladies! Perhaps one day, take on the dreaded Blyth Spartans in a touch-and-go final? I am so proud of you, Cissy.
Your letters were redirected to my new aerodrome at Villeseneux, as I was finally assigned last week back to 100 Squadron. While the depot at Candas kept me busy, it is in my beloved squadron that I wish to serve. I daresay that after my first sortie of '18, I experienced a touch of anxiety. It is minor, and I know I will be ready for whatever mission we are assigned, especially since we have that evil old lunatic Ludendorff on the run. Imagine thinking he and his ragtag army could run through our troops, now fortified by millions of beloved Americans.
The squad tomorrow begins a move back to a prior aerodrome, closer to the fleeing Hun. Things are changing so quickly. I can feel victory, perhaps more than I would feel if I were in merry old England. This belief keeps me going and helps bring my spirits up.
My darling, I so wish for us to be together, to hold one another the way we did last winter. I remember my hunger for you while flying last October, being satiated only when we

finally met. Well, I feel the same desires, the same wish to hold you in my arms and to whisper over and over and over that I love you!

Stay safe, my darling.

Bob

Chapter 41

May 1918

With the Hun on the retreat, the elation of our mid-month return to Ochey felt good, similar to the spirit and camaraderie in the fall of '17. The swift move to regain our old aerodrome brought drama, but the most rewarding sight was seeing French and Belgian citizens reclaim their villages and their homes. The personnel makeup of 100 Squadron kept changing with new faces, but most noticeable was our synthesis as a completely different force. On 1 April, the RFC joined with the Royal Naval Air Service to become the Royal Air Force. Sam Hardy's return with me to the familiar aerodrome provided comfort. Well, mostly.

I swung my leg off the back of the Douglas motorcycle and chuckled as I looked at Hardy's impish grin. "Ahhh, I think it's safer to fly a Fee over hostile enemy territory than to sit on the back of that thing holding on for dear life, Sam!" We had just traveled the twelve miles through woodlands and past farmers' fields, flying over potholes as big as bomb craters, to get to the Nancy café that was a favorite of our airmen.

We took a table on the Café Impérial patio overlooking the shopping area in central Nancy. "You're such a baby," said Hardy. "Squealing and whinging at every turn and over every bump."

"Ha! I'm as bold as Jack Johnson, only he doesn't fight lunatics!"

"You need to lean into the curves, Bob. You need to relax. And speaking of Americans—"

"Who's speaking about Americans?"

"You did. Just then you mentioned Jack Johnson."

"Oh." I scrunched up my face in a confused smile—I had used a euphemism out of habit instead of its underlying meaning—as the waitress set our espressos down. Hardy was sizing her up somewhat hungrily. "Sam! She's someone's daughter."

Sam held his gaze on her as she sashayed her way back to the bar. "She sure is. Must be a damn good-looking family, I'd say."

I waved a hand in front of Hardy's face. "Hey, get your eyes off her ass. What about the Americans?"

"Oh ya, my point. That jackass Brown who just joined treats us like servants, treats all the mechanics that way."

"I've heard things myself. The fly-boy from Jamestown. Acts like he was the very first English settler in America, that he alone began the colony three hundred years ago. You'd think he was handpicked to lead this war on behalf of the Americans."

"He's dangerous, Bob. I've seen that type in this war and I saw it at the Boer. All about him. Sweet as pie to the major, then a downright cruel ass to the rest of us."

I grimaced. "You know I'm flying with him tonight?"

Hardy held up his hands, palms out defensively. "What? Bob, you can't; you need to say no. This isn't just a motorcycle ride; it's a sortie, and a dangerous one across the German lines."

"I don't think Tempest would put me in excess danger, Sam."

"Or the major's testing you, perhaps. See if you can tame the bloke."

"We'll see. I suppose—" Sam's eyes had wandered away again, looking over my shoulder dreamily. I turned to take in his view. "Sam! She's beautiful, I know, but we're due back soon."

A blissful Hardy pretended to melt into his seat, letting his arms fall to his side in a gesture that meant he was helplessly in love. "Perhaps another Genevie. So sweet, so beautiful."

"So come back later, maybe tomorrow."

"I may just do that."

I felt like throwing a wrench in the works, a little mischief. "Or maybe find a red lamp or even a blue one. Take the edge off?"

Sam stopped me in the tracks of my teasing by pointing to the cobblestone street just in front. "Done that, Bob. Two blocks down and three over."

...

The sortie to the strategic Thionville Railway Station was considered a success, as all aeroplanes dropped their bombs on the building and tracks around it, returning safely. For me it was a failure. I was angry, livid at the cowboy style of flying demonstrated by my pilot, Brown, not to mention his smug attitude about it.

As Hardy placed the chocks against the wheels, I climbed down the port side of the aircraft and onto the grass. I paced away, thinking of all the tough returns I had experienced with Wellsey and the need for the two of us to work as a team, without which we would not have survived. I thought of the misunderstanding with Vic, which was sorted in a civilized manner. Tonight was to be straightforward flying. If we had faced weather issues or enemy aircraft, we could have had a fatal outcome. I was mad, fucking mad.

Brown jumped confidently from the aeroplane, brimming with delight. "What'ya think of that ride, huh, Pitman?"

I raged at him, "I think you're a bloody loose cannon, Second

Lieutenant Brown! Not fit to fly with 100."

Grinning, Brown crowed, "Whoa, pardner, settle down a bit. No need for drama here."

I put my face inches from his, seething. "It's not drama, you fool. I'm up front in the nacelle without a cozy seat like yours, kneeling as best I can. Standing, balancing in the slipstream to drop our bombs. And you, you decide to have a joy ride on our return."

Brown rose up, standing over me to intimidate. "No harm done, friend. Let's say we go have a drink."

I glared, held his stare for a moment before speaking. "I am not your friend. Clearly you don't understand. Swerving and sideslipping and diving like that, all for your personal joy. It's my job to keep us safely—"

The Vicar came over, listening to the exchange. He cut in. "My gunner and I were immediately behind and are equally appalled at your flying."

Responding to the growing sentiment, he took on an authoritative stance. "I'm a fucking good flyer. Listen to you both—a couple of stuck-up Brits who don't know that practicing sudden maneuvers makes us more agile, increasing our ability to outfox the enemy."

"We are bombers, you clown," spat the Vicar. "If you want to be a fighter pilot, join a fighter squadron where you can fly alone and risk your own life."

Brown rotated his body toward the Vicar as Hardy moved in closer, clenching his fists. "I attended the best flying school in the US, so you listen—"

"None of us care to listen to your pretentious attitude," retorted Hardy. "God knows I put up with enough of it in the hangars."

"You're an air mechanic; stay the hell out of this discussion. What the fuck do you know?"

The Vicar turned to Brown, teeth clenched and hands curled

into fists. "Stand down, Brown. I'm a senior officer to you, and I order you to your hut. Go sleep it off."

Brown stared at the three of us, shaking his head in apparent disgust before sauntering across the dark airfield.

"What now?" asked Hardy.

Breathing heavily, the Vicar spoke quickly and decisively. "I'll speak to the major in the morning. This can't go on."

We avoided the mess, as the tone had turned so sour. I lay in bed for a long time unable to sleep, tossing the sortie around in my mind. This was not what I had signed up for. We had enough grief just surviving this war without having to deal with the Browns of the world. I knew a lot of Americans, knew them to be a proud lot, fair, kind, and always jovial and positive. Brown was none of those things at all, which had nothing to do with his nationality.

...

Night after night we continued to target the Thionville railway system, as well as its blast furnaces and electric power station, at the border apex of France, Belgium, and Luxembourg to keep constant pressure on the movement of German troops and transport that were protecting nearby coal mining and steel production in the Saar Basin.

The Vicar's talk with Major Tempest had its effect, as I was assigned the next night to fly with John Chambers, a respected pilot who had joined 100 Squadron back in January. Brown remained flying but with Naylor, a novice lieutenant-observer. Our mission was for twelve aeroplanes to each carry two 112-pound bombs onto the Kreuzwald power station, which was the first sortie inside sovereign German territory. As Hardy and I walked the perimeter of the Fee, I mentioned my anxiety.

"I can't quite finger it," I admitted. "I don't know if it's the emotional effect of flying across the German border or whether my courage may be slipping away."

"You're not losing your courage. You've been outstanding in your service to this squad. Don't let that Brown affair throw you off."

I relaxed a bit. "You're right, yet last night I lay awake questioning my role. Things have changed. You know, having to fly with different pilots each time."

"You know the reason for that—the increasing number of new replacement pilots that need to build experience."

"Ha! That doesn't inspire confidence, as it implies others have either had enough, have been reassigned, or are now POWs!"

Hardy touched my sleeve. "Sorry, Bob. Didn't mean to cause more anxiety, just trying to help."

"Oh, I know. It's not your fault. You are correct; it's just the way things are now."

"Chambers is a good pilot. I've spent time with him on practice runs. Solid chap."

I shook Hardy's hand, appreciating his understanding. "Thanks for the comfort, old friend. I'd better get up there."

"Good luck, good sortie! Give 'em hell!"

The beautiful moonlight made the ground underneath radiant as we flew north, up the valley and over the rounded peaks of the Vosges while following the silver ribbon of the Moselle River. Meadows and lakes were easily distinguished from the dark pools of forestland. The peaceful scene gave me thoughts about perhaps returning there after hostilities ended, mingling with its French inhabitants, who would want nothing but to exist in peace. While I could imagine the peacefulness of Cissy hiking along with me—dressed in the fashion of the day, of course—on this sortie, I couldn't shake the foreboding that radiated from my stomach and traveled the lengths of my limbs.

I turned to look at Chambers, who offered a reassuring smile and a nod that signaled we were united. Angling starboard just south of Metz on our course for the German border, I pondered my apprehension. I felt confident with my flying skills, bombing precision adapted to a science. The old excitement was gone, though, leaving behind an impatience to get the job done and fly home. I wondered if my angst symbolized an unconscious change in my attitude to a kind of defensive preservation.

Crossing the border, we cut the Beardmore for the long, silent glide into the station, wires and planes whistling through the cool spring air. I fought back equivocal thoughts to fully focus on dropping our 112-pounders onto the electrical station. Nine in our sortie were ahead of us, already headed home after dropping their pills, the Hun by now amply warned. Searchlights were swinging wildly across the skies, searching for us while we hid behind our only surprise, silence.

I stood up in the front nacelle, extending my Lewis down toward the intimidating light, holding back until they locked on. The station had erupted in spot fires, signifying where the squad's bombs had hit. As the lights caught hold, I dispensed regular short bursts—*five rounds, release*. I was confident Chambers had the resolve to hold the ship steady in the face of the attack even though I felt dryness in my mouth, anxiety churning in my stomach.

Five rounds, release. I hammered away on the lights as we continued our glide to the target, holding back the bombs to strike at Kreuzwald's heart, its power house. *Five rounds, release.* With its silhouette outlined by moonlight, the large square building finally loomed in front of us, so I let go of the Lewis and, with steady hands and full concentration, grabbed for the release levers.

I heard the pills clank as I yanked up the wires to release them, the aeroplane lurching with split-second uplift when their weight pulled away. As the Beardmore roared to life, we were away, climbing quickly. I turned and took a fleeting look at Chambers. I nervously smiled at him as I grabbed the rear Lewis, pulling it up on its swivel over the top of the plane. I used the gravity created by the upward angle to lean against the wing strut, firing down into the lights.

Steady, Chambers, was my only thought as I balanced precariously with one foot on each side of the nacelle. As we broke free of the lights, darkness left me standing still for a moment, suddenly aware of my racing heart and quick, short breaths. Facing backward against the slipstream, the red exhaust seemed comforting, a sign of power surging through the black sky. I let my eyes adjust, needing the moment to ensure a safe return down into the nacelle.

...

28 May, 1918

My Darling Cissy,
I think about you all the time. In the air and on the ground, you are on my mind. I close my eyes and see us walking along the estuary, absorbed arm in arm in the warm spring air with birds soaring and butterflies flitting from flower to flower.
I've heard from flyers new to the squad that Englanders are able to hear artillery from where you are in the Midlands, from London too. We've done our bit to keep you safe, my love, as the Hun continues his retreat back to his homeland. Do not worry, as we are keeping the pressure up and the enemy's guns will eventually be silenced.
I miss you, and I miss a stable life and routine. Perhaps it is the spring air, or perhaps I'm just getting tired. It has been two and a half years since I left my Canadian home, enough time to wonder how much things must have changed there, how much my sisters have grown, and what this war may have done to Canada. Lest I sound emulous, I try not to compare British men's home leave except to say that most Canadian, Anzac, South African, and Indian soldiers haven't seen their homes for a long, long time.
I know I'm getting tired, perhaps because those of us in the

fight for civilization can smell success, if that word can be used to describe utter horror. Sometimes with expectant success one loses the sharp edge. I wonder if my decision to continue flying into '18 was a good one, wonder if changing to technical service might have been better. Yet I do remain committed to the cause.

I know you don't hold the answers to my questions, and I adore you for letting me sound off in our letters. I'm glad you are getting out with the munitionettes, girls whom you've grown close to. I was delighted when you described in your recent letter that during your last football match you were awarded a foul when defending the ball. That shows the grit you bring to the game. I lay on my bed holding that letter thinking about you dressed in knickerbockers and jersey with grime smeared across your face. Against your protests, I do imagine you as adorable!

I miss you, Cissy, and long to be with you, to hold you. Be safe, my darling.

With deepest love,
Bob

...

As a weather system blew into the Vosges, we were grounded for a few days. While Hardy worked to entice me to ride on the back of the Douglas into Nancy, I declined to get soaked in the constant drizzle and fog just for an espresso. I told him that his Café Impérial beauty would just have to wait for his dazzling blue eyes. Besides, Tempest had told all flyers to remain close to the aerodrome, an order I decided was not worth defying.

When I entered the mess, the Vicar was comfortably seated in one of two overstuffed armchairs facing the old French filigreed brazier. After stomping the wetness off my shoes at the entrance,

I wandered over to see him speaking quietly to another flyer, one whom I had not yet met.

The Vicar smiled warmly as he said, "Bobby, how are you, old chap? Do come sit down." He pointed to a third chair, a wooden dining seat. "Bob, I'd like you to meet Howie—Frederick Howard Chainey."

Before sitting, I shook hands. Chainey was one of those men who held an over-firm grip for an extended period while confidently looking into your eyes without blinking. His were dark brown, a coloring which complemented the rest of his complexion. His lanky frame, defined cheekbones, and longish, middle-parted hair gave him an aristocratic air. "My pleasure, Howie. Just join the 100s?"

"To a degree. Did one sortie a few weeks back; I believe you were just arriving. I went back to Hythe to complete Night Flying Aerial Navigation. Army style ass-before-head kind of schedule. You know, assign the chap, then send him back for training, wot?"

"We're not the army any longer. Now the RAF, dear boy," said the Vicar.

"Right," said Howie. "And Bob, you've been around for a while, I hear."

"Uh-huh. Seems I was one of the few to return in '18." I paused to think for a moment. "Say, that a London accent you carry?"

"Of a sorts. Chingford, actually."

The Vicar lit a Gitane as Chainey and I worked through our introduction, the extraordinarily strong tobacco smell filling the area. It was a smell I knew would always remind me of France, of the war. It turned out Howie's family home was less than three miles from my Walthamstow neighborhood. Our shared Essex background quickly established a bond. Also similar was our infantry action before becoming flyers, he with the Suffolk Regiment.

Talking about Essex took me back to childhood, fond experiences that would always be a safety zone and which brought forth comparison of memories past. The Vicar sat forward and turned to me in a friendly manner, knowing that if he allowed, I would reminisce all night. "Spoke to Tempest the other night before I set off to bed with this damn cold."

"Yes," I said. "Seems he listened since I was partnered with Chambers. It was a solid and safe mission. What a difference."

"From the one with the American, the one who's causing issues?" asked Howie.

"Quite," I said. "The lad Brown. He took me on a joyride that risked both of us. I was hopping mad. No need for that kind of lunacy."

"What's his game, then?" asked Howie.

"We don't know," exclaimed the Vicar, "and we don't care. He needs to toe the line before he hurts his observer and himself."

"Yet Tempest's hands are tied," I interjected. "He can't get new flyers over here fast enough." I ignored the mess door closing immediately behind me. "Still, we can't wait for—"

"Ahem." The Vicar's finger was jabbing forward from the arm of his chair, a warning that someone was approaching from behind.

Brown was with Larry Naylor, his observer on the last sortie, who evidently looked beyond the foolish flying. "Evening, lads," said Brown. Naylor held back in a deferential pose, mumbling a greeting.

"Evening," we repeated in chorus, but Howie only nodded his head.

Brown began to walk away toward the bar before turning on his heal, Naylor following so close as to bang into him. The American looked defiant as he snarled, "You know Tempest has me sitting out the next sortie, whenever that will be."

We stared, all of us struggling to respond but failing to find empathetic words, so we held back. The Vicar broke the deafening silence. "Does that mean anything to you? Did he explain why?"

"Yes, he spoke of respect for my fellow officers and respect for me."

I looked at Brown, wondering where his smugness came from,

wondering why in the face of disdain from most 100 Squadron flyers he kept it up. "Do you?" I asked.

Brown swung his head to glower at me. "Do I what?"

"Respect yourself?"

Through clenched teeth, he responded irritatingly, "I told you, Pitman, I was just practicing flying essentials in the event we need to escape enemy aircraft."

The conversation continued in this manner, Brown checking his temper but not altering his position, certainly not apologizing to me for his recklessness. His arrogance was unbroken, making it unlikely any of us would be willing to ever fly with him again. He was well spoken and held a nice smile, yet there was something in it that on close examination gave away a cunning, better-than-thou attitude. First me, then Dyson—and I suspected Naylor too—as his observers, all saw him as a bully with an unsafe lust for power when controlling an aircraft. I sat there after Howie and the Vicar said good night, thinking about how wars could be lost through such individualism.

...

27 May, 1918

My Dear Sisters, Ethel and Hilda,
Thank you for your sweet letters that both arrived today. It is taking more time for them to reach me perhaps because we are increasingly on the move. I am so happy that you are both well and working hard at your jobs. Soon enough Europe and the rest of the world will see peace. I am sure of it.

Papa's latest letter said you two had grown so much, inwardly as well as physically. In that case, I now have two beautiful young women as sisters that I haven't yet met! Can you believe it is now over two and a half years since I've seen either of you, since we've been able to talk about our lives and laugh with one another?

I think often of the day we will all meet again, when we can enjoy life as free citizens of the world. I know that sounds dramatic, but over here in Europe that is on everyone's mind, at least among our fighting men. We are all tired, tired of the mud and the slaughter and the starvation we see across France and Belgium. It surely has to end soon with one side or the other suing for peace.

Ah, but I am showing sadness when I should be expressing the best for our future. It is out there, my sisters, lest we believe otherwise.

God bless and love to you both,
Bob

...

The next sortie went as planned on Monday, 27 May with Brown sitting out like a child sent to the corner for some thoughtful reflection. Chainey was a welcome addition as he joined the sortie over to Kreuzwald. With a couple dozen 112-pounders dropped, we knew we had done extensive damage, with a few aircraft actually witnessing the power station on fire.

The next night the squad was assigned to a precision strike on the Metz Railway Station, forty-five miles northeast of Ochey; however, only four aeroplanes were on the raid. As neither the Vicar, Chainey, nor I were included, I decided on a stroll across the field to the hangars after dinner. The dusk sky was dark blue against a bright western horizon.

Hardy emerged from the mechanics' mess with a brimming smile. "Hey, Bob!"

"Hello, Sam. The machines primed to go over?"

"Not tonight. Quiet for me, I'm afraid."

"Hmmm. Thought you might know what's what."

Sam looked puzzled. "In terms of?"

"Well, there are four machines being sent over what is known to be a benign target, but flown by new crew. Chambers and Brown have some experience but limited. And choosing one of your air mechanics to sit observer for Brown? What the devil is Tempest up to?"

Hardy held his palms up in question. "Unusual, I know, but it's only a twenty-five-mile run up the Moselle after all. Surely nothing could go wrong. Perhaps Tempest is testing them."

In a pensive mood, I chewed on my pipe stem as I wandered back to the mess to join the growing festivities of those squadron flyers who had the night off. Howie and the Vicar were playing bridge with Box and Inches, the latter two holding the squadron record for the most sorties flown.

I alternated into the Vicar-Howie partnership, but even with changing tactics, we still consistently lost to the formidable Box-Inches duo. The hours passed with enough ale consumed to mellow everyone, some eventually drifting away in retirement for the night. The flyers that remained witnessed a late-night commotion at the door as an ashen-faced Chambers emerged into the dimly lit, smoky room and was immediately surrounded with curiosity.

John Chambers had been charged by Tempest to be the squadron leader for the sortie. Vic, Chainey, and I had earlier speculated that he might be tasked with watching Brown's flying technique. Chambers explained that the bombing unfolded according to plan, that he had followed Brown over the target and ensured he stayed the course along the narrow corridor just west of enemy lines. We knew others had flown that run countless times in and out of Ochey. It was easy to determine the demarcation line by sighting the string of nighttime trench bonfires. All you had to do was stay west of them.

Yet somehow Brown and his observer, Private Second-Class Johnson—one of Hardy's air mechanics—disappeared in that corridor. They reportedly just vanished. Chambers had flown up and down looking for evidence of a forced landing but with no success. He reported that Tempest was livid, giving him a thorough up and down, yet we all knew Chambers was not to be held responsible. Night bombers don't fly in formation and are trained to individually navigate themselves to and from the target.

No one in the mess wished one of ours ill, but we had all silently believed Brown was a disaster waiting to happen. It apparently just had. And it was Private Johnson whom we were most upset about, a teenage lad who had no idea of the danger he was put into, nor had the choice to avoid it. Both were gone, and in the absence of a fiery crash, we held on to a dubious hope the team was at least picked up as prisoners of the Hun.

I processed the news with more foreboding, tossing and turning in a fitful sleep filled with dreams and the acting out of terror. Perhaps I was subconsciously fearful of my own vulnerability. My dreams took me back to the Somme trenches, the artillery barrage raining down, being buried alive and not breathing.

I awoke at daylight in a cold sweat with erratic breathing, a headache, and unclear thoughts. I lay there staring at the parallel planks in the ceiling, following their line from wall to peak, thinking about my dreams, the morning quietness allowing me to recall them clearly. I knew I was getting tired, emotionally tired. I kept telling myself that I must hold on for the end of the war, which surely must come soon, and that then I would be released from these horrors.

I arose to face a beautiful spring day, the chirping birds confirming that, with all things considered, life was good. The others had arisen and gone to the mess some time before. I knew what I would do, had to do, if I was to hold onto sanity. I walked to the mess with a relief that comes with having made one's mind up. I would enjoy breakfast with my colleagues and then act.

...

I savored my meal with the other flyers amid small talk but discussed my plan with no one, stifling it inside my overactive mind. I guarded against the possibility that my colleagues could intervene with convincing me of some alternative course of action. After breakfast when the others drifted away, I strode across the grass toward squadron headquarters while working up positive thoughts to portray confidence and commitment for what I was about to do. I entered into a hive of busy activity, aides plotting over maps, sergeants in intense discussion, and the unbroken clicking sound of the telegraph machine.

The CO's adjutant gave a cold, suspecting stare. "Yes, how can I help?"

"I'd like a word with Major Tempest, please."

The adjutant studied me for a moment, not sure how to react to this unannounced intrusion on a busy HQ. "Is he expecting you, Lieutenant?"

I authoritatively squared my shoulders. "No, I am arriving on the strength of his open-door policy, Sergeant."

Locking eyes, neither of us said anything for a few moments. I knew that once in front of Tempest the tone would be conciliatory; I just needed to get beyond this pencil pusher. "Indeed, let me see if he has a moment."

I glanced at the wall maps and looked at piles of documents lying on tables behind the adjutant's desk and the files he was working on. It occurred to me this war was creating reams of documents that would all have to be filed somewhere after it was over. These would be documents the King's clerks would not be willing to part with.

I watched as the sergeant returned, weaving his way past soldiers and aides who took no notice of his presence. "Major Tempest will see you now, Lieutenant Pitman."

I noted the change to the more formal, respectful salutation, which meant that Tempest was quite open to an impromptu meeting. With renewed confidence, I made my way past the desks, tables, and stand-up hallway meetings to arrive at the major's office at the rear of the building. "Well, this is a surprise. What brings you in on this fine morning? Not ill, I daresay?"

I saluted and then stood at ease when told to. "Oh no, sir, I'm feeling fine. It's my mind, really. Just dreadfully tired, nightmares, cold sweats, lack of sleep."

"That's expected, Lieutenant. You lads are striking hard at our enemy; I know firsthand how it knocks you down."

I poured out my feelings with little concern that I was in front of my senior officer, explaining that recent sorties had become increasingly stressful since we were flying directly into enemy country with inexperienced crews. Yet that wasn't the whole issue—after two and a half years, fatigue was becoming a dysfunctional force. While I knew I was being selfish and knew many soldiers had endured longer terms of service, I wanted a change.

Tempest offered a well-grounded response by acknowledging that the long stalemate on the Western Front was affecting morale, but used the fact that the Hun were being pushed back to the Hindenburg Line to lay out a strong appeal: experienced flyers were needed more than ever.

I smiled to show my confidence. "Major Tempest, it has taken a lot of courage to come forth like this, but in my heart, I know it would be cowardly to carry on by, well, simply burying my concerns." I looked directly at the major, his empathetic expression giving me the determination to go on. "I believe I would be more valuable behind the scenes, where I could coach the newer chaps, or perhaps serve at Home Establishment."

The major remained quiet with a look of thoughtful contemplation in his eyes. I wanted to give him space, time to digest what I had just requested, so I busied myself by gazing over to the wall photographs and military paraphernalia.

"I see where you're driving this, Pitman. Tell me, though—is it this Brown business, is that the dour effect?"

I had hoped that topic would not surface. "Certainly got to me, sir. I as well as many others worried it was coming, but no, my concerns have been developing for a while."

Tempest seemed pensive as he whispered, "Yet his actions did bother you?"

"Of course, sir. Losing any of our team is of concern. That is why I feel I could better serve the squad as a coach to new flyers, perhaps in a technical role, sir."

A more authoritative looked appeared on the major's face. "Very well. But I need to weigh the alternatives, consider what is best for the squadron. For now you will continue to fly, is that understood?"

"Yes, sir, with as much dedication as ever."

"Have a safe flight tonight, Lieutenant. Dismissed."

I saluted. Passing the smiling adjutant, I left HQ for a stroll over to the hangars for a chat with Hardy, my trusted friend, who I knew would support my initiative but keep it confidential.

Chapter 42

June 1918

100Squadron continued to pour bombs down onto the Hun infrastructure into June as the German Spring Offensive continued to break down, and our infantry kept up a relentless drive to push them ever farther backward. As French and Belgian citizens returned to their homes and towns and villages, the damage caused by the enemy seizure of staples and their burning of buildings was apparent, and it was hideous. Every bomb we dropped was justified by its destruction of Hun resources.

The mixing of new and experienced flyers finally resulted in increased precision, assisted by an escalated focus on dropping the 230-pound bomb. I flew with a Captain Bright and alongside the Vicar—with Howie as his observer—on tours that disrupted the railways in Thionville and the Metz-Sablon triangle. Britain knew Kaiser Wilhelm obsessed about keeping the direct Metz-Berlin line open, so we particularly enjoyed battering them at its western terminus. While the sorties were successful and the teams worked well together, I didn't settle into harmony; more than ever I desired a transfer to ground responsibilities.

In my letters, I didn't tell Cissy of my requested change, as I felt it would be worse to provide bad news later than good news earlier. Our letters were full of love and desires, sometimes scheming for ways to see each other. I prayed that I could see to that sooner than she might expect.

After the sortie on the night of 6 June, the squadron's bombardments were suddenly halted when it was announced that the RAF had created a new Independent Air Force under the command of Major-General Sir Hugh Trenchard. We were now part of a strategic initiative composed of five squadrons that would concentrate on around-the-clock bombing of German targets deep within the Rhineland.

...

"That's it, Sam? That's as far as you've gotten? Just a name, 'Bernadette'?"

"These things take time, Bobby!"

In fine early-summer weather, the track from Ochey was hard packed, and that allowed the Douglas to dart through the forests and along the fields in good time for us to secure a place on the Café Impérial patio. Although evening, the long seasonal solstice offered bright sunshine, bathing us in warmth. "Hmmm. The war will cease and all you've got is a name and a place."

"Worth waiting for when you look into those exotic eyes and—*oh là là!*—the way she sways that—"

"Ahem!" I dropped my voice to a whisper. "Incoming at your left shoulder." Hardy stopped himself just as Bernadette approached with her winning smile that could disarm any soldier anywhere.

"Bonsoir, Messieurs. Êtes-vous bien?" Without waiting for an

answer, Bernadette grinned while looking into his eyes and said with a heavy accent, "Hello, Sam. It's nice to see you again." I began to understand Hardy's infatuation as the whispered voice itself oozed sensuality.

"*Et toi. Où est ton papa?*"

"*Dans la cuisine.*" I caught Hardy's momentary disappointment in knowing that her papa's presence meant no evening walk with Bernadette, but he quickly regained his infectious smile.

"*Ah bien,*" jested Hardy.

As Bernadette walked back toward the *estaminet* door to fill our drink order, I watched his obsession with Bernadette's delightful derriere. "She's a beauty."

Our talk turned to speculation about the new IAF and whether my role would be in the air or on the ground, as I had requested. Hardy was supportive of my request to serve as a technical officer and felt I would be a good teacher, an experienced coach. Shortly our conversation was interrupted by the laboring engine of an approaching lorry, becoming louder as its tires squelched over rough cobblestones. Sam's attention focused behind me over my shoulder, and as I turned in my chair, I saw a Crossley tender emerging from the southwest corner of the town square.

"See who I see, Bobby?"

I squinted into the setting sun. "That's the Leeds boy driving, your air mechanic Blythe, but who is sitting up there beside him?"

Sam clipped me on the shoulder. "That's the Vicar, Bobby!"

"Say it's not true."

As the Crossley came to a stop in the center of the town square, we walked over to investigate. Some in their new blue RAF uniforms, our flyers began to jump down from the back of the lorry as if invading Nancy at its center. I called up to the open cab, "What the devil is this about, Vicar?"

"Celebration! We looked for you but couldn't hold the commandeered tender any longer. But here you are!"

"Celebrating what?" Hardy asked.

The Vicar now stood with us. "Word came through that Brown and Johnson have been located, much alive but in a German POW camp. With that good news and our being grounded, we figured it was best to enjoy an *estaminet* dinner. C'mon, let's go!"

With Hardy catching up after he said *au revoir* to Bernadette, there were sixteen of us marching our way down narrow, twisting cobblestone streets lined with two- and three-story stone buildings. We stopped at a bistro known to one of our flyers. He assured us the proprietor was a good sort, but to be doubly clear he gave him a substantial advance of francs to ward off any wariness and compensate for any unplanned but very possible collateral damage. One could never be too careful. An outbreak of gaiety and frolicking—perhaps altering a wall here or crushing a table there—could lead to the summoning of military police. The francs would help allay such an eventuality.

A couple of hours enjoying fine food were followed by more drinking. Everything from *vin rouge* to Champagne to *bière* to Armagnac and even absinthe was consumed in copious amounts. It was good to let loose.

Equally outrageous was my hope that our dinner celebration would cap the night and we would travel back to the aerodrome in various states of consciousness. But I was not surprised with the sudden call from one of our finest, "Off to see the girls!" was met with hurrahs and a breakout of "God Save the King." The Vicar caught my eye with a look of concern, perhaps prompted by his proper Oxford upbringing and ties to the Church. However, I knew he faced no vows of celibacy. Nevertheless, I interposed my thoughts on the way out by explaining that, while one is obligated to follow the pack in the spirit of *esprit de corps*, nothing is required but to join the forthcoming sing-along.

I caught up with Hardy to ask if he knew where we were going. His impish grin was all the confirmation I needed, but he answered anyway. "Two blocks down and three over." We laughed knowingly at our inside joke, the Vicar looking at us in puzzlement.

We marched down streets and up alleys until we arrived at the plain black door over which the blue lamp hung; the discreet sign that this brothel catered to officers. Didn't we feel special, not having to queue up under a red lamp? After a sharp knock, the eye-level slide in the door was pulled aside to reveal a beaming, rouge-tinted smile. "*Bonsoir. Qui est là?* Who is there?" queried a sultry yet gravelly voice.

"100 Squadron from Ochey reporting for duty, Madame Dodu," answered one of our finest, apparently a regular.

The door opened immediately, exposing a madam clad in a loose robe of silk draped off her shoulders. "*Ah, les aviateurs Anglais! Bienvenue!*" It seemed she was a merchant with a keen head for finance.

We filed into the cramped foyer and up the stairs behind Madame, whose plumpness, only partially hidden under her silks, filled a good portion of the staircase. As we followed her into a vast room, looks of delight mixed with expectation filled our faces, some frozen in surprise and others of wanting after so long in the war arena. For in that opulent room amid the chairs, settees, erotic hangings, and mirrored walls sat some of the most gorgeous women any of us had ever seen. Certainly, our collective intoxication and desire made the girls that much more exquisite, but seeing them draped in sheer tulle, stockings, and heels—some only partially *tulled* from the waist down—painted a man's fantasy of the true Venus masterpiece.

It wasn't long before someone was tapping away on the rickety piano tucked away in the corner, causing the rest of us to break into song.

*There is a tavern way down in Brittany
Where weary soldiers take their liberty.
The keeper's daughter, whose name is Madelon,
Pours out the wine while they laugh and carry on.*

Our troop sang the patriotic verses with passion, some belting out the lyrics while others sang softly to one mademoiselle or another. So passionate was the classic French ballad that many of the *filles* sang along in its native French style.

*Oh, Madelon, you are the only one;
Oh, Madelon, for you we'll carry on.
It's so long since we have seen a miss;
Won't you give us just a kiss?
But Madelon, she takes it all in fun;
She laughs and says, "You see it can't be done;
I would like, but how could I consent
When I'm true to the whole regiment?"*

The girls worked their way through the room, some sitting in laps while others stared dreamlike into officers' eyes as they swayed to and fro, still others kissing passionately in darkened alcoves. The combination of scent, powder, and the haze of cigar smoke made the large room unmistakably erotic. Madame kept drinks refreshed while deftly ensuring each flyer subtly handed over the one franc cover for the privilege of being here. Other, heftier donations would be settled more discreetly.

Time seemed to evaporate amid the euphoria made present by the sexually charged atmosphere. Within an hour or so, many of the mademoiselles, lads in tow, disappeared through a pair of hardly visible doorways, presumably leading to chambers. Madame was never far away, making sure her business enterprise was funded according to the rules. But the Vicar and I, with the exchange of a discrete look, agreed we had done our bit in support of the team and needed to take our leave.

We thanked Madame graciously, smiling lavishly against her

protestations that we had not been duly provided the love that her establishment so delightfully dispensed, but nonetheless, we sidled toward the door carrying wide grins. Making our way out into the cool night air, we had a good laugh at the whole escapade. I looked up at the Vicar and said in poor imitation, "Oh, my *'andsome ah-via-tor, do you not want a leetle loove before you take your leeve of mon boudoir?*" We stumbled along the cobblestones in laughter.

It was good for the team to experience such release, even for those who did not partake in any bordello love. Glancing at my watch as we returned back to the town square, I noted we had another hour before the corporal was to drive the commandeered Crossley back to the aerodrome. We caught up with him dozing in the driver's seat. "Leeds, is it?" I asked.

He bolted upright. "Yes, sir!"

"Listen, Leeds, tell Sergeant Hardy—y'know, Hardknocks—that the Vicar and I have returned ahead with the Douglas, all right?"

The Vicar stood tall in a pose of incredulity. "I can't handle that damned thing, Bobby."

"I can, Vic, and I will."

I walked over and straddled the Douglas motorcycle, pushing it off its rear wheel stand just as I'd seen Hardy do many times before. After jumping on the kick-start lever a few times, I realized I had not flipped the magneto switch. Once done, she fired up and purred like a kitten.

"Jump on, Vicar!"

He hesitated before taking a stride forward, then looked back at Leeds, who was holding his stomach in laughter. "C'mon, Vic, get aboard before Mr. Funny over there tells the squad that we couldn't bloody well get airborne on a 9 hp motorcycle." That did it, and the Vicar straddled the rear seat.

We cautiously moved forward before I realized the acetylene headlight was not illuminated, so after squeezing the brake lever a little too hard, we lurched to a stop. The Vicar slammed up against my back. Neither of us looked back at Leeds, as there was no sense giving him more fodder. And then we were off, bumping over the cobblestones before we reached the dry, flat roadway. I guardedly changed to a higher gear after staying in the lower one too long, the engine screaming its protest. Once gaining speed, I felt as if the entire world's problems had been lifted, and I bellowed out a boyish "Woo-hoooo!" as we barreled along.

We arrived safely back at the aerodrome with the Vicar clutching the back of my flying jacket just as I had done with Hardy. He was in much need of a nightcap, so we headed over to the mess, where we compared stories of the evening shenanigans. We knew that a few of the lads would not make their ride back, but men as resourceful as RAF flyers would figure out what it took to report to the aerodrome by the next morning.

I lay in bed and thought of Cissy, trying not to compare her to the *filles* in Madame Dodu's brothel. Yet I did, and although I felt a twinge of shame, I wallowed in the knowledge that, on a physical level, she outshone them. But above all, I knew she was special. She was smart and witty, and she valued and fostered women's courage. I fell asleep in the knowing comfort that I loved her so much.

Chapter 43

June 1918

16 June, 1918

Dear Wellsey,

    I trust you are well, dear old friend. I miss you at the squadron amid all of the new faces and its ever-changing character as flyers come and go. Yet I have met and flown with some decent lads in our endeavor to end the conflict.

    It will be some time before you receive these words, and there will surely be more developments in this war by the time you do, but update you I will. Today Major Tempest left 100 Squadron on a promotional posting to London. It seems 100 Squadron is graduating majors to senior brass at a brisk rate. Major Cyril Burge, a career military man at the tender age of twenty-six, has replaced him. While we don't yet know much about him, we all agree he has large shoes to fill, as both Tempest and Christie were solid chaps.

I have been granted a reassignment for ground duty as a technical officer. While not Home Establishment, it will keep me active behind the action in my service to 100 Squadron. I know that you more than anyone will understand. After returning to the squad in early May and flying eight sorties, protracted fatigue set in. Sure, I was concerned about letting the squad down, but felt I could no longer keep up a façade of false confidence while in the air.

So I am off to Henley-on-Thames, the RAF Technical Officers' School, for a few weeks of training before returning to France. Of course, I was cautioned that if necessity presented itself, I would be returned to flying duties. One would hope that hostilities cease before that could occur.

The presence of the Americans continues to advance as they pour into the trenches and the skies. I am, of course, forbidden from speaking of specifics, but I can disclose an exciting development: the American flyers at nearby Neufchâteau Aerodrome have taught us to play American baseball. It's a bit like rounders, but with a longer bat used with two hands instead of one. The friendly rivalry is tops, and they beat us every time, but with practice, the Ochey crew may yet win a game or two.

Much as you were excited to reunite with your wife, I am over the moon about seeing Cissy for a couple of days before my training. I'm quite sure as an act of benevolence before he left the aerodrome, Major Tempest subtly manipulated my timing, as he has released me from the squad effective Tuesday, yet I don't report to Henley until the following Monday.

It is wonderful to write to you, Wellsey. You are dearly missed, and I'd like you to know you will forever remain a close friend. Do take care and protect your homeland.

Bob

...

Summer was in full bloom as I sat at a small bistro table outside Chequers listening to the song of a nearby oriole. She confidently approached from the left. Standing, I reflected that my Cissy outshone any French *fille* or Bernadette. Her smile was wide, as engaging as I'd come to appreciate but would never get too much of. "Hello, Bobby," was all she needed whisper to melt my heart.

Wrapping my arms around her, I whispered, "Hello, darling." Keeping hold of her shoulders, I stood back and said, "You look wonderful. What a beautiful dress, and in my favorite color, blue."

She giggled, then murmured, "I know."

"You're naughty, Ciss, you know that?"

"Uh-huh."

When the excitement of our greeting waned a little, I noticed a small, well-worn carpetbag lying at Cissy's feet. Following my eyes, she bent over to lift it by its leather handles so that it became concealed by her flowing skirt.

I grinned with expectation. "What's that, Ciss?"

She proffered a schoolgirl grin. "Oh, a bag to carry just a few of my things, much like you would use for a day trip."

"Or an overnight trip?"

"Yes, I suppose." She was now nervously swinging the bag from one hip to the next.

"Are you thinking of traveling today?"

"Mm-hmm. And I've arrived. Why are you making me feel nervous?"

"Because I love to see you vulnerable, just a little!"

Cissy clouted me on my leg with her bag. "You are rotten. Rotten, rotten, rotten!"

I pulled her to me, kissing her lightly, denying her accusation without any need for words.

I extended my hand to the bag. "Here, let me put this in my room before we walk. I'll be quick."

We talked excitedly as we strolled down High Street. I listened to Cissy's stories of life at Chilwell over the intervening weeks. She was most animated about her developing football skills and her scoring a goal. It was invigorating to listen to her speak, to hear about the basics of life away from war. Absorbed in her presence, I lost my sense of time, yearning to pay attention against nagging thoughts about having to leave in a mere two days.

Suddenly Cissy looked grim, her sweetness melting away to angst. "Bobby, I have something to tell you. Should I say it now?"

My mind raced with thoughts of what could have happened. Could Cissy be with child, reinfected, or something else? "Of course you should say it now." I tried to sound calm.

After studying the ground with intensity, she looked at me with flushed red cheeks. "Well, I can't do anything."

"Do anything?"

"Well, you know. It's a woman thing. The need for a pause, you know ... in activity. I'm so sorry, darling, but I can't change the timing, and well, you were only able to provide short notice—"

I felt relieved and put my finger to her lips. "Shhh, it's all right, it's fine. You know the best times I have are when I'm just holding you."

"I'm relieved, Bob. I thought I would be a disappointment to you."

"No, my love for you goes way beyond just that. But thinking about it, hmmm ..."

She wound up her arm and hit me on the shoulder. "Oh, you are rotten!"

With grins and giggles like adolescent lovers, we continued our stroll down High Street with arms locked before turning toward the estuary, our favorite walk. As the sun began to throw longer shadows from the west, we turned up to the sixteenth-century Wollaton Hall located behind the University of Nottingham, admiring the estate's roaming deer. We remained well east of the arms factory, as Cissy preferred to seclude herself, having told her manager that she was making an overnight visit with an aunt and felt I would not fit that bill if seen with her.

We lingered over dinner, as these were the longest days of the year, sharing a bottle of claret on the patio of a restaurant near the university. The setting reminded me of my beloved University of Saskatchewan, and I could feel the anxiety and stress of bombing over nighttime Germany melt away in the moment.

One of Cissy's gifts was to allow me momentary private thoughts, having an intuitive sense to remain silent to allow me periods to think. I appreciated her understanding of the sometimes brief moments that I drifted into deep thought. She looked over at me with such compassion, studied me until she felt I was ready to resume our talk.

"You went far away, darling. Do you want to talk about it?"

"I'm so sorry. I was just reflecting on how long I've been away from home. This university reminds me of Saskatoon, of what I was doing with my life before the war."

"You miss that, I know. But you'll get back to it, dear."

"I miss it, yes, and I miss my sisters. I'm confused about what I should do about my education, and you, as we've not spoken about our future."

"Oh, there is time for that, love. I've learned to take one day at a time, as there is so much in this wartime that fills our minds with loss and grief. We mustn't expect too much. I love you, Bob, and I know you love me, but do let us see an end to war before we make plans."

"It wouldn't hurt to make plans, something for each of us to hang on to."

"Don't you see, darling? We are of two classes from two countries. There is much to work through—"

Spreading my hands out for emphasis, I protested, "No, don't say that. The English class system was breaking down before the war, and it will never return. But aside from that, you and I are the same, think the same, and share the same values. I just had a better break than you. And I am also English as sure as you are."

"Yet our roots are different. Well, I don't really know my roots. Employed by the Beauchamps in Belgravia, I was so lucky, but I have no family history."

I smiled and leaned into the table. "There, see? You are refined by the same training as any society girl! And you're smart, smarter than most, with a fiery character as well."

Cissy looked pensive, doubt spreading across her face. "I don't know. All of this is unexpected. Can we not let it go for now? See what happens?"

"Of course, but I want you to know that my love for you is deeper than I've ever felt before, and I want us to be together." As the setting sun highlighted the flawlessly smooth skin across her high cheek bones, Cissy leaned across the table to kiss me, a long, smoldering kiss.

...

Saturday was a whirlwind of activity, as Cissy wanted to complete another estuary walk before she turned up for football practice later in the afternoon. We had spent a marvelous night in our Chequers bed snuggled in close, with me tucked in behind her after we took about an hour to kiss good night. I felt so intimate, so close, and so protected when lying as one.

We did not rise until ten, missing breakfast but managing to enjoy a scone with espresso at a café near the university. We walked over to the Wilford Suspension Bridge before heading to the Old Ground, disappointed not to see a Saturday-morning Nottingham Forest FC match. Making it back to Chequers by one, we had time to relax in my room.

Feeling the fresh-air goodness that comes with summer exercise, we fell back onto the bed in our undergarments, again tight with each other, Cissy in front. While we dozed for a bit I couldn't help but think about having to leave, not sure when we would again share these intimate moments. Cissy pushed into me while nestling the back of her head into my face, her hair tickling me, an erotic moment created by unbound intimacy.

She whispered softly, "I'm so sorry."

"For what? What could you be sorry for at a time like this?"

"For making you feel like this." She pushed her behind into me even farther. "For getting you that way and not being able to . . ."

"It's all right, I'm fine with—"

As she turned toward me, she flourished that naughty Cissy smile and murmured, "I think I know how to make it right, darling. Roll over onto your back."

...

We agreed to meet at the football pitch at four. Cissy preferred to return to the dormitory with her carpetbag in tow, explaining that the jealousies exchanged among the women lodgers meant it was best to keep our overnight visit a secret. Besides, she was to have been with an aunt!

The practice match was a thrill to watch. The energy on the pitch, as well as the incredible skill shown by many of the women, was outstanding. I would dearly love to have seen a scheduled match, but this was a bye week. Cissy played both thirty-minute halves, delighting me with her ball-maneuvering skills. After bathing and changing she was to meet me in front of Chequers at seven for our supper, after which we would have to separate once again.

Cissy arrived at Chequers in splendor, wearing a chic white dress flowing slightly out from her waist and a taupe corseted top, both of which perfectly outlined her figure while off-white heeled shoes and wide-brimmed hat provided unspoken elegance. I smiled at the contrast of a couple of hours before when she was in football shorts and jersey.

Her warm smile was alluring. "Hello, darling. Ready to stroll to dinner?"

"I am. You look so beautiful."

She beamed. "Thank you, Bobby. I love to look nice for you."

We dined at the same restaurant as the previous night, cherishing the time together before we had to part after saying good night. I had an early-morning train, and Cissy's shift began at six. The lamb chops and mash were a special treat when so much was being rationed, but we wanted to honor our love. I drank most of the wine, as Cissy wanted to have a clear head for the morning, which took extra time but was a perfect excuse for lingering on such a beautiful, warm evening. The night was magical!

The next morning, I was absorbed with thoughts of Cissy as the train unhurriedly steamed down the line toward Paddington where I would transfer to Henley. Pure bliss was how I would forever describe my two-day diversion from military duties.

...

The RAF Technical Officers' School was pleasantly located at the Imperial Hotel on the banks of the river Thames with both theory and practical classes held in various locations within walking distance. Although the full syllabus was eight weeks, Major Burge used my flying experience to justify an abridged version. Stripping away such topics as accounts, property surveys, paymaster duties, and mess organization, my lessons focused on procurement and maintenance of engines, aeroplanes, gunnery, bombing, radio, and photography. I was expected back at 100 Squadron by mid-July.

I attended classes and worked on advancing my skills with the fervor of a schoolboy. Without the burden of bombing sorties and with thoughts of Cissy constantly on my mind, I settled in to contentment about the future. With the Hun being defeated in battle after battle and rumors of attempted peace talks, some were suggesting that the end could be in sight before 1918 turned over to a new year.

Over the following couple of weeks, I wrote to Cissy every few days when I had time alone from the three officers I was lodged with. As we were all Canadian, we hatched a plan to celebrate Dominion Day at the Little Angel pub on the opposite shore of the Thames, across the Henley Bridge near the cricket grounds. Whether the other fourteen officers were interested in how we celebrated our 1 July confederation or just wanted a reason to party didn't matter; all were welcome.

Chapter 44

1 July, 1918

It was hot and sticky in the late afternoon, but our student delegation decided to sit outside in the shady side of the pub's garden. We were of diverse backgrounds but had all seen the war front, some infantry, some flying corps, and some both. Most admitted to being war fatigued, yet none were mired in grief; they all believed the war's end must come soon.

I was explaining what I knew of Canada's confederation, although I stumbled when questions arose about the status of Newfoundland. Why was it still considered a British colony and not part of the confederation? We were discussing this nuance when there was a faint boom that was matched by a slight rumble of the earth. Because it was instantly over and not repeated, the moment was lost on the majority of the pub's civilian patrons.

Yet, as we were veteran soldiers, the moment resonated since the sound had the familiar characteristics of artillery. There was neither a second nor a third clap nor any discernible flash, so after discussing it briefly, the celebrations resumed. For unknown reasons, though, the moment unsettled me. I tossed it off as lingering anxiety about shell explosions.

The next morning, I walked into the hotel's restaurant, taking in the seductive smell of hot breakfast, eggs, chips, oatmeal, and toast. Sitting down with my plate full, the officer opposite me pushed the *Henley Standard* across the table. I froze, feeling all the blood drain from my face as I took in the front page. The three-inch headline read, **MIDLANDS SHELL FACTORY EXPLOSION!** *134 Lives Lost at Chilwell. Approximately 100 to 150 Injured.*

Fuck! Oh God, Cissy! Was she all right? How would I find out?

I headed out the open door to the gardens, wanting solace, seeking relief from the sudden fever, newly formed sweat spreading down my face. Outside in the summer air, I leaned back against a wall, fumbling with a cigarette in one hand, my other shaking so badly I couldn't line up the flame to light it. As I threw it to the ground, I felt a churning in my stomach, a deep, intense pressure from within, that didn't dissipate as I bent over and retched.

Gathering my thoughts, I stood back up, thinking about the likelihood of harm coming to my girl, reminding myself there were some ten thousand employees up there. The chances were good that she was unharmed, alive but shaken by the blast. Cissy was a survivor, could handle just about any threat, having shown courage in many ways. But this was not about courage; it was about being randomly selected by our Lord. That was why dull anxiety continued to overtake my whole being.

How would I know for sure? Her employer from before the war wouldn't know, and neither would the innkeeper at Chequers. I suddenly realized there was no next of kin to contact, no family who would be notified. Cissy was alone in this world, except for her dorm mates, me, and Daisy. Daisy! Cissy would have registered Daisy as a contact, wouldn't she? I had to talk to her.

I brushed past my fellow officers who had stepped outside to see that I was all right, leaving them staring at me in wonderment. I banged on the bell at the reception desk until the clerk emerged from the hotel office.

"All right, I know it's brass, but don't break my bell!" He scanned my face. "Are you all right?"

I wasn't. I knew I was a pale-faced, nervous, shaking wreck. "Yes, f-fine," I stammered. "I need you to ring a friend." I paused to breathe, to think. "In London."

"Do you have the number?"

I struggled to think, to focus. "Yes! Well no, not just now."

"All right, could you please write the name and address down here?"

I quickly scribbled the contact information: *Mr. Eric Pitman, 34 Honor Oak Park, London.*

"All right, sir, I'll have the operator locate Mr. Pitman's number and place the call. That will be a tuppence for the three minutes, please."

I placed the coin on the desk and sat at the edge of the guest chair, anticipating immediacy. "Ahem. Mr. Pitman, it could be a while for the post office operator to locate the number and place the call."

"Oh" was all I could think of saying.

"I will have a junior come find you when we have successfully connected."

I wandered out into the bright sunshine, stunned, not remembering when I had felt this impatient. Forced to remember my responsibilities, I walked over to the ballroom where engine theory was being presented, thankful we were not away from the hotel on a field trip. My anxiety peaked and waned as the morning wore on and I overthought the situation, only half hearing the wear factors of pistons and valves.

Finally, toward eleven a young boy holding up a small chalkboard with my name on it entered the large room. "Phone call," he bellowed. "Phone call for Lieutenant Pitman!" I jumped up and impatiently followed him over to the reception area. *Can't he bloody move faster?*

"Daisy, you know why I called?"

"Oh yes, Bob, yes, Eric and I heard the bitter news this morning. I've heard nothing."

"We must go there; we must find out if she's—"

Daisy raised her voice over my edginess. "Bob, please listen to me. Eric inquired up at the Metropolitan Police. The Nottingham authorities won't let anyone near the area; it's been sealed off. Even if we could get there by train, they wouldn't allow us to go near the factory."

I sobbed, pleading over the telephone, "We could try. We must try."

We spoke as long as we were allowed. I was desperate to find a way to get to Chilwell, even on the pretense of military business. Yet I knew Daisy made sense; I would not be allowed access. The question stabbed repeatedly at my mind: *Why has Cissy not sent word, why has she not contacted Daisy?* But I knew things there would be chaotic.

The operator interrupted with her practiced nasal tone, "You have thirty seconds left, thirty seconds to complete the call."

"Daisy, are you there?" Without waiting for a response, I asked her to promise to contact me as soon as she heard anything. She confirmed she was Cissy's next-of-kin contact. "Daisy, you will let me know as soon—"

She was crying. "Yes, y-yes I will. I know how much you love Cissy. We will find out—" The call ended abruptly with a click as the timepiece in the telephone exchange reached exactly three minutes. I held the phone receiver in my hand for a long time, frozen in thought.

"Sir, may I take the phone?"

"Oh. Yes, of course."

I stumbled out into the bright sunshine, the type of day that Cissy and I loved to enjoy strolling along the Chilwell estuary. My mind reeled with emotion, hoping she would turn up all right but at the same time fraught with grief about the possibility of a dire outcome. And being one whose nature is to dive in, I was frustrated to think she was in peril and I could do nothing to help her.

Chapter 45

July 1918

The following days brought increased agony as I worked to convince myself that Cissy was fine, willed her to be fine. In the chaos of the situation, she could not possibly get a phone call or telegraph out. Could she? Yet I knew the longer time marched, the bleaker things looked. As the nation became embroiled with the disaster, speculation grew as authorities released scant bits of information: sabotage, spy work, poor safety practices, and negligence—it was all there. My classmates came to understand the situation and tried to protect me from the news, but on the third day, the headlines spoke of the intensity of the blast—eight tons of TNT. I foolishly got myself worked up as I calculated that eight tons would fill 450 of the 112-pound bombs we were dropping on Germany. The news reported those who perished were buried in a mass grave, so mutilated were their bodies. I wept silently.

That afternoon the young clerk approached with a telegraph, marked from Eric Pitman.

4 JULY, 1918
REGRET TO INFORM CONFIRMED CISSY ANNE TAYLOR PERISHED STOP WARNING NOT TO TRAVEL TO AREA STOP ERIC AND DAISY SYMPATHIES ON TRAGIC LOSS STOP YOU MUST VISIT BEFORE REDEPLOY STOP

I sat completely stunned. Silence cloaked the room as my classmates inferred the news, the instructor canceling the class for the remainder of the day. I was vaguely aware of muttering as they passed by, some gently placing their hands on my shoulder. When the room emptied the instructor pulled up a chair in front of me.

"Lieutenant, do you wish to talk?" With my arms wrapped around my stomach, I leaned forward in the chair and studied the floor, noticing for the first time the elaborate rose pattern in the carpet but keeping my silence. "She must have been very special, holding the tenderest place in your heart. I am so sorry for your loss."

I nodded, watching my tears drop onto the roses, making the petals darker, somehow more intense and prettier.

The instructor honored my moment with silence. After rocking a bit, I sat upright, looking into his face for answers I knew he didn't have. But I could see his compassion, feel his warmth. "Have you lost a girl, sir?"

"Yes, Bob. Yes I have. My wife died of cancer in 1912. I've learned to live life alone, but never a day goes by without my thinking of her. Perhaps I'll remarry after the war."

"I'm sorry, sir. My situation must seem trivial—"

"No, not trivial. Love is love, and you need to grieve. Do you have anyone to assist?"

"Yes, my cousins in London."

"Look, it is almost Friday afternoon. You can miss the weekend activities. I'd like you to go into London, try to deal with things, and return Sunday night."

I looked at my instructor, not saying anything, my emotions choking me. At that moment, with news so raw, I felt relief at my instructor's incredible gift. I knew he was setting aside a war in respect of my personal anguish. Eventually, I stood to shake his hand and thought there really were some good sorts in this military. I mumbled, "Thank you, Captain. You are so very kind."

...

Late Friday, Daisy and Eric met me at the Honor Oak Park station. We walked slowly along the largely deserted street in the dark. Few words were spoken. I had kept a shell around me on the train down from Paddington as the Friday-night revelers came and went at each station, but now felt compelled to fill the void. I squeezed Daisy's hand. "Are you doing all right?"

"Thank you for asking. I'll be fine. I'm worried about you. Love between couples is different, at times stronger than between girlfriends."

"Maybe different, but the loss is equally painful."

Eric put out a bottle of Chianti with bread and cheese. We spoke of the tragedy in whispers, about the mechanics of the blast but avoiding the tender discussion about Cissy. Yet I went to bed holding a horrible image of the way Cissy died, she now lying in a cold mass grave at St. Mary's Church. I knew there was nothing else they could have done, being unable to identify the bodies, but it hurt to think she could not have been honored better.

My head was pounding as I lay on the bed questioning. Why had Cissy been chosen out of thousands of others? When flying sorties I had selfishly feared for my life so many times, and now Cissy had been taken, when she hadn't once complained? Like Perce, why were the good ones taken so violently?

I forced myself to think fond memories of Cissy, to fill the emptiness that was now such a painful reality. My eyes filled with tears and my breathing shortened, chest heaving up and down as I imagined her as a lively, happy, and beautiful being. I needed time to soak up those memories, carry them in capsules I would never forget, and to bury the sorrow—time which war did not accommodate.

I didn't hear Daisy creep into the room to kneel beside me. I hadn't realized, didn't at all remember moving to the floor, nor my uncontrollable sobbing that woke her in the early dawn hour. She held me, stroking my head, as I leaned against the wall, knees to my chest. "Shhh, shhh." It felt comforting as I opened myself to her compassion, realizing this was her manner of grieving as well.

At dinner Saturday, I confided in Eric and Daisy something that I hadn't fully realized but that seemed inevitable once the war ended, something that I had tried to engage Cissy in. "You really loved Cissy enough to marry her?" asked Eric.

Emotion raced through my veins, coursing into my heart, as I gulped back the urge to cry, even though I had already sobbed myself dry. "Yes, I know I did, and I know we would have figured out a way to make that work, different countries and all."

Daisy filled my glass, which I eagerly accepted though I had drunk enough Chianti. "You deserved her, and she you. Time heals, and as sure as I will nurture more friends, you will too as life cycles forward."

I left for Henley at noon on Sunday and returned to classes Monday morning, feeling as good as I could expect. I respected Daisy's prophecy, loved her for energizing my strength with thoughts of a future someone else, but not for now. My love for Cissy was too strong to think that anyone else could hold my heart the way she had.

...

It was a beautiful summer morning as I stepped from the Crossley tender that had fetched me from the Nancy train station. All was as I had left it, the familiar conjoining of chirping birds with whirring engines, and the green grassy airfield lying under a deep blue sky while insects buzzed and airmen scurried. This was my home, my refuge, my stability.

Following an afternoon walk alone in the woods, I was returning to my hut that Howie and I now shared when I heard my name called out from Hangar No. 2. "Bob! Hey, Bobby!" Hardy raced toward me. "How are you? How was training?" he yelled before he got close enough. "Are you all right? You look—aw, bloody hell, you don't look so good."

In spite of my puffiness, I looked straight at him. "It's all right; I know I look terrible. I expected to be asked."

"Something happen? Don't mean to press, but is your family well?"

If there was anyone at the aerodrome who could help me transition back, it was Hardy. I trusted him, trusted his understanding. "It's Cissy. She's dead." I knew my voice sounded barren.

He looked at me, absorbing my grief, then stammered, "D-dead? Cissy? Are you sure? I mean, how—"

"Explosion." Tears welled. I needed to hold it together, so I looked away to check myself before turning back. "The Chilwell Ammunition Factory explosion."

"Chilwell. Ammunition. Oh, Bob, she wasn't one of—"

"Afraid so. She was such a fine girl, a real darling, my sweetheart."

"Would you like to talk? Would that help?"

"What I would like is to get on that motorcycle of yours, take a trip over to Nancy for coffee, perhaps. Would you do that for me?"

"I'm sure it's fine. Let me just go explain to my lieutenant. I'll pick you up in front of your hut in, say, ten minutes?"

The sound of the Douglas approaching was soothing, providing a comfort so often embedded in the type of tones that deliver memories of past pleasures. We flew along country roads, past farms and green fields, up rises and down road grades before reaching the flats leading into Nancy. I didn't let go of Hardy's tunic even as we bumped slowly along the cobblestones leading to the café. I was feeling the best I had felt since the sad news.

Bernadette, ever so excited to see Hardy, greeted us by arranging a table on the terrace. While I had thought her presence would set off more emotion, seeing her innocence and beauty actually worked the opposite, creating a sense of peacefulness.

I explained everything, feeling at times inadequate as I was not able to answer Hardy's understandable questions about what had actually happened and why. "They aren't saying much, so I don't know if there was a safety lapse, an irresponsible rush to increase production, or some inevitable accident when a factory produces thirty-five hundred high-explosive shells per day."

He looked at me with complete attention and sympathy. "Nasty position to be in, not being family but losing the most loving soul of your life."

"Yet even family don't know. She didn't have family. So I'm in the same position, I mean, *I* was her family, my cousins Daisy and Eric were her family. I, all of us, can only cling to the Minister of Munition's sympathies."

"Churchill? What did he say?"

I gathered my thoughts in recall of the exact words. "I'll never forget it. 'The courage and spirit shown by all concerned, both men and women, commands our admiration.' Cissy had courage, and gads, did she have spirit!"

"She did. I could see it in her eyes, see it in her movements, when I met her way back at the Savoy that night. She was lucky to have had such wonderful times with you before her life . . . oh, I'm sorry, I didn't mean to—"

"You can say it. Before her life was cut short. Well, it was, dreadfully short, which I've got to accept. But thanks for saying those kind words. Means a lot."

Bernadette kept espressos coming until we protested and realized we had to return to the aerodrome. She sensed a level of grief at the table, so Sam explained there was a loss in my life. As we stood to say goodbye, she gave me a warm hug and an endearing kiss on both cheeks while whispering, "*Mes condoléances.*"

Chapter 46

August 1918

For weeks my thoughts and emotions had been aerobatic, like a Sopwith fighter caught in a constant loop-the-loop. Returning to the familiar hum and routine of the aerodrome not only invigorated my spirits but also provided grounding as I attended to my new routine duties.

The Vicar, Howie, and others were unconditionally supportive without overcompensating. I knew I was adjusting well when I felt a healthy jealousy over Vic and Howie forming that same pilot-observer bond that Wellsey and I had once had, having flown numerous sorties as a team. But I had made my own bed as a ground technician.

My mind was geared for the challenge of understanding the intricacies of a new bird that was just then arriving to replace the Fee, the giant Handley Page O/400. While it had been employed in other squadrons since its introduction in April, 100 Squadron was just receiving these massive long-range bombers. The activity around our first arrival was frenetic.

I stood on the field, and after staring up at its foreboding height, I followed the long shadow of its underbelly. My eyes focused on the elongated propellers that gave the illusion of extending across the airfield to the mess. I thought how lucky I was to work with Hardy and his team on the new craft. I may have been appointed Technical Officer, but he was the brains of our technical unit.

Against the summer breeze, I waved the lit match over the fragrant tobacco that I had just packed snug in the bowl of my pipe before looking up to see Howie and Hardy waving. "Hello, Howie. Hey, Sam."

"Checking out the big bird, are we?" asked Howie with a grin. "Those bastards over in Hun-land will not sleep under threat of these aerial dreadnoughts, wot?"

I again looked up and down the aeroplane to assess its alleged capability before locking eyes on the massive bomb racks. "Suppose you're right when you put it that way."

Hardy followed my line of sight. "Sixteen 112-pounders or eight 230-pounders. Now, that's some firepower."

"Slow as a Zep, though?" I asked.

"Oh no," he said. "Two 360-horse Rolls Royces and a 100-foot wingspan pulls her along at quite a clip. Can make Frankfort, perhaps even Berlin, from here."

I laughed. "Sure, but can she make it back?"

Howie spoke up, "The factory lads say seven-hundred-mile range."

"That's comforting. Frankfort at two hundred miles is an easy in and out, but Berlin at five hundred miles would be fine if you were staying for dinner with the kaiser!"

Howie understood the flawed claim as he quipped, "Or unless our genius generals hatched a harebrained plan to refuel somewhere on the return."

Hardy weighed in, "Or just plan to leave you to your own resources?" Realizing that sounded insensitive, he followed up quickly.

"Oh, that was not funny." Howie pretended to proffer a schoolmaster glare before wielding a friendly punch on his coverall sleeve.

I turned to face Howie, grinning not because of the sideways joke but rather feeling exhilarated to be part of the squadron life again. "The flight roster shows you and the Vicar are getting some practice runs in this bird."

"Somewhat. But as more HPs roll in, we'll have more chance to become acquainted with the new gal. Meanwhile, we continue plugging along with sorties in our ole Fee."

Hearing a thump above our heads, the three of us looked up to a bottom in blue coveralls beginning its descent down the ladder leading from the cockpit. With feet finally on the ground, the grinning mechanic turned to face us. "Hullo."

Hardy picked up the initiative. "Charlie Crickmore, this is Lieutenant Pitman, our new Technical Officer, and you know Lieutenant Chainey, of course."

"Ah, you're First Air Mechanic Crickmore. I've heard good things," declared Howie.

"Nice to meet you, sir! I'm Crick. Promoted to corporal when I transferred over from the 216s. I also passed aerial gunnery, sir."

"Quite, Crick. My apologies, it slipped my mind what with coveralls hiding your rank and all."

Crick beamed with enthusiasm. "That's all right, sir. With three large squadrons on this aerodrome, it's not easy to remember everything, wot?"

I studied Crick's innocent-looking face and ruddy complexion, wondering if an officer's mustache would provide more maturity. "You're quite young, are you?" I asked.

His enthusiasm was catching. "No, sir. I recently turned twenty-one, but I was eighteen on enlistment. It's been a long three years, I'll say."

"With that experience and as a trained gunner, I'm surprised you haven't been selected for a commission," I said.

"Oh, not possible, Lieutenant Pitman. You see, I'm only a brass fitter by trade, so I wouldn't qualify as an officer."

I thought about the ridiculous protocol the British military still practiced after four years of hellish war. It was shameful that university students with no military background were still being commissioned while a more capable type like Crick would forever be denied a leadership role. "Shame. You seem a good fellow with good intuition."

His grin wouldn't quit. "Thank you, sir."

"Please call me Bob."

"Crick, just so you know, Bob is a wizened flyer having performed numerous sorties for 100 Squadron over Hun-land since mid '17," declared Howie.

"Pleased to serve with you, Bob. One of the originals, I'd say."

Howie saw my embarrassment so cut in to change the focus. "Explain this machine to Lieutenant Pitman, if you please."

"Yes, Lieutenant—er, may I call you Howie?"

Howie nodded his approval as we walked the length of the O/400. Rounding the tail planes, all of us agreed this must be the largest aircraft ever produced. Crick was animated, full of excitement as he pointed up and along the starboard wing. "Hundred-foot wingspan, twenty-two feet from ground to that top wing, 360-horsepower twin engines, and weighs eight-five hundred pounds empty. You might think she's black, but she's actually olive green, which hides better in the dark. About seven feet to the bottom of the cockpit, Bob."

"And fully loaded? Bombs, petrol, cooling water, crew—what's it rated then?" I wondered.

"That takes her up to about thirteen thousand pounds, sir."

"Speed?" asked Howie.

"Oh, maximum ninety-seven mph at five thousand feet, about eighty at maximum ceiling of eight thousand. Two hundred gallons of petrol in four tanks will keep her up for eight hours."

Hardy had been quiet to respect his junior's enthusiasm but showed encouragement. "And tell them about weaponry, Crick!"

"She can take up to five Lewises, two in front and three in the rear gunner's station. And two thousand pounds of bombs. A real war machine, if I may say so."

Hardy was proud of his air mechanic and grinned to show it. "Yes, you may say so, and we agree with you."

Crick looked honored. "Would you like to go on up and have a look about, Bob?"

Standing in the cockpit, I was awed by the large steering wheel—similar to that of an automobile—that the pilot would use to control the aircraft. The full seat beside him gave the observer access to the same instrumentation. The design in the forward gunnery was closer to the Fee with two Lewises and the bomb release levers, but it seemed odd to access it through a small portal from the cockpit.

I turned to view the length of the aeroplane from the cockpit and was taken aback by its immenseness. The rear gunnery was located about two thirds of the way back, armed with two Lewises atop and one underneath for rear firing. Curiously, there was no capability for voice communication between the cockpit and the rear gunner.

Standing on the field below, Howie cupped his hands around his mouth for a stronger voice. "You two gonna wait out the war up there?"

I watched Crick easily navigate down the cockpit ladder, noticing just how high the drop was. It struck me that a crew in need after a forced landing would require a lot of pluck to descend, unlike the Fee where one could easily jump to ground.

"Quite the aeroplane," said Howie. "We're lucky to have you leading the mechanics pool and ordnance, someone to bust through the usual military bunk-de-bunk."

I looked at Hardy before winking at Crick. "My task is made significantly more efficient with mechanics like these two, Howie!"

...

There was abundant reason to be buoyed by the turn of events in the war as the Hun continued to give up ground. Most promising was that General Pershing, with his American forces, was working well with Field Marshall Haig to prosecute effectively and eliminate enemy resistance. So quick were events changing that 100 Squadron ceased their attacks in order to move the aerodrome another fifty miles deeper into the Vosges at Xaffevillers during the second week of August. Yet, in spite of my concentration on work, I was weighed down with melancholy.

I was feeling good for a few days after that fine afternoon with Hardy over at Nancy, but the nights kept getting frightful. With dreams of explosions and bursts of flame, I relived the Somme, connecting my near death to Cissy's savage demise. So real were the sensations that in slumbered wakefulness I could smell cordite and choked from smoke that was not there, before waking to realize I was safe. The cold sweat would dry quickly as I lay back, staring at the ceiling in the wee hours of the hot summer.

Howie was always there for me, my bunkmate who was turning out to be as much a dear friend as Wellsey, if not as easygoing. Before the recent aerodrome move, he and the Vicar had been active with many night sorties in support of the push, returning late, then bright and cheery in the morning.

On a hot, sticky morning toward the last week of August, we made our way to the mess, where many of the airmen had set up outdoor tables in the shade. The Vicar was reading a London newspaper he had pilfered from somewhere, probably Burge's office.

"Why bother reading the news when we're making it right here?" chortled Howie.

The Vicar looked up, always ready with a quip. "I like to read about it over and over, to stroke my ego, perhaps!" He smiled brightly and nodded. "Hello, Bob."

"Mornin'. A fine one indeed."

With platefuls of the ubiquitous eggs, chips, and toast that never seemed to vary for breakfast, we tucked in. I looked at the Vicar, then Howie. "You boys have been going at it hard since we resettled, eh?"

Howie chewed while the Vicar considered the question. "Quite. Enemy aerodromes, night after night over Morhange, Buhl, Freisdorf, and any others we can locate. And we hit them again and again."

I visualized the Fees cutting their engines as they coasted down to drop their heavies. "Hun must be losing a lot of ground, eh?"

"And aircraft," said Howie. "Albatross, Fokkers, and even a couple of Gothas have been smashed. Not to mention morale."

"Yet the bastards won't lay down their arms," I declared. "Do we need to bomb Frankfort itself?"

The Vicar suddenly looked at me with hard, questioning eyes. "Have you been brought into the fold, Pitman?"

He made me feel like a schoolboy caught dipping a girl's pigtails in the inkwell, but I didn't know why. "No," I protested. "Just seems we may have to push that far to get them to surrender."

The Vicar studied me before lowering his voice. "That is exactly the plan with the new O/400. If they don't give in, we attack their urban homeland."

I whistled. "That's aggressive, but I see the point."

I did from a military perspective, but I knew that attacking their cities was a new path we were crossing. I understood the rationale that we would target railways and other industrial sites—in spite of starving troops being defeated in an increasing manner, the Germans refused offers of armistice. Yet I also knew civilians would be employed in German factories and railway networks. Never mind that the Germans themselves had bombed our innocents in England and France. Thoughts of earlier bombing and strafing rose to my mind's surface, the horror of it still real after all these months. Yet this was war, *c'est la guerre*.

...

That afternoon all officers were called to a special briefing; it was to be a historic day. The boyish-looking Major Burge stepped into the mess, his reputation as a fierce fighter of the skies preceding him as a commanding authority. Yet his gentlemanly, polished manner—honed during his Indian Army stint—was always precise. "At ease, officers. This is a particularly special evening, the first use of our O/400s on a sortie." Brief applause broke out and spread across the room before Burge extinguished it with a raised hand. "Three Fees with crews of two will fly alongside three Handleys with crews of three. The six aircraft will join 97 and 215 Squadrons over Boulay."

Burge's adjutant announced the teams. Leading off was Box and Inches with Crick as their gunner. We all applauded Corporal Crickmore, who looked so proud to be chosen for his new gunnery skills and more so for being trusted on a historic run. It was not unheard of for a mechanic to fly a sortie, but unusual. The Vicar, Howie, and Jamieson would follow with the Savery, Gilson and O'Donoghue team as anchor. The CO's assistant surveyed the room, then agitatedly asked, "I say, where are Box and Inches?"

Crick jumped at the opportunity to defend his officers. "They are out on a practice run and missed the announcement, sir."

I looked over at Burge, who broke into a slight smile, perhaps realizing just how dedicated Box and Inches were. "Blast, they're practicing again?" He knew that the two relentless flyers had flown together for a squadron record thirty-two sorties in only seven months' service.

We all admired George Box and Bobby Inches for their unflinching courage and dedication to flying. They seemed to embody the British Isles, George with his fine Yorkshire manners, Bobby with his Scottish brogue, and tonight, Crick bringing his easygoing Kentish ways.

At 2000 hours, the six machines were set to meet those from the other two squadrons over the lighthouse before pushing on to the Boulay aerodrome, where they would drop thousands of pounds of explosives. All squad personnel who did not have duty assignments came out to watch 100's inaugural HP mission. The Handleys would take off first, led by Box in the pilot's chair and Inches beside him as observer. And there was Crick, beaming as he waved down to the crowd from the rear gunner's slot.

The mighty Rolls Royces roared to life, the immense aeroplane sounding invincibly powerful as Box throttled up to test the pitch. Signaling their number by Morse, they waited and received their green light from the control tower for takeoff. Box from way on up gave a wave of his gloved hand to the crowd below and moved the machine forward to cheers of support. Gaining speed as he roared down the flare path into the wind, the machine lifted itself fifteen or so feet above the ground and leveled out. There was a collective gasp of relief as the wheels scarcely cleared the control tower before heading toward the line of poplar trees at the aerodrome perimeter, on toward skies beyond.

Yet the big bird remained level, ceased climbing. With less altitude than required, they soared directly at the poplars. No one breathed, dared not say anything, as the red engine exhaust alarmingly aligned with the trees. *Get up, get up!* Suddenly, the right wing hit one of the trees, causing the mighty machine to keel over onto its side, falling hard to earth, bursting into flames. It seemed like forever, those agonizing seconds before we all realized what was to be next, some men diving to the ground, others for cover, and still others just staring in disbelief. The bombs exploded with such intensity that the poplars blew back as if in a hurricane, pieces of machinery thrown hundreds of yards in every direction, fire raging high into the night sky. With increasing horror, a realization dawned about the outcome of the three, praying they had perished quickly. None of us could comprehend if death inside that fire trap had been instant or whether they'd had horrifying moments to think about their inevitable demise.

I stood in place, paralyzed by my thoughts. This was how Cissy had died, wasn't it? This was the horror of Chilwell laid out in front of me. The Lord wanted me to understand, to struggle through the moment she perished. No, these soldiers were not sacrificed for that, but as long as their destiny was to offer their souls, I was to experience it. In that instant I ached again with grief, for Cissy and now for the brave three.

I snapped to, realizing I couldn't remain in place in a state of self-pity. All my senses came alive in my will to help. With adrenaline coursing through me, I surged with other flyers and ground crew toward the sickening wreckage, assuming all bombs had been detonated, perhaps not caring if they hadn't—so strong was the instinctive call to action. We saw bodies and pieces of bodies strewn all over, some charred beyond recognition, others thrown clear in their death but spared from burning. But there were too many bodies, too many pieces, when only Box, Inches, and Crick had been in the aircraft.

Time brought the answer. The armament division from 97 Squadron had been close by and had run toward the flaming wreck to help rescue our three. In the seconds it took to reach the wreck, they were cruelly met with the armament blasts and ensuing inferno. Eight were killed and fifteen seriously injured. This was the saddest day in the sqaudron's existence and in the embryonic history of the newly formed IAF.

Everyone worked through the night with the cleanup, doing whatever they could, sharing an overwhelming need to do something, anything, to help the squadrons of the IAF move forward. Atrocities of war were expected, but not when accidents like this happened. In time we would know if an innocent mistake or mechanical failure was the cause.

...

Sleep did not come at first as I lay there tossing myself across the bed and turning over and over in muddled thought. I clearly imagined the horror that had been reality just a few hours before. Minute details emerged, scenes I did not realize I had noticed, menacing particulars that I attempted to verify in my mind—did they really happen? Howie lay across from me, a dark bulge under a thin blanket that I dared not disturb even though I wanted to talk, even with slumber beckoning.

Suddenly, I lurched violently. Howie was hovering over me, his hand tightly holding my shoulder while he whispered to me. My breathing, I couldn't get my breathing under control. What was he saying? *Why doesn't he speak up if he wants to talk? Why is he shining that light on me, blinding me?*

"Bob, Bobby!"

"Wha—"

Louder now, "Bobby, wake up. Wake up, old boy. You're dreaming." He shook me gently.

I sat bolt upright. "D-dreaming?" I heaved with short, shallow breaths. "I was dreaming?" I looked up at Howie, compassion in his eyes as I remembered bit by bit. "Oh God, it was awful. People screaming, burning as they ran through the darkness, looking like lanterns, horrible-shaped lanterns."

I sat there a while as my breathing settled before again speaking. "Bloody fool I am, these dreams, nightmares. For the longest time I couldn't sleep for thinking about last night, yet I must have dozed."

"You're no fool, not at all. You're still in mourning, you know that. Last night would trigger nightmares in any of us, but especially . . ."

"You can say it, Howie. I know especially since Cissy died

that way. I know I faced that reality while I stood there last night. Horrible business, fucking horrible." I wrung my nightshirt, absentmindedly pulling it away from my clammy skin. "Not just the innocents like Cissy, like Crick, like my good friend Percy, but all of the horrible deaths, all of the disgust and terror."

"Bobby, best you get yourself dressed, get washed and shaved. It will be light soon. I'll do that too. No sense laboring over the vagaries and revulsions of war. We are almost at the end, got to see this through."

I smiled weakly. "You're right, Howie. Thanks for being a good friend."

Chapter 47

August 1918

Major Burge and the other COs at Xaffevillers aerodrome understood that morale was dangerously low and immediately grounded all sorties for a few days. Attempting to break the gloom, Major-General Hugh Trenchard, commander of the IAF, addressed the personnel on the airfield. His unusually loud voice was a stark reminder of his nickname, Boom.

"Good afternoon, RAF flyers and ground crew. It is with sadness that I stand here today to formally acknowledge the loss of one of our new O/400s along with the crew who perished, including those of 97 Squadron who ran in pursuit of rescue. I daresay those heroes will be remembered alongside all who have given their lives for King and Country.

"Yet these events do happen in times of war. It is with much pride that I can confirm there are trained flyers to fill in behind and plenty of Handley Page's rolling out of factories as we speak. We wage war in all circumstances and at all costs if we are to gain the peace. That we will do.

"We will continue to prosecute my targets with assets that are delivered on time and in top shape. You will not be short of aircraft, matériel, or supplies. Armed with such power, we will get cracking! Thank you, and God save the King."

While the airmen respectfully returned a murmured "God save the King," they stood there dumbfounded. Major Burge had listened with his head bowed to the gridiron flooring, unable to look at his squadron. In the priority of shame, Trenchard seemed to have felt it was more important to have lost an aircraft than its crew. Evidently to him there was a ceaseless supply of airmen and crew at his disposal, a disgusting reference to the commodity that was human lives.

All men and the few nursing sisters standing there that day felt the bad taste of his seeming lack of remorse. His targets! His aeroplanes! Get cracking! All during a memorial for irreplaceable lost souls.

The next day I was summoned to Major Burge's quarters. "At ease, Pitman. Sit, please."

"You requested my presence, sir."

Burge appeared uncertain, which belied the image he crafted of himself with carefully Brilliantined hair, heavy but well-groomed eyebrows, and dark authoritarian eyes, all of which hid his youthful face. Yet there he was, acting nervous. Did Trenchard light into him for something? "Yes, quite, things to discuss. I've spoken to your fellow Lieutenants Conover and Darby as well. Lay of the land as it were."

Would he jolly well get to the point? "Yes, sir."

"You're one of my longest-term officers, my technical man with a strong moral compass too. It has come to my attention that there may be some discord among the flyers. That true?"

Which way was he leaning? Was I to be a rat scurrying along the grassy field to squeal tasty bits of discord for the major just so he could come down hard? I couldn't read Burge well. "Sir, the disaster put the wind up, you know."

"Come now, Pitman, I know that. What is the tone, the morale, just now?"

I needed to ease into this, aware that Trenchard's mighty ego might have forced Burge to seek out any dissonance. "Talk of the Handley Pages perhaps not being battle ready, maybe as a result, you know, of the brass pushing the aircraft to be ready when there may still be development work to be done." There, it had been said, and I hoped without attributing any blame other than to those up top.

"Speak freely, Lieutenant."

"The lads are scared, sir, fearful of another disaster. There are many rumors circulating that the cause of the crash was mechanical, not pilot error. No one wants to blame poor dear Charlie Box, sir, nor Bobby Inches, instead of believing the crash was caused by a malfunction of some sort." Damn! Did I just implicate the ground crew?

Burge was stoic. "Any theories?"

"Well, sir, there is word that the rear elevator controls may have accidentally been kept strapped down, you know, such that they would remain stationary while on the ground to avoid damage."

"Yes, I know why they'd be strapped down."

Finally, the known Burge was emerging, the one who wanted to get on with the story. That was a good sign. I resumed, "Well, if the straps hadn't been removed before flight, the aircraft would have little lift, perhaps forcing the nose down, entangling the aircraft in the poplars."

Burge stood, pondered what I had just stated while moving across the room. His back was to me while he stared out the window, before turning.

"Cigarette, Pitman?"

Why was he stalling? What had I said that might be worth mulling? "Definitely, sir."

He studied me as I moved forward to suck in the draft, lighting the Gitanes from his silver lighter that showed the words "Gott mit Uns" emblazoned on the side. The irony of "God with Us" on an enemy lighter raised the question of how our good Lord could be with both sides of the conflict. The story of why Burge even owned this implement would have to wait for another time.

Burge evidently trusted my judgment, as he disclosed the possible cause. "The aeroplane was so badly burned that our mechanics have little evidence from which to make a determination. What you are saying and what I believe is that there was indeed ground crew error."

"There are some that would agree, some not, sir."

He pressed on: "However, and you know this from your many sorties, Pitman, the pilot and observer have equal responsibility to inspect their aircraft."

"I agree, sir. It could have been that Box and Inches had been out in the aircraft most of the afternoon and perhaps assumed it would not be banded."

"I won't carry this any further, Lieutenant, except to bless Box and Inches, and the young lad Crickmore. Bloody sad turn. This is terrible business, and we must get this squadron on its feet, so I ask you to keep our discussion quiet. That's the end of it. No fault laid."

That was not an order, instead a confirmation of trust and mutual respect. "Yes, Major. I'll do everything I can to assist with tonight's sortie."

"Good, good." Burge looked pensive and again turned to the window, uncertain of further comment, but then seemed to relent as he shifted inward again. "Ah, one other thing, Pitman. I'm aware of the effect the major-general's words had on the squad. I'm also aware that he is a man of keen dignity, of loyalty to his airmen. His position is very difficult, trying to be seen as a caring parent, if you will, yet run an air force during the worst conflict mankind has ever seen. He did not express his sorrow in a manner that was easily interpreted; however, he has the best interests of every one of us at hand. I'd like you to help me support him, Lieutenant."

"Yes, sir."

"Dismissed, Pitman. And ah, well done!"

So I was to be a trusted ally to watch over the squad's morale, but also an unwitting recruit to allay any animosity toward the brass. That was an ugly torch to carry since I couldn't withhold breakdowns in the squad's resolve, yet I had no inclination to be—*what was I thinking in that meeting?*—that scurrying rat. And if that weren't enough, my guts still churned and nightmares persisted about the agony of this war and of losing Cissy.

Chapter 48

September 1918

The weather remained stable, and for the most part the Fees had been retired, picked up for domestic use by the United States Air Service, or sent to air depot graves. Bombing power increased as a smaller number of giant O/400s ferried larger amounts of explosives over to German targets. All of this meant that the Vicar and Howie had been busy in the air most days since the beginning of the month. One evening, the mess was a hive of activity as they arrived after a raid, the other aviators having a night free.

Howie stepped up to the bar, while the Vicar strolled over to the corner table where I was glancing through a newspaper. I chortled, "Hello, Vic. Was it lonely being the single aircraft flying over to Metz tonight?"

"Bobby, how are you? Thanks to your chaps for seeing us in safely."

"Pleasure is mine, Vic. Successful?"

"Uh-huh. Sixteen 112-pounders on the railway leading into the station will keep them busy with repairs. I know the kaiser wants his bloody line kept open to Berlin, but why don't they just give up the ghost, eh?"

"Speaking of the kaiser, I'm hearing the Austrians want to sue for peace, but he won't have it."

"What maniacal mind would keep throwing men at a losing cause? The rumor is that he is dragging convalescents and Spanish flu victims out of hospitals and sending them to the front."

Listening as he arrived with three pints, Howie interjected, "Terrible business. We're pushing them hard north of here, and they're ceding ground at Amiens and Bapaume, but still their generals remain stubborn."

"And the Americans were successfully engaged at St. Mihiel in a similar vein," added Vic.

Vic and Howie were really wound up, and I fed their egos. "Not to mention the hate you two are raining down on their transport capabilities."

"Thanks, Bobby, but somehow they seem to recover in short order."

I sipped my ale, pondering the perspective of the Germans. They were with little food and supplies, but still able to keep their airfields and railways operational after our continual bombing onslaughts. "Say, what of Jamieson? I saw you subbed Blakemore in as gunner tonight?"

"Jamieson's a trooper. He rode with us on the Handley straight through until tonight," said Vic.

Howie put down his glass, quick to intercede. "Even troopers get tired, though."

I thought about how tired I myself had become while flying last spring, night after night in a wood-and-fabric aeroplane, on watch for enemy aircraft and Archie shrapnel through weather that played havoc, or mechanical hiccups that constantly gnawed at my nerves. The spraying arc of gunfire that chopped down the enemy from five hundred feet was merciless, injuring and maiming in open spaces or killing them, if they were lucky. Only that unique soldier, the one who flew on those sorties, would ever truly know the horror and the success wrapped into the same bundle of emotion. Yes, the term *trooper* was appropriate.

The Vicar looked over at me, compassion in his smile. "You all right, Bob?"

"Oh, yes, yes. Just thinking about ole Scottie Jamieson. Hope he's not burning out."

"He's grounded for now, I'm afraid," said the Vicar. "Blunt thing is he can't properly protect our rear when he's tired, run down as it were." He drew himself in closer to the table, which Howie and I instinctively followed, somehow knowing there was to be secrecy. "The inaugural Frankfort raid is due to proceed in a few days. We're just waiting to hear from London. We need a seasoned gunner for a sortie of that magnitude."

I was feeling a bit defensive of myself. "Well, there's any number of qualified observers—Segner, Pascoe, and Shillinglaw for instance."

"Sure, there is a pool," said Howie, "but it all depends on their condition and availability. This will be a long, arduous journey, and we need the right gunner."

The Vicar wore a knowing look and canny grin. "We'll see how things pan out."

...

Daisy and Eric's letter was a boost I needed, full of compassion, love, humor, and understanding. It wasn't that letters from home didn't offer those, but theirs provided a different level of understanding, one that only a shared love for Cissy could grasp. Due to the pain, I had decided not to tell anyone in the family about my relationship until after the war. If at all.

13 September, 1918

My Dearest Cousins Daisy and Eric,
I was elated to have received your letter dated 25 August, finally catching up to me at a new aerodrome. Being located ever more easterly than at any time in this war is certainly a good sign of our progress. To see the end of the conflict this year would be heaven sent.

It was so heartfelt of you to inquire after my health, especially my frame of mind. Daisy, you mentioned you were beginning to accept Cissy's death, replacing it with fond memories of who she was instead of what she could have been. I feel I, too, am beginning to remember her in that manner. Although I miss her in the most infinite way, I feel lucky to have been touched by such a loving soul. She will never be far from my thoughts.

Thank you for visiting the gravesite at St. Mary's Attenborough and for remembering me to Cissy. You describe such a peaceful setting with the tree canopy and flower gardens I know she adored. I will visit myself just as soon as I am able.

Eric, it is wonderful that you have been re-employed at the newspaper, and getting your old job back as development editor is tops! As I remember from Walthamstow, you would sit up nights writing and writing. We had such a creative household between music, writing, and that bit of cabinet making. Our current reality makes one appreciate those times when we had such enviable choices.

I laughed at the image you described of young Stanley marching up and down your street as an officer of our King's army. I am pleased, Eric, that you and I had such an impact. I only hope and pray he never has to fight for the liberty we are struggling to protect. May this be the war that ends all conflict. Please give my youngest cousin a great-big, loving squeeze for me.

Well, my dearest cousins, I must sign off now with a promise to visit just as soon as any leave is granted. I am not holding my breath since, in this latest push, all British, French, and American soldiers are engaged to the fullest. May this then be the final surge to victory!

Yours with love,
Bob

Chapter 49

15 September, 1918

"Pitman, enter. Thank you for coming at a moment's notice. I trust my adjutant managed a smile when he rousted you."

With a salute I looked upon Burge sitting at his desk with none of the disquiet he had shown the other day, looking as authoritarian as ever with a strong physique evident under his tight-fitting, impeccably tailored tunic. London money and title were well alive!

"Sit, please." Burge motioned to the area behind me as he moved across the floor with purpose.

I turned and was startled to see Vic and Howie casually sitting around a meeting table with wide, discerning grins. The Vicar warned, "No gawking, Bobby. Not becoming at all."

While my two comrades cast a breezy look, I was suspicious as I took the only seat remaining. I decided a friendly tone was best. "Hello."

Burge seemed impatient. "Look, I've been reviewing a bold plan with your cronies here. It's time you are brought into the fold."

I intuitively knew why I was brought into this meeting, but decided to deflect as nicely as I knew how. "Yes, sir. The shortage of supplies and parts may absolutely be affecting, ah, bold plans, but I assure you we have a healthy parts-trading arrangement with 97 and 215 Squadrons on the opposite side of the aerodrome."

Howie humorously winced at my feeble attempt to avert Burge's plan, immediately seeing through my ruse. Vic looked at him to share a knowing smile as I looked back at the major.

"That's not quite the issue, Lieutenant. We are sending two O/400 crews over to Frankfort. That is about a six-hour run that has not been attempted before. Idea is to force the Hun's hand, deliver shock and terror, if you will."

I ran my fingers along the side of my khaki side cap, turning it from end to end, unable to stop a building nervousness. I became aware that the rapid thoughts shooting through my head gave me an anxious countenance. I refused to look at Vic and Howie, as they would grimace at my further protest. Yet I persisted: "I don't understand my connection—"

"Well, Jamieson is out. I think you know that. I've been pressuring these flyers here to provide alternates for their rear gunner. Your name kept surfacing."

I then had to look, first at Vic and then Howie, hoping for some recognition that this was some sort of prank. Their pan faces answered it wasn't.

The Vicar assumed a serious tone. "Look, Bob, you are an excellent observer, extremely proficient on the Lewis, proving that time and again in the Fee."

"We need you," added Howie. "We understand each other, how we act as a team." I knew I looked worried, knew the three understood my overriding thought—I had not expected to sortie again. "In these new O/400s, we have considerable protection from the Hun's fire, whether ground defenses or enemy aircraft." But I also knew that when I was permitted to pursue technical ground duties, I could be ordered into the sky at any time.

As Howie and the Vicar attempted to ease me into the assignment, Burge stepped in. "Lieutenant Pitman, I'm afraid that unless you provide a suitable reason for not accepting this order, it stands."

I did not wish to irritate the major with the trepidation I was feeling. My mind was rebelling since I had allowed myself to believe I would be grounded for the balance of the war. Yet there I was, being ordered into the largest aeroplane ever built, to fly to the enemy's front yard with a bomb load that could raze the Palace of Versailles in one go.

"Well, sir, I've not seen duty in the Handley Page, so perhaps that brings a risk to the other crew members." I could not stop my drivel. "The Box-Inches disaster has been explained as exceptional, but just Saturday, the American lad Gower was forced to land his Handley with a shot-out propeller." Bloody hell, I was not sounding very much an officer, and I hoped that Burge overlooked my indiscretion at referring to the Box-Inches disaster.

"Understood, Lieutenant; however, you have not convinced me to stand down my order. You will be supported by Johnson and Chainey here, whom you will join for a practice run this afternoon."

Knowing I had been committed, I needed to move beyond my doubts by showing a confident military persona, to promptly accept the assignment. "Yes, sir. I am honored that you and my fellow flyers have such confidence in me."

"Noted. This sortie will take place tomorrow evening, so I suggest you get cracking."

We stood and collectively saluted. "Sir!"

"Dismissed, gentlemen."

...

I held my curiosity as we crossed the field in silence to the front of the mess, where we were able to take advantage of a nicely set lunch table in the late-summer sun. I was reflective of the major's conversation, of his orders now that they had been exercised. I took a moment to glance up at the willowy clouds separated by spaces of deep blue, rising majestically as if to beckon me back to their domain. We sat, and with thoughts of returning to flying I broke the quiet.

"Burge commented that my name kept popping up. What's behind that?"

In a deferential manner, Howie looked at the Vicar, his extended hand urging him to respond. "You're respected, Bobby, not just for your character but for your skills. You know the Lewis, you know bombing accuracy, that sort of thing."

"You've got lasting experience to help get us into Germany and back," added Howie.

I contemplated their shameless compliments as I decided whether they were truly sincere or just serving the immediate cause. Yet I knew in times of war that really didn't matter since courage and survival were the overriding precepts. I wondered if my earlier request to step back from flying was subconsciously spawned by a need to survive for Cissy. That was when she was still alive, and I perhaps subconsciously knew that our future lay together. But I was to be flying again. And she was gone.

"Your words are kind, but surely—"

"Bobby," said Howie, "we spent a thorough time discussing many candidates, but for this length of show, we cannot risk deficiency." He stopped chewing and made an awful face. "What is this concoction, anyway?"

The Vicar smiled knowingly. "Meat pie mixed with sauerkraut. We're in German-influenced France now. Listen, don't know about

Jamieson, but I do know his lack of confidence presents risk. You don't, old boy. Be honored!"

I contemplated, sighed, and forced a smile before confirming, "We will be a formidable team over Frankfort, I daresay."

...

"Hey, Bob! Heard you are flying again." Hardy looked at me with a grin, his blue eyes sparkling in the bright sun.

I grinned back with an easy demeanor, having fully accepted my assignment. "Yes, I'm the chosen one, as they say. Ha!"

"Let's show you around before your practice run." I followed Sam and ambled up into the rear gunner's station, lower to the ground than the front section. Standing up, the view forward to the cockpit was some distance, far enough to deny any conversation with the pilot and observer, especially when the Rolls Royce engines would be at high pitch. As I waved to Howie standing in the cockpit, I realized the isolation would be daunting.

Sam studied me. "I'm reading your mind, Bob. Happens to all gunners the first time. Take notice of the communication system just there." He pointed to a steel wire that ran around pulleys and extended from the gunner up to the observer with a small container attached to send messages back and forth.

Hardy again contemplated my thoughts. "I know. At eight thousand feet, the slipstream and freezing air will make it difficult to write messages, so there are also two torches on board for Morse exchange."

"All right, that's civilized," I said. "The rear-facing seat makes sense, I suppose, yet it seems to increase the isolation, don't you think?"

"You're only really sitting there for takeoff and landing. Other gunners have said they are too busy organizing the Lewises and watching for threats to bother with too much sitting." Hardy showed me how the hinged seat lifted out of the way to reveal a platform from which the gunner was able to stand with a good view of the rear and sides while swinging the machine guns into any position in a 270-degree arc.

The setup was quite remarkable, from the massive amount of machine-gun drums efficiently stacked in the sidewalls to the ventral gun placement at the bottom for rear protection and for directing at searchlights. I kneeled down to peer through the floor opening with a clear view to the rear and then turned forward to see the daunting bomb rack that would vertically hold either eight 230-pounders or sixteen 112-pounders. There was even a small pocket with a recessed shelf that held emergency food supplies in the event of a forced landing.

The practice flight went off without a hitch. The Vicar commanded the warm skies over friendly landscape, which allowed me to become comfortable with the feel of the aircraft and the gunner's operations. Hardy met us on landing. "Feel good to you?"

I felt much better about things, actually brimming with excitement after soaring in such a powerful, daunting machine. "Oh sure, I feel better. I've tried everything out, well, as best I can without actually engaging the enemy. Yet!"

"You'll do well." He held a saucy grin. "Say, how about a coffee in the village? The ole Douglas is raring to go."

"The village?"

"Oh sure, a new village just down the road, a place called Baccarat."

I smiled warily, thinking of Hardy's exploits at local French *estaminets*. "Afraid I'm under orders not to leave the aerodrome, Sam. Unusual, I know, but related to tomorrow's mission."

"Unfortunate, but I won't probe. I may take a ride over there myself."

"What, another Bernadette?"

The grin spread a mile wide, covering his face. "Not yet, Bob. Looking, perhaps!"

...

I lay in bed listening to Howie's contented breathing across the room, myself again dozing but unable to find deep sleep. The moonlight streaming in through the top of the drapery illuminated the shadow of a dragonfly, which danced against the opposite wall. Its flight was with purpose, seeking a way through to safety. I thought of rising to help it but realized the inevitable stumbling in the dark would disturb the night. The distressed night flyer would remain unaided, left to its own devices for survival.

I thought of the many sorties I'd flown, how I slept well the night before knowing I had the next day to keep myself busy preparing for flight night. This was no different, yet I was wakeful with a gnawing anxiety that I needed to identify if I were to get any rest. As the early dawn replaced the brightness of the moon, it hit me: I had always had Cissy with me when I was about to fly, right from my first training flight. No, not in person, but in my heart, she had been there. Her presence made real by the knowledge that on next leave or with the next letter, she was there. Not this time.

I was to fly alone without my true love, yet I had her memory. While generally a realist, I believed, truly believed, that I would be closer to touching her in heaven while traveling up to eight thousand feet. Memories flooded in with that first time our hearts connected at Mrs. Clarke's. The tea kettle whistling as I answered the door, pleasantly surprised to see her in mauve and black silk, her eyes beaming at me from under that wide brim hat. Although I pushed back tears, one or two dripped onto my pillow. Vividly seeing, feeling, her being in my mind was at once intense pleasure and bitter pain.

Remembering the joy she had brought to everyone and her strong, determined character made me wonder why she had been chosen and why I had been spared after countless nights wreaking havoc over our enemy. I had to reject guilt; I knew that was not the character Cissy had fallen for. She had sought the best out of life, and it was for me to honor that. In my recent letter I had committed to Daisy that I was walking alongside her in accepting Cissy's death, and I needed to dignify that. Eventually, I felt peaceful enough to close my eyes in slumber.

Feeling a presence, I opened my eyes to the grinning Howie inquiring whether I was to remain in bed all day or join him for a late breakfast. With his hand squeezing my shoulder, his gentle grip of compassion told me he knew yet wouldn't break into my thoughts unless I invited it. Friends don't get closer than that.

Chapter 50

16 September, 1918

Twenty hundred hours. Darkness had set in after a fantastically warm day on the aerodrome, but the air temperature tonight would be frigid. Annoying sweat permeated our Sidcot suits and hip-length sheep-lined boots, but we would soon need them.

Our Handley Page O/400 loomed large just outside Hangar No. 3, its tail illuminated under misty lights that showed our registration, D8302. Hardy appeared from under the framework, holding that familiar wrench as if it were an extra limb. "Howdy, Bob!" He embarrassingly looked down. "Er, Lieutenant Gower from Colorado taught me that!"

I grinned, always admiring his enthusiasm, and teased, "Hmmm, not becoming for a flatlander like you! Am I the first?"

"No, the others are on the opposite side."

We caught up with Howie and the Vicar to walk the perimeter of the Handley as Hardknock's crew dodged and ducked in their tinkering before flight time. After inspecting this and questioning that, we halted at the bomb cage. Packed in were four crates of Baby Incendiaries with thermite cores that would ignite fires after the detonation of the 112-pounders, which were also racked up.

The Vicar motioned for us to gather as Hardy eased away in respect of privacy. "Look, Bob, it's time you understood the raid we are about to undertake." I stood erect, attentive under his somber tone as he continued. "The Cassella dye factory in the Fechenheim sector of Frankfort."

I looked at Howie, puzzled. "Why would we bomb a dye factory?"

"I know—I asked the same question. An honorable German company, Cassella originally manufactured artificial dyes. But the same coal by-product, something called aniline, is being used by the Hun to make chlorine gas."

I whistled. "The very stuff being used to choke our boys to death in the trenches. Well, I'll be damned. We are going to eliminate that weapon."

Vic seemed to take in what I had just said, pondering his response. "Well, one source, but who knows how many more factories producing all sorts of chemical weapons there are? Our spy network found this one, and now with long-range aircraft, we are able to deal with it."

Howie interjected, "The factory is right on the deep curve between the river Main and the Frankfort rail tracks, kind of like in a salient, so we will be well guided. You will need to be at the ready with your ventral gun. Searchlight duty."

I nodded as the nearby firing-up of surrounding aircraft broke our contemplation of the raid. After exchanging handshakes in the twilight, I walked to my separate rear entrance, musing that it felt as if we were departing in separate aeroplanes. Standing in my station, I could see Howie and Vic make cockpit adjustments before turning to give the thumbs-up. Two mechanics guided by torchlight ambled up the ladders leading to each massive wing.

The silhouette on the starboard side shouted to Howie while cranking a handle on the giant Eagle engine before it sputtered, emitted black smoke, then whirred to life. Once the port engine harmonized with its twin, the technicians descended their ladders and disappeared into the night. The Eagles hummed in a powerful concert as Vic thrust forward the throttles.

I pushed down the hinged seat as the big bird lurched forward for the taxi downwind to the end of the field. It felt odd to be facing to the rear, yet I was grateful to have a seat at all after so many sorties kneeling in the front of a Fee. And the slipstream would be behind me!

A familiar apprehension gripped me as we swung around into the wind. The Rolls Royce Eagles were powered to maximum strength as we picked up speed down the flare path, barely feeling the bumps and dips below our great weight. I could feel the tail rise when the aircraft leveled itself as we gained lift, soaring into the darkness toward Frankfort.

With lighthouse approval, we rose over the Meurthe River and into the mountainous Vosges darkness. I stood to face the front cockpit and saw the figures of Howie and the Vicar illuminated by instruments, huddled over in animated discussion. It was daunting not to be able to speak to them, yet there was no reason to be concerned. I had my station to attend to in preparation for the attack.

Nothing had shaken loose on the takeoff; the Lewises were securely mounted. I pointed one downward to check the sighting then raised it to the sky to check its balance in the slipstream. Peering along the barrel, my eye caught the cloudless night sky. Against the black canvas were endless stars ranging from port horizon across to starboard. The magic at eight thousand feet was mesmerizing, an exhilarating feeling as my mind expanded with thought.

Buried alive at Mouquet Farm two years before, gasping for air. The confusion in the clearing station where I woke, then ending up at the Maudsley. Happy thoughts about meeting Eric and Daisy, little Stanley, Wellsey, letters from my family. Sad thoughts about losing Perce, shell shock, disease, and flyer fatigue. And foremost of those thoughts spinning around my head were memories of Cissy.

The peaceful setting with stars twinkling in the dark vastness brought calm, which gave me the courage to believe her spirit was somewhere out there and that she wanted me to be all right. At that moment, I knew I would pursue life to its fullest, take the course I desired, and allow myself the freedom to make choices, but Cissy would never travel far from my heart.

I was jolted back to attention as we traveled through an air bump. Looking forward, I saw an illuminated Howie turn with a reassuring thumbs-up, but didn't know if he saw my dark shrouded acknowledgment. The moonlit silver line below was the Rhine. My watch and a rough calculation of time told me the lights to starboard were Mannheim. Although my navigational training was not required for this flight, it gave me peace of mind to follow our course.

Thoughts of being well into the German heartland kept me standing on my platform, gazing keenly, looking out for threats of enemy aircraft, and knowing that in a short while we would approach Mainz, fifteen minutes this side of Frankfort. The purpose of our visit was fast approaching.

Torchlight caught my attention—Howie indicating something, flashing out a signal: dash-dash, dot-dot-dot, dash-dash-dot. *M, S, G.* Ah, a message! I felt down behind the raised seat to open the container and directed my torch to the note. *Approach target in twenty, engines cut two miles out, glide in, be alert be safe, no need reply.* I waved my torch to and fro, and Howie waved his back.

Those twenty minutes felt like an eternity while standing on my platform in tense anticipation of an enemy attack bounding out of the darkness. I fingered the trigger of the port Lewis. Thoughts of searchlights suddenly illuminating our underbelly to make us the target instead of the other way around rose up from my stomach.

Suddenly, the night was eerily quiet except for the whistling of wires and the slight humming of wing fabric as the mighty engines were cut. For an instant in the silent blackness, memories flooded in about the many nights coasting toward our prey in the smaller Fee. Except this time I was secure in an aircraft office with high sides and a plethora of weaponry at my reach. With our downward descent, I had a full view in front of the Handley, amazed to see the Fechenheim industrial center beside the river Main lit as if on exhibition. I thought it such an unsuspecting spectacle.

With movement in the forward cockpit, I watched Howie's outline bend over the bomb sight. Rapid calculations of wind, air speed, and drift would instruct him. Or would he rely on visual instinct to drop the bombs? It didn't matter since I heard the first bomb release from the rack as we lined up over the factory compound. Wanting to do my bit, I pointed the rear-facing Lewis down onto the target, squeezing the trigger that rapidly projected round after round of random destruction onto the enemy. Excitement soared through my body from fear, power, or perhaps something else.

As each of the heavy bombs dropped, I felt the seven-ton aircraft lift away from their weight. Archie exploded around us; no need for Hun searchlights as we were illuminated as clear as day by the factory lights, our monster bird bouncing and bucking with each explosion. I sweated, felt the beads of water from under my leather helmet streaming down my face. I leaned down to open the V hatch below as I knew I would soon need the lower Lewis. Each heave of my chest felt like that fist punching up from within as I struggled to control my erratic breathing, to swallow back my heart that had disgorged into my throat.

The roar of the engines coming back to life was a relief, propelling us away as I lay down to dispense machine-gun fire through the bottom hatch, strafing everything in the area. We soared into the freedom of darkness, but we were not to be released, not yet. Searchlights flooded the sky and caught us, Hun machine guns spraying upward, bullets thwacking into the wooden frame and pinging on struts. I aimed for the lights, shooting irregular spurts of fire as I fought to control my breathing. Through the din, the roar of the engines, I could hear Howie's guns doing the same at the front, welcome proof that he was equally alive and well.

The pull of the engines was strong, taking us upward and away from the menace—that threat of our own instigation—as we soared south toward Darmstadt before the planned turn west over the Vosges. We were out of machine-gun range now, but not Archie. Puffs continued exploding around us, the lumbering machine climbing slowly, not with the agility of the Fee. We were tons of material straining upward, slowed by our own weight, lumbering into the night. The Vicar steered the craft to port sideways with a graceful southerly turn that would take us back down toward the Vosges and home.

As suddenly as the lights had caught us, we were in blackness. Relief seared through me as we pulled away from danger, my breathing coming back under control, nerves relaxing their grip. Pulling up from the V hatch, the thought came to me—this was a historic night. We were the first British bomber to attack an industrial target deep within German territory, as far as the city of Frankfort!

I felt good, but wished I were up front with my comrades to share congratulatory smiles. I instinctively turned toward them, cherishing my lone grin in the darkness.

As attentive as ever, Howie was peering over into the bomb crate. I could see into it as well, could see that all bombs had cleared, but perhaps from his angle he could not. The ever-attentive Howie! But then the Vicar stood up, with his figure illuminated by the rising moon, tapping Howie on the shoulder before pointing to starboard. My gaze followed his finger to its engine, and my smile faded to an anxious frown. The propeller was stationary, not moving. What did this mean? Could we fly forward with one propeller, with the strength of only one engine?

Howie stood up and carefully leaned toward the engine, one leg in the cockpit, the other braced on the starboard wing, yanking on the propeller while risking his life against a strong slipstream and unbalanced aircraft. The engine was not reacting, remaining frozen in the night. My mind raced with thoughts about the engine failure Wellsey and I had endured, of our shot-up Fee limping home. But back then we were not hundreds of miles away in German territory. Was this happening again, could this happen twice to one flyer in the same long war? With Howie returned to the cockpit, Vic was trying to correct the listing of our ship, manipulating the wheel to keep us stable. I became aware of sweating again, my heart pounding in my chest.

Howie leaned over the Vicar, an animated silhouette whose flailing arms belied the hurried speech and the intensity of the situation. In an instant, Howie stood tall, waving to gain my attention, shining his torch against his left hand, signaling, pointing downward with his index finger. Fuck, we were force landing! On German soil! Just after bombing them, attacking their very soul at Frankfort!

This was the moment of truth about dealing with the fear that had stalked me throughout the war. My mind raced, recalling words such as *bravery* and *grit* and *fortitude*. I had flashes about the inner strength that would be needed to survive the landing, then to deal with the inevitable German retribution. About the courage to find strength, the sheer drive to work with Howie and Vic to ensure we survived. Unless... Was evasion possible?

I peered over the side and saw flat fields, but couldn't see directly in front of the aircraft. Damn! Nothing I could do but wait. With the port engine shut down for stability, we coasted at a helpless clip, with wings vacillating from side to side. I knew the Vicar was struggling to keep the aircraft stable. Bloody hell, we were losing altitude quickly; any choices for landing were going to be made for us. I was tense, focused on hope. The Vicar must have been feeling the same fear and trepidation, possibly worse. But abruptly it happened. He set our broken machine down in a ploughed field as if it were the one safe place destined for us, rocks and debris flying up high, smashing at the nacelle as the massive airship shivered under stress, eventually lurching to a stop. We were alive, safe! Except that we were in fucking hostile Germany. Survival depended on our next move. We had to act quickly.

·

Chapter 51

17 September, 1918

I glanced at my wristwatch, presented to me by Judge McLorg of the Saskatchewan law courts upon commending me for enlisting, a moment forever engraved into my mind. It had endured years in the mud, in the air, in Cissy's arms, and now told me it was thirty-five minutes past midnight.

I was the first to alight, dropping the short distance onto the soft, dark soil before running to the front to assist Howie and Vic in their seven-foot drop. At this point we did not need leg or foot injuries. We stared momentarily in disbelief, processing the last fateful twenty minutes that had changed our destiny. Looking beyond our little circle, the Vicar broke the silence, alarm in his voice: "Fuck, there are torches approaching; looks like civilians." I had never heard the Vicar swear.

That the ground temperature was significantly warmer became painfully evident as we sweated in the confinement of our bulky Sidcot suits. "Await their arrival and help, or flee—what do you think?" I barked.

With beads of sweat pouring down his face, I had seldom seen the Vicar look so worried. "How can we bloody trust them, Germans loyal to their kaiser? It's obvious that we are an enemy bomber!"

Howie peered behind us through the darkness. I followed his sightline and saw the same dark mass that he did. "Over there, looks like a forest. Let's run for that, make our plans from there."

We ran. Reaching the trees, we threw off our flying clothes while catching our breath. The locals had now reached the Handley, their torches shining all over it, some trying to climb up. We were blessed for a moment, as they were more curious to look over the large machine than to find its crew.

Unanimously, we agreed not to give ourselves up, but debated the regulations that required us to set fire to the aircraft and its armaments. The idea of waiting out the locals' curiosity was not enticing, so we agreed to forgo the burn and concentrate on a prompt escape—we weren't even sure if our matches worked. We pooled our meager provisions, pulling goods out of our Sidcots that were stored for just such an event: a torch with a battery box, Nestle's milk chocolate, bully beef, biscuits, and soap. The Vicar looked amazed as I uncovered two maps that were strapped at the back of my knees, one for German territory down to the Swiss border, the other showing the Dutch frontier. Gathering the tiny compasses we each had secured in the heels of our shoes, we set out.

Nervously, we moved across the field, constantly looking back at the excitement that was still occupying the Germans, buying us time to move away. We stopped behind shrubbery to risk shining a torch on the map. "It looks like we are 130 miles east of the French lines, but crossing the Vosges could be nasty. Besides, the whole region is crawling with German soldiers," whispered the Vicar.

I knew we were in serious trouble. My mind was working fast, trying to think of ideas for a solution. "Remaining east of the Vosges will avoid bad weather, but any way we look at it we are going to encounter German citizens—starving, resentful, angry Germans."

Damn, this was pointing out problems, not helpful. I stabbed at the map. "But look, the Swiss border is directly south."

Howie frowned as he measured the map by finger lengths. "But that looks like 175 or so miles, longer than walking to the lines."

"Howie," I protested, "it is flat land, no mountains, and although we could encounter German citizens, we are less likely to be seen by soldiers this far back."

The Vicar remained silent, letting us fret out the options, but then Howie placed a hand on my shoulder. "All right, I agree. Our best shot is to remain clear of armed soldiers. Little use our Webleys will be if we had to engage."

"All right, it's agreed. We make our way to the Swiss border," said the Vicar. "But even if we cover fifteen miles each night, it will take over ten days. We'll have to forage and plunder whatever we can."

"Thank goodness it's harvest time, then," snickered Howie.

"And perhaps we could stow away on a train. I saw hobos do it on the Canadian Prairie." Howie and the Vicar shot a glance at me for my attempt to lighten the stress.

We traveled about nine miles before sunrise, when we settled in a small but dense wood. The biscuits, tinned beef, and chocolates that we had pooled didn't last the morning, as the three of us were famished.

Chapter 52

September 1918

After sleeping through the day, we awoke with intense thirst and set out as soon as the cover of darkness allowed. Quenching ourselves was frustrating since all stream beds were seasonally dry. Eventually finding a roadside pump, we approached it with caution, pumping it painfully slow to avoid the squeaking of the handle as much as possible. It alarmingly wanted its high pitch to burst out. At that moment, the taste of fresh water was better than the best French wine. Passing through yet another village and doing our best to remain extremely quiet, we again settled into a nearby wood just before daybreak.

The wood was dry and the vegetation rich, so we had an easy time hiding. But the lushness of the foliage also brought gnats, clouds of nasty, buzzing, biting pests, which caused erratic waving of arms and slapping of skin. "Bobby," whispered Howie, "you're gonna get us noticed, eh?"

My whispers were even softer due to exhaustion after

forty-eight hours of little sleep and gnawing hunger. "Sorry, lads, it's just that I'm going to go crazy. I wonder if giving ourselves up to the hostile Hun would be better than swatting these invisible creatures."

The Vicar looked alarmed. "No, don't say that." We settled back to an irritable rest. But then at midday, women and children arrived to forage in the wood, their innocent voices creeping closer. *"Hier, Mama, ein Pilz!"* we heard as they located mushrooms in their bid to provide for their starving families. To avoid being spotted, we moved deeper into thick shrubbery, avoiding threatening thorns as best we could.

At dark, we continued our southbound trek. In a field, we were able to lay our hands on some turnips and beans that filled us for the moment, raw as they were. We stumbled upon another roadside pump, which again provided a good long drink of quenching fresh water. Howie stood up from our crouched position but quickly dove onto his stomach. The Vicar and I were startled but raised our heads above road level to see a parallel-running railway line. The Vicar silently pumped his fist, and I smiled at the thought that perhaps we could snatch a stolen ride down to Mannheim or further. We would be hobos in Hun-land!

With hopeful promise, we followed the line, eventually coming to a dilapidated guardhouse appearing vacated. But a dim porchlight was suddenly illuminated as an elderly man, perhaps a gateman, not heretofore visible behind a Dutch door, jumped out at us. *"Halt! Wer sind Sie? Wohin gehen Sie?"*

I shrugged my shoulders and looked for any evidence of a gun on the old fellow while the Vicar turned to Howie and asked, "You understand?"

"No, but based on his tone my guess is he wants to know who we are and where we are going."

Even in our shabby, dirty uniforms that made us look like ghosts coming off the fields, the Vicar steeled himself with the most confidence he could muster. "Hello, we are Swiss ah, *Schweizerisch, gut ya?*"

The Vicar looked from Howie to me, nervousness showing in his eyes. "I don't know about this, fellows."

The silence was deafening as the old guard stood there sizing us up, looking from one of us to the other, but saying or doing nothing.

"I don't think he's armed, so I say we keep moving south like we are walking home to Switzerland," I said.

We took a few steps backward under the gatekeeper's protests before he waved a hand in disgust. He was probably aware we were not German. Perhaps he thought English was the dominant tongue in Switzerland. Or he may have been simply too tired of conflict and poverty to care, since he shook his head back and forth as he re-entered the gatehouse. We walked on and did not turn around.

There was no activity on the rail tracks, but by map I reckoned it was another twelve miles to Mannheim where we were sure to link up with southbound trains. But we were overcome with fatigue, causing us to stop short of the target. We holed up in yet another small shrubbery for the entire next day. Again, we were almost spotted, this time by young boys picking berries. Worse, the weather turned into blustery rain, which caught us in nothing but our summer khaki uniforms.

That night, the third after our forced landing, we started out again, determined to get to Mannheim and that southbound train. But very quickly we were soaked to the skin, hungry, and losing spirit. We huddled under a lone tree, looking at one another, wondering what the other was thinking. I knew we were determined to get to safety, but at the same time knew in our hearts that this walk to Switzerland was becoming increasingly improbable. In the cold and wet—let alone the hunger—I was losing resolve, so I decided to cautiously broach the situation. "Fact is we are weak, cold, and tired. We can't deny it."

"We are that," Howie put in, his teeth chattering against the cold, driving rain.

I pushed a little more. "Out here we could get sick, unable to help ourselves. We don't know what is ahead of us as we continue walking. If we do find a train, we don't know if it will be heavily guarded."

"Are you giving up, Bob?" whispered the Vicar, himself looking glum.

"No, not giving up as much as being practical so that we can survive and return to our families. I don't know which way is best, but we need to talk this through, that's all I'm saying."

Howie stepped in. "If we surrender, they will have to feed and shelter us, correct?"

"Technically, yes," said the Vicar. "If they have food. You saw those women and children foraging. And they were farmers, closer to food than most."

I knew we all felt conflicted but close to admitting we were seriously run-down and likely losing the physical ability to make the walk to the Swiss border. Howie offered, "Let me float this idea—how about we stop at the next village and simply knock on some doors, see what reception we get?"

"Could be hostile, but I'm in," said the Vicar.

"And I'm definitely in," I added.

...

We pushed forward, slouched against the driving rain. Making a decision seemed to energize us to move forward, no matter what the outcome. Within hours we came upon a village, thankful that the first person we encountered was a civilian. The Vicar asked him to take us to the nearest police station. To him we must have appeared alarming, looking like wet refugees sprung out of the dusk, but he thankfully remained calm. *Polizei, ja?* He understood and led us away, first making a stop at his home, where his wife kindly gave us some bread.

While that German citizen and his wife were a blessing, the village jailers were not, locking us up for the night and refusing us food. We were chilled to the bone in our drenched uniforms. The next morning the local police brought a British POW from a nearby factory to speak to us. But we defiantly provided no information other than our names and ranks. And we remained famished.

Later that morning an armed escort marched us to the train station. We arrived in Mannheim and were paraded through the streets under jibes and threats from the local citizenry. Again in prison, they kept us together for questioning, enticing us to give up information with the promise of food and hot drink. We soon got the gist of the game—there was no food, never would be, so we kept quiet. In disgust, our jailers transferred us back to Mannheim station. As burdens, they wanted us out of there.

With the rolling lull of the train and in exhaustion, Howie and the Vicar dozed. As we sped along the banks of the Rhine, I struggled to keep my anxiety in check, the anticipation of what was to come robbing me of the ability to sleep. I irritably watched the guards watching me, their bodies as gaunt as to belie their authority. I faintly smiled at the thought that without their threatening *Maschinengewehrs* strapped over their shoulders they would be defenseless.

...

At Karlsruhe we were hustled to an old hotel on the prominent Ettlinger Strasse, a clearing depot from which prisoners were transferred to permanent camps. It was whispered to us by orderlies—themselves POWs—that the inmates referred to this as the Listening Hotel since it was devoted to intelligence collection. Even though we had little strength or appetite for talking among ourselves, it was good to be forewarned of the eavesdropping practices.

The constant uncertainty about where we were to wait out the balance of the war was wearing on me. And we were missing the euphoric atmosphere that had been building among 100 Squadron flyers about a likely armistice. Howie was locked in one room, while the Vicar and I were in another. Our prison garb smelled, and the hot soup we were given tasted like decaying kitchen rubbish. The room we were assigned, while once of upper-crust décor, was now unclean and unkempt, smelling of earlier prisoners' presence. Early the next morning, I was summoned to an elaborate room decorated in gaudy gold and maroon to meet a cheerful blue-suited civilian, fiftyish. He stood from his desk to shake my hand but did not introduce himself. I immediately sensed a dislike for him.

"Lieutenant Pitman, how are you?" The masquerading civilian did not wait for an answer. "I am a historian, having permission from the German military to conduct research. Will you answer my questions?"

This impeccably dressed man with a perfect command of English aroused my suspicion. I was cognizant that I had recently bombed his homeland and should appreciate any courtesy offered, but his demeanor was irritating. Perhaps that was part of a strategy of breaking down prisoners to make them talk.

I shrugged. "Perhaps."

"You are an Englishman, yes?"

"No."

"Your accent is not Flemish, nor French?"

"No."

"You are perhaps Canadian, then?"

I knew he would recognize my positive body signal. "Yes."

"You are Protestant, yes?"

"Yes."

"You are a British subject?"

"Yes."

"You are career British military?"

Jutting my chin out, I hissed, "No."

Blue-suit strode toward me, stopping just in time to avoid banging his nose into mine. He stared into my unblinking eyes and feigned an accusatory tone. "Yes, you are!"

I shook with rage, risked losing control, knowing that is what he wanted. "No."

"For how long?"

"Three years."

"Ah, joined up for the cause, for your King, to fight his German cousin, yes?"

I stared straight at his face but with a detached feeling that, for the moment, removed emotion. However, I did feel the deep-seated hunger striking at my patience.

"Canada! O, Canada! You haven't seen your family for three years, yes?"

I hated this man, obviously German intelligence, skilled in manipulation. "Yes."

"And your girl, you miss her?"

I knew he was planting a wild guess, but he hit the target. Seeing me well up, he knew it. "Yes, very much."

The suit chuckled annoyingly as he crowed, "Ah, you do speak in sentences. Well, a little." I sensed he counted on having me emotionally contained. "You miss your girl, haven't had the *ficken-ficken* for a long time, *ja*?" That struck me as intolerably crude and had the opposite effect, as I was not going to allow this Hun to irritate me with boorish references.

He strolled casually around the room, while I remained in place, and then lit a cigarette before leaning back on the front edge of his desk. "Now, from where did you fly before your aeroplane became a gift to the kaiser?"

"The other side of the lines."

"How long was the flying time to reach Darmstadt?"

"I don't recall."

"How much petrol did you carry?"

I continued to stand rigid, staring ahead. "I do not know. I am not an air mechanic."

"Another sentence—very good. What bombs did you carry?"

"Cannot answer."

"Do you refuse to answer these questions, to interrupt my research?"

I stood there, steeling myself against hunger and against this man's crudeness in reference to Cissy, not knowing if I was making things worse for myself but refusing to let his manipulation win. "Yes."

And still the interrogator held a calm level of patience, which I responded to with a rigid countenance, again jutting out my chin and pursing my lips. "What is your peacetime occupation?"

"Student."

"Ah, perhaps a student of history, like myself?"

"No."

"What then?"

"The law."

"Oh-ho! The British common law. Tsk, not the Book of Civil Law, the more cultured German code."

I shook my head.

"You are in the British air force, yes? The Royal Air Force?"

"Yes."

"You were crew on what type of machine?"

"No comment."

"You were attached to what aerodrome?"

"No comment."

"Where was this aerodrome located?"

"No comment."

"Come now, Lieutenant, your comrade in the room opposite provided this information. Perhaps you could cooperate like him so that my records are impeccable, yes?"

There was no way that Howie had responded any differently from me, nor would the Vicar when it was his turn. "No comment."

"Lieutenant, these questions may seem to be of military importance, but really they are for my invaluable research that will be used to save millions of lives in the future. Where was your last bombing target?"

I'd had it. Listening to this spy lie about his reasons for the information and knowing it was for military purposes sent me to the edge. I abandoned care, resigned to whatever repercussions I would have to face. "Sir, you are aware that I am under instruction from my government not to respond to military questions, and yours are frankly of a damned military nature. You do not fool me, and I will not provide any further answers. I'm done!"

I was shocked at my impulsive response. Immediately after uttering it, I wondered if it was courageous or just plain stupid. Yet he pulled back, his expression showing surprise at my obstinacy. Blue-suit returned to his desk, and in the time it took to light a cigarette, the guards miraculously returned to escort me back to my cell. The Vicar was in turn taken away, allowing no opportunity for me to prep him.

...

The next seven days were difficult, as we were allowed only one outside hour a day for air. Howie was permitted to rejoin us in our "hotel" room, and we were not badgered any further for information. We talked to calm each other, but questions hung over us like a black shroud. What if this war lasted another year, another two years, and Germany could no longer feed its people due to our continued naval blockade? What if the Central Powers won with a dictatorial Germany leading the Western world? In either case, our welfare was doomed, yet we continued to talk down such fear. We needed to have faith that our side would prevail. Throughout, I kept my sanity by talking to the others and by thinking of safe places, just as Cissy had so tenderly suggested. In fact, it was thoughts of strolling the Chilwell estuary, arm in arm with my beloved that kept me most sane.

One day our uniforms were returned, and we were abruptly marched to the train station along with other prisoners. We rumbled through lovely countryside, passing villages and rich farmland untouched by bombs and trenches or the cratered churches that were seen all over France. The invader had utterly destroyed foreign countryside without as much as a blade of grass in his own backyard knocked out of place. Any expectations that we were to be quickly imprisoned in a lush, green environment were destroyed by the rumor we were to be on the train for thirty hours.

Howie was looking pale, sweat dripping off his forehead. "I'd rather be dead. It stinks in here, can't breathe."

The Vicar sat up, looking as pastoral as he could manage in the rare air. "No, you don't, you really don't, because we will survive this. Right, Bob?"

As I attempted to speak, I coughed, the dryness in my mouth reminding me that I felt similar to Howie. "Yes, we will get through this together, all of us." I stood to open the fold-down window above my seat in the fourth-class compartment, but was pushed in the back with a guard's rifle muzzle.

He screamed loud and clear, turning the rifle butt up to the window to slam it shut. "*Nicht offnen!*" An Irishman in the row beside us explained about the Hun's obsessive concern over escape. I looked back up at the window.

The Irishman watched my puzzled look. "Aye, I agree, smallest-possible child couldn't fit through, an' to tink they've even locked up our boots." He held out his stocking feet as if to prove the point.

Chapter 53

October 1918

"*Welcome* to Landshut Sanitation Camp." The red-haired brute was daunting, not just for his size but also for his fierce Kaiser-like mustache, crimson-cheeked face, and massive eyebrows. Looking agitated, tired, and without patience, he pronounced, "I am your *Kommandant Hauptmann* Hahn at this most sterilized camp."

The fresh air felt exhilarating compared to the fetid inside of the train, notwithstanding the wire fences that surrounded us as we stood two deep at attention. "You were not expected, no information of your arrival, so you *vill* not have food for now. Meanwhile, you *vill* be *insulated*."

Muttering occurred between neighbors and those standing behind with speculation about what the captain had meant by *insulate*, though no one was willing to raise the question. Hahn raised his fist for silence, and with a firm "*Achtung!*" stabbed his left index finger into his right upper arm.

It became obvious that the *Hauptmann* intended to inoculate us when two doctors in white lab coats appeared from around the corner of his quarters. The dreary clouds suddenly made the refreshing air feel cold as we were commanded to strip to the waist to allow the medical team to methodically inject us. Word traveled quietly that, as cholera was known to present a risk in German prison camps, this was for our protection, yet some wondered if the injections were a form of experiment. Regardless, there was nothing we could do.

Hauptmann Hahn stood erect in quintessential Teutonic fashion throughout the inoculation process, which finished when the doctors faced him and with half bows clicked their heels. "You *vill* provision with good beds. You *vill* obey orders. You *vill* be good, *ja*? You *vill* not be *sinking* of running away!"

In his broken English, Hahn spelled out food rationing, even though he had earlier pronounced there would be none. It seemed if we agreed to sign weekly chits against our British bank accounts, he would organize meals from a local pub. We knew there was little chance of surplus food being available in Germany at the time, and that the scheme involved moving prisoner food out of the camp so that it could be sold back to us offsite. We didn't care whether our banks honored the notes nor that he was laundering funds with the help of the pub owner, so agreed to the plan. We wanted to eat.

"Now, four officers to one room, boots taken every night to prevent the *Flucht*."

What began with a slight chuckle became infectious laughter as neighbor looked at neighbor, unable to contain themselves. The *Flucht*? What was he talking about?

Hahn's face turned a brighter red, his anger spreading until one of our flyers who knew a little German appealed to him for clarification. When our lad announced that the *Kommandant* was concerned over escape, the collective nod of understanding caused Hahn to beam. "OK, you think I say no fucked, *ja*? No, I say *Flucht*, no running away. Ha ha ha!" In a dangerous display of impulsiveness, he held his Luger up high above his head and squeezed the trigger. We instinctively ducked with the pistol's explosion, but none of us broke rank. His point was emphasized and understood.

After Hauptmann Hahn returned to his quarters, the guards stepped in to allocate huts. In the confusion, Vic, Howie, and I strode purposefully off to the nearest one and claimed our beds with no regard for permission. The hut was a simple square wood frame, obviously purpose built for the war. The inside was dank notwithstanding a small central brazier with a sheet-metal pipe to the roof. A small table with a mirror leaned vertically at its far edge and a bowl for washing rounded out the Ritz-like adornments.

Howie peered down from the top bunk at me after he had tested his mattress. "You better not have been allotted more straw than me, Pitman!"

"Not possible. You could fold my mattress up and stuff it in your tunic pocket. How about you, Vic?"

"Same, but good Lord, we are dry and this place is fairly clean." Howie smiled over at him. "But it ain't an Oxford dorm, Vic!"

There was a pause as we contemplated our unknown future. I wrapped the end of the flimsy gray blanket around my arm as I tested it for warmth. "The question is: How long will our stay be?"

Howie again flung his head over the edge of his bed, smiling. "How long will this war last?"

"That's the question," declared the Vicar, "so we ought to just settle in for whatever duration that is."

"Ah hell, Vic," I said. "It's been only two weeks since our capture and already the tedium is driving me a little crazy." I looked up and over at our fourth bunkmate, the previous interpreter. He nodded congenially, so I decided to proceed with a soft voice. "What of escape, eh?"

"Not a chance, Bobby," said the Vicar.

"Not so fast," thundered Howie. "That could make sense, especially if our boys are pushing east toward us."

"Then we will be released," protested the Vicar. "Besides, if I understand the geography, we are in Bavaria, a couple hundred miles from Switzerland. I, ah, believe we tried that idea before. Walking to Switzerland is not going to happen."

Howie knelt up on his bed, excited. "But we could follow the Danube, perhaps even hitch on with a river boat."

"Howie," I said, "the Danube flows from the Black Forest east through Hungary, all through hostile territory. I take back my comment, as I agree. We are far too deep into Germany."

Howie continued, "At least think about it."

I looked straight up at Howie and with a stern face said, "No *Flucht!*"

...

In the cloudy gloom of that October day, I lay back on my mattress and did ponder escape but dismissed it with remembrance of the miserable walk out of Darmstadt. More-pleasant thoughts took me away to that small Nottingham bistro near the university where I so enjoyed that summer meal with Cissy, one of the most pleasant memories of our relationship. Of my life. Looking at her beauty bathed by that flowing blue dress, her faintly painted lips in a perpetual smile, caused me to beam as I lay there. We had spoken of the future—I wanting a definite plan and she wanting to wait for peaceful times—as we both confirmed our love for one another. Then, standing on the arched bridge spanning the river Trent, we had lightly kissed. We were undeniably, deeply in love.

I committed to myself that image, the memories that would be my refuge, a safe place to shield myself from whatever was to come. If I were to die in this prison, I would carry that gentle remembrance to my charnel. I didn't recall falling asleep or my cellmates attempting to wake me for evening rations until I awoke with the dawn chirping of the jackdaws. While the others slept, I momentarily crept out into the misty morning, which foreshadowed the winter cold that was to come. The kommandant had agreed that for an extra mark a week, I would be allowed two sheets of paper and two envelopes. So, before morning rations, I returned to the hut and sat at the wash table to write.

2 October, 1918

Dear Papa,
You will have received the telegram that I am now a German prisoner of war. While I am forbidden to disclose my location, be assured it is well within the German territory, not at one of the outposts in their crumbling empire. We are well protected, if you understand my context.
As officers, we are supposedly treated with dignity and with better provisions, such as food and shelter. Well, if these are defined as better, I feel sad about what our regular troops are enduring. As agent over my affairs, you may notice that in addition to my regular pay entries, there will be deductions for prison food. These should be less than one Canadian dollar per week since we agreed with the kommandant's four-deutsche-mark levy.
While on the topic, Papa, if something were to happen to me, please distribute all of my savings equally to my darling sisters. I know that is a drastic request, but if the war is prosecuted for a long time yet, I'm not confident that many of us interned will survive. The poverty and suffering that we have seen among Germany's citizens is testament.
Meanwhile, one of our darkest enemies is tedium. The days have turned decidedly wintry under dark, dreary clouds and drizzle. We have little to occupy us since, according to the Hague Convention, officers are not permitted to perform work duties. While I understand its intent, I curse its effect since it makes

the days long and boring. One can only play put-and-take for so many hours with pebbles for currency without submitting to indifference with that as well.

As you can see, my one sheet of paper is filled, so I will bid you adieu. Please hug Mama and Grannie for me and send my love to Ethel and Hilda.

Your son, Robert

...

2 October, 1918

Dearest Eric & Daisy,

It's only been a little more than two weeks since I last wrote, but what a change that short time has brought. I am a prisoner of war held in the German heartland, although I am not permitted to explain how that occurred or where I'm being imprisoned. Be assured I am all right and in good health.

With an abundance of time on my hands, I think of you often, especially you, Daisy. I wanted you to know that I've managed to find the courage to throw off my grief over Cissy, to move beyond frustration and anger to emotions that are filled with fond, happy memories. I know we both miss her dearly. I sincerely appreciate your allowing me to indulge my feelings, to share our common remembrance. While selfish, that helps me get through the days in cold, cold Germany.

For all our sakes, I trust it is God's will to presently see an end to hostilities.

With love to you both,
Bob

...

We were inoculated every four days, but as time passed were no closer to understanding why. The fifty or so flyers who were interned kept pretty much to their bunkmates except for exercise periods. Orderlies, mostly Italian regular soldiers, performed cleanup and other duties, which made our time waste away even more slowly. As the days dragged on, I found myself drawing on memories more and more, the safe place I had stored away in order to ward off increasing melancholy and the sinking back into dark nightmares.

One rainy day, we were sitting on our bunks whiling away the time, except for Howie, who was sitting on the floor with his back to the wall, bouncing a ball off the opposite side. While the rhythmic sound was annoying, we did not interrupt out of sympathetic respect for his having a job to do. Suddenly the rhythm stopped.

"Ever think about the night we force landed?" Howie muttered.

"In what way?" I asked.

"Well, we just disappeared. Xaffevillers wouldn't have known where we were or whether dead or alive. D8302 gone, vanished! We've experienced nights like that, prayed when one of ours didn't show up. We would then guffaw and trundle off to bed when reality became clear—*oh, they're lost.*"

The Vicar sleepily looked over. "What's your point?"

Howie looked defensive, impatient with Vic's question. "This time it was us, vamoose, gone, disappeared!"

"Within a few days, the Hun would have wired our whereabouts to Geneva," I retorted. "Eventually Burge would have received word, you know, *Information received from reliable sources . . . Frederick Howard Chainey, previously reported missing, now reported POW.*"

But I saw Howie's point. I knew he was losing faith, perhaps slipping into gloom. Fear was artful, could creep up in the guise of many forms to conquer one's decency and self-worth. Talking about the event typically helped. "I see your point. We've all stifled this conversation for weeks since our capture, and it's time to air our misgivings, to stop the manly façade and admit we are scared. I know I am."

"Scared of what, Bobby?" asked the Vicar.

"What our loved ones know or don't know. Whether they are in mourning or experiencing some other grief."

Howie stood up and paced. "Or when they received the telegram, did they feel better or worry the days away? After all, they know the Hun is getting desperate and can hardly afford to feed us."

The Vicar sat up, now alert. "Listen here, chaps. This talk is not good, just getting us worked up."

"Not necessarily," I countered. "I think these things need to be said so that we can support one another, be more aware of each other's feelings to help us through."

"There's reason!" said Howie.

Yes, reason was the only thing keeping me sane. My faith had been to keep busy when my deepest courage was threatened. Yet there were no physical tasks here, no keeping busy. In spite of cold nights, poor food, and being incarcerated by a Hun who had lost the resolve to care, I decided to employ a positive voice as my daily work. And after all, I had my safe place.

Chapter 54

October 1918

Later in the month, we were informed of a move to a more permanent facility. Hauptmann Hahn seemed pleased to send us packing deeper into central Bavaria. This time the closed train windows did not create oppression, as the weather was cooler and the journey was a short three hours. At Ingolstadt station our boots were returned for the five mile march to a country fort, appearing rather out of the Middle Ages with its crenelated walls, moat, and drawbridge.

"*Velcome* to Fort Prinz Karl, officers of the enemy. I am *zee Kommandant*, and I ride, how you say, *zee* high horse. I see everything."

This greeting was from Hauptmann Fuchs, who talked strong but looked weak with hunched shoulders, unkempt dark-brown hair, blue Aryan eyes, and a mustache he had evidently been trying to grow since puberty. He looked uncertain as he explained that, since we were not expected, there was no food, but for four marks a week we would be fed well. Being familiar with that story, we freely accepted it and instead conspired about ways to manipulate this vulnerable soul.

After settling in, the days again passed with tedium, but the three of us were together. In spite of the brick walls and haunting grass roof of the castle, the room was quite warm. We were free to move around and to make acquaintances without interference from the guards. Escape talk again surfaced, albeit not serious, as we bantered about how easy it would be to negotiate the moat. Even if we did, we would not last long in the near-freezing temperatures.

One day I strolled alone through the hallways and passages of the complex building, smoking a Turkish Murad. After moving past a grand stairway that led to the main level, I came to a cordoned-off section, which had chairs and rustic tables lined along the wall. An elaborately decorated double door was just visible in the darkness at the end of the hall.

Stubbing out my cigarette on the concrete floor, I pushed past the movables to get to the doors. Locked! I hesitated, looked behind me for spying eyes, and then pushed gently. There was a little give. Pushing harder, then shoving, the right door opened so hard I had to catch its handle to stop it from violently banging the inside wall.

As my eyes adjusted to the darkness, I could see before me a magnificent ballroom with enough space to hold all of the three hundred prisoners held at Prinz Karl. I moved cautiously inward, being careful not to trip over unnoticed furniture, and was able to pull aside large velvet draperies. As light filtered in and dust drifted down onto my shoulders, I saw more chairs, long tables, small sideboards, and a lectern at the front.

But the prize was sitting there in the center of the far wall—an old Bechstein. I strode to it, gently rubbed dust off the signature plate, *C. Bechstein*, and looked at its inlaid woodwork casing. Ah, the German obsession for precision in their hand manufacture was embodied in that instrument. Staring at the piece under the dim light took me back to central London where my grannie would sometimes take me for tea. We would pass Bechstein Hall and its related shop on Wigmore Street as we returned to Marble Arch station. Pianos that were built for British royalty and shipped all over the world were on display. I wondered if the currently deep-seated anti-German sentiment in Britain extended to such brilliance as the Bechstein piano.

I carefully raised the cover to expose the keys, gently plunging one black, one white, then another black. Not wishing to draw attention, I quickly covered them. How long had they been asleep? Who had owned this musical masterpiece?

...

"You gotta come quickly!" I had burst through the door of our room, startling both Howie and the Vicar from afternoon slumber. After rebuffing my excitement, they hurried after me down the stone corridor and into the large room off the inside passageway. Emboldened by the attendance of my new accomplices, I ambled over to the piano and brashly opened the cover.

Gently tapping out "Chopsticks," I asked, "What do you make of this?"

The Vicar looked delighted. "I make happier days ahead."

"Quite so, Bobby!" howled Howie.

Both of them turned to take in the room, glancing from end to end, looking up at the giant, gaudy crystal chandeliers. The delight in their eyes spoke loudly that they were thinking as I was. "Do you think they will allow us to use it, to have sing-alongs?"

The Vicar nodded as Howie spoke. "Why don't we find out? But let's not ask, let's just do it. Fuchs is soft, and surely even the Hun can see the usefulness of a music hall, eh?"

I beamed with excitement. "All right, let's call for a concert, shall we? I think I can render up some songs from memory. After all, we had lots of practice at Ochey and Xaffevillers, Villeseneux too."

"Splendid. You work on those ivories, and I'll spread the word." Howie's grin filled the room. "How about tomorrow evening for a couple of hours before curfew?"

I sat at the keys and thought of tunes that I had played in Walthamstow. Ten years back to that Easter in '08, back to all the wonderful times that the piano inspired. Music had such a wonderful ability to transport one to events, happy and sad, but memorable nonetheless. It was through music I would most remember Cissy, from the music at the Savoy, and the music at Fortnum tea, to the music of our love, from quiet hums to loud orchestras.

And as Dr. Mott used the piano as therapy at the Maudsley, I would bring music to this jail. I wanted to bring comfort to the other prisoners. This was my chance to meet my commitment to be a positive voice, their positive voice.

The next evening's concert involved most everyone, from inmates to jailers. We had left little choice for Hauptmann Fuchs but to accept our intrusion into the ballroom since, by the time the guards had rousted him, we were already well underway. We counted on his indecisive nature to give way to acceptance. With this little bit of manipulation, it thankfully did.

Even for the guards who had been hastily placed at the entrance and in every corner—after all, the kommandant could not know if our British flyers were hatching some secret, sinister plot—this was a welcome diversion as they tapped their toes and hummed along.

Oh, Mademoiselle from Armentieres, Parlez-vous.
You might forget the gas and shell,
But you'll nev'r forget the mademoiselle!
Hinky-dinky, parlez-vous.

We were careful to select songs that were not obviously offensive to our enemy or those that mentioned war, for to provoke them now would be pointless. The hostility we all carried in our hearts would not find anger, at least not through these means.

Dusk and the shadows falling
O'er land and sea;
Somewhere a voice is calling,
Calling for me.

This rule made our selection somewhat difficult due to the vast number of anti-German songs sung over the war years and lyrics that made traditional songs bawdy. Still, we were able to sing with gaiety many songs that the Germans in the room did not understand to represent the free, decent life we had all been fighting for.

I've got a lovely bunch of coconuts;
There they are all standing in a row.
Big ones, small ones, some as big as your head.
Give them a twist, a flick of the wrist—
That's what the showman said.

In this way we passed the days practicing and the evenings singing. Having stumbled upon the ballroom that day, and exposing that beautiful piano was a heaven-sent message that we were to be all right, to endure our time left in captivity.

Chapter 55

November 1918

Toward the middle of November, during an interval at one of our concerts, rumors were circulating that an armistice had been signed between the Austro-Hungarians and the British-French entente. That night we went to bed optimistic, excitedly chatting until the wee hours in the darkness.

The next morning, at our typically precise eight o'clock roll call, we were assembled in the yard under a light snowfall, waiting for the kommandant to emerge from his quarters. With shuffling to keep warm, we all wondered why an officer who invariably practiced precise Germanic punctuality would be late. Eventually he emerged in a clear state of agitation.

Hauptmann Fuchs sputtered a few words in his native German, his body gestures signaling a troubled mind. He stopped, stared at the ground, then with much gusto raised his head and shouted out a message that none of us understood. Breathing heavily, he focused on us, peering up and down the rows as his chest heaved in and out.

With cheeks puffed and his blue eyes popping, he spoke in English, necessarily slowly and methodically.

"*Zee* German army is strong, more than any other. Love for Germany is forever in the minds of its people. Germany defended its land against the cruelty of France and of England and later from the Americans, all of whom cut off our food supply by illegally blockading our ships. *Zee* ships were peaceful, only trying to supply our starving citizens." Fuchs puffed himself out while his voice went suddenly shrill. "You! You who bombed our cities and killed innocent people, you are evil and you are wrong."

I thought of how zeppelins and massive Gothas had spread terror among Londoners and Parisians night after night, raining bombs down on innocent people. How Germany started this conflict by first invading neutral Belgium, then France, and only then did the British army sail cross the Channel. And only then did America intervene.

Nearing exhaustion, the hauptmann's voice shrank as though he was defeated. He stared stoically at us. We listened to every word, anticipating his message through the tears welling in his blue eyes, willing him to say what we wanted to hear. "You who bombed my people, you know that Germany fought best. Germany did not lose *zee* war; Germany did not surrender." And with a bellowing voice, shrill with passion, *"Deutschland ist Mutig."*

Your troops may have been brave, but your leaders were craven, I thought.

He paused, not giving us what we wanted to hear, holding back as a tear rolled down his cheek. He was too proud to check it. "You had many numbers, many men. The Americans with their millions caused this stop. Count von Oberndorff has not surrendered; he has only signed *zee* armistice."

A roar of cheers erupted, a deafening chorus as hats and anything loose were thrown into the air, each of us hugging whomever stood near. The kommandant was in a rage, unable to understand this undisciplined, chaotic outbreak, eventually turning in disgust to return to his quarters.

...

Later that day we learned the armistice had been signed one week earlier on 11 November. In spite of asking and badgering, there was no information about our release. While the German penchant for documentation and order was well known—we would expect them to be diligent at double-checking their prisoner roster—they were acting capricious by not opening up about our liberation.

While we continued with the sing-alongs, they were not well attended as thoughts of freedom affected hearts and minds. Other distractions such as signing a parole document allowed freedom every afternoon from one to five to walk anywhere, from the countryside to the villages. We had the luxury of going around to various settlements along the Danube River to buy food. Some of us even walked the five miles to Ingolstadt, as the exercise was another happy diversion.

Walking through the countryside, we noticed how poorly the local people were and realized there was opportunity that would benefit both sides. The camp was well stocked with rice, tea, and other staples, and as the kommandant had all but disappeared, security was slack. We were able to make exchanges with the villagers for butter and eggs. In perspective, the situation seemed dire since we knew we were returning to a better life, whereas these people would be left behind in extended misery. What had Germany achieved?

Chapter 56

December 1918

While life got better, we were still not free, nor were we given the hope of a repatriation plan. With such apprehension, the mind plays tricks such as obsessing about being left behind. The tedium wore us down as the days turned into weeks. "How much longer, Bobby? It is our right to be returned, yet here we fucking sit," complained Howie one day. "This endless waiting—can't take it much more."

I put my hand on his shoulder in the same manner he had soothed me those many times in our Fee. "It's cruel, I know. Surely it's in violation of the Hague Convention."

The Vicar sat up. "The Germans don't care about conventions. They violated them from the outset. A war they damn well started, a war in which they introduced chemical gas and slaughtered Belgian civilians. Damn and blast them!"

"I'm fucking mad too," I said. "No one telling us anything, and now we sit here forgotten. So many other chaps in France and

England must be returning to their families by now."

After his prior outburst, Howie sat in a contemplative mood, seeming to mellow as he sank into a deeper level of thought. "Well, I suppose those like us that didn't die are frustrated, but when you think of it, the millions left behind dead in the mud, those poor bastards don't have the hope we have now."

His comment made us uncomfortable, the Vicar taking on a reflective look. "Yes, that is true, and we must be patient. No point chomping at the bit. I doubt even our guards know what's happening."

I leaned toward the Vicar in an affirming gesture. "You know, that's a good point. It's rumored the kaiser is in Holland, the German government has all but disappeared, and who knows who is running their defeated army. These chaps have been left to fend for themselves, probably as frustrated as us. Chaos, I'm guessing."

"Perhaps it's better to be locked in here than loose on German soil," opined the Vicar. "And thinking about it, I heard there are over a million of us POWs to liberate. Now, that must be chaotic."

Howie sat upright, some of his impatience returning. "Still, we've been here almost a month after the hauptmann's sermon, and there's been no word from anyone about anything. It'd be nice to know something!"

"Quite," said the Vicar. "I've heard it's getting the better of many prisoners. One just has to hear the chatter about escape that seems to be on many officers' lips."

"Say, what about that, Vic?" asked Howie. "We agreed that escape was too risky while the war was on, but we're less likely of being stopped now. Think of all the POWs, returning German soldiers, wandering civilians. And there must be occupying British forces here by now. Think anyone would notice if we were to simply not return one afternoon?"

"The difficulty," I said, "is getting on the railways without a pass. Two weeks ago in Ingolstadt, I noticed numerous guards patrolling the railway stations."

The Vicar looked troubled. "No, it's not happening. Didn't I just say it is better to be locked in here with patience than to be loose on German soil with no effective government? Besides, it's too cold, too dangerous, and too stupid."

Howie and I looked at the Vicar and grinned with acceptance of his sage advice. We knew it was good for us to debate such things, even if we had no intention of acting.

...

The cheering was loud and boisterous, not dissimilar from those attending a home football game. "Can you believe this day has come?" crooned Howie. On Tuesday, 17 December, the thirty-seventh day after the armistice was signed, the three hundred prisoners of Ingolstadt were settled in comfortable cushioned seats on a train headed to the Swiss border.

The march to the station through driving rain—similar to that encountered those few days after our forced landing—felt different. There we were in the comfort of first class. The Vicar took a long look, first at me and then at Howie. "You two look like you showered with your clothes on—hair plastered to your head and tunic to your miserable bodies."

Dripping onto the upholstered seat, Howie beamed. "Perhaps it's a good omen that the Lord cleanses us as we leave this horrid camp, eh?"

"You may have a point, Lieutenant Chainey," the Vicar said aptly. "You may very well be on to something."

"Listen to the two of you sounding like squawking school children let out for holidays," I blustered. "I feel cleansed too, but I'll feel a lot more absolved when we cross into Switzerland."

"Isn't it a relief that this is finally behind us? Back on English soil for Christmas, a wonderful feeling, wot?" said the Vicar.

I wanted to share as much excitement with my friends, but couldn't shake thoughts of their being settled with their English families for Christmas, whereas I had many more hurdles to face. While feeling good about my coming freedom, I couldn't escape a tinge of sadness about having to wait in England for my demobilization papers, queueing for passage across the Atlantic, then entraining out of Montreal for three days travel to Saskatoon. The Vicar interrupted my thoughts. "And you're amazing, Bobby. Three and a half years absent without seeing family or friends, and you've survived well under those conditions. You, your fellow Canadians, the Americans, the ANZACS, the Indians, the South Africans—you've all given more than us."

"Thank you for saying that, Vic. It means a lot. Now, are you going to share that package of Red Cross biscuits I saw you stuff into your tunic?"

"I surrender, gents. If only we could find some tea, eh?"

Howie had drifted into slumber with a contented look on his face. We were all exhausted, relieved but feeling drained after the surge of excitement. The anticipation that we held from the time of waking that morning until we took our seats on the train had ebbed. The motion and noise of the wheels clicking and clacking eventually silenced most in the carriage. Some of us fell asleep, and some were lost in thought as they watched Germany pass by the window.

...

The gentle rocking slowed as the steam whistle declared our arrival into Munich station. As we stretched our legs, we took humor in seeing so many of our Prinz Karl comrades walking along the platform with still-wet backsides, the rest of our uniforms dry after the two-hour journey from Ingolstadt. Those of us with a few deutsche marks had enough time to fetch a tea or a beer before re-boarding.

The run over to Stuttgart, then down to Konstanz on the German side of Lake Constance would take twice as long, so we were happy for the refreshment.

With the change in geography came improved weather as the sun burst through the carriage window, making a cold winter day feel warm inside. I looked out at the landscape, lightly snow-covered fields interspersed with forest, the Alps off in the distance. The wonder of this beautiful land made the kaiser's decision to mow through Belgium to attack France more of a mystery. When there was so much richness to live for at home, why was it necessary to invade?

I was drowsy as the train gently rocked. How different my thoughts were compared with my arrival at Amiens those many years ago. Then, my fears were intense, full of anxiety about what was to come in a war so mechanized that it erased the traditional concept of individual valor in favor of mass slaughter. About army generals who had become so self-absorbed they could only see mass movement and massive machinery, blinded to the courage of those millions of individuals who perished.

The landscape passed in a blur as the train picked up speed, moving us along to our freedom. The sun felt soothing on my face as it lulled me again. Had I come any closer to understanding what courage was? It kept itself veiled, didn't it? The killing of an enemy soldier was concrete enough; the mass spraying of bullets at great velocity onto troops marching along a road was real, but whether those acts of war were courageous remained obscure.

The train slowed along a branch rail as we slipped through Stuttgart, then picked up speed again heading south, the snow-laden fields on both sides glimmering in the sun.

I again wondered: Could I say I was courageous? I thought so, yet due to the arcane nature of the war, I realized that others might see the conflict differently based on their experiences. That was why one never spoke of it, a soldier's dark closet. I had led my platoon with pluck; I had bombed targets in death-defying circumstances, and I had learned to remember Cissy in a positive way. Yes, it took all the courage I had to accept that she, and so many others, like Perce, who had affected my life, were gone. I would use that spirit to ensure memories of them lived forever.

I awoke with a start, sweat dripping from my forehead, this time not from a nightmare but rather because I had fallen asleep against a sunny windowsill. I cleared my head by quietly admiring beautiful Lake Constance, its alpine Rhine water shimmering in the afternoon sun. "Must be Konstanz coming up, lads," I burst out in an unthinking manner as Howie and the Vicar were dozing.

"Hmm?" said Howie.

"Your auntie Constance is calling, Lieutenant Chainey!"

"Wha—I don't have an Auntie Con . . . Oh, ha ha, very funny, Pitman."

The Vicar and I looked at each other, then smiled at the waking Howie. "That's one for us, Bobby," he chortled.

"Howie, we are almost in Konstanz. You know, near the Swiss border," I said. He sat upright, looking out at the lake through bleary eyes.

...

"Achtung! Zeig uns deine Unterlagen!" The uniforms worn by the German border guards were as extraordinarily neat as the men were well groomed. Even appearances shown by a surrendered country were being kept up, at least in front of foreigners. Well, they can demand *Unterlagen*, but we had little to show for documents, only the release handed to us by Hauptmann Fuchs as he had ticked off our names on his clipboard before we crossed the prison moat.

The process was a little ridiculous as a guard stood over us to check our papers. One would think our British uniforms and accents would be proof enough for permission to exit Germany.

Howie whispered as the guard moved along, "At least he has a job."

We chugged forward ever so slowly, crossing the viaduct over the Rhine and through the southern part of Konstanz. We heard raucous hoots and hurrahs from the more forward carriages, revealing they were in Switzerland. We were right behind.

"Ah, the Swiss are incredible," commented the Vicar as he accepted gifts through the open window. "Showering us with chocolates, cigarettes, biscuits!"

On the platform, Howie took on the look of a school chum, moving around, hugging any girl or woman he saw, men also. "They are so nice, such warm people!"

I bounced over excitedly. "And the coffee, lads. Try the coffee—it's real, no acorns!"

A small boy of about seven ran up to us after leaving other soldiers, wrapping his arms around the Vicar's legs. *"Danke,"* he murmured, *"Danke fürs kämpfen."* His mother ran over, her English broken but easily understood. "Oh, I'm so sorry, but ever since his brother died, he has been thanking you soldiers for fighting."

The Vicar's eyes welled up, and I simply let it out, stood there holding my coffee and cried tears of sorrow for this little guy, but also tears of relief as we stood in neutral Switzerland. Howie knelt down and hugged the boy. *"Danke* back to you. Thank you, little one."

It was then we felt some release, raw emotion escaping the core of our hearts, releasing pent up anguish, allowing ourselves to rejoice. Watching his mother lead him away, I realized that what that little boy had done could heal countries if they, too, were prepared to open up their hearts.

"Penny for your thoughts, Bobby?" Howie faced me from the opposite seat as I stared out the window into the darkness. The Vicar slept as he leaned slightly forward on the soft cushioned seat, rocking gently with the movement of the train. We were well on our way to Geneva via Zurich.

"Thinking of that young lad, how his innocence pierced our feelings, his inherent sensitivity to our grief."

"Well, he got to us at that vulnerable moment when we crossed into freedom, but yes, he seemed to instinctively understand the sacrifice of soldiers."

"Thinking about what his mother said, you know, losing his brother. That was obviously her other son. Yet she taught the youngster to love. That is something."

The Vicar stirred in his seat, mumbled, then drifted away against the constant drone of our conversation. "Yeah, Bobby," said Howie. "The things we've seen over here, how the people have survived under such terrible conflict, surrounded by death, destruction, and armed conflict, never knowing what might happen from one day to the next..."

"And to think that our families will never know what really went on over here," I mulled.

"How's that?"

"Well," I justified, "even if we did explain, they would never truly understand, couldn't possibly grasp, the horror that went on."

Howie stared into the darkness at the eerie flashes as telegraph poles swept past before turning back to me. "True. I don't know how I would explain the war to my family. How do you explain pieces of bodies rotting in the mud or bayonetting a Hun before he does that to you?"

"You don't, because even if they believe those things happened, they will question why you didn't do something to avoid such tragedy. They will believe we had a choice, because they simply don't know any better."

Howie again turned away to peer into the blackness outside the window. I watched him for a moment, thinking that the darkness was symbolic of the only way to move on from war. To throw all those experiences into a dark hole, not to be disturbed, as a way to move forward. I let him be as I turned my thoughts to my own family, the joy of seeing my beautiful sister Hilda, who had turned eighteen last January, now a young woman who would put on grown-up airs. When I last saw her, she was fifteen with the innocence of a young girl. What would she say, what would Ethel say, and what would I say? Would we still have the togetherness we had always had?

There would be fanfare for those of us returning home, and in spite of the lack of true answers, questions would be asked. How to explain the fear of flying in fierce weather at eight thousand feet to bomb an enemy target? Listeners would want to romanticize it as they had done in other wars, yet it was difficult for me to find romance in any of it. How did you justify strafing rows of marching soldiers from an aeroplane? Being told it was an ethical military command—protecting our cause the same as those young men in the German army were told—seemed glib. You killed because you had to kill, not because you wanted to.

The Vicar's body did not shift from its relaxed state, but he turned his head to face me. "Were you scared, Bob?"

"Vic, you're awake."

"Quite. Been listening to you two. It occurred to me that after we force landed the Handley, I never asked you if you were afraid back there in the gunner's slot."

"Yes, I was afraid. Of not knowing what was happening, that was the worst. Afraid of not seeing my sisters again, my parents, and my school chums. And once we landed, I remember thinking it would be a terrible way to go, to be mowed down by an excitable Hun while on their soil. Yes, I was scared."

"Yet you were the one who rallied us to that wooded area, encouraged us to take the action of walking away from the danger," said the Vicar. "If we had remained, who knows what a fired-up Hun might have done?"

"Ah well, my mind just happened to be focused that night, that's all."

Chapter 57

21 December, 1918

High up on the hill, I looked past the Place d'Armes watchtower at the ship docked under the harbor lights, which would transport us across the English Channel to Dover the next morning. After traveling eleven hundred miles, the train that had delivered us from Ingolstadt in five days rested in the nearby Gare de Calais.

I would momentarily rejoin Howie and the Vicar in the dockside *estaminet*, which was teaming with soldiers returning from the front, all charged with excitement. As I desired a little time in the fresh wintry air to think, I strode up the long pathway that ended at the lookout.

On this first day of winter, peace was on everyone's mind, yet my thoughts summoned the inevitable spring that would bring flowers, green grass, darling foals, warm air, and all the other new growth that refreshes our earth. For me this was a renewal by basking in daydreams while shedding nightmares.

The world was free; even those who had sought to bring evil were free of their horrific burden. It was true the British way of life had broken down, that England, France, Germany and others were nearly bankrupt. But choices would open up in a restoration after everything settled down to become normal in a new way. As mankind's effort to build destructive war machinery transformed to building homes and workplaces and factories for the benefit of all, our world citizens would adapt to renewed lives. Even the losses would heal with time.

I struck a match to light my pipe as I leaned back against a man-sized rock, peering up at the waning moon that was full enough to brighten the night. The shadow of the wispy clouds passing across its surface reminded me of the many nights traveling high above in the open air. I was thankful for that moonlit image that would always be etched in my mind as a reminder of the people who had taught me how to face fear and embrace courage—Perce, Cissy, Wellsey, Hardy, and so many others.

The faint voice of the Vicar calling from below reminded me that he and Howie were also key influences in the shaping of my future. Oh yes, I would go back to Saskatoon to weigh my choices, knowing the university held open my seat at the law school. Yet I also knew I had a tidy sum of war-allowance savings tucked away at the Bank of Montreal, which would give me the freedom to travel, maybe to Vancouver to see my sister Ethel. Perhaps Hilda would go too. There would be choices that for the past few years I had not permitted myself to consider.

As I now pondered those options, the moon silhouetted a distant aeroplane passing through its brilliance as if proving for me the point about its image of courage. The distant hum of its engine propelling it through the night sky and its flickering wing lights had been transformed from images of war to one of peaceful passage. Perhaps Cissy was directing it as a signal of love—daydreams could happen at night too.

"Bobby, you out here?"
I had better go and begin living again.

Historical Note

The history depicted in this story follows an accurate timeline and is true to general events as they unfolded from the 1916 through 1918 portion of the Great War.

When the Archduke Franz Ferdinand, heir to the throne of the Austro-Hungarian Empire was assassinated in Bosnia on June 28, 1914 the stage was set to ignite simmering tensions across Europe. Those agitating for war were to see it by August, although few expected it to last through the end of 1918.

The Triple Entente of France, Russia and Great Britain was formed to counterbalance the Triple Alliance of Germany, Austro-Hungary and the Kingdom of Italy. This set up conditions for the first true world war, especially when sovereigns such as the Ottoman Empire, Togoland, West Africa, Japan and China became involved. Neutral Belgium was thrown into the fray by an aggressive German maneuver to invade it unlawfully.

Canada – alongside Australia, New Zealand, South Africa

and Newfoundland – was a Dominion of the British Empire and therefore integrated in its defence. Canada mobilized immediately after Britain declared war on Germany, its young men joining up in respect of 'King and Country'. Its first field action took place by the Canadian Expeditionary Force at Ypres, Belgium in April, 1915, during which Canadian Lieutenant-Colonel John McRae penned the poem "In Flanders Fields" to honour a fallen friend.

Canadian participation grew, joining the Battle of the Somme which commenced on 1 July, 1916, a scene of horror and colossal loss of life. All of Canada's divisions – with Newfoundland – participated and as noted in the story, the Royal Canadian Regiment joined that muddy battlefield in August, 1916. Taking count of both sides, the Somme accounted for over 1.2 million casualties (8,600 soldiers per day).

The Canadians participated in the other major WW1 battles such as Vimy Ridge, Passchendaele and Amiens. Out of a population of 8 million, 620,000 young Canadian men enlisted, with 425,000 serving overseas. Sixty thousand did not come home.

While Canada did not have a flying corps until after the Great War, it contributed many flying officers to the cause. The descriptions of training, aerodrome capers and flying sorties are all based on historical records.

Characters

Robert (Bob) Pitman existed and was the author's maternal grandfather. His characterization is based on historical record and personal knowledge. Surviving being buried alive under bombardment with subsequent shell shock is fact. The contraction of disease is fact.

Most of the soldiers mentioned – Percy Sutton, Malcolm Isbester, Heber Logan, John Forbes, Henry Egar, Eric Pitman, Frank Wells, Frederick Chainey, VE Schweitzer, Francis Johnson and others – fought in the Great War. Where physical description of each character is lacking, or personality uncertain, characterizations were invented.

Sam Hardy and Cissy Ann Taylor are purely fictional, but essential to the flow of the story. Their characters are based on similar personages who Bob Pitman likely encountered based on known preferences for people he associated with.

Places

Places where the various events occurred – the marches through towns in the Picardy Département and Albert in the Somme Département – are accurate. The Somme battlefield along the Albert-Bapaume Road is exact.

There existed Casualty Clearing Stations at the Somme and at the Albert School House. The hospitals existed in the places mentioned, including the Maudsley in London. The aerodrome locations are accurate as recorded in various histories of 100 Squadron. Each bombing target on each night described is historic.

The Brunner Mond Munitions Factory at Silvertown (now part of Greater London) produced arms and did experience a disastrous explosion on 19 January, 1917 while Cissy was in hospital. The National Shell Filling Factory, Chilwell produced munitions from early 1916, employing up to 10,000. The 1 July 1918 explosion involving eight tons of TNT is accurate. Of the 134 that perished, only 32 could be positively identified; while in the story Cissy is described among them, she truly wasn't based on her fictional nature.

Situations

The description of shell shock and its treatment is true to historic accuracy. The Maudsley Hospital, under Dr. Frederick Walker Mott, did practice an 'atmosphere of cure' as described. The hospital stands today as one of London's leading psychiatric hospitals.

The contracting of venereal disease was controversial in the Great War. While military brass initially held its existence with disdain, they accepted that millions of young men – facing a high chance of death or maiming – desired to have an encounter when away from the trenches or airfields. That Commonwealth soldiers contracted diseases in greater proportion is understandable since they had more disposable income (paid more than their English compatriots) and when given leave were not within reach of home. Additionally, French brothels were quite legal and openly enticed soldiers in the advancement of their business.

Munitionettes were engaged in arms production throughout the Great War as so many men were involved in the war effort. These were extremely dangerous jobs as described in the story, and oft times presented life-long chemical side effects. Social effects are also notable: as the restrictions of Victorian England were being cast off women realized they were equally adept at performing manual labor, placing them in a position to earn significant wages (outside of the paltry earnings from service/servant jobs).

The suffragette movement, on a slow burn from Victorian Britain times, finally succeeded in 1918 when women over 30, with property, were allowed to vote. Sadly, Cissy would have just missed the success in women's rights she was so passionate about. Canada was slightly more progressive by granting voting rights to women during 1916-17.

Aircraft

The FE2b was the night bomber employed by 100 Squadron from its inception in February, 1917 through August, 1918, when the Handley page O/400 replaced it as a long range night bomber.

The 'Fee' was a lumbering 2-seater aircraft of the pusher type with propeller located rear of the engine (versus the tractor, front propeller pull type). The advantage was that the observer/gunner, who sat in the nacelle forward of the pilot, had a very wide, unobstructed arc of fire. Its bomb load was typically a center loaded 112-pounder with four 25-pound Coopers bombs under each wing.

Beginning in 1917 with 100 Squadron the Fee night bombed German held industrial targets such as aerodromes, factories and steel plants, as well as rail track and stations, although it did not have enough endurance to fly sorties very far into Germany.

The Handley Page Type O/400 came into 100 Squadron service in August 1918 when the Fees were retired. It was the largest bomber that Britain operated in the Great War. The targets remained approximately the same, except that Britain could then reach farther into Germany itself as described in the story.

While the O/400s could carry a new 1,650-pound bomb, 100 Squadron mainly carried multiple 112 and 230-pounders. Armament consisted of five Lewis-type machine gun systems mounted at various defensive positions about the fuselage; two up front for the observer and three for the rear gunner.

Summary

The story of *Seeking Courage* will be judged by the reader on its merits as an entertaining romance as well as an instructive history. The goal was to demonstrate a bravery that so many young men and women practiced over one hundred years ago in order to make our lives safer today. It is through each character's experiences and passions – woven from historical fact – that reaching this goal will be decided.

Please visit www.seekingcourage.com
for detailed historical notes.

GLOSSARY

Achtung: German for "attention" or "regard"

Adjutant: a military officer who acts as an administrative assistant to a senior officer

Aerial Bomb: 112- and 230-pound heavy explosives dropped from WW1 aircraft; provided good penetration and fragmentation when dropped on buildings, railways, roads and bridges

Aerodrome: equivalent to airport or airstrip; a military air base; aka 'drome

Aeroplane: British term for airplane

AM: air mechanic

Archie: anti-aircraft fire

Armagnac: oldest distilled brandy in France, produced in the Armagnac, Gascony region

Army: typically, four or five infantry divisions; changes throughout wartime

Artillery Gun: longer barrel than howitzer and mortar; smaller shells, higher velocities, flatter trajectories

Baby Incendiary Bomb: weapons packed with thermite designed to start fires; 6.5 oz. appliances packed in containers of 272 bombs

Barrage: barrier of excessive, continuous artillery or machine gun fire in "lines" on a specific area designed to destroy the enemy or make them keep their heads down

Battalion: four infantry companies, plus other units; roughly 1,000 troops

Beardmore 160 HP: British six-cylinder, water-cooled aero engine built by Arrol-Johnston and Crossley Motors for William Beardmore & Co (licensed from German Austro-Daimler)

Bessonneau Hangar: portable timber and canvas aircraft hangar used by the RNAS and the RFC during WW1

Blighty: Britain: 'Blighty wound' required a trip home for treatment and convalescence

Boer War: war between the British Empire and Boer (Afrikaner) states, over the Empire's influence in South Africa; Oct 11, 1899 – May 31, 1902

Bonne chance: French for good luck

Brigade: four infantry battalions plus other units; roughly 4,000 troops

Brilliantine: hair-grooming product by French perfumer Edouard Pinaud, consisting of a perfumed and colored oily liquid

Bully beef: tinned meat common in British armies

CAMC: Canadian Army Medical Corps

Captain: commissioned officer rank historically corresponding to the command of a company of soldiers; a senior flying officer beginning in WW1

Casualty Clearing Station: British Army term for military medical facility behind the front lines that is used to treat wounded soldiers

CEF: Canadian Expeditionary Force; field force created by Canada for service overseas in WW1

C'est la guerre: French for 'It's the war.'

Chat: lice; to chat is to talk in a group while extracting lice from uniform

CMR: Canadian Mounted Rifles, infantry unit of the CEF

CO: Commanding Officer

Company: four infantry platoons plus other units; roughly 230 troops; labelled A,B,C and D

Coopers bomb: fragmentation bomb, designed to throw showers of fragments like those of the high-explosive artillery shell; 20-lb

Cordite: odorous explosive used as propellant for shells and bullets

Corporal: the lowest non-commissioned officer (NCO)

Corps: two or more divisions; roughly 50,000 troops

Crossley tender: light truck (British: lorry) assigned to RFC/RAF squadrons

Danke: German for 'thank-you'

Deutschland ist Mutig: German for Germany is brave

Division: three infantry brigades, plus other units (engineers, medics, signallers, etc.); roughly 18,000 troops

EA: enemy aircraft

Esprit de corps: a feeling of pride, fellowship, and common loyalty shared by the members of a particular group; common in military

Estaminet: French for tavern

FE2b: Farman Experimental biplane operated originally as a fighter then a day and night bomber by the RFC/RAF during WW1

Flamethrower: mechanical incendiary device that projects a long, controllable stream of fire

Flare path: a lamp or flare lit runway, necessary for aircraft to take off or land after dark

Floppin; fok: swear word of the day, a euphemism for 'fuck'

Flucht: German for escape

Geordie: relating to Tyneside (NE of England), its people, or their accent or dialect

Gone (go) west: die, or be killed

Gotha: a heavy night, long range bomber used by the *Luftstreitkräfte* (Imperial German Air Service) during WW1

Gott Mit Uns: German for 'God with us'

Greatcoat: large overcoat typically made of wool designed for warmth and protection against the weather; issued to officers in WW1

Handley Page O/400: heavy biplane bomber used by Britain during the WW1, at the time the largest aircraft that had been built in the UK and one of the largest in the world

HE: high explosive

Howitzer: short barrel artillery gun; propels shells at high trajectories

Howzit: common South African English greeting

Hun: slang for the German soldier; technically Asiatic nomadic warriors; Attila the Hun

Hundreds, I'm: Afrikaans for good, fine

Ja: both German and Afrikaans for yes

Jack Johnson: first African American boxer to become heavyweight champion, one of the greatest heavyweights of all time

Jeune fille: French for young lady

Jolie fille: French for pretty girl

Kaiser: Wilhelm II (1859-1941), the German Kaiser (emperor) and king of Prussia from 1888 to 1918 with a reputation as a militarist

Kampfen: German for fight

Khaki tunic: khaki: from the Hindi for dust-colored; tunic: the full officer dress jacket

Kommandant: German for commander

Lee-Enfield: bolt-action, magazine-fed, repeating rifle used by the British Empire and Commonwealth during WW1

Lewis gun: American designed lightweight machine gun used in British infantry/flying corps

Lieutenant: most junior commissioned officer in the armed forces

Lieutenant-colonel: commissioned officer above a major and below a colonel, typically in charge of a battalion in the army

Lorry: a large, heavy motor vehicle for transporting goods or troops; a truck

Maschinengewehr: German for machine gun

Madame: boss of a brothel

Maxim one-pounder: the *pom-pom* due to the sound of its discharge, was a 37 mm British autocannon; an enlarged version of the Maxim machine gun

MG: machine gun

Minenwerfer: 'mine thrower'- German short-range mortar on wheels; nicknamed 'Minnie'

Mon pilote: French for my pilot

Morse Code: an alphabet or code in which letters are represented by combinations of long and short signals of light or sound, much used by armed forces

Mortar: artillery gun with higher angles of ascent and descent than howitzers

MP: military police

Munitionette: female worker in a British munition's factory during WW1

Nacelle: a housing for the aeroplane's cockpits; located at front for the pusher-type FE2b

NCO: Non-Commissioned Officer, ex. a corporal or sergeant

Neurasthenia: aka 'shell shock'; psychological disorder resulting from explosion of shells or bombs at close quarters; characterized by chronic fatigue and weakness, memory loss, hallucinations, flashbacks, insomnia, nightmares and depression.

Nicht offnen: German for do not open

No-mans-land: dangerous land between two opposing trench lines

OC: Officer Commanding

Office (of aeroplane): pilot's cabin or cockpit on an aircraft; also, observer's cockpit

Pacifist: person who believes that violence, even in self-defence, is unjustifiable under any conditions and that negotiation is preferable to war (viewed as traitorous in WW1)

Parachute flare: flare fired from aeroplane like a rocket, but with small parachute attachment to slow landing

Phosphorous shell: chemical element phosphorus that is used in smoke, tracer, illumination, and incendiary munitions; 40 lb

Pill: RFC/RAF WWI slang for bomb

Platoon: four infantry sections; roughly fifty troops; smallest unit led by a commissioned officer; labelled 1st, 2nd, 3rd and 4th

*Po*lizei: German for police

Pom-pom: 1 pound bomb, known as the pom-pom due to the sound of its discharge

Port side: left-hand side of aeroplane, facing forward

POW: prisoner of war

Princess Pats: Princess Patricia's Canadian Light Infantry regiment of the CEF, named for Princess Patricia of Connaught, then daughter of the Governor General of Canada

Private: soldier of the lowest military rank

RAF: Royal Air Force; formed in April 1918 when the Royal Flying Corps and the Royal Naval Air Service joined together

RAMC: Royal Army Medical Corps

RFC: Royal Flying Corps; British air corps from inception to April 1, 1918 when integrated with RNAS to form Royal Air Force (RAF)

RCR: Royal Canadian Regiment - infantry regiment of the Canadian Army (Canadian Expeditionary Force, WW1)

Regiment: a popular name for an infantry battalion; more technically, a permanent unit of an army of several battalions

RNAS: the naval wing of Britain's Royal Flying Corps established 23 June 1914

Section: each platoon had four sections of twelve troops led by an NCO; labelled A,B,C, and D

Sergeant: the highest rank of non-commissioned officer (NCO)

Shell shock: medical condition caused by prolonged exposure to trench warfare. See 'neurasthenia'

Show: action or attack on the enemy

Shrapnel: small metal balls exploded from a shell in flight (not pieces of the shell itself, which are called fragments)

Sidcot suit: RFC/RAF one-piece flying suit developed late by Sidney Cotton (thus Sidcot) for protection the piercing cold of the high altitudes

Sideslip: where an aircraft is moving *somewhat* sideways as well as forward; used as an evasive move during wartime

S'il vous plait: French for please

Sky Pilot: slang term for military chaplain

Snaaks: Afrikaans for jocular, humorous, playful

Sortie: deployment of a military unit such as an aircraft from a strongpoint; French for exit; a mission

Stand-to: highest state of military alert where troops stand for immediate action with weapons at the ready, usually at dawn and dusk when attacks were most likely

Starboard side: right-hand side of aeroplane, facing forward

Strafe: fired upon by shells or machine guns

Suffragette: a woman seeking the right to vote through organized protest

Tin hat: British facetiousness for a steel helmet

TNT: Trinitrotoluene is an explosive material used as a filling for artillery shells

Triple Alliance: partnership between Germany, Austro-Hungary and Italy signed in 1882

Triple Entente: partnership between France, Britain and Russia signed in 1907

Very light/Very flare: flare gun typically used for signalling, from the ground to aircraft and vice versa, and between in-flight locations

Victorian: a person who lived during the Victorian period; by WW1, was beginning to refer to prudish or outdated attitudes

Vin rouge: French for red wine

V.R.I.: 'Victoria Regina Imperatrix', Latin for 'Victoria, Queen, Empress'

Vrou: Afrikaans for wife

Webley: a British arms manufactured revolver often carried by junior officers in WW1

Zeppelin: large, hydrogen-filled, airships named after Count Alfred von Zeppelin; used for strategic bombing by the German army and navy

CPSIA information can be obtained
at www.ICGtesting.com
Printed in the USA
FFHW010914200619
53089212-58737FF